THE WITCHLIGHT IN THE WEB

THE WITCHLIGHT IN THE WEB

CHLOE COPELAND

The Witchlight in the Web:
Book 1

DEDICATION

This book is dedicated, as always, to my beloved husband, Thomas. It's a reminder that even when things get tough, you must push through to find your rainbow at the end. I'd also like to extend a very special thanks to my friend, Ross, who helped brainstorm many of the finer details with me. Lastly, I'd like to thank my fans and followers for making my creative endeavours possible. I wouldn't be motivated without you all!

Content Warnings

Please be advised that this story contains depictions of the following sensitive subjects:

- Child Abuse
- Sexual Assault
- Slavery

Contents

Chapter 1

I couldn't help but chew nervously on my lip as I stood straight as a board beside Lady Amaranta's desk. The Lady herself sat quietly, her head down as she regarded the documents before her. I stole a glance at her; she was always so enchantingly beautiful, and today was no exception. A cluster of small witchlights sat perched upon her silvery hair like a glittering crown. The little fiery creatures always seemed attracted to her as they floated and rearranged themselves in her hair. I couldn't stop myself from openly admiring her.

Even though I wore my best robes, I still felt dull and out of place in comparison. No matter how fancy or elaborate the design, I would only ever be allowed to wear shades of brown. Colours and accents were reserved for magi, and I was not one of them. I was simply a mundus, a pawn to be used for Amaranta's games and nothing more.

And today, Amaranta would make her first move in a new game. She would place me on the board to infiltrate her rival's ranks, to be her eyes and ears behind enemy lines.

The target?

Elieason Railan, the newest and youngest of the Prime Mages.

I'd heard many rumours about the man; some called him ruthless, others brave, but the common consensus was his exceptional combat prowess. I did not doubt his skill. At just nineteen years of age, he had proven himself worthy of the Celestial Lady's sight and been granted the position of the Twelfth Prime Mage. A most prestigious title bestowed upon the select few most favoured by our patron goddess.

A part of me was worried about how such a person would act. Prime Mages were not known for their kindness. Would he look down upon me? Should I be worried about my safety? Of course, I should be worried. I was a plant, a spy, an agent of Lady Amaranta. I'd spent years training at her bequest. It was only because of her that I was here right now. Without her, I would be nothing, another body left to freeze on the streets of Maentaea. She saw something within me, a usefulness that would have otherwise gone untapped. I looked promising on paper, and now it was time to demonstrate everything learnt. Lady Amaranta had specifically chosen me out of all her agents for this assignment. I was, and still am, uncertain why, but I had to believe in her judgment. I couldn't let her down.

She wanted me to watch over this new Prime Mage, to make sure he stayed within the bounds of her game and played by her rules. She wanted me to spy on his every move, to make sure he remained loyal to the Celestial Lady and her grand plans. It was, in theory, a simple assignment. The only unknown variable would be Railan himself.

There was a sudden, loud knock on the door, and I flinched as my eyes darted towards it. I could hear Lady Amaranta let out a soft sigh as she turned over her papers. She cleared her throat before she spoke.

'Come in,' her voice was mature and sounded like the vocalisation of warm, melted butter.

The door swung open with unexpected force, and that was when I finally laid eyes upon him: Railan. He was tall and lean, his copper hair was short and messy yet styled in such a way as to perfectly accentuate his sharp features. He wore his vibrant red and navy uniform with an air of casual elegance, and the way he carried himself made it clear he was no ordinary mage. As he entered the room, he cast a glance at me.

Railan's eyes locked onto mine, and I felt my cheeks flush as my heart skipped a beat. They were a deep blue, like the depths of the ocean, with a hint of mischief hidden behind their lustre. The way he looked at me was unnerving, like he could see right through me. He strode confidently into the room, the sound of his footsteps echoing off the walls.

'Lady Amaranta,' he greeted her with a nod, and then turned his attention to me, 'and who is this?' His eyes raked over me, assessing me with a critical eye.

'This is Isla, a recent graduate from the academy. She has been assigned to be your assistant,' Lady Amaranta introduced me. 'She'll be working closely with you, Railan.'

Railan's lips curved into a small smile, and I couldn't help but notice how his eyes crinkled at the corners. 'Ah, I see. Well, it's a pleasure to meet you, Isla,' he said, extending his hand towards me.

I couldn't help but feel self-conscious under his scrutiny, but I quickly reminded myself that I had a job to do. I stepped forward and bowed respectfully before accepting his hand. I was met by the feeling of electricity, as if zapped by a spark, at his touch. His grip was firm, but not overpowering, and I found myself holding onto it for a little longer than necessary.

'It's a pleasure to meet you too, my Lord,' I said, keeping my tone polite and professional as I let my hand slip free.

He gave me one last glance before he returned his attention to Amaranta. 'So, what's on the agenda for today? Or is this it?' Railan asked.

Lady Amaranta raised an eyebrow, looking a little taken aback by Railan's brusque manner. 'This is just the beginning, Railan. Today, you will get acquainted with Isla, and then you will start your official job as Prime Mage. You still have much to learn.'

Railan let out a small scoff. 'Learn? I thought I was already qualified. That's why I was chosen to be a Prime Mage, right?'

Lady Amaranta leaned back in her chair, looking unimpressed, 'Being a Prime Mage requires more than just strength and fighting ability. You need to learn strategy, diplomacy, and most importantly, loyalty.

You need to know when to act and when to hold back. A Prime Mage's lessons are never over, and that is why you will require an assistant. Her main directive is to first and foremost serve you, but also to guide you.'

Railan seemed to be considering her words, his eyes flickering over to me for a brief moment. 'Fine, I'll play along. But I'm not here to waste my time on meaningless tasks,' he said as he draped himself on the adjacent chair.

I tried not to let his dismissive attitude bother me as Lady Amaranta began to explain the schedule for the day. I already knew the schedule by heart. In fact, I knew the next week well in advance, that was assuming Railan would cooperate. However, I had a sinking feeling in the pit of my stomach that he would be resistant. I had my work cut out for me.

He was young, powerful, and overly confident. That would most definitely mean trouble for me, but I was ready. I'd been trained in many things, and pleasing people was one of them. If I could distract him with complete compliance, my job would be a lot easier.

I can do this.

I subtly watched Railan as Lady Amaranta spoke. He lacked the respect that I was used to from members of the Creed. Amaranta was one to be admired, and as the third Prime Mage, she was powerful in her own right. However, Railan seemed to be unimpressed by her rank, and I wondered if he was just trying to act tough or if he was truly that confident in his own abilities. His eyes flicked towards me briefly again, and I felt a shiver run down my spine. It was like he could see through me, like he knew exactly what I was there for. I quickly looked away, trying to focus on Lady Amaranta as she continued to speak.

After she finished, Railan stood up and stretched, looking at us with a smirk. 'Sounds like a blast. Let's get started then, shall we?'

I followed them out of the office and into the bustling halls of the Lady's Citadel. People moved out of our way, giving us a wide berth as we passed. I could feel Railan's eyes on me every now and again while I kept my gaze fixed forward, determined not to let him see any fear. It was going to be a long day.

We did a thorough tour of the Citadel, more specifically, the restricted zones. The building was large and expansive, and more than half of it was heavily restricted to those with certain rank privileges. As an agent of Lady Amaranta, I was one such person, though from now on that privilege would outwardly appear to be granted by Railan.

Lady Amaranta was careful to avoid this fact as she presented the tour to us. I remained quiet except when spoken to, and I made sure to keep a glimmer of awe in my eyes. I had to give the impression that everything was new and exciting.

As we walked, I noticed Railan seemed uninterested and disengaged, only nodding or grunting in response to Lady Amaranta's explanations. I couldn't help but wonder what his true intentions were. Was he as uninterested as he appeared, or was he just playing a part? I would have to keep a close eye on him to determine what kind of player he would be.

Finally, the tour ended, and we were back in Lady Amaranta's office. She dismissed me with a nod, signalling that my assignment had officially begun. As I turned to leave, Railan called out to me.

'Hey, you,' he said, and I turned back to face him. 'Make yourself scarce,' his tone was cold and commanding, and I could feel the weight of his gaze on me.

I nodded respectfully and left the room, my mind already racing with strategies to avoid drawing attention while still completing my task. This was going to be a challenge. I knew I would need to earn his trust, somehow, if my mission was going to be successful. But trust was the one resource that was sorely lacking in the world of the Prime Mages. It would be an exhausting task. In any case, failure was not an option. But what was I going to do? I would simply have to watch and learn. Then I would be able to start predicting his moves.

What did he mean by making myself scarce?

What exactly was he expecting? From now on, my job was to practically be his shadow. Perhaps if I just kept my head down, I would simply fade into the background, just another painting on the wall or a nondescript decoration. I didn't need to be more than that.

I stood outside the door, making sure to stand out of the way. I already found my mind full after spending barely an hour together. I couldn't quite read Railan. He seemed both hot and cold, charming yet guarded. He was a puzzle I would have to figure out. Lady Amaranta wanted the full picture of who he was, and I would deliver it to her.

The door abruptly opened, and I kept my head down, though my eyes instinctively stole a glance. Railan stepped out of the room, his eyes meeting mine briefly before he strode off down the hallway without a word. I let out a breath I didn't know I was holding and continued to stand there for a moment, trying to compose myself.

I couldn't afford to let my guard down, not even for a second. I reminded myself that I was there to do a job, and that meant being professional at all times. With a determined nod, I walked down the hallway, hot on his trail. I made sure to keep a reasonable distance between us as I followed him.

Like a shadow. I am a shadow. I can do this.

I eyed him carefully as he strode ahead. I figured if he didn't notice me watching, then a stolen glance here and there would be fine. I needed to understand who I was working with.

He was quite tall, with nearly a whole foot on me, and he walked with a confident swagger. His long legs also meant he was covering more distance than I, and thus I had to pick up my pace just to keep up our current distance. His fluffy, ginger hair was vibrant and easily recognisable, which was a little unusual for a Maentaean since we typically either had very fair or dark hair. I didn't need to see his eyes to remember exactly what they looked like. My heart fluttered uncomfortably at the thought. I didn't understand why. I'd seen many beautiful eyes before. Perhaps it was simply the intensity that inspired fear within me.

As we walked, I took note of the way he carried himself. I already knew he was confident, but there was also a natural grace to his movements, and his body seemed almost perfectly sculpted. He was fit and toned, the muscles in his arms visible even through the fabric of his clothes. His attire was stylish yet functional, and I could tell he took care of his appearance. He had a certain air of raw power about him, which was both intimidating and intriguing. I made a mental note to keep my distance, both physically and emotionally. This was a job, after all.

He seemed to be going somewhere, and it also seemed to be oddly far. I scanned our surroundings and immediately realised we were heading directly away from the next location on our schedule. I tilted my head in confusion as I glanced down at my notes and confirmed that we were, in fact, heading in the wrong direction. I looked back up at Railan, and my stomach dropped.

Oh no.

I immediately realised that I had to confront him, to set him on the right path, and the thought alone terrified me. It was literally his first appointment, and he was already diverting off course. He might be off track, but I was also there to gently correct him as necessary. It was my job to make sure he knew who, what, and where he needed to be and go at all times.

I cleared my throat as I clutched my notebook.

'Lord Railan, I must remind you that your next appointment is in the West Wing... we are currently heading to the South,' my voice trembled slightly, unsure how he would react to my correction.

Railan stopped in his tracks and turned to face me. I held my breath, waiting for his response.

He gave me a long, hard stare before speaking. 'I'm aware of where my appointments are. I'm taking a detour,' he said, his voice unyielding. I could feel my heart sink at his words as I realised that he was purposely disregarding the schedule.

He began to walk again, and I quickly followed, not wanting to fall behind. I mentally went over the rest of the day's schedule, trying to think of how I could adjust it to fit in this "detour".

Before I could say anything else, Railan suddenly turned to me and asked, 'Do you like to swim?'

I was caught off guard by the sudden, seemingly random question. 'I...I'm not much of a swimmer, my Lord,' I replied hesitantly.

Railan nodded thoughtfully, 'Perhaps I can teach you sometime. It's a good skill to have, especially with the weather here.'

I wasn't sure what to make of his offer, but I knew I couldn't outwardly refuse. 'Thank you, my Lord. I'd be happy to learn.'

We continued in silence, the atmosphere between us tense and uncertain. I couldn't shake the feeling that I was in for a long and complicated journey with Railan, and I was already internally screaming. Why did he ask about swimming? It seemed so random considering there wasn't exactly anywhere to, well, swim. Maentaea was in a perpetual state of winter. The only readily available water sources were constantly frozen over. My eyes flicked to the softly glowing pendant that hung from his belt. It was his focus, a holy symbol that allowed him to control the power of his chosen element. It was a deep blue, similar to his eyes. Deep blue symbolised the water element.

Water element.

My breath briefly caught in my throat for a second as my chest tightened.

Water.

I was taken aback as realisation dawned on me.

H-had he just threatened me?

I blinked in confusion at him as he continued on his detour. Surely he hadn't meant it as a threat? It had been less than two hours since I'd first met him, and there was no way he could hate me so fast, especially when nothing had happened. I'd simply tried to get him on track for his appointment. Could he sense my fear? Was that it? Was he like some kind of predator toying with its prey? Or was he just teasing me?

Not only had his words filled me with terror, but so did this detour. We were way off course. I looked nervously at my pocket watch. At this rate, we would be late. Why was he doing this? This was his very first day as the new Prime Mage. Didn't he care about upholding any kind of reputation? More so, it wasn't just a reflection on him, but also on me and everyone else under his command. I needed to be firmer. While I was expected to follow his orders, I was also supposed to guide him when necessary.

I cleared my throat again. 'My Lord, at this rate, you have thirty minutes to make it to your appointment with Lord Danila in the South Golden room. It takes fifteen minutes to walk from the West Wing to the South Wing. If your detour cannot be completed within fifteen minutes, we will be late,' my voice was more stern this time.

Railan didn't seem to react to my stern tone; he simply continued walking as if my words hadn't registered with him. My heart was pounding in my chest, and I was unsure of what to do. Should I push harder? Should I let it go and just hope we make it in time? As we walked, my mind raced with possible reasons why he was doing this. Did he want to test my loyalty? Was he intentionally trying to make us late? Or was he simply trying to throw me off my game?

I only grew more concerned as we exited the Citadel and entered the snow-covered gardens. I felt like I was about to have a heart attack as a large frozen pond came into view. Why? Why was he doing this? Was he intent on pasting me on the ice?

Railan turned to face me with a sly grin. 'Well, here we are,' he said. 'I thought it would be a nice change of pace to take a little break and enjoy the scenery.'

I stared at him for a moment as I tried to comprehend his words. A break, as in from work? We'd barely started the day! Though I had to admit it was a relief to see that he hadn't meant his earlier words as a potential threat. But at the same time, I was frustrated that we were now even further behind schedule.

I took a deep breath and tried to remain calm. 'My Lord, while I understand the desire to take a break, I must remind you that time is of the essence. We have a tight schedule to keep and cannot afford to be late.'

Railan raised an eyebrow and chuckled. 'Relax. We'll make it to our appointment in plenty of time. I just thought a little detour wouldn't hurt. You seem to be the type who's always focused on the task at hand. I simply want to remind you that it's good to take a step back and enjoy the world around us.'

I nodded, not entirely convinced, but there was little I could do at this point. I followed him to the edge of the pond and watched as he crouched down and reached a gloved hand towards the ice. A moment later, the ice began to crack and split, and before I could react, Railan fell directly into the freezing water. I gasped in shock and horror.

Oh, sweet Celestial Lady!

W-What in the name of the Lady was going on? The water was ice! Panic surged through me, and I threw myself to the edge of the pond. I needed to get him out. He was fully clothed! What was he thinking? He could drown!

He resurfaced a short distance away, and I immediately noticed that Railan seemed to be enjoying himself as his laughter echoed across the ice.

I called out to him, my voice tense and worried, 'Lord Railan, please come back to the edge. It's dangerous to be in the water like that; it can easily freeze over.'

Railan turned to me, still grinning, 'Relax, I know what I'm doing. I've done this plenty of times before. Plus, I can control water at my whim.'

I shook my head, still in dismay. Just because he could control water didn't mean it couldn't still kill him, especially the icy waters of Maentaea.

'But the water's freezing. You could get hypothermia, or even worse, drown.' I tried my best to impress the gravity of the situation upon him as I reached out to him.

Railan's smile faded, and he slowly made his way back to the edge of the pond. 'You worry too much,' he said as he ignored my hand and climbed out of the water, his clothes dripping with icy slurry.

Relief washed over me as he stepped out of the water, but I also felt a sense of frustration at his recklessness. 'Please be more careful, my Lord. As your aide, I must ensure not only that you are on task, but also your safety.'

Railan rolled his eyes, but nodded in agreement. 'Fine, I won't do it again. Happy?'

I nodded, still feeling a bit shaken from the scare. 'Yes, my Lord. Thank you.'

Even if his words were lies, it was something. I had no idea what he was trying to prove with this little stunt. He was indecipherable. More importantly, not only were we going to be late, but now he was also soaking wet. I quickly unfastened my outer coat and held it out for him to take.

'Please take this, you'll catch a cold in this weather. It only takes fifteen minutes for a wet person to become unconscious and fifteen to forty-five minutes to die, and that would be even worse than running late,' I offered him an uncertain smile, even though my heart raced with dread.

Punctuality was expected as the Prime Mages only ever met with the most elite individuals. This would reflect poorly on both of us. What would Lady Amaranta think? I couldn't even complete one simple task. Would she feel like her faith in me was misplaced, that I wasn't as special as she'd hoped? That I was truly worthless and that all her time, money, and effort had been wasted? If I were to be dismissed, then I would have nothing; I'd be back on the streets. Worse still, my family would be back on the streets. My heart ached at the thought of my innocent little sister at the mercy of the relentless winter. It was only by Lady Amaranta's grace that we lived, and it was my responsibility to keep my family safe and looked after. But what if I couldn't? Would she sell me off to try and scrape back some of the money she had invested in me? I didn't want to go back to being a slave, not again. My thoughts were spiralling. I could feel I was on the verge of tears.

No, I need to squash them.

'P-Please, let's go. We don't want to keep Lord Danila waiting too long,' I couldn't hide the nerves, and I didn't want to at this point.

I needed to be distracted, and work was the one thing that would keep me in check. Railan silently accepted the coat and shrugged it on, water dripping from his hair and clothes. He didn't seem to be affected by the cold; his gaze locked onto mine as if he was trying to read me. I couldn't help but feel like a failure, a disappointment, even though I had done everything in my power to prevent this situation.

I led the way back to the path, walking as quickly as I could without slipping on the icy ground. Railan followed closely behind me, his steps quiet and deliberate. My mind raced with possible excuses and apologies, but I knew they wouldn't do any good. The damage was already done.

We arrived at the West Wing several minutes late, and I quickly apologised to Lord Danila as he greeted us at the entrance. Fortunately, Lord Danila seemed unfazed by our tardiness and welcomed us inside without comment. I breathed a small sigh of relief as we followed him to the meeting room, but I knew I couldn't relax just yet. The day was far from over, and I still had to keep Railan on track.

I stood quietly beside the door as Railan made himself comfortable. Lord Danila was a prominent figure from the Golden Circle Bank. Their meeting was to discuss Railan's accounts and access. The bank was established and managed by Lord Lyrkus, the fifth Prime Mage and Railan's soon-to-be most valuable associate. Well, that was if this meeting went well.

There were far too many ways that he could mess this up. He was very lucky Lord Danila had turned a blind eye to his tardiness, let alone the fact that he was soaking wet like a rat fresh from the sewer! Oh, the shame! No doubt the Fifth Prime Mage, Lord Lyrkus, would hear about this farce, and that could cripple my Lord's access to funds. Funds he'd need for any operations he intended to undertake. I prayed that he would at least be able to pull out some honeyed words to win Lord Danila over.

I watched with bated breath as my young Lord began the meeting. As Railan began to speak, I tried to focus on his words, hoping that they would be enough to convince Lord Danila of his capabilities. But my attention kept wandering to his appearance, and the worry continued to gnaw at me. The water was still dripping from his hair and clothes, and the room was beginning to smell damp. I hoped that Lord Danila wouldn't notice, or worse, be disgusted by the sight and smell of my Lord.

I couldn't help but feel responsible for this failure. As his attendant, it was my duty to ensure that he arrived on time and presentable. But I had failed in that regard, and now I feared that it could have serious consequences for both of us.

I took a deep breath and tried to steady myself. I needed to focus on the present and do whatever I could to assist Railan in this meeting. I made a mental note to keep a cloth and some perfume on hand for future emergencies and to always be prepared for the unexpected.

As the meeting went on, I watched as my Lord spoke confidently and charmed Lord Danila with his words. Despite his appearance, he seemed to have a way with people that I could only admire from afar. I hoped that it would be enough to secure the partnership he was seeking and that the consequences of our lateness would not come back to haunt us.

I checked my watch again. I prayed this meeting wouldn't go overtime. Even though there was a good hour before the next appointment, that time would have to be utilised to make my Lord presentable. His appearance was probably even more important for the next meeting.

Next, he would be introducing himself to his direct subordinates. These were the people who would serve him in every aspect of his life from now on. They would depend on him and, more importantly, his reputation.

If he presents himself as anything other than respectable, then he will lose face with his people before he even gets started. A Prime Mage was powerful alone, but their true power came from their ability to lead. If the Creed sensed even the slightest fault, they would not hesitate to write him off. Without the unwavering support of his subordinates, he would be little more than a glorified figurehead. As confident as Railan appeared, he still needed to earn and maintain the support of his people.

To face the Creed and other Prime Mages alone would be disastrous. Every plan or thought would be met with objection, and he would become stagnant, unable to rise within the ranks of the Prime Mages until he eventually lost the favour of the Celestial Lady. Her favour was fickle, and the Prime Mages lived in constant fear of demotion, constantly fighting over each other for the converted First Prime Mage position. While Lord Railan had impressed her enough to become her twelfth favourite, one mistake would see him expelled from the council and back into obscurity. That was a long way to fall, and I was now along for the ride. I couldn't let that happen. Yes, I was supposed to watch him and report on his actions, but I was also supposed to make sure he was being effectively used to further the Creed's agenda and bring glory to the Celestial Lady.

As I was lost in thought, Railan's meeting with Lord Danila came to an end. My Lord's expression was unreadable, but I couldn't help but feel a little relieved that it was over. Lord Danila left the room, and my Lord turned to me with a nod.

'Let's go,' he said simply.

My eyes fell briefly upon the water stain on the couch, and a sigh escaped me. Railan would certainly need that bank account to charge the damages. No doubt there would be many more at this rate.

I followed him out of the room and down the hall, my mind still racing with thoughts of what was to come. This meeting would be just as important as those with the nobility. My Lord's ability to lead them would be paramount to both his and their success. I could only hope that he had the necessary skills to do so.

'My Lord,' I spoke up, my voice a little quiet with nerves. 'Might I suggest quickly changing before the next meeting?'

Railan stopped in his tracks before he turned to face me. 'No, I'm fine,' he said flatly.

I blinked at him for a moment. 'But...'

'It'll be fine, you worry too much,' Railan casually waved me off as he turned and continued walking.

I let out an exasperated gasp as I chased after him, shaking my head. 'I worry for good reasons, my Lord.'

'And what reasons are those?' Railan replied rather sarcastically.

I opened my mouth to list off the reasons, but quickly shut my mouth as that would be the worst idea I've had yet. 'Oh... y-you know, the usual reasons associated with this job...' I ended up saying vaguely.

Railan raised a brow at me. 'No, actually, I don't know,' he narrowed his eyes at me, a slight smirk touching the corners of his lips as he put me on the spot.

'O-Oh...' I bit my lip, feeling flustered as he called me out. 'I-I... w-well-'

'Relax, I'm just messing with you,' Railan let out a hearty laugh. 'I know you have good reason to worry, but still, have some faith.'

The discomfort persisted, but I nodded my head slightly. 'I'll try...'

Railan nodded in return before continuing on his way. He was right, I needed to have some faith, but that was easier said than done.

Chapter 2

Railan's subordinates were waiting in one of the Citadel's many meeting rooms. It was large and spacious, decorated with lush, vibrant upholstery. The room was abuzz as we entered, but soon quieted down as the occupants realised who we were. Railan strode immediately to the front of the room, his head held high despite his damp appearance. I cringed internally. He was brave, I would give him that.

The crowd was a mixture of Railan's direct subjects, including retainers, knights, and servants alike. In total, I would have said there were about fifty people crammed in here. I would have to try to memorise their faces as I would be working closely with the servants soon, once Railan had acquired his estate.

I followed along before standing to the side of the front row of the crowd. Railan had a warm, friendly smile on his lips, and it made my stomach drop. He needed to assert his authority now, not make friends. The subjects in this room were all either new to their roles or requisitioned from the previous Twelfth Prime Mage's household. Either way, no one here would hold anything more than the bare minimum amount of respect for Railan.

Railan cleared his throat, drawing everyone's attention as the room fell into awkward silence. He didn't seem fazed as his posture remained slight but relaxed.

'In the name of Her Eminence, the Celestial Lady, and on behalf of the Creed, I am honoured to stand before everyone here today. My name is Elieason Railan, the Twelfth of the Prime Mages, and I am here to guide you into a glorious future. I'm aware that some of you might have reservations about me and my abilities, given my age, but I can assure you that the Celestial Lady's judgment remains as sound as ever.

I have full confidence that, working together, we can achieve greatness and prosperity. Under my command, I can assure you that you will all be treated with fairness and respect.

I guarantee that your loyalty will be rewarded as I ascend the ranks of the Prime Mages. However, if anyone here has any doubts, then I invite you to challenge me right here and right now in a duel. If you believe the Celestial Lady's judgment to be flawed, then by all means, step forward and test my strength.

You will not be punished should you take up the challenge now, but be warned, any challenge to my authority after this meeting will be met with swift retribution.' Railan's expression turned serious in an instant as his eyes scanned the crowd. 'Step forward now, or I shall assume that everyone acknowledges me as your new Lord and commander without question.'

My entire body went tense at his proclamation. It took every ounce of my willpower and strength not to facepalm in shame and disappointment. Why would he do this? Why would he allow someone to challenge his authority at this pivotal moment? My breath hitched in my throat as I glanced around the room to see if anyone would take up the challenge.

Most of the crowd looked as uncomfortable as I felt. In particular, the other mundi kept their heads down, not wanting to draw attention to themselves or appear in any way confrontational. That was the smartest move for those in our position.

The magi in the crowd, however, were a bit bolder, as fitting of their positions. They kept their heads high and their expressions guarded. Some of the more confident members shifted slightly, the hum of vague whispers filling the air.

I prayed to the Celestial Lady that no one would step forward, that everyone here had at least a little bit of self-preservation. Besides, this was clearly a test. Anyone foolish enough to challenge Railan would undoubtedly be challenging the wisdom of the Celestial Lady herself, exposing themselves as heretics and dissenters. And no matter the outcome, they would be branding themselves as untrustworthy and someone to be disposed of.

Railan raised a brow as he moved his hands to his hips, pushing out his chest slightly. 'So no one here wishes to challenge me?'

The crowd remained silent.

'I can't hear you.' Railan's voice was a little louder, a little firmer. 'Does anyone want to challenge me?'

A few people cast glances at each other, as if uncertain what to do. I was also unsure what Railan was expecting, but then it clicked for me, and I straightened up slightly.

'No, sir!' I replied loud and clear, hoping this was the answer he wanted and that I would set an example for everyone else.

Railan's gaze turned to me, and I naturally lowered my head in sub-servience. 'I can't hear you!' he repeated, his expression now stern as his eyes narrowed at the crowd.

'No, sir!' I forced my voice to project louder, and to my relief, a few more voices joined me.

'Louder!' Railan commanded.

I could see his eyes flash with a blue glow. It was subtle, but I noticed that some of the more resistant people seemed to be inspired to comply.

'No, sir!' the whole room seemed to shout.

Railan seemed satisfied with our compliance as he relaxed once more, his smile returning to his lips. 'Good. Now that that is cleared up, I look forward to working with you all. I expect nothing short of your full compliance and your best efforts. Together we can achieve great things, and that is exactly what we will do under my leadership.'

Railan proceeded to lay out his full expectations and the delegation of tasks that he would assign each group based on their rank and skills. It was all very monotonous and standard stuff, perhaps even suspiciously so. He didn't seem to deviate from standard protocol in the slightest, choosing to take on a more reserved and safe allotment of his resources. This surprised me, given his rather rash behaviour so far. Regardless, it put my mind at ease, and I was able to mingle a little more comfortably with my fellow subordinates. I, too, would need to build up a good rapport with the people in this room. Most of the magi would be reporting directly to Railan, but the mundi would more than likely go through me, especially those who would be joining Railan's household after his debut and subsequent assignment of estate title.

As his assistant, I would also become his household manager. In fact, that was going to be the majority of my role once things were settled. I'd have oversight of his entire house as well as manage his schedule and meetings. It was the perfect position to watch his every move, just as Lady Amaranta intended.

I flicked my gaze over towards where Railan was chatting with some of his knights. He seemed comfortable as they laughed at some joke I couldn't quite hear. At least he seemed to be making a good impression. That was all I could hope for.

Railan seemed to notice me staring as he looked directly back at me before excusing himself from the group and striding right for me. I quickly averted my gaze and glanced around to see if there was someone important behind me whom he might be interested in talking to. But to my dismay, he came right up to me, and I gripped my notebook tighter.

'I believe I'm done here, let's go,' Railan declared matter-of-factly.

'Oh... um,' I checked my pocket watch nervously. 'You still have a few more minutes left to mingle, my Lord.'

'I know, but I said I am done.' His voice was stern and unyielding, his eyes piercing me even as I avoided them.

'Yes, my Lord,' I bowed my head slightly in compliance.

I wasn't about to argue with him, and I didn't have a reason to keep him here now that the official introductions were over. Railan nodded before grabbing me by my elbow and yanking me along with him as he made for the exit. I let out a little gasp and wanted to protest that I didn't need to be dragged along, but I knew that it was probably for the best to let him do as he pleased with me.

I kept my head down until we were out of the room. I could feel the crowd's eyes at the back of my head, or more precisely, I could feel their eyes trailing Railan. Most of them probably didn't even notice me, and if they did, then this was nothing out of the ordinary.

I wasn't sure where Railan intended to go, so I glanced at the schedule one more time. To my relief, there was a nice little three-hour break, and thus, nowhere to be in any kind of hurry. To my dismay, it was also the allotted time for him to prepare for his honorary dinner with the Creed officials. The only sliver of relief I could find was the knowledge that at least this dinner did not include the other Prime Mages. I was confident they would eat him alive, even with his gift of the gab.

'My Lord, we should prepare for tonight's dinner. It would be uncouth to be late to your honorary party,' I spoke up. 'This will be your first official opportunity to ingratiate yourself with the gentry. I suggest it be your main priority.'

As soon as I finished, I immediately regretted it. It wasn't my place to lecture him.

'Ah, forgive me, my Lord. You do not need me to tell you such things. You know what you must do,' I couldn't help but lower my

head further, and I shrank back as much as physically possible, prepared to be reprimanded.

Railan chuckled as he let out a soft, wistful sigh of defeat. 'There's
no need to apologise. You're right, of course,' he paused for a moment,
a look of quiet contemplation and resignation upon his features. 'I've
set a bad precedent with you,' he looked at me, and something I
couldn't quite distinguish flickered behind his ocean-like eyes. 'I
wanted to test my new boundaries...' he trailed off as if talking more
to himself than to me.

Railan finally let my arm go, and I took a small step back. His
gaze was somewhat distant for a moment, and I raised a brow slightly.
What a strange young man. His mood was so erratic and unpre-
dictable. I could understand why he was regarded as a wild card. He
went from jumping in a pond to quiet contemplation within a few
hours. It was enough to give me emotional whiplash.

An air of awkward tension rose between us. I still needed to corral
him towards dinner preparations. Perhaps I should just relax a little
bit. Maybe then he would be more willing to comply.

'We should do something about your clothes, they're still wet,' I
gave him a light-hearted smile.

Railan grinned and gestured down to his damp clothes. 'Ah, you're
right. Thank you for reminding me,' he said, his eyes crinkling at the
corners. 'Let's find some new clothes for me to wear, shall we?'

He led me through the winding corridors of the Citadel, his demeanour much lighter now. I couldn't help but notice how easily he
navigated through the building, his confidence shining through. I suppose he had been paying attention during the tour.

He eventually stopped outside an unassuming room. He paused
and regarded it for a second before he entered. I quickly followed
after him to find a room filled with neatly organised clothing racks. I
frowned as I entered, confused why such a room was here and whose
clothes these were. Railan quickly scanned through them and pulled
out a set of dark blue garments that would complement his hair.

'Perfect,' he declared as he began to change.

I let out a sharp breath and quickly turned around, not expecting him to act so brazenly. My heart raced and my cheeks burned. Why was he like this? Why did Lady Amaranta decide I would be suited to serve him? He would give me a heart attack before I could make any progress at this rate. I clutched my notebook to my chest and tried to calm myself. I could hear his musical laughter behind me, as if he were amused by my reaction. How else was I supposed to react to a strange man stripping right in front of me? I felt my eyelids flutter as my eyes rolled in annoyance.

'My Lord, would you not prefer to return to your lodgings and change into your own clothes?' I asked as I decided to move out of his line of sight.

'No,' he said simply.

Oh, sweet Celestial Lady.

'I'm concerned the owner might be less than thrilled to find their garments requisitioned,' I commented as I opened my notebook.

'Relax. These aren't owned by anyone. Everything in this room is simply a manifestation of my current desire made by a Room of Things. Not that I expect you to know that,' he said rather sarcastically.

'I know what a Room of Things is...' I retorted quietly.

I didn't like his condescending attitude. Though I was rather used to it by now. As a mundus, I was used to being looked down upon by magi. I tried to distract myself, to focus on my notebook, scribbling down notes about my observations so far, details of our meetings so far, but my mind kept drifting back to Railan. It was hard to ignore his presence, especially when he was standing so close by, his distant warmth seeping into my back. I felt a jolt of electricity run through me as I suddenly felt his breath on my neck, and I quickly turned around to face him.

'Lord Railan,' I said, my voice shaky. 'What... what are you doing?' I tried desperately to keep my eyes locked on his face, but I couldn't do it and quickly covered my face with my book.

He looked at me with a grin, his eyes sparkling mischievously. 'What? Just changing clothes. It's not like you haven't seen a man before, right?'

I felt my cheeks flush as I tried to compose myself. 'I just... It's not appropriate,' I stammered, sure that I would keel over right then and there.

Railan shrugged, unfazed by my discomfort. 'Relax. We're both adults here. And besides, it's not like I'm asking you to undress with me.'

I felt a mix of relief and annoyance at his words as I whipped back around. Part of me was glad that he wasn't expecting anything more from me, but another part of me was irritated that he seemed to think it was okay to act so cavalierly around me. I took a deep breath and tried to focus on my notebook once again, determined to ignore him as much as possible. But as he began to hum a tune under his breath, I couldn't help but feel a strange sense of something unfamiliar. I couldn't put my finger on it. All I knew was that it made me deeply uncomfortable.

'I have to admit,' Railan spoke up abruptly, his tone suddenly soft and more sincere. 'It's nice to have someone looking out for me for a change. I'm used to doing everything on my own,' he caught my gaze in the reflection of a nearby mirror.

What was he talking about?

'Hm?' I couldn't help but tilt my head in confusion. 'I'm just doing my job, my Lord. I'm here to be utilised by you however you see fit. Your success is the Creed's success. I have faith in the Celestial Lady's judgement, and therefore I have faith in you. I will try my best to help you shine,' I spoke passionately, perhaps a little too passionately.

I quickly caught myself and broke our line of sight as I cleared my throat and straightened up. I believed in our shared mission, but it was far too early to put any real faith in Railan. Faith alone was not enough to ensure his success. Besides, if I were to be successful, Railan would never rise above his current station. Lady Amaranta did not desire another rival for the Celestial Lady's favour, and if she could not use him, she would rather he be expelled from the Creed entirely. I almost felt bad for him; he seemed almost a little too naive and childish for the world of the Prime Mages. I had to quickly remind myself that I shouldn't feel too bad. It wasn't personal for me. I was just here to do a job.

Railan's expression softened as he listened to me, and he let out a small sigh. 'You're a good one, aren't you?' he said, his voice calm and quiet. 'I appreciate your dedication to the cause. But don't forget, we're not just pawns in the Lady's game. We have our own agendas, our own desires. I won't let anyone stand in the way of mine, and I expect the same from you.'

His words sent a chill down my spine. What did he mean by that? Was he talking about his ambitions? Hearing him talk so carelessly about the Celestial Lady made me shift uncomfortably. He really did have no respect. I decided to keep my guard up and remain cautious around him, no matter how charming he may seem at times. Words like that could be easily misconstrued. Words like that were exactly what Lady Amaranta wanted to hear.

'Of course, my Lord,' I replied, trying to keep my tone neutral. 'I understand that we are all working towards our own goals, but I will continue to serve the Creed and the Celestial Lady to the best of my abilities.'

Railan nodded, his gaze still fixed on me. 'Good,' he said simply. 'Now, let's get going. We have a dinner to attend, and I don't want to keep our esteemed guests waiting.'

I followed him out of the room and into the hallway, my mind still swirling with thoughts and doubts. But for now, I knew I had to focus on the task at hand and do my best to make a good impression at the dinner. The fate of Lord Railan depended on it.

Chapter 3

For the first time today, we arrived at something punctually. I couldn't help but be washed with the sweet sensation of relief. Still, I found myself fixated on Railan's earlier words.

His own agenda.

What did he mean by that? I suppose that was something I would have to find out. I just hoped whatever he desired didn't put him at odds with anyone else, not yet. Unrestrained ambition was often the bane of Prime Mages. The desire for more, to be more, to have more, was a corrupting force. Lady Amaranta had maintained her position by showing restraint, even though she still coveted the position of First Prime Mage. I did not envy them.

I let out a heavy sigh as I leaned briefly against the drawing room wall. I was thoroughly exhausted, and I couldn't wait for this day to be over. However, no matter how tired I felt, there was no excuse for laziness, and I quickly straightened up again. My Lord had only just started mingling, and that meant I was in for a potentially long night.

As my eyes swept across the room, I couldn't help but take note of the grandeur of the event. The room was filled with an array of high-society individuals, each dressed in their finest attire. I had always been fascinated by the elite; the way they carried themselves and interacted with one another was so different from what I was used to.

But as much as the atmosphere intrigued me, it also made me feel out of place. I couldn't help but feel like an impostor among them, a mere commoner dressed in a uniform meant to blend in. I didn't belong in this world, but I would do my best to serve my Lord in it.

I scanned the crowd, looking for any potential threats or obstacles that could hinder my Lord's success. He needed to make a good impression tonight, as it could open up many opportunities for him. And if there was one thing I had learned about Railan in our short time together, it's that he knew his way around people.

I spotted him chatting with someone whom I immediately recognised from my training. Lord Advas. He was a prominent nobleman with strong economic ties due to his ownership of Maentaea's main port. My heart simultaneously rose and fell. He was a perfect, strong ally to have and an even more fearsome foe. Railan needed to win over Lord Advas; otherwise, he would find his access to resources severely hindered.

I made my way closer so I could try to overhear their conversation. I knew Advas was renowned for his pomp and grandeur. The key to his favour was simply to stroke his ego. However, I found myself increasingly concerned with every step, as I also knew that Railan had his own ego. I stopped beside the closest canapè table and focused my ears towards the two Lords. I was ready to intercede with a tasty distraction should the need arise.

As I listened in, it was apparent that Railan was handling him well. He spoke with an air of confidence that was undeniable, even to a nobleman as powerful as Advas. I couldn't help but feel a sense of pride in my Lord's abilities. He was a natural at this sort of thing.

But my focus was short-lived as I noticed something out of the corner of my eye. A group of masked individuals silently made their way into the room and moved towards us. Their smooth, blank masks spiked fear through me, and I recognized them instantly as members of the Silvyan Order. What were they doing here? They weren't on the guest list. More importantly, what were they planning to do?

I quickly scanned the room for any nearby Creed agents, but none were in sight. I would have to act fast. I quickly made my way towards Railan, trying not to draw too much attention to myself.

'My Lord,' I whispered urgently as I reached his side. 'We have a problem. The Silvyan Order is here,' I subtly gestured towards the group of masked individuals who were still moving towards us.

I had to assume he knew at least something about them. Still, the Silvyan Order was a fresh ally of the Celestial Lady, much like Railan himself, and that meant they could not be trusted, not yet. His Lordship would need to keep his guard up. Their motives for their alliance were unclear, though this could also prove to be the perfect time to learn more about them.

Railan looked up at me before his eyes flicked towards the late guests. I took the cue and quickly made my way over to the entrance, bowing politely to the arriving guests and directing them towards the main hall.

'Welcome, distinguished guests, please make yourselves comfortable. Food and drink are at your disposal,' I kept my head down, not daring to look directly at them, even if their faces were covered.

They didn't pause or acknowledge me as they simply kept walking. My stomach twisted with unease. These were powerful people, and any misstep could lead to disastrous consequences for the Creed's plans. A shiver ran down my spine as I realised that the last delegate of the Silvyan Order had stopped near me and was seemingly staring right at me. My palms felt sweaty. What could they possibly want?

I hesitantly lifted my eyes to meet them, but as soon as I did, they turned away to keep following the rest of their group. How strange. I watched them leave, their beautiful robes flowing behind them like wisps of wind. I made a mental note to keep an eye on them throughout the night, to discreetly observe their conversations and movements.

'Keep an eye on them, would you,' Railan whispered in my ear, his breath tickling my neck and startling me.

I let out a muffled squeak as I flinched and quickly spun around. I wanted to chastise him for scaring me, but I bit my tongue as I saw him laugh at me.

'Relax, nothing is going to happen to you, not while I'm around,' Railan continued to chuckle, clearly amused by my reaction.

I pouted ever so slightly before I composed myself. 'I understand, my Lord. I'll keep my eyes and ears open,' I replied quietly.

Railan nodded to me before he resumed making his way around the room. I watched him for a moment before letting out a sigh.

Great, now I have multiple targets to watch.

This was going to be a long night.

As the sun set and the moon rose, I found myself growing increasingly tired, but I couldn't let my guard down. Railan was still working the room, his charisma and charm on full display, and I knew that I had to be ready to assist him at a moment's notice.

Luckily, or perhaps unfortunately, the Silvyan Order representatives kept mainly to themselves, and while there was a tense aura that hung in the air, Railan seemed to be mostly unfazed.

I made sure to offer them food and drink to keep them satisfied, but they declined everything. Of course, they weren't exactly human, so it was not surprising that they would be uninterested. Perhaps that was what made them so uncomfortable to be around.

On the outside, they were humanoid enough, but every inch of their bodies was concealed under layers of fine clothing. No one knew what lay underneath, and that was what made them scary. My imagination was already running wild, projecting images of fearsome beasts just waiting to burst forth and tear my throat out.

No, stop that.

I couldn't let my fears get the better of me. For all I knew, they could just be normal people playing dress up. Yet even I could sense that there was something more to them than meets the eye.

As the night wore on and a few hours passed, the party was starting to die down without any issues. The officials started to slowly trickle out, one by one, until only the Silvyan Order remained. I watched nervously as Railan finally made his way over to them. They hadn't done anything all night, so I knew I shouldn't really be worried, but still, I could feel my heart pounding in my chest as Railan stopped by the Silvyan Order representatives and attempted to work his magic. I couldn't hear what they were saying from where I was standing, but I could see the tension in their body language. My mind raced as I tried to think of what I could do to help if things went awry.

I took a few steps to join the conversation when suddenly one of the Silvyan Order representatives turned and started walking away. The others quickly followed, except for the same teal-clad representative who had stopped to gawk at me earlier. They tilted their head slightly as they stared at Railan before pressing their hand to their chest and bowing their head. They seemed to notice me approaching as their masked face snapped towards me before they turned to catch up with the rest of their companions, leaving Railan standing alone. He looked disappointed, but not surprised. I approached him cautiously.

'Is everything alright, my Lord?' I asked, my voice barely above a whisper. 'What was all that about?'

Railan sighed, his shoulders slumping slightly. 'It seems they weren't interested in anything I had to say. But that's alright. We'll just have to find another way to gain their trust.'

I nodded, relieved that the situation had been diffused. 'Is there anything I can do to assist you, my Lord?'

Railan smiled. 'Actually, yes. I need you to compile a report on the Silvyan Order. I want to know everything there is to know about them. Their history, their motives, their strengths, and their weaknesses. Everything.'

I nodded, my mind already racing with ideas. 'Consider it done, my Lord. I will start it first thing tomorrow.'

Railan clapped me on the back. 'Good. I knew I could count on you.'

I couldn't help but flinch, both surprised and uncomfortable by Railan's casual touch. I raised my brow but didn't say anything. I supposed that meant he approved of me now? I just hoped his mood wouldn't change in the morning.

As we made our way out of the room, I couldn't help but wonder what the Silvyan Order was really up to, if they really had good intentions, or if their goals were something more nefarious. Then again, what was I thinking? They hadn't exactly given me any reason to distrust them; after all, they were theoretically our allies. Still, they were foreign, and their very nature made my body stand on edge. I could sense that Railan felt the same. I would have to make that report promptly.

'My Lord, I shall see you to your lodgings,' I said. 'Hopefully, your estate will be prepared soon. I imagine it will be nice to have some space and not just a single apartment,' I smiled lightly in an effort to relieve some of the tension in the air.

Railan nodded in agreement, the tension in his shoulders visibly easing. 'Indeed. A change of scenery would be welcome.'

We made our way out of the building and into the cool evening air. The stars shone brightly in the sky, and a gentle breeze blew through the streets. As we walked, I couldn't help the unease that settled into the pit of my stomach. The Silvyan Order was still a mystery, and I couldn't shake the feeling that there was something off about them. Lady Amaranta was suspicious of their return. Though I was sure she was also working to secure their allegiance. I didn't doubt that she saw some kind of potential to manipulate them for her machinations. She always had a plan to use people.

We arrived at Railan's temporary lodgings, and I bade him goodnight before turning to make my way back to my apartment. As I walked, my thoughts continued to race. The events of the night had left me with more questions than answers, and I knew that I would have to work hard to ensure that Railan's mission was a success. But for now, all I could do was rest and prepare for the challenges that lay ahead.

Chapter 4

I awoke nice and early with a renewed sense of purpose and determination. It was a new day with many wonderful possibilities. While I knew Lord Railan would no doubt throw everything into chaos, I still had some time to prepare myself and enjoy the quiet calm of the early morning.

I sat at my desk, a warm hot chocolate in one hand and my notebook in the other. I flicked through my notes. I let out a wistful, defeated sigh. Indeed, my Lord was the embodiment of chaos. He was very much my opposite, and I couldn't help but wonder why Lady Amaranta picked me for this job. Perhaps she thought I could balance him out. Sure, I could do that, but still, it felt like an unexpected burden.

I let out another sigh as I turned to today's schedule. Thankfully, the first appointment was a little later in the morning and thus I had ample time to begin my investigation into the Silvyan Order.

I finished off my drink before I proceeded with my morning ritual. I would need to visit the Archive, and that meant a little trek in the snow. I glanced outside. A light shower of snow fell steadily. It was perfectly mundane and beautiful, and it also meant that I would need to rug up. As they say, when it rains, it usually pours, and I wasn't about to take any chances. I knew full well the consequences of underestimating the cold. I slipped on my biggest coat and slung my satchel over my shoulder. No doubt, I would need it to carry any potential books I would borrow. Content that I was prepared for the day, I made my way out of my apartment and into the cold streets of the Capital.

The cold, crisp air was a nice little shock to my body. If I weren't awake yet, I definitely would be now. The Archive was, unfortunately, not a part of the Creed Citadel since it was more akin to a public library. That meant I couldn't slip in through the Citadel's nice, cosy halls even though they sounded perfect right now. I could feel the fresh flakes as they touched my cheeks and turned them red. Cold. I pulled up my cloak hood to better shield my face.

The walk was not exceptionally long, but the weather was cold enough to leave me feeling chilled despite my many layers. I was grateful to see the grand building that was the Archive as it came into view, and I hastily scurried inside the main entrance. I couldn't help but shiver, and I was hit by a wave of welcoming warmth. A large fire roared in a grand fire pit at the centre of the foyer. Its flame had a unique sparkle to it, one that suggested it was most likely magic. Of course, that would explain the lack of suffocating smoke in what was otherwise an unventilated area.

I took a moment to catch my breath and warm up as I took in the lavish fixtures. It was nice and familiar. I'd spent a lot of time here over the years, perhaps to the point that I now knew it better than the back of my hand. Of course, it was clean, quiet, and brimming with knowledge. Everything I liked.

I peered over to the far back of the foyer, where the information desk was located. A small, involuntary smile spread across my lips as I spotted a familiar face.

A slightly chubby older man with a thick, blonde beard sat behind the desk. His head was down, and it was apparent he was deeply engrossed in the text before him. I recognised him instantly as the head librarian, Pavel. He was indeed a welcoming sight as we'd become well acquainted over the years. In fact, he felt more like an uncle than a stranger at this point, and I was reminded that it had been far too long since I'd last visited the Archive. I'd spent the last month training specifically for my assignment to Railan and thus been a little too preoccupied for any personal or general research.

I eagerly skipped over to the desk and tapped on the marble top. 'Good morning, Mr Pavel!' I chirped merrily.

My sudden arrival seemed to startle the man as he let out a surprised yelp and fumbled the book in his hands. A frown briefly sat upon his brows before he saw me, and they quickly turned into big, happy arches. Though his smile was mostly hidden, I could still make out the faint outline as his beard raised slightly.

'Oh, Issy! How good to see you, it feels like it's been an age! I was beginning to think you'd been assigned out of the country,' he chuckled.

'I wouldn't leave without saying goodbye! Plus, I promised I'd collect your exotic text wish-list to take with me, didn't I?' I laughed as I shook my head. 'No, things have just been rather hectic lately. I know news travels fast around here, so you shouldn't be too surprised to learn that I've been promoted to Lord Railan's assistant. He was formally introduced to the Creed yesterday and will publicly debut as the official Twelfth Prime Mage during this weekend's social ball. Of course, you already know this since you will be attending, right?' I raised a brow expectantly.

Pavel let out an almost nervous laugh. 'Assistant to a Prime Mage, huh? You sure are moving up in the world, aren't you?'

'You didn't answer my question,' my smile narrowed into a more sly smirk.

'Yes, of course, I'll be there. If not to see who this Railan fellow is, then to at least steal a dance or two with you,' Pavel gave me a teasing wink.

I chuckled as I shook my head. 'You know I'm not one for dancing. Besides, I will be working. I don't anticipate much, if any, free time.'

'This Railan fellow will work you to the bone, even on a social outing?' Pavel raised a brow.

I couldn't help but shrug. 'Perhaps. I'm still getting used to him at the moment. He's rather... lively,' I put it as politely as I could.

Pavel's expression dropped slightly, and he lowered his voice as he leaned closer to me. 'I've heard... things... about this Lord Railan. You should be cautious now and take care of yourself,' his voice was stern and filled with concern.

'And what have you heard of his Lordship?' I tilted my head as I narrowed my eyes at him.

I knew Pavel meant well, but I was also curious to hear exactly what kind of rumours were currently spreading about my Lord.

Pavel stared at me as he pressed his lips into a firm line. I softened my expression and fluttered my eyelashes at him. 'I'm genuinely curious. You can be honest with me,' I reassured him.

His lips turned into a grumpy pout as he instantly melted at my overly sweet inflections.

'Well...' Pavel leaned in even closer so that he could whisper to me. 'I heard that Lord Railan is particularly ruthless, and that is why he was promoted to Prime Mage. Some even say he was an assassin. That does not bode well. Someone like that likely has no honour.'

I frowned at his words. 'And who told you those lies?' I glowered.

'Look, that's just what I heard from no one in particular,' he was immediately defensive as he withdrew and held up his hands.

Fantastic.

I knew my Lord's reputation wasn't... great. But even Pavel had heard the rumours. I'd have to run some counter-interference to try and quell the rumours, even if they were true. Lady Amaranta hadn't specifically instructed me to sabotage him just yet, so I would do my job and defend him.

'Well, whatever you've heard is emphatically false. Lord Railan is, on the contrary, a very nice and approachable young man, and I have no idea where this assassin nonsense has come from. He is, in fact, a very honourable warrior, and that is why he was chosen by the Celestial Lady,' I said with confident conviction.

Pavel searched my face for a moment before he let out a soft sigh. 'Well, if that is your experience, then I have no choice but to reserve my judgement.'

I gave him a bright, contented smile. 'It is.'

Pavel shook his head as his smile returned. 'Well, enough about that. What brings you here today?'

Oh, that's right. I'm here for a specific purpose.

'I'd like access to the restricted archives,' I said as I pulled my Creed sigil from my pocket and flashed it at him.

'The restricted archives?' He raised a brow as he shuffled his chair over to his locked drawers. 'And what would you be needing from there?'

I shrugged, not willing to give away too much. 'I'm doing some research, and what I need is more than likely there.'

Pavel rolled his eyes as he unlocked the drawer and shuffled through its contents. 'Hopefully it's nothing you can get in trouble for.'

'I have access, so there's nothing in there that can get me in trouble,' I reminded him.

'Still, best to be cautious,' he said as he passed me a shiny silver key with a red ribbon tied to it.

'You know the rules for this,' Pavel said firmly. 'If you try to leave the building with it, it is a criminal offence. Also, a reminder that the key is embedded with elemental magic so that it can be traced.'

'I understand,' I nodded as I closed my palm around the key. 'I'll drop it off as usual.'

'Alright, I hope you find what you need,' he gave me one last gentle smile.

I returned his gesture before I made my way into the Archive proper. I would consider the inner Archive to be one of, if not the most, beautiful works of art in all of Maentaea. It was wall-to-wall elegant shelving that reached to the ceiling. The layout was almost maze-like, and if one wasn't careful, they could easily become lost. I could recall that a few of my first visits had ended with me crying down some random section with seemingly no end. I smiled at the thought. I had been a dumb child back then. Now I knew every aisle by heart, and getting lost seemed impossible.

I confidently made my way through the Archive, striding with purposeful intent. The restricted section was located at the very back, hidden away from regular visitors and locked behind a door reminiscent of those found in bank vaults. Only certain Creed members had the privilege to access this section, and I was lucky enough to be one of them.

The restricted section was exactly what one would expect. It contained sensitive and restricted texts. It was mostly controversial historical and religious accounts that had been deemed heresy, but there was also intimate knowledge of certain Creed secrets. Mostly old military records, but there were other, more dangerous things. However, my interest was in the Silvyan Order. Until recently, they had been thought to simply be myths and legends. Though that was obviously no longer the case. I wasn't even sure if the information available would be anywhere close to accurate, but I would collect it nonetheless.

I entered the restricted section and headed straight for the "S" section. The shelves were a lot more sparse in the private room and thus, easier to peruse, especially given my time limit. I ran my finger along the spines of the books and folders, inspecting them closely as I scanned for anything relating to the Silvyan Order. To my surprise, there was nothing. I frowned, slightly confused. Perhaps it was under the "O" section instead. I wandered deeper into the archives in search of anything useful. I let out a small sigh of relief as I found a few books tucked away under "Order". I pulled them from the shelf and brought them over to the nearest table. The books appeared worryingly thin, and I didn't have much hope that they would be of any help. I opened the first one and was aghast to discover that a good portion of its pages had been torn out. I held it up to inspect it.

Odd.

I looked over what remained and found it was mostly vague descriptions of the Silvyan Order's hierarchy. A few keywords had been blacked out. I bit my lip as my mind raced. Who exactly were these people, and why would information on them be censored? Perhaps they truly were more dangerous than I'd first thought. I turned to the next book. It had been similarly defiled with very little in the way of useful information. All six of the books on the subject had been heavily doctored and censored. It was very strange.

I leant back in my chair, frustrated by the lack of, well, anything. I tried my best to scribble down as much as I could, but it all seemed superficial and useless. Frustration bubbled up within me, and I closed my eyes, taking a deep breath to calm myself down. I couldn't believe that there was nothing useful about the Silvyan Order in the Creed's restricted archives. It was impossible. They had to have some information on them.

'Are you having trouble finding something?' a gentle, feminine voice suddenly called out to me.

I quickly sat up and flicked my eyes in the direction of the voice. A mature-looking woman stood not too far away, a pile of books in her hands. She flashed me a friendly smile, and I quickly returned the gesture. She wore brown, just like me, which meant she was also a mundus of the Creed. I couldn't recall ever having seen her before, but she must have been quite senior to have access to the restricted section.

'A little,' I chuckled lightly. 'Most of these texts are censored.'

I held up one of the books and waved it with a sigh.

'What are you researching?' she asked as she made her way over to me and placed her books on the table.

I passed her the book to inspect. 'I'm just compiling a little something on the Silvyan Order. Their return has sparked some curiosity, but alas, it appears I won't be able to satisfy that itch.'

The woman regarded the book, turning it over in her hands before flipping through the pages. She pursed her lips into a line as she saw the lack of substance.

'They are rather fascinating, aren't they? Though you won't find anything useful here,' she chuckled as she placed the book down.

'Oh?' I raised a brow. 'Pray tell, if you know somewhere more suitable?'

'Well... I shouldn't really say,' she suddenly drew back all coy, as if she'd said too much.

'As an academic, I'm now far too curious,' I gave her a sly smirk as I rested my chin on my hand. 'You can't just casually mention an alternative source and not expect me to enquire further.'

The woman let out a light, musical laugh. 'Forgive me, I didn't mean to stir you. I understand the desire for knowledge can be quite addictive,' her demeanour relaxed again.

'Indeed, this subject may just lead to many sleepless nights,' I joked.

The woman simply laughed again before her emerald eyes settled upon me with a look of gentle delight. 'I'm Lauralai.'

'Oh, I'm Isla, it's a pleasure to meet you,' I quickly stood to give her a proper greeting.

'Isla...' she repeated my name quietly, as if committing it to memory. 'Pretty, like an island.'

I nodded at her observation. 'Indeed. And I believe Lauralai refers to a siren.'

Lauralai also nodded, and we shared a delightful chuckle at our extremely nerdy observations of our names. It was rather pleasant to feel at ease, especially after the stress of yesterday. I hadn't even realised how much I missed mingling with other academics.

She regarded me for a moment before she spoke again. 'Well, I suppose it won't hurt to give you a little clue.'

I raised a brow, inviting her to continue.

'If you want to learn more about the Silvyan Order, I would suggest you go to the old ruins in Arcanist's Village in the inner ward. The latest findings suggest they are an old Silyvan temple, though the Silvyan's themselves have neither confirmed nor denied this. Perhaps you might find something useful there,' she revealed.

'The ruins...' I pondered the information. 'Wouldn't any information from there already be recorded?'

'I suggest you go and see for yourself,' Lauralai gave me a knowing wink. 'Now, I must be off, but I hope you find what you're looking for.'

She collected her books and headed out of the room. I watched as she left, my mind abuzz at her little hint.

The ruins in Arcanist's Village.

I'd heard of them, but only in passing. They had been excavated quite some time ago, so I doubted they would really provide me with any real insight. Still, I couldn't help but feel that perhaps it would be worth it just to check it out anyway. I looked at my pocket watch; it was indeed time to start thinking about leaving. I let out a soft sigh. I would have to investigate the ruins later.

I packed up my things and returned the books before I made my way out of the archives. I discreetly deposited the key back into Pavel's care and stepped out into the cold air of Maentaea. I felt a sinking sensation in my stomach. It was almost time to fetch Railan for his first appointment, and I couldn't help but dread what was to come. However, I tried to prepare myself mentally, reminding myself to expect the unexpected. I just hoped that he wouldn't do anything too reckless today. Regardless, I was ready for whatever came my way.

Chapter 5

As I made my way to Railan's lodgings, I silently prayed that he would still be there and hadn't just wandered off somewhere. The thought of another embarrassing encounter made me cringe. I needed to try harder to rein him in, but the thought alone was intimidating. I would have to overcome my fear; otherwise, I would be useless to him. If I were useless, then he would get rid of me, and Lady Amaranta would be furious. I could only imagine her punishment. Would she expel my family onto the streets or hurt them? Would she sell me to someone else? Would she kill me? I couldn't think of such things.

I stopped by the entranceway and confirmed that there was a sleigh waiting for him. That was a relief. Trying to arrange transport on such short notice would have been a nightmare in and of itself. Today's business was outside the Citadel, and thus we would need to have a sleigh on hand at all times. I was almost looking forward to it since I usually just walked everywhere.

When I arrived at Railan's door, I knocked briskly and held my breath, listening for any sounds from inside. As I waited for a response, I couldn't help but feel anxious. I really didn't want to have to search for him for hours, especially not in this weather.

After a few moments, I heard shuffling inside the room and the sound of the lock turning. The door creaked open, and Railan peered out from behind it, his hair still damp from what I could only assume was another one of his impromptu swims.

'Ah, you're here!' he exclaimed, his eyes lighting up with excitement. 'I was just getting ready. Give me a minute, and we can head out.'

I was relieved that he was still here and not off on some wild adventure. I nodded and waited as he disappeared back into the room to gather his things. A few minutes later, Railan emerged, dressed in his usual elegant, if not a little flamboyant, attire, and I led him outside to the sleigh waiting to take us to his appointment.

As we rode through the streets, I couldn't help but feel a sense of unease. I knew that Railan's appointment was not going to be an easy one, and I worried about how he would react. I knew it had almost certainly been slipped into his schedule as a test by Lady Amaranta. Today, Railan would have to face the Grand Cardinal, Vasili Raskolnikov, the acting voice of the Celestial Lady for the common folk. He was renowned for his serious, no-nonsense attitude and his complete and absolute devotion to the Celestial Lady. He believed in following her words to the letter, and any suggestions otherwise would be branded heresy.

He was by far the scariest official within the Creed, besides the Prime Mages themselves. The only reason the Cardinal wasn't a Prime Mage himself was that he was unfortunate enough to be born a mundus. Perhaps his fanaticism came from the belief that the Lady would one day change his fate. Regardless, Railan was expected to schmooze the cardinal and reaffirm his faith and devotion to the Celestial Lady. The slightest slip of the tongue would turn the cardinal against him instantly, and thus, the people.

I found myself growing more nervous the closer we got. The Cardinal's estate was on the far side of the city in Highsword Borough, and thus, there was a little too much time to think.

I glanced at Railan and swallowed nervously. His clothes were, thankfully, dry, but his hair was still damp and somewhat unkempt. I prayed it would be somewhat dry by the time we arrived. Regardless, his appearance was serviceable, and that was all that mattered.

'My Lord, I must inform you that Cardinal Vasili can be rather... strict,' I hesitated to describe the man.

Railan just chuckled and flashed a grin at me. 'Don't worry, I can handle him. Besides, what's life without a little challenge?'

His confidence was reassuring, but I couldn't help feeling anxious. I had to hope his charm would work on the Cardinal.

As we reached the gates of the estate, I could feel my heart pounding in my chest. The cardinal's imposing mansion loomed ahead of us, its grandeur intimidating me even from a distance. The guards at the gate greeted us and checked our credentials before allowing us entry. We made our way through the frozen gardens, and I couldn't help but admire the immaculate scenery and perfectly shaped ice sculptures. Everything about this place reeked of power and wealth.

Finally, we arrived at the door, and I took a deep breath, trying to calm my nerves. The butler led us into a grand sitting room, and we were left waiting for a few minutes. Every second felt like an eternity, and I couldn't help but fidget with my clothes as I stood quietly beside the lavish couch.

'Relax, this will be nothing,' Railan tried to reassure me as he lounged casually.

I simply nodded, his words not inspiring any faith within me. He was acting far too comfortable for my liking.

Finally, the Grand Cardinal entered, and my heart skipped a beat. He was even more imposing than I had imagined, with his stern expression and piercing gaze. I could feel him scrutinising us, looking for any hint of wrongdoing.

Railan quickly stood and stepped forward, greeting the cardinal with a bow. 'Your Eminence, it's an honour to be in your presence.'

The Cardinal nodded, his expression still stern. 'I trust you under-stand the gravity of this appointment, Lord Railan. The Celestial Lady requires unwavering loyalty from her subjects, and any deviation from her will is unacceptable.'

Railan remained calm and collected, his confidence unwavering. 'Of course, Your Eminence. I am fully committed to the Celestial Lady and her vision for our nation.'

The Cardinal nodded again, and I could feel a small sense of relief wash over me. But the tension in the air was still palpable, and I knew we were far from safe. We would have to tread carefully in the pres-ence of this formidable figure.

I keep myself small, with my head down and my hands wrapped tight around my notebook. Now was not the time to draw attention to myself. I had to remind myself to have faith in my Lord. His ran-domness yesterday seemed to have been more like a test than anything else, and somehow I'd passed. I hoped his otherwise personable nature would be enough to carry him through, though now was the perfect time to gauge his loyalty to the cause.

The Cardinal's eyes shifted over to me, much to my dismay, before they returned to Railan.

'This is a private matter; your aide is not required. Dismiss her for now,' he said firmly.

My chest tightened as I flicked my eyes to Railan, who met my gaze immediately. Railan's expression was unreadable as he turned to face me. I could see the slightest hint of worry in his eyes, and it gave me some comfort knowing that he was still human, still capable of feel-ing fear and uncertainty. I nodded to him and stepped back, bowing slightly to the cardinal before turning to leave the room. I closed the door behind me and leaned against the wall, taking a deep breath and letting it out slowly. It was going to be a long wait. I pulled out my notebook and pen, scribbling down a few notes from what I'd over-heard so far. It was my job to keep track of everything, to ensure that nothing was missed, no detail was too small to be recorded. I had to be ready for anything. My eyes darted to the door every time there was a sound, hoping that Railan would emerge soon. But the minutes ticked by slowly, and I couldn't help but wonder what was happening inside.

I briefly pressed my ear to the door to eavesdrop, but it was far too thick and sturdy to hear anything other than a soft, muffled drone. I quickly gave up on the idea as it was clear the cardinal was more than prepared for this kind of situation. I couldn't help but chuckle to myself. Of course, the Cardinal worked with sensitive information and was generally a private person, so it made sense that he would have taken extra precautions to keep things confidential. Though that did make my job harder.

I wiped the smile from my lips as I adjusted my posture. I needed to be professional. I glanced around the grand hall. Everything about the cardinal had an air of grandeur. It was almost a little too on the nose, as if he was overcompensating for something. I let my eyes wander and took in every detail. I was in for a potentially long wait.

My mind wandered back to the Silvyan Order. I couldn't help but wonder if there really was anything useful in the old Arcanist's Village ruins. One would have thought it would have been picked clean by now. Still, perhaps just a little look wouldn't hurt. Besides, it would be interesting on premise alone. I'd never personally visited the ruins since I was more interested in the theoretical sides of things rather than the practical. I made a mental note to stop by on the way home if today didn't drag on like last night.

I was so engrossed in my thoughts that I didn't even notice when Railan emerged from the cardinal's office, looking somewhat dishevelled but also strangely triumphant.

'Ah, there you are,' he said, a grin spreading across his face, 'I have good news. The Cardinal has given me his blessing.'

I felt a surge of relief flood through me. This was the outcome we had been hoping for, but I couldn't help but wonder what Railan had said or done to win over the cardinal. I decided to worry about that later.

'Congratulations, my Lord. I knew you could do it,' I said.

'Did you, though?' Railan narrowed his eyes at me, and I felt my skin prickle nervously.

'O-Of course, my Lord,' I stuttered as I looked at the ground.

Railan let out an amused laugh. 'Relax, I'm just messing with you.'

I squeezed my eyes tight as I took in a deep breath. How could I possibly relax around someone so... just, ugh! I couldn't let him get to me. The day had only just started. I needed to take it one step at a time. I could relax at the ruins later.

'We should get going. You need to make some progress on the social ball preparations. As the guest of honour, your specifications must be met,' I forced out a smile.

To my delight, Railan simply nodded in agreement, and we made our way out of the cardinal's estate.

As we got seated in the sleigh, I was hit with sweet relief. The hard part was finally over. The rest of the day was to be spent on more casual arrangements, mostly to do with the upcoming ball. As I glanced over at my seemingly high-spirited Lord, I couldn't help but feel somewhat guilty. There was a boyish, naive charm about him, and I knew full well that he could be ruined at any second. There was a reason that the Prime Mages were not only revered but also feared. One did not remain a Prime Mage for long unless one could manoeuvre around the other Prime Mages. Staying as the Twelfth would not remain feasible in the long run. The ultimate goal of a Prime Mage was to rise through the ranks, to gain more power and favour with the Celestial Lady. But the other Prime Mages were also vying for the same positions, and that meant that their world was one of fear, uncertainty, and betrayal. Sabotage, mistrust, scheming, these were the skills of the Prime Mages. This was the world we were now a part of. If it was not Railan, then it would have been someone else. I had to quickly remind myself that this wasn't personal. I was just doing what had to be done to protect not only myself, but also my family.

As we continued on our way, I took the opportunity to ask Railan about his plans for the upcoming ball. 'My Lord, have you decided on your costume for the ball yet?' I asked curiously.

Railan chuckled. 'Not yet, but I have a few ideas in mind,' he replied. 'I was thinking of going for a more... dramatic look. Perhaps something inspired by the Prime Mages themselves.'

I raised an eyebrow at that. 'Are you sure that's wise, my Lord? The Prime Mages are feared by many, and it might not be the best idea to draw too much attention to yourself so soon.'

Railan simply shrugged. 'I have never been one to shy away from attention, my dear aide. And besides, it's just a bit of harmless fun. No harm can come from dressing up, can it?'

I couldn't help but feel a sense of unease at his words. The Prime Mages were not to be taken lightly, and I couldn't shake the feeling that something dangerous was lurking just around the corner. But I knew better than to voice my concerns to Railan. He was his own person, and he would do as he pleased. My job was simply to support and advise him to the best of my abilities.

'The next appointment is with the seamstress, and ample time has been delegated to ensure your vision can be properly conveyed. Whatever my Lord decides, I'm sure you will be the centre of attention. The ball is being held in honour of your debut, after all,' I gave him a weary smile even though I dreaded what kind of monstrosity of an outfit he would request.

Railan chuckled, 'Oh, you wound me, my dear aide. Have a little faith in my fashion sense, won't you? I promise not to disappoint you or our guests at the ball,' he said with a wink.

I couldn't help but roll my eyes at his teasing. Despite my reservations, I knew that he had impeccable taste when he wanted to, and I needed to trust him not to make a complete fool of himself or the Creed at the ball.

'Of course, my Lord. I do not doubt that you will be the talk of the town after the ball,' I said with a small smile.

Railan beamed at my words and leaned back into the cushions of the sleigh. As we made our way to the seamstress, I couldn't help but feel a sense of contentment. Despite the dangers that lurked in the shadows of the Prime Mages, I had to have faith that Railan would be successful.

We soon pulled up outside the most exclusive boutique in all of Maentaea: Aizel. Getting an appointment here was exceptionally hard; even the richest of the elites had months-long wait times just to spend a few minutes inside. It was only by the grace of the Celestial Lady's request that my Lord even had the opportunity to set foot inside with such prompt timing.

I felt the butterflies stir in my stomach as I stepped out of the sleigh and saw the truly luxurious building. Solid marble walls embossed with golden leaf. It oozed with pomp and wealth. This was a place I could never have dreamed of visiting, yet here I was. My mouth felt dry as I eyed the lovely outfits perfectly positioned in the windows. A single piece would cost more than I could ever hope to earn in a lifetime.

You can look, but don't touch. I reminded myself.

I followed Railan in through the heavy, ivory door, and my breath was taken away by all the glittering fabrics on display. The scent of gentle rose incense filled the air and mingled with the smell of newly spun fabrics. Everything was pristine and clean and a little intimidating. I didn't really know where to look as every surface seemed almost too dazzling.

Focus.

We were here for a reason. I shook off my daze and scanned the room for the attendant. To my relief, an elegantly dressed woman was already heading straight for us. She held her head high and had an air of superior professionalism about her. I pushed forward to greet her with a respectful bow.

'Good evening, Lord Railan is here for his appointment with Lady Aizel,' I gestured towards my Lord.

The woman narrowed her eyes at me before following my hand. Her face immediately softened into something more charming, yet insidious as she laid her eyes upon Railan. She quickly brushed past me, ignoring me completely as she sauntered over to Railan.

'Ah, Lord Railan, we have been expecting you. Follow me, Lady Aizel has been eagerly waiting to meet you,' the woman beamed as she got a little too close and placed her hand upon his arm.

I couldn't help but feel a twinge of discomfort as the attendant practically fawned over my Lord. I followed closely behind them as they made their way through the boutique, my eyes darting around at all the beautiful fabrics and intricate designs. Lady Aizel herself was waiting for us in a private room, surrounded by an array of fabrics and patterns. She was a regal woman with perfectly styled silver hair and sharp, calculating eyes.

'Lord Railan, it is an honour to finally meet you in person. I have heard so much about you,' she said with a small smile as she rose from her seat to greet us.

Railan gave a polite bow. 'The pleasure is all mine, Lady Aizel. I am looking forward to seeing what you have in mind for my outfit for the ball.'

Lady Aizel's smile widened. 'Of course, of course. But first, let's get you properly measured and discuss your preferences. We must create something that perfectly complements your unique style and personality.'

I watched as they got to work, discussing fabrics, colours, and designs. It was clear that Lady Aizel was a true master of her craft, and Railan was in good hands. As they worked, I couldn't help but wonder what kind of outfit Railan would choose. Would it be something bold and daring, or more classic and refined? I suppose only time would tell.

I almost felt perverted as I covertly scribbled down my Lord's measurements for future reference. I could feel my cheeks growing hotter and hotter as I looked between the numbers and him. I couldn't deny that my Lord was conventionally attractive, after all, I was still a woman with semi-functional eyes.

Stop that.

I quickly closed my eyes to clear my head and the colour from my cheeks. I could look, but never touch. Besides, I still wasn't sure what lay beneath his charming exterior. He had a wildness that could only stem from his youth. I had to hope he would mature with time, and then my job would become easier. I hoped Lady Amaranta's concerns were unfounded and that I could remain by his side. At least then I could pretend to be a semi-autonomous person.

I really need to stop overthinking.

I averted my gaze and decided to focus on Lady Aizel. It was clear why she was regarded as the best seamstress in all of Maentaea. She had a friendly air about her, and she knew exactly how to handle her clients. It was also apparent why her designs were so exclusive and expensive. She did not have any assistants besides her boutique attendant, and that meant that every design was hand-made personally by her. A renewed sense of awe washed over me. Lady Aizel was truly amazing.

As I observed Lady Aizel's work, I couldn't help but feel a pang of jealousy. Here was a woman who had achieved everything I had ever dreamed of: success, respect, and admiration. I wondered what it was like to be her, to have the talent and dedication to create something so beautiful from scratch. But then again, I reminded myself that every path was different and that success came in many forms. I was content with my job, and I was sure I would grow to enjoy serving my Lord.

After a few more hours of measuring and discussing, my Lord was finally finished with his appointment. We stepped out of Aizel feeling satisfied, yet a little overwhelmed. The day had been long and arduous, but we had accomplished what we set out to do. My Lord's outfit for the ball was in the works, and preparations had begun.

To my pleasant surprise, my Lord had been perfectly agreeable today, and I hoped that attitude would continue going forward. There were only a few more days until the ball, then he could afford to be more relaxed. Until then, I needed him to stay focused and presentable.

'There's nothing more scheduled for today, you should get some rest,' I suggested.

Railan nodded in agreement. 'That sounds like a good idea. I have a feeling that the next few days are going to be quite busy.'

I offered him a small smile. 'Indeed, but I'm sure it will be well worth it.'

He gave me a nod of appreciation before turning to leave the boutique. I followed closely behind him, relieved that the first day of preparations was over. As we climbed back into the sleigh, I couldn't help but feel grateful for this opportunity. The world of the elite was a fascinating place, full of hidden wonders and mysteries. And here I was, experiencing it all firsthand. I leaned back in my seat and took a deep breath, relishing in the moment.

There was still a lot to be done, but I was confident that we would be able to manage it all in time. I couldn't help but feel a sense of anticipation and excitement for the upcoming ball.

Chapter 6

I bid Railan good night and started back towards my apartment. There was a chill in the air, the same as every other night, yet it seemed to have a little extra bite. I cast my eyes up to the sky. It was probably because of the new moon. The darkness only made the winter harsher.

Darkness.

I suddenly remembered that I wanted to make a slight detour. Well, more like a large detour. I had said to myself that I would stop by the old ruins in Arcanist's Village tonight after work. Lauralai's tip had piqued my interest, and I knew it would continue to gnaw at me until I scratched the itch.

I diverted my path and started towards Arcanist's Village. It was quite out of the way, being a district of the inner city. I was just lucky that my shift had ended earlier than expected. A quick investigation, and then I could get some sleep. I trudged through the snowy streets with excited determination. It was always fun to learn new things, and though I wasn't overly optimistic, the thought of uncovering something that was long forgotten made my insides tingle.

I passed through Greatsword Ward and the Sword District into the Arcanist's Village. It was so named for obvious reasons, as it was where the majority of the magi had coalesced over the years. Tiny motes of elemental light fluttered in the breeze throughout the streets. Known as witchlights, the little orbs gathered on the eaves, painting the buildings in gentle, prismatic light. Power lived here. I reminded myself to be cautious and keep my head down. I didn't need nor want to draw the attention of the magi, especially not this late at night. I was able to follow the witchlights to the old ruins that were hidden away in the abandoned portion of the village. The witchlights were particularly drawn here as they clung to the crumbling stone. Old magic flowed through these ruins.

I carefully climbed over the partial wall that was meant to deter visitors. While the ruins had been excavated, that didn't necessarily mean they were safe. The structures were unstable, bandits could be lying in wait behind any corner, and unstable wild magic could lead to trouble if I didn't keep my wits about me. I moved slowly, quietly as I scanned the area. The witchlights provided quite the illumination despite the moonless night, and I couldn't help but briefly admire them. They were manifestations of elemental magic. Some believed them to be sentient creatures, while others simply viewed them as raw power. I was uncertain where my opinion landed. They moved on their own and were either pulled or repulsed by people. I couldn't say for certain if it was simply because they were drawn to strong elemental power or if it was a more conscious choice. Either way, I wasn't here to study witchlights; I was here to study the Silvyan Order.

As I crept through the ruins, I couldn't help but feel a sense of unease. The Silvyan Order was a group of powerful creatures who had one day simply vanished from the world, only to just as abruptly return. They were mysterious, unknown, and not to be trifled with. Where had they gone, and why had they returned? These were good questions that had yet to be answered.

The deeper I went, the more unsettled I became. Even with the glow of the witchlights, I felt like I was in a very dark place. I began to notice that partial depictions of murals and symbols were still visible upon the ancient stone. Curious, I pulled out my notebook to cross-reference the symbols with the ones I'd copied from the books in the Archive. To my surprise, I was able to find a few matching symbols. Something about a "Sil". I could only speculate that it was about a high-ranking member of the Silvyan Order. Had this place been the residence of a powerful member of the Order? I'd always kind of assumed it had been a temple of some kind.

As I moved in deeper, new, unknown symbols started to appear. I copied them down in quick succession. They could prove useful in the future. I even made some rough approximations of the partial murals. While the ruins were fascinating, they hadn't exactly provided me with any useful insights. At least, not any insights that Railan would be interested in.

I took in a deep breath and felt the subtle nagging of sleep as it pulled at me. I checked my pocket watch; it was after midnight. I closed my eyes for a brief moment. It had been a long day, and I deserved some sleep. I stood to leave, but a strange glint caught my attention out of the corner of my eye. I ambled over to the source and found a little witchlight hidden under some crumbled stone. To my surprise, it sat atop a small wooden box nestled between the rocks. I frowned, wondering what such a thing was doing there. The box looked old, the wood a deep brown, and etchings adorned its surface. I reached for it, hesitating as my fingers grazed over its smooth surface. A shiver ran down my spine, and I pulled my hand back, almost as if the box was cursed. But then my curiosity got the better of me, and I grabbed it firmly.

I studied the box intently, trying to figure out how to open it. There was no visible lock or latch, no sign of how to get inside. It was like a puzzle, and I loved puzzles. I twisted the box, turned it upside down, and shook it, but nothing happened. The little witchlight clung tightly to the box despite my efforts to open it. Something powerful must be inside. Perhaps the box was locked by elemental magic? In that case, I didn't have any hope of opening it. I was just about to give up when I noticed a tiny seam running along the edge of the box. I traced my finger along the seam, and with a soft click, the box opened.

I let out a soft gasp of shock. I cautiously peered inside to find a single piece of paper, yellowed with age, and a small vial containing a black liquid. My heart quickened as I carefully pulled out the paper. It was written in an almost illegible script, but I could make out a few words. "Silvyan Order...ancient...power...dangerous...use caution." I frowned, wondering what it all meant. Was the black liquid in the vial connected to the Silvyan Order somehow? Was it a poison or a cure? I had no idea. But I had a feeling that this discovery was going to be important.

This discovery was unexpected. I had no idea what to make of it or what to do with it. I glanced around to make sure no one had seen me before I carefully put the paper and vial back in the box. I made sure they were secure before I placed the box in my satchel. I had to get back to my apartment, where I could examine them more closely over the next few days.

I slipped out of the ruins and back onto the barren streets. I couldn't help but glance over my shoulder every few feet as I hurried home. No matter what I did, I couldn't shake the feeling that I was being watched. My mind raced with thoughts of the Silvyan Order and what I had discovered. I couldn't wait to analyse the contents of the box more closely and hopefully gain some insight into who they truly were. However, my excitement was dampened by the persistent nagging feeling that I was being followed. I quickened my pace, turning down alleyways and side streets to try and shake off any potential pursuers, but the feeling persisted.

Finally, I arrived at my apartment building, breathing a sigh of relief as I quickly made my way inside. As I climbed the stairs to my room, I still couldn't shake the feeling that I was being watched, but I tried to dismiss it as paranoia. Once inside my apartment, I locked the door behind me and pressed my back to it as I let out a small sigh of relief. I'd made it back without issue. I made my way to my desk, where I carefully extracted the box from my satchel.

I studied the yellowed paper for a moment, trying to decipher more of the writing. "Silvyan Order...ancient...power...dangerous...use caution," I repeated the words in my head, trying to fill in the blanks. A dangerous, ancient power. Naturally, that did not bode well, and I turned my attention to the vial of black liquid. It was sealed with a cork covered in blackened wax. For a second, I contemplated opening it, but then I decided against it. I had no idea what it was, and I was most certainly not qualified to find out. My eyes flicked to the little witchlight that still clung to the wooden box. I might not have been brave enough to open the vial, but I was still curious. I held up the vial to the witchlight and watched carefully to see if it would react. The little blob of light rolled ever so slightly away from the glass, and I let out a little disappointed huff. I guess the vial was nothing. I started to pull away when the witchlight abruptly leapt onto the bottom of the vial. It rolled around the smooth surface, nudging at the wax stopper to try and get inside. I blinked in fascination. Perhaps the liquid really did contain magic.

I carefully placed the vial back in the box, making sure it was secure. I had to do more research on it and possibly consult with some of my colleagues in the field. If it was anything, I knew both Lady Amaranta and Lord Railan would be interested. My eyes fluttered with a pang of anxiety. Both Prime Mages could theoretically try to use the vial to improve their respective ranks, but who should I give it to? Of course, my first thought was Lady Amaranta, but would that be wise? I could, in theory, use the vial to gain Lord Railan's trust. Both options had their perks and drawbacks.

I couldn't worry about the Prime Mages and their little games. For now, I needed to focus on the Silvyan Order. I took a deep breath and refocused my attention on the yellowed paper. It seemed to be a warning about the Silvyan Order, but what exactly were they? I racked my brain, trying to remember if I had come across any mention of them before in my studies. Nothing came to mind, but that didn't mean there wasn't information hidden somewhere. I wanted to know more, and the only way to get it was to keep digging. If the restricted section of the Archive was fruitless, then I would have to turn to more... obscure sources. That would require a little more effort on my part, but I desired answers, and I would get them.

Chapter 7

The next few days flew by abnormally quickly, perhaps because they had been so jam-packed with ball preparations. I hadn't had a chance to further my investigation on the Silvyan Order or the mysterious vial, despite my curiosity nagging at the back of my mind.

Today was about the ball's finer details, and Railan was neck-deep in meetings with vendors. The menu and drinks were on the agenda, prompting a knot of nervousness in me. The prospect of Railan sampling drinks sparked both intrigue and concern; alcohol often loosened lips, revealing more than intended. While it was a potential information goldmine, the fear of unexpected consequences gnawed at me.

Railan's gaze shifted from the window to me, a brow raised in question. 'What are you worrying about now?' he inquired, cutting through my thoughts.

'I-I'm not worrying. I don't know what you're talking about,' I replied, attempting nonchalance. I turned my gaze away, fixating on the passing scenery outside the sleigh.

His chuckle filled the air, and he shook his head. 'Oh really? Then what's with that expression on your face?'

Caught off guard, I stammered. 'I'm not making any expressions. This is just how my face looks,' my attempt at composure faltered, leaving me feeling more exposed than ever.

The sound of his laughter was infectious as it pierced through my ears. It was a pleasing sound, yet it unsettled me. Railan suddenly reached over, his hand going for my face. I flinched, closing my eyes as I expected him to hit me. To my surprise, his touch was soft as he gently tilted my chin to face him.

'You're adorable when you try to hide things, you know that?' he said with a teasing grin before his expression became a little more serious. 'But what was that just now?'

I couldn't help but blush, feeling the warmth spread across my cheeks as I averted my gaze. 'It's nothing,' I insisted, attempting to maintain a composed expression.

Railan's eyes narrowed at me for a moment before he leaned back, his fingers leaving my chin. 'Alright, let's see if I can guess. You're worried about the menu? Or perhaps the drinks?' his playful demeanor returned as he settled back into his seat.

I sighed, relenting with a small smile. 'Maybe a bit about the drinks. I just...' I contemplated telling him about my reservations, but decided to simply hold my tongue.

Railan's brow remained raised at my response, and he shook his head before running his hand through his ginger locks. 'Ah... do you think I'll have poor taste, hm?' He asked a bit sheepishly.

'Huh?' I glanced back at him, not expecting him to interpret my words that way. I quickly shook my head in return, putting up my hands defensively. 'No, no, no! T-that wasn't what I meant...' I bit my lip as I averted my gaze. 'I'm sure my Lord has excellent taste...'

I could feel Railan's eyes on me, but I didn't look up.

"Then... what is it?' He continued to press for an answer.

'It's nothing, I'm just overthinking, my Lord. Please forgive my lack of decorum,' I blurt out, wanting him to drop the issue.

Railan stared at me for a bit longer before clicking his tongue and whipping his head back towards the window. A sort of pout sat upon his lips as he looked away. A pang of unease churned in my stomach. I hadn't meant to upset him or be so defiant, but I couldn't tell him my real concerns.

The rest of the sleigh ride was awkwardly silent as neither of us uttered another word. I checked through my notebook and pretended to scribble down things to make myself look busy, but really, I just couldn't stand the tension, and I wished this day would just end already.

We eventually arrived at the vendors, and Railan jumped out of the sleigh with lightning speed. He was already striding off inside without me as I quickly scrambled to stuff my book in my bag and follow him. I stumbled a little in the snow as he left me out in the cold. I guess I really had upset him.

Railan had already removed his coat and had been received by the attendant by the time I stepped inside. He didn't even glance at me, which only made my anxiety spike. I had to take a breath and brush it off. I took off my coat and scurried after Railan as he was already heading to the tasting area.

The attendant led us through the building, chatting with Railan while I was left to follow in their shadow. My nose was immediately filled with all kinds of smells. It was enough to make my mouth water and my head hurt. It wasn't long before the smells grew more intense, and we soon entered the sample room.

A wide array of decadent foods had been prepared for Railan's tasting, and my eyes almost bulged out of my head when the sample table came into view. I'd never seen so many delicacies in one place before, let alone had the chance to taste them, not that I would be tasting them now anyway.

Railan was the only one tasting today, and I had to remind myself to stay calm. Railan sat on one of the two chairs by the table while the attendant quickly took up the other. I glanced around to see if there was another, but of course, there wasn't. I shouldn't have expected so much, after all, I was a lowly mundus. I took up my place against the wall behind Railan and pulled out my notebook to take notes of his preferences and order.

Chapter 8

The next few days flew by. In fact, I hardly noticed that today was the day! Tonight was the ball, the payoff for all of our preparations, and I was absolutely terrified. I mean, I was excited, but I also couldn't shake the sense of dread that loomed in the back of my mind.

Railan had been behaving himself after that rough first day, but still, I couldn't help but be concerned. I'd yet to officially see his costume since I'd been instructed to wait outside during the fittings. I'd even collected the bag yesterday after his final fitting, but it had been specifically packed to avoid tampering. I'd looked it over to try and find a way around it, to sneak a peek, but Lady Aizel was truly a master. It had been sealed tight with magic, and that meant I would have to rely solely on my faith in my Lord's judgment.

Regardless, the hour was drawing nearer faster than I'd like, and I hastily made my way to Railan's lodgings. I couldn't wait until his estate was officially ready, then I wouldn't have to trek through knee-high snow every day just to see him. I straightened out my ceremonial Creed uniform as I stood outside his door. It was practically my regular uniform with a few extra embellishments to make it more formal. I didn't need a costume, after all, I was still on the job. There was going to be no time for fun and games at the ball. I still needed to keep my Lord out of trouble and assist him as required.

I looked at the door and hesitated for just a moment. If only I could pause time. I didn't feel nearly as prepared as I would like. Almost everyone in the city would be introduced to Lord Railan tonight, even the other Prime Mages. The thought of meeting them made my legs feel weak. Lady Amaranta was also a Prime Mage, but she was a known factor. The other Prime Mages, however, were more volatile. I didn't know much about them other than the fact that they were scary, and I worried about how they would react to Railan, since his nature seemed to be the exact opposite. I wanted, no, needed him to succeed tonight.

I knocked on his door, unsure what to expect. The door swung open almost immediately and startled me. Railan greeted me with a wide grin. He was already dressed in his costume, a sleek black suit with silver accents that complemented his vibrant orange hair. A black mask covered the upper half of his face, leaving only his sharp jawline and full lips exposed. My eyes widened in surprise and admiration. He looked stunning. Relief washed over me, and for a brief second, I almost felt like I could relax. Maybe, just maybe, tonight would go smoothly. I took a deep breath, trying to calm my nerves.

'Well, well, well, don't you clean up nice,' I quipped, trying to hide my nervousness.

'Thank you, I try,' he replied with a playful wink. 'You look lovely as well.'

I blushed at the compliment, feeling both grateful and embarrassed. My uniform was, well, a uniform. It wasn't anything special, but it was the best I could do.

'Shall we?' Railan gestured towards the open door, and I nodded, following him out.

With that, we made our way out onto the cold Maentaea streets. A sleigh already waited to take us to the Citadel Ballroom, where a crowd had already gathered outside. The air was thick with anticipation and excitement, and my heart was pounding in my chest. This was it, the moment of truth.

As we entered the ballroom, I was momentarily blinded by the glittering chandeliers and dazzling golden decor. The room was a sea of people, all dressed in their finest attire, and I felt like a very small fish in a very big pond. I took a moment to take in the scene. The room was absolutely breathtaking, with elegant decorations and twinkling, grand chandeliers made from fine crystals. The music was soft and melodic, adding to the enchanting atmosphere.

I looked around, scanning the room for any familiar faces. I could see Lady Amaranta off to the side, talking with a few of the nobles. I couldn't tell who they were, but I didn't want to draw attention to myself by staring.

Railan's presence was a small comfort, but also a major source of anxiety. He was like a beacon, drawing attention wherever he went. I couldn't afford to let my guard down for even a moment. As we walked, I couldn't help but feel like all eyes were on us. I could hear whispers and murmurs as we passed by, but I tried my best to ignore them. This was all part of the job, after all.

I turned my attention back to Railan, who was scanning the room with interest. He looked completely at ease, which only made me feel more nervous. I had to remind myself that he was the one who would be in the spotlight tonight, not me.

We made our way over to a small group of people, who I assumed were part of the Creed. I recognized a few of them from the offices, but I didn't know them personally. Railan greeted them all with a smile and a nod, and they in turn welcomed him warmly.

I breathed a small sigh of relief. Maybe this night wouldn't be so bad after all.

Soon, we were approached by a group of elegantly dressed women, all vying for Railan's attention. He greeted them politely, but it was clear that his eyes were scanning the crowd, searching for something or someone. I couldn't help but wonder who would draw his attention. Was he really so disinterested in these women that he had to look for someone else? They were all exceptionally beautiful. Perhaps he already had his sights on someone? I didn't know since we hadn't exactly gotten personally acquainted yet. Our schedule had been relentless and left me little time to interact with him outside of business.

Suddenly, I felt a hand on my shoulder and turned to see Lady Amaranta standing behind me. She was dressed in a flowing red gown that hugged her curves in all the right places, and her silver hair was styled in an elegant updo. A cluster of fiery witchlights dotted her hair and dress, giving her a powerful, ethereal look. Despite her stunning appearance, her expression was stern and unyielding.

'Good evening, Lady Amaranta,' I greeted her with a bow.

'Good evening, Miss Isla,' she replied, her voice laced with a hint of amusement. 'I trust everything is going smoothly?'

'Yes, my Lord has been very cooperative,' I answered, glancing at Railan, who was still scanning the crowd.

Lady Amaranta followed my gaze and smiled slightly. 'He is a curious one, isn't he?'

I didn't know how to respond to that, so I simply nodded.

'Don't worry, I'm sure he'll make a good impression tonight,' she assured me. 'After all, he is one of us.'

I couldn't help but feel a sense of relief at her words. If even Lady Amaranta had a scrap of faith in Railan, then perhaps everything would turn out all right.

'Thank you, my Lady,' I said, bowing once more.

Lady Amaranta gave me a nod and a small smile before gliding away into the crowd. I watched her go, feeling a sense of awe and respect for the woman who had been a constant presence in my life. She was a mystery, but also a source of familiarity.

'Hey, you okay?' Railan's voice pulled me out of my thoughts.

I turned to face him, a little startled. 'Yes, sorry. Just lost in thought.'

'You look like you're about to pass out,' he teased, his blue eyes sparkling with something I couldn't quite distinguish.

'Do I?' I suddenly felt very self-conscious. 'I'm fine, just distracted. Please forgive me,' I had to pull myself together. 'Are things to your liking?' I asked as I quickly glanced around the room. 'Lady Amaranta is here already, you mustn't forget to greet her,' I reminded him.

Everything seemed to be in order, though I had yet to see any of the other Prime Mages besides Lady Amaranta. Though it was a little hard to tell since half the people here were wearing some style of mask.

Railan chuckled. 'You know, you sure get flustered easily.'

I felt my cheeks heat up at his comment, but before I could retort, the sound of trumpets filled the room. I turned to see the Master of Ceremonies stepping onto a small stage at the front of the ballroom.

'Ladies and gentlemen, Prime Mages and honoured guests, welcome to the Annual Creed Ball!' he announced, his voice booming throughout the room. 'Tonight, we celebrate the unity and strength of the Creed, and we also welcome the Twelfth Prime Mage, the esteemed Lord Elieason Railan.'

The crowd erupted into applause, and I turned to Railan to see him watching the proceedings with a small smile on his face. Despite my nerves, I couldn't help but feel a sense of pride at the sight of him. He looked every bit the part of a Prime Mage, and the way he carried himself spoke volumes about his confidence and ability.

As the night went on, I kept a watchful eye on Railan, making sure he didn't get into any trouble or do anything untoward. He chatted with various guests, including several of the other Prime Mages, and I could see that he was holding his own. I was impressed with how easily he seemed to adapt to the situation, even though it was his first ball of this nature.

As the evening wore on, I found myself relaxing slightly. Perhaps things were going to be alright after all. Just then, I caught a glimpse of a figure in a silver mask watching us from across the room. It was one of the other Prime Mages, and for some reason, their gaze made my blood run cold. I couldn't quite place why, but something about them seemed off, almost menacing. I made a mental note to keep an extra close eye on Railan, just in case.

'Isla!'

A familiar voice drew my attention, and I turned to see Pavel. A large, jolly grin spread across his face. I could even make out a hint of his lips as he trimmed his beard.

'Mr Pavel!' I beamed at him as he made his way over to me, 'I'm so glad to see you made it.'

'Of course, I said I would,' he chuckled. 'I'm glad to finally find you.'

'Oh, I haven't been that elusive, have I?' I teased.

Pavel gave me a shrug. 'Maybe not, but this crowd is something else,' he gestured to the packed ballroom.

Indeed, the turnout had been more than even I had anticipated. No doubt everyone wanted to catch a glimpse of the new Prime Mage, especially with all the rumours surrounding him.

'I know. It's a little intense, but everything is going smoothly. Thank the Celestial Lady,' I said.

'I'm glad to hear that. Now, I believe you promised me a dance,' Pavel gave me a cunning smirk.

I narrowed my eyes as I returned with my own smirk. 'I did no such thing.'

'Well, I'm here, so it won't hurt to have just one little dance,' he was practically begging me.

'I told you, I don't dance,' I reiterated.

'Oh, come on. I'm not asking for a waltz, just something simple and fun,' he chuckled. 'Surely you can take just two minutes to relax?'

I let out a defeated sigh. Dancing was not my strongest suit, but with such a dense crowd, who was really going to notice if I looked a little awkward? I relented and held out my hand.

'Fine, two minutes,' I said firmly.

Pavel's smile somehow grew even wider as he took my hand and led me to the dance floor. My stomach twisted nervously, even though I was sure no one was paying us any mind. Pavel and I took our positions and began a simple two-step. I found myself hyper-focused on my feet as I tried not to trip or be tripped over.

'No need to be so stiff, just go with the flow of the beat,' Pavel reassured me as he spun me around the floor.

'That's easy for you to say, all I hear is sound,' I groaned.

Pavel chuckled at my observation. 'If you relaxed, you might be able to distinguish things.'

I let out a grumpy huff, even though I knew he was probably right. *Relax.*

Everyone was always telling me to relax as if it were easy. Nevertheless, I could do that for just a minute.

I took a deep breath and loosened my shoulders. *Relaxed.*

I found myself stepping on Pavel's toes, but to his credit, he didn't complain, and soon I did indeed find myself having fun. All my stress and worries seemed to disappear for just a moment as we moved across the room.

As the dance came to an end, Pavel dipped me down low, and I let out a small laugh. He pulled me back up, and we both grinned at each other.

'See, that wasn't so bad, was it?' Pavel asked, his eyes sparkling with amusement.

I had to admit, he was right. It had been a nice break from the constant stress of the event.

'No, it wasn't,' I said, returning his smile.

As we made our way back to the edge of the dance floor, I spotted a familiar figure across the room. It was Lord Railan, standing alone and looking slightly lost in the sea of people.

'It was good to see you, but you must excuse me,' I said to Pavel as I made my way towards my Lord.

As I approached, I could see the tension in his shoulders and the furrow in his brow. He was more anxious than I'd ever seen him. Perhaps it was the late night, or maybe it was something I'd missed in my short period of distraction.

'My Lord?' I said as I came up to him. 'Is everything alright?'

He turned to look at me, and I could see a flicker of relief in his eyes.

'Yes, I suppose so,' he said hesitantly.

'Would you like to dance?' I asked, extending my hand to him.

I wasn't sure why I offered; perhaps I was still riding the high of my dance with Pavel. Railan looked at my hand, then back at me, clearly surprised by the offer.

'I'm not much of a dancer,' he admitted.

'That doesn't matter, anyone can do a simple two-step,' I said with a smile. 'It might take your mind off things.'

After a moment of hesitation, he took my hand and we made our way to the dance floor. The music was slow and easy to follow, and soon Railan was moving with more ease. I could feel him relaxing in my arms, and I couldn't help but smile. Contrary to his humble words, Railan was, in fact, an excellent dancer. Once he got into the swing of things, I found myself hardly able to keep up. I might have been regretting my earlier confidence, but at least he seemed to be back to his more chipper self.

The song soon came to an end, and I was thankful to finally be released from his grasp. He lingered ever so slightly, and I tilted my head as I took a step back.

'Is there something on your mind, my Lord?' I asked, noting his hesitation to let go.

Railan cleared his throat, his gaze flickering away from mine for a moment before returning.

'I just... wanted to thank you,' he said softly. 'For the dance and for your company. It's been a difficult few days, and it was nice to forget about everything for a moment.'

I smiled at him, feeling a warmth in my chest. 'Of course, my Lord. I'm always happy to help in any way I can.'

We fell into a comfortable silence for a moment, the music and chatter from the party surrounding us. I glanced around, taking in the sight of the ballroom filled with nobles and high-ranking officials, all mingling and enjoying themselves. It was easy to forget about the dangers and tensions that loomed over our world in a setting like this.

'Eli! Eli!' A high-pitched squeal suddenly cut through the serenity, and we both turned to see a young girl running through the crowd towards us.

Railan's face immediately lit up as the girl flung her arms around him. She had distinctive ginger hair and wore an extravagant, adorable dress of bright blue. I knew immediately that she must have been one of Railan's relatives.

'I found you, finally!' the girl beamed, her eyes sparkling as she looked up at him.

Railan chuckled, ruffling her hair affectionately. 'You certainly did, Seraphine. Where is everyone else?'

'Coming. This place is so big and you're so small!' the girl pouted.

Railan let out a more earnest laugh at her comment as he shook his head.

'You found him!' another voice suddenly called, and I flicked my eyes over to see a young boy who looked almost identical to the girl pushing his way through the crowd.

'Ailen!' Railan beamed at the boy.

The children were soon followed by an older woman and man, who I could only assume were their parents. Railan's smile was so large and radiant that I almost felt like I needed to shield my eyes. I let out a little sigh of relief; these must have been the people he was looking for earlier in the night.

'Mother, Father, I'm so glad you could make it!' Railan quickly stepped past the children and scooped the woman up into a tight hug. He then turned to his father, giving him a firm handshake.

'Of course, we wouldn't miss this for the world, my boy,' the older man beamed, clearly proud to be here.

'You look so handsome, Eli,' the woman swooned, taking a good look at Railan, who did a little spin to show off his custom attire.

I took a step back as I watched the family reunion. I imagined it had been a while since they had seen each other, as life as an adult was. A soft smile tugged at the corners of my lips as my mind briefly wandered to my own family. I would have loved for them to be here, too, but alas, it was impossible. A hint of sadness tugged at my heart, the warmth from earlier fading somewhat.

My family.

I missed them so much, especially at times like this. Seeing Railan laughing and chatting so casually with his family just reminded me of how alone I was right now.

'Oh, and this lovely lady is my assistant, Isla. She's been helping me adjust to my new role.' Railan's voice suddenly shook me out of my thoughts, and I felt my cheeks flush as he gestured towards me.

I shifted awkwardly, caught off guard at suddenly being drawn into the conversation. 'Oh, um, it's a pleasure to meet you, my Lord and lady,' I quickly bowed, keeping my head down.

'Ah, I see, it's a pleasure indeed,' Ralian's father stepped forward to shake my hand. 'No doubt you're half of the reason this party is thriving.'

I shook his hand, my own trembling slightly as I chuckled awkwardly. 'Oh, you flatter me, but I assure you, Lord Railan is to thank for the festivities, after all, without him we wouldn't be here at all.'

I was swiftly drawn into conversation with Railan's parents as we waited for the rest of their family to arrive. They were kind and friendly in a way that was unexpected from people of their standing. It was odd, but I wasn't going to deny the hint of warmth and acceptance that emanated from them.

After a few minutes, the rest of the family arrived, and we were introduced to a host of aunts, uncles, and cousins. All of whom had come just to see Railan's debut. They all seemed to be in high spirits, and I found myself caught up in their energy, laughing and chatting with them as if I had known them for years. Railan was beaming with pride, and I couldn't help but feel grateful to have been included in this fleeting moment of family joy.

As the night wore on, I found myself dancing and laughing with Railan's younger siblings, while Railan mingled with his extended family. It was a strange and unexpected turn for the evening, but one I found myself thoroughly enjoying. The music and lights of the ballroom faded away, replaced by the warmth and love of this family gathering. For a moment, I felt like less of an outsider and more like a friend.

I found myself faltering at the thought. I wasn't here to be a friend; I was here to watch Railan's every move. A pang of sadness rose within my chest as I twirled around the dancefloor with Seraphine and Ailen. I once again found myself wishing that my own family could have been here to experience the grand splendour of the evening. They had been confined to Lake Village for ten years now, ever since I'd been bought from the slave markets by Lady Amaranta when I was a young girl. I trained and worked for Lady Amaranta in exchange for their safety. However, safety did not mean freedom. They were essentially prisoners in a gilded cage. Lake Village was decent enough and self-sustaining, but residents could not come and go as they pleased, not even to the annual ball. I had to remind myself that I couldn't let my guard down so easily. One mistake could see my family suffering the consequences. Their lives rested in my hands.

'Are you alright, Miss Isla?' Seraphine asked as she tilted her head up at me.

I hadn't realised I'd stopped dancing. I quickly shook my head and recomposed myself. 'Yes, I'm fine. I just got distracted by how cute you are!' I forced a smile as I pinched her cheek.

Seraphine giggled and swatted my hand away, her cheeks flushing pink. 'You're so silly, Miss Isla,' she said, before turning her attention back to her brothers, who were chasing each other around the dancefloor.

I watched them for a moment, my heart aching with a mixture of longing and fear. Longing for the family I could never be a part of, and fearing for the family I had to protect at all costs.

'Miss Isla?' a voice interrupted my thoughts, and I turned to see a familiar young woman in formal brown clothes reminiscent of my own.

'Lauralai!' A smile quickly spread across my lips. 'I didn't expect to run into you here.'

'Of course I'd be here,' she chuckled. 'Practically the entire city is here.'

I nodded in agreement. That was very true. Lauralai suddenly extended her hand to me.

'Shall we have a dance?' she raised a brow at me.

More dancing. I was already exhausted from pandering to everyone else and let out a defeated sigh. What was one more dance at this point? I placed my hand upon hers and gave her a nervous smile.

'I must warn you, I'm not very good,' I said sheepishly.

Lauralai shrugged as she placed her hand on my waist. 'I'm not so much interested in dancing as talking with you.' She spun me away into the crowd. 'I'm curious, did you happen to find what you were looking for? If I recall correctly, you were looking for information on the Silvyan Order, yes?'

'Oh,' I was surprised she would bring up such a thing in public like this. 'I... can't say I found too much more than what those books could provide,' I said, keeping my voice low.

'Did you end up visiting Arcanist's Village?' Lauralai prodded curiously.

'I... I did, but I can't say I found anything of much use for my research,' I shrugged, trying to remain calm and casual.

Lauralai's pretty lips pressed into a disappointed line as she furrowed her brows. 'Really? I was certain it would be helpful. Alas, it would appear I was mistaken. Forgive me, I didn't mean to send you on a wild goose chase.'

'Oh, you have nothing to be sorry about. I appreciate your tip, even if it didn't turn out how I wanted. I still learnt a few things, and that is what is important. The pursuit of knowledge is one fraught with wrong turns and dead ends, I wouldn't be an academic if I couldn't handle all the detours,' I gave her a playful wink.

Lauralai chuckled at my words. 'I suppose that's true. But please, do be careful in your pursuit. You never know what dangers await around the corner.'

Her words sent a shiver down my spine, and I couldn't help but feel a twinge of fear. I knew all too well the danger I was embroiled in. I had to be careful. I needed to balance my duties to Lord Railan with my duties to Lady Amaranta. I walked on a knife's edge; one slip in either direction would be the end of me.

'Thank you for your concern, Lauralai,' I said sincerely. 'I'll be careful, I promise.'

We continued to dance and talk for a while longer, and I found myself enjoying her company. She was easy to talk to, and her intelligence and wit were a breath of fresh air compared to Railan's teasing.

As the music came to a stop, Lauralai released me from her arms and curtsied. 'Thank you for the dance, Miss Isla. It was a pleasure as always.'

'Likewise, Lauralai. Until next time,' I returned her curtsy and watched as she disappeared into the crowd.

I couldn't help but feel a sense of unease settle in the pit of my stomach as I made my way back to Railan's side.

As I approached him, Railan turned to me with a charming smile, his eyes twinkling mischievously. 'My dear Isla, you look positively flustered. Have you been dancing with a suitor behind my back?'

I rolled my eyes, but couldn't help the blush that crept up on my cheeks. 'Don't be ridiculous, my Lord. I was just dancing with a friend.'

'A friend?' he repeated, raising an eyebrow. 'Is that all?'

I opened my mouth to give a smart retort, but decided against it. 'Yes. And I don't believe it's any of your business who I dance with,' I said with a cool, professional tone.

Railan chuckled, his eyes twinkling with amusement. 'Ah, but everything is my business, my dear Isla,' he suddenly closed the gap between us, his voice slightly lower than usual. 'Especially when it comes to you.'

I fought the urge to roll my eyes again, as my cheeks were set ablaze. He was just messing with me again. I let out a little huff as I darted my eyes to the ground. I could hear his amused chuckle, and my blush only darkened further.

'S-speaking of business, my Lord, I believe you have yet to ingratiate yourself with the Cardinal tonight,' I quickly tried my best to shift his focus.

Railan's expression turned serious, and he nodded in agreement. 'Of course. I can't forget about his eminence. Duty before pleasure. Thank you for reminding me.'

I nodded meekly as he wandered off into the crowd, leaving me to catch my breath. Tonight had proved to be a little more exhausting than I could have ever expected. Luckily, Lord Railan seemed more at ease as he returned to mingling with the other guests and engaging in conversation. More importantly, he left me alone. As the night drew to a close, he finally returned to find me. A smile remained on his lips, but his eyes seemed weary.

'Shall we turn in? The hour is rather late,' I asked.

Railan nodded in agreement, 'Yes, I think that's a good idea. It's been a long night, and I'm feeling quite exhausted.'

I signalled for the sleigh to be brought around while Railan said his goodbyes to the remaining guests. Soon enough, we were on our way back to his apartment.

As we rode in silence, I couldn't help but reflect on the night's events. It had been a success, and Railan had exceeded my expectations in terms of his interactions with the other guests. I couldn't help but feel a sense of pride in him.

Railan seemed lost in his thoughts, but eventually, he spoke up. 'I have to admit, I was nervous about tonight. It wasn't as bad as I thought it would be. In fact, it was quite enjoyable.'

'I'm glad to hear that,' I smiled at him. 'You did very well tonight, and I'm sure the other Prime Mages will be pleased with your performance.'

Railan gave me a nod. 'Thank you, Isla. I couldn't have done it without your guidance.'

I was a little flustered by his gratitude and simply gave him an approving nod. We arrived at his apartment complex, and I helped Railan out of the sleigh. As we walked towards the entrance, I couldn't help but feel a sense of apprehension. It was one thing to manage Railan's public appearances, but another thing entirely to work alongside the other Prime Mages. They were a notoriously difficult group to please, and I knew that I had my work cut out for me. But I was determined to do my best and make a good impression.

I walked Railan to his door and gave him a small bow.

'Please get some rest. While I've made sure your schedule is more lax tomorrow, there are still many things to be done that need your full attention,' I said. 'A good night's rest is a necessity.'

Railan nodded in agreement, his fatigue showing in the lines around his eyes.

'Thank you, Isla. Your guidance has been invaluable. I will see you in the morning,' he said before disappearing into his room and closing the door behind him.

I sighed, feeling a sense of relief that the night had gone smoothly. But at the same time, I couldn't help but worry about the challenges that were sure to come in the future. The weight of my responsibility settled heavily on my shoulders, and I knew that I would need to be vigilant and prepared for anything that came our way. With a deep breath, I turned and made my way back to my quarters, my mind already racing with plans and strategies for the days ahead.

Chapter 9

The next week was, for the most part, uneventful. It was mostly business as usual, or more so, what I'd grown accustomed to. Lord Railan was handling his new position well despite his initial hurdles, and I honestly couldn't be prouder. My first report to Lady Amaranta was due, and thankfully, it was rather short and boring. Railan was a model citizen despite his flamboyant personality, and there had been no signs that there was anything to be concerned about.

I let out a small sigh of relief as I sealed the report and tucked it into my satchel. I needed to personally deliver it to the drop-off point before I could pick up Lord Railan for the morning. Luckily for me, today's schedule was rather empty, with a large chunk of free time between lunch and dinner. I could finally take a proper breather for the first time in what felt like forever. My gaze turned towards my desk drawer. Unease poked at me as I pulled it open and stole a glance at the old wooden box. I hadn't had any time to further my research or investigate the vial. I placed the box on my desk and carefully opened it. I wasn't exactly expecting any new revelations, but I couldn't help but be curious. The little pale green witchlight still clung to the vial. A part of me was surprised that it hadn't faded away yet. I couldn't help but smile as I poked at the little creature. It was naturally repulsed by me and quickly skittered to the opposite end of the vial.

Of course, I was a mundus. There was no power within me to be attracted to; I was just mundane. I was grateful that Lady Amaranta saw at least a semblance of value within me. I needed to try my best to serve her. I also needed to do the same for Lord Railan. Having two masters was precarious. I didn't like it, but I didn't exactly have any choice in the matter. I simply needed to keep my head down and not rouse suspicion.

I put the vial back in its box before I tucked it safely back in my drawer. I would need to try and squeeze in some time to get some actual research done. Once I knew exactly what the nature of the contents was, I would then be able to decide who I could give it to. For now, I needed to hand in my report and start the day. I shrugged on my cloak and made my way down the frozen streets, heading towards Palace Borough, where Lady Amaranta had arranged a nondescript dead drop location. I would simply leave my report, and another of her agents would retrieve it later. I would have to be careful, but I wasn't exactly worried. The location was quite safe and just public enough that if anything should go awry, I could simply slip away into the crowds.

As I made my way to the dead drop location, a sense of unease settled in the pit of my stomach. Perhaps it was simply the bitter chill, but I couldn't help but notice that the streets were eerily quiet, and the few people I did pass by were bundled up tightly against the cold, their faces obscured by scarves and hats. It was as if the entire city was holding its breath, waiting for something to happen.

I quickened my pace, my hands automatically pulling my cloak and satchel closer to me. I knew it was foolish to let my guard down, especially with everything that was going on, but I couldn't shake the feeling that I was being watched.

Finally, I reached the dead drop location, a small alleyway tucked away between two buildings. I looked around nervously before slipping the envelope containing my report into the designated spot. I waited for a few moments, half-expecting someone to jump out at me, but nothing happened.

Thank the Celestial Lady.

Feeling a sense of relief wash over me, I let out the breath I hadn't noticed I'd been holding. I turned to leave, but before I could exit the alley, I came face-to-face with a group of men in dark clothing, their faces hidden behind masks. My heart was pounding in my chest, and I tried to back away and take the other exit. However, as soon as I turned, I heard footsteps close in behind me. I tried to run, but was halted as many hands latched onto my cloak. My mind raced as I struggled to free myself from their grip, but the men were too strong. I could feel the panic rising in my chest as they pulled me closer to them, their masked faces looming over me. I tried to scream for help, but a gloved hand swiftly covered my mouth, silencing me.

One of the men spoke, his voice cold and menacing. 'A mundus should know better than to walk the streets alone at this hour.'

My heart sank as I realised that these men were most likely part of the Magi Primacy movement. They viewed the mundi as beneath them, mere animals, and I was at their mercy. Tears pricked at my eyes as they forced me to the ground. I tried to struggle against them, but they were too numerous, too strong.

Help me, Celestial Lady!

'What's going on here?' a familiar voice boomed.

The men came to an abrupt halt, and I caught a glance of bright orange hair through my ice-stained glasses.

Railan?

What was he doing here? It didn't matter. I tried to call out to him, but the hand over my mouth prevented me from doing so. The men turned to face him, their masks hiding any expression, but their body language showed they were wary of him. Railan stood tall, his fists clenched at his sides, and his expression was inscrutable.

'I asked you a question,' he repeated, his voice low and dangerous.

One of the men stepped forward, his hand going to his waist where I could see the glint of his bright red focus in the moonlight. 'This is none of your concern.'

Railan's eyes narrowed. 'I beg to differ,' his hand moved to reveal the deep blue focus of his own, a subtle warning to the group of men. 'Now, release her.'

The man laughed. 'You think you can stop us? It's five against one.'

Railan smirked, an almost delighted glint in his eyes. 'I like those odds.'

He stepped forward, and suddenly the air around him crackled with energy. A few of the men loosened their grip on me, unsure of what was happening. Railan abruptly lunged towards us, a strange grace and fluidity in his movement that I had never seen before. In a flash, a sword of swirling water appeared within Railan's hand and just inches away from the man's throat. The man stumbled backward, and Railan caught him by the collar of his shirt, pulling him close.

'I suggest you let her go before things get ugly,' his voice was low, almost a growl.

The man's eyes widened in fear as he looked at Railan. He seemed to have realised his mistake, and with a nod to the others, they released me and took off running. Railan let the man go, letting him stumble before he too scurried off into the darkness.

Railan let out a breath he had been holding, letting his sword dissipate before he turned to me. 'Are you hurt?'

I blinked up at him, unsure what had just happened as my heart raced. Railan? Why was he here? Had he been following me? Had he seen me make the drop-off? This was bad. I quickly scrambled to my feet, half tripping in the icy snow as I tried to escape past him.

Railan caught me by the arm, stopping me in my tracks.

'Hey, wait. It's okay, I'm not going to hurt you,' his eyes searched mine, concern etched on his face. 'What are you doing here, Isla?'

I shook my head, still trying to process everything. 'P-Please let me go,' I could feel the tears swelling in my eyes as I tried to pull myself out of his grasp.

Railan immediately released my arm and stepped back, his expression softening. 'I'm sorry, Isla. I didn't mean to scare you.'

I took a few shaky steps back, putting some distance between us as I tried to steady my breathing. 'Why are you here?' I asked, my voice still shaking.

'I asked you first,' he retorted as he kept his eyes on me, watching my reaction carefully.

'I-I was just....' I had to think quickly; I couldn't reveal the truth. 'I just wanted to see if I could visit Listeia's library, so I can complete the report you requested,' I focused my eyes on the ground, careful to avoid his gaze.

Railan raised an eyebrow, clearly sceptical of my explanation. 'Is that so?' he said, his voice dripping with sarcasm.

I nodded, my heart racing. I had to keep up the facade; I couldn't let him suspect anything. 'Yes, that's all. I... I didn't mean to cause any trouble,' I shrank back, pulling my cloak tight around me.

Railan sighed and ran a hand through his hair. 'You should know better than to wander around this district by yourself. It's not safe. I can't have you getting hurt.'

I nodded, feeling a pang of guilt. He was right, I had been foolish to come here alone, yet I didn't have a choice. 'I know, I'm sorry. I won't do it again,' I lied as I hid my face behind my scarf.

Railan's expression softened as he studied me for a moment. 'Let's get out of this weather.'

I nodded, feeling relieved that he was taking me away from this dangerous area. 'Thank you, my Lord,' I whispered, grateful for his protection.

I desperately wanted to run away, but I knew I wouldn't be able to escape him. I followed along behind him, keeping my head down as I tried to think of what to do next. Had he seen me make the drop off?

And more importantly, what was he doing here, especially at this time of morning? I couldn't just leave since I was supposed to meet him in a few hours anyway, but this was unexpected. I stole a glance at Railan. He strode forward with his usual swagger, his posture tall and straight with no hint of discomfort or unease. I couldn't help but wonder if he was upset with me. Would he punish me for causing him trouble? I hadn't meant to get caught, not like that. I felt even more anxious as I noticed we'd entered Arcanist's Village. I could sense the distinct shift in the air as I felt the abundance of magic surge around me. Why were we here? Did he know I'd been here too? I didn't see why being here would have been a problem. Or did he know about the mysterious box?

My heart continued to pound in my ears as we walked in palpable silence. Was I done for so soon? I blinked in cautious awe as a cluster of bright blue witchlights fluttered down from the sky to rest upon Railan's hair and clothes. He quickly went to brush them off, and I couldn't stop myself from letting out an involuntary gasp.

'Don't-' I started, but quickly covered my mouth.

Railan turned to me with a raised eyebrow, clearly surprised by my outburst. 'What?' he asked, looking a bit perplexed.

'I'm sorry,' I said quickly, trying to regain my composure. 'It's just...those witchlights. They're...' I didn't know what I was trying to say, and I shook my head. 'It's nothing.'

Railan looked at me for a moment before his lips curled into a small smile. 'They're just witchlights, it's not like you haven't seen them before, right?' he said, his voice tinged with amusement. 'They are drawn to me when I come here.'

I nodded, feeling a bit embarrassed by my reaction. 'I see,' I said, trying to sound nonchalant.

''They recognise power and I have an immense amount of it,' his voice was suddenly low as he stared directly at me.

I felt a shiver run down my spine at his intense gaze. I knew he was powerful, but hearing him say it so directly sent a jolt of fear through me. I couldn't help but wonder exactly how powerful he truly was, and what he could do with that power. The Celestial Lady had chosen him as one of her favourites specifically for that power.

'But enough about that,' he said, breaking the silence as his usual, jovial expression returned. 'Let's grab some breakfast.'

Railan led the way through the bustling streets of Arcanist's Village, weaving in and out of the slowly emerging crowds of people and magical creatures. I kept my head down, trying to avoid drawing attention to myself, but I couldn't help but be awed by the sights and sounds around me. It was almost like stepping into a different world, one where magic was commonplace and anything was possible. It was a stark contrast to how it had been in the middle of the night. It truly was a case of night and day. I caught glimpses of enchanted shops and market stalls, selling everything from potions to spellbooks to exotic ingredients. There were street performers and musicians, entertaining the crowds with their magical talents. It was overwhelming, yet exhilarating at the same time.

Eventually, Railan led me to a small tea shop tucked away in a quiet corner of the district. It was cosy and inviting, with low tables and cushions on the floor. Railan gestured for me to sit down, and I did so, feeling a bit awkward as I tried to find a comfortable position. I couldn't deny that the place was nice, but it also seemed a little too plain for someone of his standing. He ordered some tea and a few small pastries, and we sat in silence as we waited for them to arrive.

His eyes were on me, and I tried my best to avoid them.

After a few moments of uncomfortable silence, Railan spoke up. 'You know, you don't have to be so nervous around me,' he said, his voice soft. 'I'm not going to hurt you.'

'Aren't you?' I asked, my voice barely above a whisper.

Railan seemed a little taken aback by my response, and a small frown formed upon his brow. 'Have I hurt you so far?'

'No...' I admitted.

'Then what makes you think I will?' he leaned in closer, his full attention on me as he gave me an expectant, curious look.

I opened my mouth to respond, but quickly shut it as I pulled my scarf up over my cheeks.

Railan's expression softened, and he reached out to gently touch my arm. I naturally pulled away. Even though I knew he didn't have bad intentions, I was still sceptical.

'Hey,' he said, his voice gentle. 'It's okay. You can be frank with me.'

I took a deep breath, trying to steady my nerves. 'Can I?' I asked, uncertain if I could trust his words.

'Yes,' Railan let out a small, frustrated sigh. 'How do you expect to be an effective assistant if you don't feel like you can talk to me?'

I shifted in my seat, feeling a mix of guilt and anxiety. He had a point. If I were going to work with him, I needed to be able to communicate openly and honestly. But the fear still lingered in the back of my mind. I didn't know how much he knew, if anything, and I knew I couldn't let my guard down no matter what he said.

'What were you doing in the Palace Borough?' I asked, bluntly, my eyes searching his face for any hints of his true intentions.

Railan shrugged as he leaned back, casually letting himself flop down upon the pillows. 'I was just out for a stroll.'

I didn't believe him.

'Before sunrise?' I raised a brow.

'And you were going to a private library at the same time?' Railan raised his brow back at me.

I pressed my lips into an annoyed line as we fell into a silent stalemate. I wasn't about to reveal anything, and neither was he. Still, I was grateful that he had been there to save me, even if he had been following me. I hadn't expected to run into trouble on my very first dead drop. I would need to use more caution next time.

'My Lord... thank you for coming to my rescue...' I mumbled aloud.

Railan waved a hand dismissively. 'No need to thank me. I can't allow anyone to think they can just walk over me and assault my subjects.'

I frowned, feeling a little annoyed by his nonchalant attitude. 'But still, I appreciate it...' I said quietly.

Railan regarded me for a moment, his expression unreadable. 'You're welcome,' he finally said, his voice softer this time. 'Just be more careful from now on, okay? If you need to go somewhere, I can escort you.'

A small sense of something, perhaps relief, filled my chest. He seemed to genuinely care about my safety, and that was... surprising. It was a small comfort, but it was something.

'That... won't be necessary,' I said, my cheeks flushing. 'My Lord has far more important things to do than waste time on me.'

Railan chuckled softly. 'Don't underestimate your importance,' he said. 'And besides, I wouldn't want anything to happen to my brand-new assistant. It's barely been two weeks.'

I couldn't help but feel a little touched by his words. Maybe he wasn't as bad as I had thought. Maybe there was more to him than met the eye. But still, I knew I had to be careful.

'Thank you,' I said, giving him a small smile. 'I'll be more careful from now on.'

Railan nodded, looking satisfied. 'Good.'

The rest of our time at the tea shop was spent in a more comfortable silence. I sipped on the tea and nibbled on the pastries, trying to enjoy the moment of peace before the chaos of Railan's schedule would consume me, even if there was just a little break in the middle. Railan seemed content to simply sit there, his eyes closed as he listened to the ambient noise of the district.

Railan sure was a strange man.

Chapter 10

The rest of the morning went as expected, and neither Railan nor I brought up the events of the early hours. I wanted to just forget about it. It was an embarrassing blunder on my part, and I wouldn't let it happen again. I could only pray that Lady Amaranta wouldn't somehow find out. I was also extremely lucky that Railan didn't seem to suspect anything, at least not outwardly. He said he wouldn't hurt me, but I couldn't trust his words if he found out I was a spy. A covert agent only lived as long as they remained just that, covert. I needed to live, if not for my own sake, then for my family. They still needed me, and I couldn't let them down.

The morning's meetings finally came to an end and would not resume until the late evening. Now was the perfect time to run any errands. Specifically, now would be a good time for me to dig deeper into the origins of the mysterious box and the vial contained within.

'Shall I escort you back to your lodging, my Lord?' I asked Railan as we exited the room and stood within the halls of the Citadel.

'No,' he said simply.

I nodded. 'If that is all, shall we reconvene here one hour before the next meeting to discuss my notes?'

'No, that is not all,' Railan replied, his expression carefully guarded.

I felt my stomach drop, and I blinked up at him in confusion. 'My Lord?'

'I need you to come with me, I have some things to do that require your assistance.'

I felt a twinge of unease at Railan's request. I wasn't sure if I wanted to be alone with him again, especially after the events of the early hours. But I couldn't refuse his request either. As his assistant, it was my duty to aid him in any way possible, even if it made me uncomfortable.

'Of course, my Lord,' I said, trying to keep my voice steady. 'Where are we going?'

Railan gestured for me to follow him as he started to walk down the hall. 'There's something I need to show you,' he said cryptically.

I trailed after him, feeling a sense of unease settling in the pit of my stomach. I couldn't help but wonder what it was he wanted to show me. Nothing in particular came to mind. Had he had a revelation during the meeting? Did he suspect me? Was he taking me somewhere private to interrogate me?

I couldn't deny him, so I just followed along in silence. He led me out of the Citadel, and after a while, we exited the city gates and wandered into the winter forest. My anxiety only increased as we wandered off the path and into a seemingly random direction. This was it; he definitely knew I was a spy, and he was going to dispose of me. I clung to my satchel. There would be nothing I could do to stop him. I could try to run, but I already knew it would be futile.

As we continued deeper into the forest, my heart pounded in my chest. Every crunch of snow, rustle of leaves, and snap of twigs sent my nerves on edge. I was ready to bolt at a moment's notice, but I tried to remain calm and collected on the outside. Railan seemed to sense my unease and slowed his pace, turning to me with a reassuring smile.

'Relax, you're always so on edge,' he said, as if reading my thoughts.

I tried to relax, but the words felt hollow. Could I really trust him? I had no choice but to go along with him.

After several minutes of walking, we arrived at a small clearing where a group of seven snow-capped menhirs stood in a circle. I immediately let out a small gasp in awe as an abundance of multi-coloured witchlights danced through the air, floating gracefully between each stone. At the centre of the circle was a more ornate, carved statue. I couldn't make out what it was since it had been partly destroyed, its top half completely missing. A rainbow of witchlights sat atop the jagged remains, spilling over like a magical fountain.

Railan noticed my reaction, and a sincere smile spread across his lips. 'I thought you might like it here since you seem to have an interest in witchlights.'

I blinked at him as my awe turned into confusion and then sudden relief. He hadn't brought me here to kill me. He was simply showing me the witchlights. I could feel my eyes prick with tears.

'It's beautiful,' I whispered, my voice catching in my throat. 'Thank you for bringing me here, my Lord.'

Railan gave me a small nod, seemingly pleased with my reaction. 'It's one of the few places where I can find peace in this chaotic world,' he said softly. 'I used to come here often whenever I needed to clear my mind and gather my thoughts.'

'Used to?' I tilted my head, curious why he would use the past tense.

He nodded, a wistful sigh escaping his lips. 'You know exactly how busy my life has become. It turns out that the power that comes with being a Prime Mage does not grant one freedom.'

I nodded in understanding, imagining the weight of responsibility that came with being a Prime Mage. Railan's life would have already been busy as a magi, but now it was exponentially more demanding. He was in a precarious position; any wrong move could see him fall back into obscurity. If he wanted to rise, he would have to start playing against the other Prime Mages, and that would leave him in an even more dangerous situation.

'I can only imagine,' I said softly. 'But it's good that you have a place like this to come to when you can find the time.'

Railan smiled at me, his expression softening. 'Yes, it is. And now you know about it too. Whenever you need a break from your duties, you're welcome to come here and enjoy the peace.'

I couldn't help but feel touched by his gesture. Despite our rocky start, Railan had been nothing but kind to me since I started as his assistant. He was a little rough around the edges, but I felt like there was potentially a genuine kindness hidden under his charming exterior. He had even taken the time to show me this beautiful place. Kindness was a rare thing to possess in this world of lies and schemes. I felt a sense of gratitude towards him and a newfound respect for the man who held one of the highest positions in our world. But I also felt a pang of sadness. Kindness was a weakness. All things kind would eventually be expunged by the other Prime Mages.

'Thank you, my Lord,' I said quietly, trying my best to mask my darker thoughts.

Railan waved off my thanks, his smile turning mischievous. 'But don't think that means you can slack off on your duties,' he said teasingly. 'I'll still need you to keep me on schedule.'

I chuckled softly, feeling a sense of warmth spreading through me. 'Of course.'

Railan seemed content with my reply, and he sat down by one of the menhirs, a peaceful expression upon his features as he closed his eyes. I watched him for a brief moment. The mild sunlight washed over him, as if specifically illuminating him in this fleeting second. Tiny blue witchlights had already started to collect around him, brushing against his hair and skin, longing to be close to him. There was something uniquely attractive about him, from his confidence to the fullness of his lips. I was surprised to see the light spotting of freckles upon his cheeks. How had I never noticed them before? I suppose there were many other things to draw my attention.

I returned my gaze to the statue, not wanting him to catch me staring. I moved closer and knelt before it. I couldn't help but wonder what it had been. Was it a person, a long-forgotten god, or something else entirely? Whatever it was, this place was brimming with magic. I closed my eyes and offered a small prayer to the statue, whatever it may be, as well as the Celestial Lady. I prayed that they would watch over me and my family, that they would keep everyone safe, and that they would show mercy to Lord Railan.

'Isla...' Railan's voice interrupted my thoughts.

I turned to glance back at him. He hadn't moved and still rested against the pillar, but now his sapphire eyes were focused intently on me. He was subtly inspecting me, and I felt a tinge of pink touch my cheeks. Did I look bad? Did he not like me praying here?

'Yes, my Lord?' I asked, nervous to hear his reply.

'You know... I don't really know anything about you. I don't even know your last name,' he observed as his gaze remained locked on me.

'There's nothing to know, my Lord,' I turned back to the statue.

He let out a loud scoff, and I couldn't help but flinch. 'That's a bold-faced lie,' he retorted.

'It's the truth,' I shot back, almost a little too defensively.

'No, it isn't. You're here, aren't you? You have a family, a home, a life outside of serving me,' he pointed out, his tone firm. 'I want to know more about you, Isla. Tell me about yourself.'

I hesitated, unsure of what to say. I had always kept my personal life to myself, not wanting to burden anyone with my troubles. I certainly wouldn't reveal the truth about my actual circumstances. But perhaps Railan was right, perhaps it was time to open up a little. Just a fraction of the truth. I took a deep breath and began to speak.

'My last name is Marielle, and I was born here in the Capital,' I started, keeping my eyes focused on the statue as I spoke. 'My parents are still alive, and I have a little sister. I was lucky enough to receive a scholarship to the Creed Academy, where I graduated with a degree in business and communication. I work hard so I can send any money I make to help my family. Things have been hard since my father was crippled by the frost. That's all there is to know, really.'

I was careful to exclude all the truly unsavoury details. Like my time in the slave market, the training I'd received in preparation for my covert duties, and the fact that I was deeply in debt to Lady Amaranta.

Railan was quiet for a moment, processing my words. 'That's quite noble of you,' he finally said, a small smile playing at the corners of his lips. 'I'm sure your family is proud of you.'

I shrugged, feeling a little embarrassed. 'I just do what I can,' I replied.

'Well, I think it's admirable,' Railan said, his gaze softening. 'And I hope to get to know you better, Isla. You seem like an interesting person.'

I couldn't help but smile at his words, feeling a warmth in my chest, 'I hope... that we can work together for a long time, my Lord,' I said softly.

'So do I,' Railan agreed, and we fell back into a comfortable silence.

I felt a strange sense of understanding wash over me. The rumours surrounding his ruthlessness had been just that, rumours. I was glad that he wasn't a cruel master. Perhaps the Celestial Lady really was watching over me.

Chapter 11

I felt a lot more at ease ever since Lord Railan had shared the secret menhirs with me. The strange tension that had hung between us had seemingly dissipated, and I felt relaxed for once in my life. That didn't mean that I could let my guard down; there were still many dangers that threatened to undo me. I simply understood that Lord Railan was the least likely to bring me harm, and that was... unexpectedly pleasant.

I awoke with a strong sense of vigour. Today would be a very busy day, perhaps the busiest so far. Today was also the day my Lord would finally receive the deed to his new estate. That not only meant he'd have his own, private space, but also that the next few weeks would be filled with all manner of shopping and interior design. I'd already arranged for a specialist architect to meet us at his estate tomorrow so that he could begin the renovation process immediately.

It was all so exciting. The first order of business was a lengthy visit to the Maentaean Land Commission to officially acquire my Lord's land title. I expected it to take up at least half the day, as I anticipated an unprecedented mountain of paperwork. A part of me was looking forward to it. Paperwork was simple. It would be nice to just relax for the day.

I eagerly made my way to Railan's temporary lodging. Soon, he would not have to return here. I knocked on the door with a spry enthusiasm. I was ready.

There was a moment of silence before I heard Railan's voice from inside.

'Come in, Isla,' he said.

I opened the door and found him sitting at his desk, poring over a stack of documents. He looked deep in thought.

'Good morning, my Lord,' I greeted him with a small bow. 'Are you ready to head to the Land Commission?'

'Ah, Isla. Yes, I'm just finishing up some last-minute preparations,' he replied, setting down the papers. 'I'm afraid I've kept you waiting.'

'Not at all, my Lord,' I said with a smile.

Railan returned my smile and stood up from his desk. 'Shall we be off, then?'

We made our way to the Land Commission, where we were greeted by a stern-faced clerk who began the lengthy process of verifying Railan's identity and reviewing the various documents needed for the land title transfer. The process was exclusively mundane paperwork and somehow even more arduous than I had anticipated. It baffled me to no end how it hadn't been modernised with magic, and by the time we were finished, it was late in the afternoon.

'Well, that was a fun day,' Railan said with a wry smile as we left the building. 'I had no idea that much paperwork could exist in one place.'

'Yes, paperwork has a way of piling up,' I agreed, feeling just a little drained from the experience.

'Let's go get some food,' he suggested.

I was taken aback by his casual offer. We hadn't exactly eaten together since the morning I'd been attacked by the Magi Primacy goons. I blinked at him as I hesitated to reply.

'I, er... I can arrange something if you'd like?' I said as I purposefully avoided looking at him. I pulled out my notebook and quickly tried to look busy. 'There is always an open reservation for the Prime Mages at any restaurant you wish to visit. Just let me know where you'd like to go.'

Railan chuckled. 'No need for that, I'm not that picky. Besides, I think it'll be nice to have a casual meal together, just the two of us.'

I couldn't help but feel a flutter in my chest at his words. It was a rare moment of intimacy between us, and I couldn't help but feel grateful for it. Railan was a very fascinating man in his own right, and having the opportunity to simply sit and listen to him filled me with awe and warmth.

I nodded. 'I would like that very much.'

We ended up at a small local tavern, a place that Railan seemed to frequent quite often. The food was simple, but delicious, and the atmosphere was warm and welcoming. We chatted about various topics over the meal, from the weather to the latest gossip around town. I found myself enjoying his company more and more with each passing moment. I made sure to make little notes on everything he told me, not to be malicious, but simply because it was important to him. He was genuinely interested in what I had to say, and I felt heard and understood in a way that was new and refreshing.

After we finished our meal, Railan insisted on paying the bill despite my protests.

'Consider it a small thank you for all your hard work,' he said with a wink. I couldn't help but smile in response.

As we walked out of the restaurant, Railan turned to me. 'I had a great time. Thank you for coming with me.'

'I had a great time too, my Lord,' I replied with a smile. 'We should do this again sometime.'

I immediately heard the casualness in my voice, and my cheeks burned red as I covered my mouth. That was awfully presumptuous of me.

'Definitely,' Railan chuckled, amused by my reaction.

For a moment, I thought I saw a hint of something more in his eyes. But before I could dwell on it, he turned and walked away, leaving me standing there, feeling both confused and excited.

My Lord was certainly a strange man. It appeared Lady Amaranta was a better judge of character than I could have ever predicted. I'd had my doubts that we would get along initially, but it turned out to be unfounded. We were rather complementary, and my confidence had grown exponentially since our first meeting.

And soon we would be living together. My cheeks abruptly burned at the thought, and I quickly covered them with my hands.

Living together.

I hadn't even given it a single thought until now. I mean, it wasn't exactly alone; there would be a full complement of staff and thus, additional work for me. But still, we'd be living under the same roof. My heart raced uncontrollably. I was going to live in a mansion. Something I'd dreamed of since I was a child.

A child.

My excitement was quickly replaced by a dull ache. The blush subsided, and my face quickly dropped. I hadn't had much time for anything other than my job. I'd been too preoccupied. I hadn't been able to spare a single thought for my family.

My family.

I wondered how they were doing. I hadn't seen them in well over a year at this point, and the last update I'd received had been well over two months ago. They had been doing well, yet I couldn't help but worry that things had changed.

I would have to arrange a visit soon, if I could find a sliver of free time. My Lord was relentlessly busy, and therefore, so was I. I could only hope that being able to host guests in his own residence would open up some more time for me. I shook off all my worries and quickly chased after him.

Railan's new estate was a little too far from the Capital proper for my liking, but it was nice and secluded. I was sure he would at least enjoy that aspect. After all, he did value his privacy, even if it was nothing more than an illusion.

As for the building itself, well, it was even more of a mansion than I could have ever possibly conceived. It was more akin to a castle if I had to be honest. While it did seem a little neglected, there was still something grand and elegant about it. The land it sat upon was vast and overgrown with snow-covered trees. It would take a lot of work to get the garden in order, but I could already envision an onslaught of charming designs that would delight my Lord.

A plump, well-dressed man met us at the gate just as we arrived. Alexi Pompanov, one of the top architects and interior designers in all of Maentaea. He was known for his daring sense of design and fearlessly bold choices. I knew he would be the perfect match for Railan.

'Master Pompanov, Lord Railan is most pleased that you could join us today,' I bowed as I introduced my Lord.

'Of course, of course,' the round man seemed almost nervous as he scurried towards us. 'Lord Railan in the flesh, it's an honour,' he bowed as he extended his hand.

It was absolutely amazing just how sweaty he seemed despite the frigid weather. I couldn't help but conceal a small smile. Pompanov had nothing to fear; Railan would no doubt enjoy his imaginative mind when it came to the renovation process.

Railan greeted Pompanov with a warm smile and a firm handshake. 'It's great to finally meet you, Master Pompanov,' he said. 'I've heard wonderful things about your work and I'm excited to see what you have in mind for my new home.'

Pompanov beamed with pride at the praise. 'Oh, you flatter me, my Lord,' he said. 'I have some ideas that I think will really make this place shine. But first, let's take a tour of the estate and get a sense of the space we're working with.'

We followed Pompanov through the gates and into the courtyard, which was overgrown with weeds and snow. The mansion loomed above us, majestic and imposing, but also in need of some serious tender love and care. Pompanov led us through the grand entrance and into the main hall, which was cavernous and dimly lit with only the cold daylight piercing through the windows.

'I can already see it,' Pompanov said, rubbing his hands together with excitement. 'Crystal chandeliers hanging from the ceiling, richly upholstered sofas and armchairs, tapestries on the walls...this room has so much potential.'

Railan nodded in agreement, his eyes roving over the space. 'I want it to feel welcoming, but also elegant,' he said. 'I want to make this place somewhere I can entertain guests, but also relax on my own.'

Pompanov listened carefully, nodding and taking notes. 'I have some ideas for the colour scheme and furnishings that I think will achieve that balance,' he said. 'But before we get too deep into the specifics, I have some questions about your personal style, my Lord.'

Railan looked momentarily flustered, as if he wasn't used to talking about himself in that way. 'I'm not sure I have a specific style,' he admitted. 'I just want it to be...nice.'

Pompanov chuckled. 'Well, we'll have to dig a little deeper than that,' he said. 'But don't worry, we'll figure it out. Let's continue the tour, shall we?'

And with that, we set off through the rest of the mansion, discussing everything from the layout of the bedrooms to the colour of the kitchen tiles. By the end of the day, Pompanov had a laundry list of ideas and inspiration, and I had a headache from trying to keep up with their rapid-fire conversation. But despite the overwhelming nature of it all, I held a sense of excitement for what was to come. With a little elbow grease and a lot of creativity, this mansion was going to be transformed into a home worthy of its new Lord.

Chapter 12

The next couple of weeks had been a precarious balance between appointments, meetings, and renovations. I'd had even less time to think, let alone rest. I was beyond tired and fueled only by the habitual consumption of highly sweetened coffee. I was certain Railan would be feeling similar.

However, it was all worth it as the day was finally here. Today, my Lord, and by extension, I, would finally get to move into his estate. I was both excited and a little sad as I finished packing up the last of my belongings. It was almost sad that everything I owned could fit into a single suitcase, not that I really needed more. I placed the mysterious box safely in my satchel, intent on keeping it close. I was still painfully curious about its contents, but time was a very limited resource, and I hadn't had any to spare. I'd long since given up on compiling a satisfying report on the Silvyan Order, and while I hadn't been happy, Lord Railan had seemed content with my work.

I glanced around at my now barren apartment. It had been my home for the last five years, ever since I'd graduated from the Creed Academy. It was a single room, but it was homely, and it had been solely mine. Privacy was a luxury very few could enjoy, yet I'd been lucky simply because of Lady Amaranta's favour. Now I would be living in a fancy mansion. I was a little nervous.

In theory, I understood household management, but I'd never had any actual experience. Railan had been content with my current abilities, so I wasn't too concerned that he would be dissatisfied. Still, I wanted to continue to prove my worth.

I grabbed my bag, and even though I would miss the place, I closed the door with confidence. One door was closed, but another was open and waiting for me.

I made my way to Railan's lodgings. I hoped he had finished packing by now, too. I'd cleared the day specifically so he would have ample time to move in and make himself at home.

I knocked on his door for the final time, eager to see him.

The door opened, and Railan appeared, his hair still damp from a recent shower. He looked refreshed and invigorated, a stark contrast to my tired appearance. He greeted me with a smile and a nod, his eyes crinkling at the corners.

'Ready to move in?' he asked, holding the door open for me.

I nodded, my excitement returning. 'Yes, my Lord. I'm looking forward to it.'

We left his apartment for the last time and eagerly climbed aboard the sleigh that waited for us. I couldn't help but marvel at the amount of luggage Railan had. He had several large trunks and suitcases that were almost precariously strapped to the back, and I couldn't imagine what he had packed. I had only the essentials.

The ride was bumpy and uncomfortable, but the scenery was breathtaking. Snow-covered trees lined the road, and the air was crisp and fresh. I leaned my head against the window and allowed myself to relax for a few moments.

As we approached the estate, my heart began to race with excitement. The mansion slowly came into view as the trees thinned out, and it was even more magnificent than I remembered, with its sprawling gardens and towering turrets. It was clear that Pampanov had been busy, and quite a bit of work had been done since our first visit.

The estate had been transformed into a true masterpiece, and I was thrilled to be a part of its history.

We made our way to the front entrance of the mansion proper, where several of Railan's staff members were already waiting for us. They bowed as we approached, their faces solemn yet welcoming. It was a stark reminder that despite the luxurious surroundings, we were here to work.

Railan introduced me to the staff members, and I greeted them with a polite smile. I would need to learn their names and roles soon, as I would be working with them closely. The thought made me a little nervous, but I pushed it aside. I had to remain professional and confident.

The staff members began to unload our belongings from the sleigh while Railan and I made our way inside. I couldn't help but feel a little overwhelmed by its grandeur. It was like nothing I had ever seen before, and I was both excited and intimidated. Railan led me through the halls, showing me the various rooms and features of the estate. It was clear that there was still a lot of work to be done, but I was eager to get started. I was determined to make this estate a true gem of Maentaea, just like its owner.

Railan seemed to have an almost childlike excitement as he showed me around the manor, pointing out all the things he'd specifically requested. He had interesting taste, to say the least. I couldn't help but smile quietly to myself. Everything was unique, yet elegant, much like my Lord himself. No doubt, the numerous guests he would receive in the years to come would be left with a memorable experience. I suppose that was the point, though.

As we continued the tour, there was a sense of satisfaction in seeing everything finally coming together. It had been a lot of hard work, but it was all worth it to see my Lord happy and content in his new home.

'I'm glad you like it, my Lord,' I said, nodding at his enthusiasm for the grand fireplace in the main hall. 'The renovations turned out beautifully. I'm sure the guests will be in awe.'

Railan turned to me with a grin. 'Of course they will be. And... I have you to thank for it, Isla.'

I felt a warm flush spread across my cheeks at the compliment. 'I only did my job, my Lord. I am happy to have been of service.'

He chuckled. 'Modest as ever. Well, come on, let me show you the rest of the rooms.'

We continued the tour, exploring each room and taking note of any finishing touches that still needed to be made. As we walked, Railan shared his plans for the future of the estate, and I could see the passion and excitement in his eyes. It was contagious, and I couldn't help the swell of anticipation in my chest for what was to come.

Eventually, we made our way to my room. It was a smaller, simpler room compared to the grandeur of the rest of the mansion, but it was perfect for me. I could feel the weight of the day settling in as I placed my suitcase at the foot of the bed and took a deep breath.

'It's been a long day,' I said with a small smile, turning to Railan. 'I think I'll get some rest.'

'Of course, don't let me keep you. You've more than earned it,' he replied with a nod. 'I'll see you tomorrow, Isla.'

'Goodnight, my Lord,' I said, bowing before I closed the door.

I paused, listening briefly to his footsteps as they moved away from me before I made my way to the bed. As I lay down, I couldn't help but be washed with contentment. I was living in a mansion, and more importantly, I was making a difference in Railan's life. It was all I could have asked for. It felt like, for a brief, fleeting moment, that I was just a regular woman living a regular life.

I had the first decent rest in a very long time, and I awoke with an almost intoxicating vigour. It was a new day, and I had a household to run. I decided to wear something a little more business casual, and I even wore my hair down for what felt like the first time in forever. I flattened my simple blouse and straightened my glasses as I inspected myself in my very own personal mirror.

Presentable.

It was kind of nice not to wear several layers. I didn't expect to leave the warmth of the mansion, and even if the need arose, it was even nicer to know my room was not far away.

I didn't have to worry about impressing any visitors today, only the staff. My Lord still had a few finishing touches to complete, then I could expect things to be business as usual. I had to make the most of what little downtime was available in the meantime. My eyes flicked over to my satchel, and I placed it upon my desk before I pulled out the old wooden box. I will finally have time to continue my investigation. I opened the lid and peeked inside. The subtle glow of the solitary witchlight still shone from within. I was still aghast that it continued to persist. The vial must be quite powerful to sustain it. I smiled to myself as I poked at the light, amused as it ran away from me, moving from one end of the vial to the other. I would definitely get to investigate this this afternoon, but for now, I had my real job to tend to.

My first task was to arrange breakfast. I checked my pocket watch. Seven. Lord Railan should still be in bed. I would arrange for a nice cooked breakfast to be brought to his room and for the maid to wake him. I merrily made my way to the kitchen, taking care to greet all the staff I encountered. I needed to establish a good rapport with them.

The kitchen was located on the ground floor near the staff quarters, which included my room and was fully stocked. I'd briefly met the head chief last night. Ivan, I believe, was his name. I intended to acquaint myself more fully with the man who would be handling all of our nutritional needs. I also needed to establish my stringent expectations. No doubt the staff had been chosen carefully, but one could never be too sure.

As I entered the bustling kitchen, the smell of freshly brewed coffee and sizzling bacon greeted me. I felt a little excited as I briefly watched the chefs expertly prepare the meal.

'Good morning, ma'am,' greeted Ivan, the head chef, as he noticed me. 'Is there anything I can help you with?'

'Yes, good morning. Ivan,' I replied with a warm smile. 'I just wanted to check in and see how things are going. I also wanted to become more acquainted with the kitchen and see if there's anything I can do to help.'

'Yes, thank you, ma'am. Everything is going smoothly, but we could always use an extra hand. If you're willing, you can help with the plating and presentation of the dishes.'

I eagerly agreed and began to assist the chefs with the final touches. I made sure to chat with the staff, getting to know them and learning about their roles in the household as I worked. I was pleased to find that they were all well-trained and efficient. But I still made sure to express my expectations for cleanliness, punctuality, and attention to detail.

After the breakfast was plated and ready, I decided I would personally bring it to Railan's room, just to make sure that everything arrived to my satisfaction. I wanted everything to remain perfect, and I had to admit, I was also curious to see how Lord Railan was settling into his new home. I made my way to his room with an optimistic pep in my step, the silver platter in hand. I plastered a genuine smile upon my face before I rapped on the door a little too enthusiastically.

When Railan answered the door, he seemed pleasantly surprised to see me. An air of sleep still clung to him, and his ginger hair was a ruffled mess. I couldn't help but blush slightly as I realised he was only half dressed.

'G-good morning, my Lord,' I greeted him with a small bow as I averted my gaze. 'I figured you would enjoy your first breakfast here in your room. I wanted to make sure you had a proper start to your day.'

He looked at me with his signature, if not a little sleepy, smile. 'Thank you, Isla. It looks wonderful. You really do go above and beyond in your duties.'

My cheeks darkened slightly at the compliment, and a sense of pride and satisfaction washed over me. It was a good start to the day. I placed the platter upon the small table that sat in the corner of the room before I made my way over to the heavy curtains that plunged the room into darkness. I drew them back with a little more effort than expected before I turned to leave. To my surprise, Railan remained in the doorway, his deep blue eyes trained on me.

'My Lord, your breakfast will get cold,' I couldn't help but turn my gaze to the ground as I felt his eyes upon me.

Railan stepped into the room and closed the door behind him, his gaze unwavering. 'I can warm it up later,' he said, his voice low and smooth. 'I'd rather spend some time with you.'

I felt a flutter in my stomach at his words, but I quickly composed myself. 'Of course, my Lord,' I replied, trying to sound as professional as possible. 'Is there something you needed my assistance with?'

Railan chuckled. 'No, nothing urgent. I just wanted to see how you were settling in and to thank you for all the hard work you've put in so far. You've been an invaluable asset to me, Isla.'

I couldn't help but smile at his words, feeling warmth spreading through me. 'It's my pleasure to serve you in any way you require, my Lord. There's no need to thank me. I'm just doing my job.'

Railan stepped closer to me, his eyes never leaving me. 'You do much more than that, Isla,' he said softly, his voice barely above a whisper. 'You make my life easier and more enjoyable. I appreciate you more than you know.'

I felt my cheeks continue to burn at his words, and I struggled to find a suitable response. Before I could say anything, Railan leaned in and pressed his lips to mine, his hand coming up to cup my cheek. The kiss was gentle at first, but quickly grew more passionate, and I found myself responding in kind.

I didn't understand what was happening. My body was acting on its own as I kissed him back. My mind was simultaneously racing and frozen. I felt his hand slip around my waist to pull me closer, and as he pressed me to his chest, my senses abruptly returned. What was I doing? This was highly inappropriate. I immediately pulled back and turned my face away and out of his reach.

'M-my Lord, what are you...?' I couldn't even bring myself to finish the sentence as my face burned hot.

Railan's expression shifted, as if he was suddenly realising what he had done. He stepped back, his hands dropping to his side.

'I... I apologise, Isla. That was out of line. I shouldn't have done that,' he said, his tone serious and regretful.

I took a deep breath, trying to steady myself. 'It's alright, my Lord. Just... please, let's not speak of it again.'

He nodded, looking almost pained. 'Of course. I-I'll... leave you to your work, Isla.' And with that, he turned and left the room, leaving me standing there, still trying to process what had just happened.

I stared at the open door for a moment. He hadn't even eaten his breakfast. But that wasn't important. My heart beat hard against my ribs, and I quickly left, practically running as I made my way out of his room. My mind raced with thoughts and feelings I didn't quite know how to process. I didn't know where I was going; I just wanted to be somewhere else.

I ran until I made my way to one of the side entrances, and I quickly slipped outside into the cold. I pressed my back against the door before I slipped down to my knees. What was that? My cheeks still blazed despite the cold that now touched them. I brushed my fingers across my lips, the sensation of the kiss still fresh and vivid. Why would he do that? Why would he kiss me, of all people? I was confused. Was it a mistake, perhaps the result of his exhaustion? My mind raced with excuses. He didn't really have any reason to think much of me; I was no one, simply his shadow. Worse still, I was only placed here to watch him. My heart ached slightly.

Watch him.

Perhaps I was slipping? I wondered what Lady Amaranta would think if she found out. Perhaps she would scold me for my hesitation, after all, there was no place closer to my Lord than his bed. I didn't really have any right to deny him, but I just... wasn't sure if I could do such a thing. I liked him, and I couldn't deny he was handsome, but I struggled to distinguish whether those were my real feelings or simply my sense of duty.

Besides, there was surely no way that someone like him could ever want someone like me. I was... less than desirable. I looked down at my hands as they started to shiver from the cold. If he knew who I truly was, he would surely be disgusted. Tainted, impure, less than human. I was all of those things. I was not someone who could be loved by someone like Railan.

I hadn't realised that silent tears had started to trickle down my cheeks until I felt the bitter sting as they froze upon my skin. I blinked, surprised, before I quickly wiped them away. I needed to be professional. I couldn't let this disrupt my mission. I needed to stay close to him, even at my detriment.

Panic suddenly surged through me. What if my rejection made him pull away from me? It would only be natural, but I couldn't afford to lose the months of rapport I'd built with him. Running away had been the wrong answer. I needed to speak to him, to clarify everything. This was a misunderstanding. One I needed to rectify.

I stood, my legs already aching from my short time in the snow. I dusted off the white flakes, even though they had already soaked into my clothes. I took a deep breath before letting out an equally big sigh. My casual efforts were for nothing. I would have to get changed already. I couldn't let Railan see me like this.

I made my way back inside and skulked towards my room. It was barely eight in the morning, and everything had already turned into a disaster. Why now? Just when things were supposed to be settling down.

'Ma'am, are you alright?' an unfamiliar voice called out to me.

I turned to see one of the younger maids nervously standing outside one of the many rooms. She seemed almost shy as I acknowledged her. I'd been so distracted I hadn't even noticed she was there.

'Oh, yes. Good morning!' I forced out a cheerful smile. 'I'm sorry, I don't believe we've been acquainted yet. I'm Isla, the household manager. What is your name?'

'Oh, um, I'm Rosalind, ma'am,' she fidgeted anxiously as she kept her head low, starkly reminding me of myself. 'I'm sorry, I just... I couldn't help but notice you seemed upset. Ah, forgive me for my presumption. It's not my place,' she spoke a little too quickly. I could hardly catch a word she said.

'Oh, no, I'm not upset, perhaps a little frazzled,' I chuckled as I boldly lied.

A small frown sat upon her youthful brow as she looked me up and down. 'Is it... because you got wet, ma'am?' she asked innocently.

I looked down at my clothes and was reminded that I was indeed, soaking wet. I let out an involuntary chuckle. I looked a bit like Railan when he'd jumped into that pond when we'd first met.

'Yes,' I said simply. 'I made the mistake of stepping outside for just a moment,' I explained. It was simpler to obscure the truth than to outright lie.

Rosalind's brows lowered, and she let out a little sigh of relief as she relaxed. 'Oh, I see, I thought perhaps...' she trailed off as she stopped herself from saying something she'd regret.

I tilted my head at her curiously. 'You thought?'

Her nerves abruptly returned, and she stared at the ground. 'Nothing, ma'am. I mean no offence.'

'It's fine. You have nothing to fear here,' I reassured her. 'Please don't feel like you cannot talk to me. If you have concerns, you may bring them to me.'

'Yes, ma'am,' she remained on edge despite my reassurance.

I gave her another soft smile. 'I must be off, I'll catch a cold if I don't change soon. It was lovely to meet you.'

I gave her one last glance before I hurried back to my room. How embarrassing! I prayed that Rosalind wouldn't spread any gossip about this. It was the first day, and I couldn't afford a scandal so soon.

I finally made it back to my quarters, and I quickly locked the door behind me. I let out a heavy sigh. Things had been going so well. Where had I gone wrong? What had I missed?

I shook my head. I'd try to figure it out once I was more presentable. I quickly stripped off my wet clothes and rummaged through my closet for my usual uniform. So much for casual. I suppose it served me right. I shouldn't have gotten so comfortable. I caught a glimpse of myself in the mirror as I laid out my fresh clothes. I stared for a moment in disgust.

Tainted.

I brushed my fingers lightly over my skin. There were no visible scars, yet I could still feel the faint ache of every touch, every bruise, every restraint that had ever been placed upon me. Vivid flashes of memory bubbled to the forefront of my mind. I didn't want to remember. I wanted to forget. But I couldn't forget.

My parents had been extremely poor and in debt before I was born. Things only got worse once I was born and my father lost his leg to frostbite. Then my baby sister was born. Little Inessa was the most beautiful baby. I wish I could have seen her grow up. Instead, I was sold to the slave market in a desperate attempt to stay alive. I was only a young girl. I didn't know anything then. I didn't know that people would hurt me, defile me, ruin me beyond saving.

I tore my eyes away from the mirror as I covered my body in shame. I started to cry again. Why did I have to be reminded of my true self? I'd been so happy to pretend I was someone I could never be, a truly respectable woman. Even after Lady Amaranta had bought me, her training had still been just as demeaning. I learnt everything I would need to watch a Prime Mage, to blend into the shadows, but also to please. Pleasure and pain didn't matter as long as I could do it. I'd almost forgotten that I was simply an object to be used. I didn't have autonomy; it had been an illusion. I'd gotten too comfortable just because Railan had shown me a scrap of kindness.

Railan.

I quickly put on my uniform and wiped away my tears. I had to keep my facade intact. More importantly, I needed to salvage my relationship with him. He had also run away from our encounter earlier. A pang of pain pierced my chest as I vividly recalled the hurt in his beautiful blue eyes. I needed to make this right before everything fell apart.

Chapter 13

I walked briskly through the halls, uncertain where to look for Railan. Everything was so new, we had yet to establish any habits I could use to my advantage. I had no clue where he would have retreated to, and that made me worry. I asked several of the staff I encountered if they had seen him, but all they gave me was "no" after "no". I spent a good hour scouring the whole manor, looking in every room. I even started opening the cupboards as my anxiety increased. Concern filled me. Where could he possibly have gone? I'd scoured the whole mansion from top to bottom.

I glanced outside, and my heart froze.

No.

The only place I hadn't looked was outside. I could feel my breath quicken at the thought. He hadn't exactly been wearing much when he'd left; there was no way he would be fine in this weather. Though it wasn't actively snowing, the weather remained well below zero. It had already been over an hour. He could be frozen to death by now.

My legs carried me faster than they ever had as I rushed out into the elements. My mind raced. Why? Why was this happening? I trudged through the snow, whipping my head frantically as I tried to catch a glimpse of his bright orange hair. I had no idea where I was going as the snow had since covered any remnants of tracks. The uneven ground seemed intent on hindering me as I found every hidden branch and hole.

'Lord Railan!' I yelled out as loud as I could.

There was no response, only the howling wind and the sound of snow crunching under my boots. I called out his name again, hoping against all other hope that he was still out here and hadn't already succumbed to the cold.

Suddenly, a blue witchlight fluttered into my vision. I blinked as I watched it carefully land upon a freshly fallen tree. It shouldn't have piqued my interest, but it was no regular fallen tree. The bark had been scorched completely black, and a subtle heat still radiated from it, leaving it oddly devoid of snow. I frowned, both curious and frightened. What could have possibly done this? Was it the Silvyan Order? Was Lord Railan in more trouble than just the looming threat of the frost? My eyes darted around, and I soon saw a trail of even more witchlights leading deeper into the forest, as if they were trying to guide me. To my confusion, both blue and red lights danced before me. Fire and water. I didn't have time to ask questions. Even if I was heading into danger, I needed to find him.

I followed the lights. Blackened marks marred patches of ground and trees, leaving behind melted puddles of half-frozen water.

Then I heard a faint noise, like someone moaning in pain. I followed the sound, heart racing, until I came across a small clearing in the woods. An abundance of witchlights filled the air, and I saw that almost all the trees that enclosed the space had been violently damaged. Their bark still sizzled, and the smell of burning wood filled my nose.

Then I saw him.

There, lying on the ground, was Railan, his body shivering violently as he lay curled in a slurry of half-melted and refrozen ice. The red and blue witchlights clung to him like a beacon.

Without a second thought, I rushed over to him and pulled off my outer jacket, wrapping it around him as best as I could as I pulled him into my arms. Cold wetness soaked into my clothes, and he felt like ice.

'My Lord, are you okay? Can you hear me?' I asked, trying to keep my voice calm despite the panic that surged inside.

Dark red blood oozed from his nose and mouth, painting the snow, and now, my blouse. What had happened to him?

He stirred briefly as his eyes slowly opened. 'I-Isla? What are you doing out here?' he mumbled, teeth chattering.

'I was looking for you. What were you thinking? You can't just run off like that, not in this weather,' I scolded gently as I trembled with both relief and anxiety.

He was still alive, but just barely. I needed to get him back to the warmth of the mansion. If he stayed out here much longer... I shook my head. I didn't want to think about it.

'I'm sorry,' he said, his voice barely above a whisper. 'I just...needed some space. I didn't...' he trailed off as his eyes fluttered weakly.

'My Lord, please hang on,' I said, trying desperately to keep my own emotions in check as tears threatened my eyes. 'We need to get you back inside. Now.'

With great effort, I managed to help him up, wrapping my arms around him to keep him steady. We stumbled through the snow back to the manor, the trail of witchlights as our guide.

'Someone, help!' I yelled out as we practically fell through the doorway.

A confused butler poked his head out from the adjoining hall to see what was happening and quickly leapt into action as he saw us splayed out upon the foyer floor.

'Blankets, we need blankets!' his voice boomed as he rushed to our aid.

A second, younger boy hesitated for a moment as he laid eyes upon us before he snapped out of his shock and he took off running. To my relief, the staff immediately took over, bringing Railan blankets and hot tea to warm him up. I sent word to the doctor, just in case anything serious had afflicted him, and Railan was eventually brought up to his room and laid to rest. The windows were firmly shut, and the fireplace fully stocked.

'Ma'am, let me help you,' Rosalind came over to me once things had finally settled down. 'You will catch a chill if you stay like that,' her voice was filled with worry.

I blinked at her, my mind clouded, and I realised that I was once again cold and wet. I'd recklessly run into the forest without my cloak and had given my outer jacket to Railan, leaving me in only a thin layer that was now soaked through.

'Ah, you're right,' I said quietly. 'How embarrassing for you to see me like this twice in the same day,' I tried my best to put on a brave smile despite the adrenaline that still pulsed through my veins.

'I'll help you get dry, ma'am.' Rosalind gingerly took my arm and gently pulled me into the staff quarters.

She sat me in front of the common room hearth to warm up while she fetched me some fresh, dry clothes. I hardly registered her return as I stared into the flames. Guilt rattled me. When I awoke this morning, I was in such high spirits. I never could have possibly conceived everything that had come to transpire in the few short hours that had passed.

'Here, ma'am,' Rosalind crouched by my side as she placed the spare clothes in my hands. She gave me a shy smile as she grasped my hand, giving it a slight squeeze. 'Would you like me to help you?'

I blinked as I looked at her, finally comprehending something, and I shook my head. 'No, I'll be alright now. Thank you...'

She squeezed my hand again before letting it go. 'I have to return to work... please look after yourself, ma'am,' she said as she stood.

'I will,' I weakly reassured her.

She gave me one last concerned glance before she hurried off to continue her duties. I sat in front of the fire for a little longer. I didn't know what to do next. On one hand, this could turn into a rather advantageous situation for Lady Amaranta. If Railan were to simply die, it would be one less opponent for her to worry about. The game board would be cleared, but where would that leave me? I was just another pawn, would I too be discarded? If he died, my future, my family's future, would be uncertain.

I also... didn't want him to die. Whatever I did or didn't feel for him, it didn't matter. I knew for certain that I didn't want any harm to come to him.

I quickly changed, I couldn't remain wet all day. I still had a job to do, and now that Lord Railan was incapacitated, I would need to deal with the day's schedule. It would be a farce to cancel everything, but I didn't have any choice. He was not in any state to see anyone, let alone conduct business. I let out a drained sigh. We would have to deal with the consequences later. For now, I would take full responsibility.

The doctor arrived within the hour, and while I avoided eavesdropping directly, I made sure Rosalind was there to hear the diagnosis and report back to me. Extreme mana exhaustion. The doctor had administered a mana potion and recommended three days of bed rest. That was three days I would have to try and reorganise. What a headache.

I tried to keep my mind busy as I worked tirelessly throughout the day. Yet, no matter how preoccupied I found myself, my thoughts continued to wander back to Lord Railan. I needed to confront him.

Chapter 14

I swallowed hard as I steeled my nerves. I paused outside Railan's chambers, my heart racing uncomfortably as I thought about entering. A part of me wanted to simply check on him, pretend nothing had happened, but the other part wanted to confront him, to chastise him for his stupidity and remind him of our positions. Confrontation was not my strongest aptitude, and even now, my hands shook lightly as I grabbed the doorknob. I needed to be strong, to stand my ground for once in my life.

I opened the door and peeked inside. The room was cast in deep shadows, the only light coming from the roaring fire that left the room almost a little too hot. I cast my gaze to the bed. Railan lay facing away from me, barely visible under many layers of thick blankets. My eyelashes fluttered, desperate for me to look away, but I kept my gaze firm.

'My Lord?' I croaked, my voice a low, uneven mess.

A part of me hoped he wouldn't respond, that I could just leave without any guilt. However, to my dismay, Railan stirred at the sound of my voice, though he didn't turn to face me.

His voice was hoarse when he spoke, almost as if he had been screaming. 'Isla... please leave. I... I don't want you to see me like this.'

Despite his words, I could sense the weakness and pain in his tone. It was clear that he was in no position to argue or fight.

I stepped inside, shutting the door behind me before approaching the bed. I sat on the edge of the mattress, looking at him with concern.

'My Lord-... Railan,' I uttered his name quietly, a slight hesitation to my informal tone, as I placed my hand upon his shoulder. 'Are you alright?'

Railan let out a soft sigh, his body relaxing slightly under my touch. 'No, I'm not,' he admitted, his voice strained. 'But it's nothing I can't handle.'

I didn't believe him.

'Why...' I felt the air catch in my throat as I struggled to find my courage. 'Why did you run away like that? You could have died...'

He turned his head slightly to look at me, his eyes searching mine for a moment before he looked away again. 'I know,' he murmured, his tone oozing with guilt.

I felt a twinge of anger mixed with concern as I watched him. 'You knew and yet you still did it,' I said, my voice low with frustration. 'Do you have any idea how worried we all were... how worried I was?'

Railan remained silent, his gaze fixed on the darkness.

'I don't understand you, my Lord,' I continued, my tone softening. 'Why would you risk everything like that just because I denied you?'

Railan's body tensed at my words, and for a moment, I thought he might snap at me. But instead, he let out a heavy sigh and rolled over to face me. His eyes locked onto mine, the dull light making them resemble the darkness of the abyss, and the emotion behind them was even more indiscernible.

'I know it doesn't make sense,' he said, his voice barely above a whisper. 'But when you denied me, it felt like everything I had worked for... everything I had sacrificed... it all meant nothing. I... I couldn't face that.'

I frowned, trying to make sense of his words. 'What do you mean?'

He let out a bitter chuckle. 'I've spent my whole life fighting for my position, Isla. I've had to do things... terrible things... to get to where I am. And I did it all with one goal in mind. To prove myself worthy, to be the most powerful man in the world. But when you denied me... it was like a slap in the face. It made me question everything I had done.'

I felt a pang of sympathy for him. I couldn't imagine what it must feel like to have everything you've worked for, everything you've sacrificed for, called into question by one rejection. But for as much as I could empathise, it also infuriated me.

'That doesn't excuse what you did,' I said firmly. 'You put yourself and everyone else in danger.'

Railan nodded, his expression contrite. 'I know. And I'm sorry, Isla. I truly am. I just... I didn't know how to handle it.'

I sighed, the anger and frustration seeping out of me. 'You could have talked to me, Railan. We could have worked it out together. There's nothing that cannot be fixed by open and honest communication,' I let out another, softer, sigh. 'I know that I ... haven't been as honest or as open as I should, but I want you to know that you can talk to me, no matter what. You don't need to run away from me.'

Railan looked up at me, his eyes shining with unshed tears. 'I know that now,' he said, his voice choked with emotion. 'But in that moment, I was so consumed by my own pain and self-doubt that I couldn't see past it.'

I nodded, empathising with his perspective but still feeling disappointed in his actions. 'I understand, my Lord,' I said, using his formal title to emphasise the seriousness of the situation. 'But you need to promise me that you won't do something like this again. I can't bear the thought of losing you.'

Railan reached out and took my hand, his grip firm but gentle. 'I promise,' he said, his voice soft and sincere. 'I won't do anything like this again. I'll talk to you, Isla. I'll tell you how I feel, no matter how hard it is.'

I smiled at him, relieved that he understood the gravity of his actions and was willing to commit to change. 'Thank you,' I said, giving his hand a gentle squeeze in return. 'I believe in you, Railan.'

He gave me a small, grateful smile before releasing my hand. 'I have a lot to make up for,' he said, briefly casting his gaze to the side before returning to me. 'I'll do whatever it takes to make things right.'

'You don't... have to do anything,' I averted my gaze, looking down at my hands. 'I know that it was wrong for me to deny you in the first place. If you desire to use me, then you are entitled to do so, I just...' I trailed off, my voice trembling as I felt weak once again. I needed to be honest, just like I'd said. I took a deep breath and continued. 'It's just that... I'm scared. You're a Prime Mage and I... I am nothing.'

Railan threw back the blankets and sat up, moving closer to me as he reached out to tilt my chin up so that our eyes met. 'You are not nothing, Isla,' he said firmly. 'You are... everything to me. And I won't use you, not in that way. I want... I want something real with you. Something more than just power or status. I want to be with you because I care for you, because... because I love you.'

I felt a burning hot flush rise to my cheeks at his words.

Love?

Why would he say such things? Why? Did he really mean it? He couldn't possibly. It was impossible. But then, looking into his eyes, I knew that a part of him did. I saw the sincerity and depth of emotion in his gaze and felt my own heart swell with a mixture of joy and fear.

'Railan...' I began, feeling my heart sink. 'I cannot accept those words. I haven't been honest with you... And if you knew me, the real me, you wouldn't say such things.'

Railan shook his head, his expression earnest. 'I don't need to know everything about you to love you, Isla. I know enough to know that you are kind, brave, and strong. That you have a heart full of compassion and a spirit that refuses to be broken. Those are the things that matter to me.'

I looked at him, feeling a mixture of disbelief and awe. Could it really be possible that someone could love me, flaws and all? It seemed too good to be true, yet I couldn't deny the warmth spreading through my chest at his words. I felt tears prick at my eyes. Why did he have to be so... so strange! His words were far too pretty, far too naive. I couldn't believe him.

'You don't understand...' I shook my head, my thoughts slipping into denial.

I wanted to tell him the truth about everything. That I was a slave, a spy, a pawn. That I was broken beyond repair. I wasn't any of the things he thought I was. I wasn't brave, I was scared, always so scared. Fear ruled me. As much as I wanted desperately to accept his affections, I knew that love would never be enough to save me.

Railan seemed to sense the turmoil within me, and he reached out to take my hand once more. 'I may not understand everything, Isla, but I know enough to know that you are worth loving. You deserve to be loved, and I want to be the one to love you.' He paused for a moment before continuing, 'I'm not asking for anything in return, Isla. I just want to be there for you, to support you, and to love you.'

I looked into his eyes and saw the sincerity in them, and for a moment, I allowed myself to believe that maybe, just maybe, he could be the one to save me. But then, the reality of my situation crashed down on me, and I knew that it was impossible. No one could save me from the life I was living, no matter how much they loved me. But even still, I couldn't stop myself from longing for this one brief reprieve. To pretend that everything was fine, to pretend I was more than just a pawn to be used in this power game.

'Do you really want me... even if all I am, all I can ever be, is lies and dreams?' I asked as my tears stained my glasses and made my vision blurry. 'Can you really accept that? Why would you accept that?' I turned my head away and pulled my hand out of his grasp.

I'd said too much, wanted too much. He could never truly want someone like me.

Railan's hand fell back to his side as I pulled away from him. He looked at me with a mixture of sadness and understanding. 'Isla, I don't care about the past. I don't care about what you've done or what you've been forced to do. That's not who you are to me. I care about the person you are right now, at this moment. And right now, all I see is a beautiful, kind-hearted woman who deserves to be loved.'

He was too good to be true, like a perfect dream. And if this was a dream, then I didn't want to wake up. I wanted to surrender fully, completely. Even if I would burn, I wanted to feel the heat of love, of passion, and desire. I wanted to be more, even if it was only temporary.

'If the illusion is enough, then love me. Love me with all your heart. But don't let it break when the illusion is gone and all that's left is bitter reality,' I sobbed.

Railan leaned in close, his eyes filled with determination as he gently touched my chin, tilting my face up to look at him. 'I will love you, Isla. I will love you even when the illusion fades and reality sets in. I will be there for you, no matter what happens. I promise.' He ran his thumbs over my cheeks and wiped away my tears. 'You don't have to be afraid anymore. I'll protect you, I'll cherish you, and I'll love you with everything I have.'

His words were like a balm to my soul, easing the pain and fear that had been my constant companions for so long. For the first time in a long time, I allowed myself to believe in a future where I wasn't alone, where I was loved and cherished, where I could be free.

I wrapped my arms around Railan's neck, hugging him tightly. 'Thank you,' I whispered, my voice choked with emotion.

Railan hugged me back, holding me close. I could feel the strength of his arms and the rapid beating of his heart. Power beyond measure surged within him, but it would never be enough.

'I'll never let you go, Isla. You're mine. Only mine,' his breath was warm against my ear and sent a tingle down my spine.

I knew his words were lies. I would always be someone else's. But right here, right now, I was his. I pulled back slightly, and I felt his grip tighten around me, reluctant to let me get away. But I didn't want to get away. Consequences be damned. I leaned gently on his shoulders, pushing myself up just enough to brush my lips against his. This was my choice.

Railan's lips parted as he responded to my kiss, deepening it with a sense of urgency. I could feel the passion and desire that had been simmering beneath the surface finally igniting, and I responded in kind. Our bodies pressed closer together, our hands roaming freely as we lost ourselves in the moment.

For a while, there was nothing else in the world except for us. No lies, no scheming, no danger, no past or future. Just the two of us, entwined in each other's embrace. But eventually, the need for air forced us to break apart, panting and gasping for breath.

Railan rested his forehead against mine, his eyes closed as he tried to regain his composure. 'Isla,' he murmured, his voice husky with desire. 'I want you.'

I knew what he meant. And as much as I wanted him too, I couldn't bring myself to say the words. Not yet. Not until I knew for sure that I could trust him with my heart and soul.

Instead, I gave him a small, meek smile and leaned in to kiss him once more. 'I want you too,' I whispered against his lips. 'But... I just... I need time.'

Railan's eyes fluttered open, and he pulled back slightly to look at me. I could see the confusion and disappointment written all over his face. 'Time?' he repeated, his voice laced with uncertainty. 'What do you mean?'

I took a deep breath, gathering my thoughts before speaking. 'I mean... I don't want to rush into things...if you change your mind.'

Railan's expression softened as he listened to me, his eyes filled with understanding. 'I get it,' he said, running a hand through his hair. 'I don't want to rush you. I just... I feel like I've been waiting for you my whole life, Isla. And now that you're here, I don't want to waste any more time.'

I couldn't help but feel touched by his words. Despite everything, Railan had shown me nothing but kindness and understanding. He had promised to love and protect me, and I could see the sincerity in his eyes. But I couldn't let myself get carried away. Not yet.

'Thank you,' I said, leaning in to kiss him softly on the lips. 'For understanding.'

Railan smiled, his eyes filled with warmth. 'Always, Isla. I'll wait for you, no matter how long it takes.'

I didn't have the words to respond, so I simply held him close, hiding my beet-red face against his chest. I let his warmth soak into my skin and the sweetness of his words sink deep into my heart. Railan had made a grand proclamation, but it was also behind closed doors. I knew if I wasn't careful, I would regret this, but I didn't care.

After a few moments of comfortable, contented silence, I finally pulled away from him, staying just within his grasp. 'I'm sorry to have disturbed you, my Lord. You need your rest, please don't let me distract you any further,' I bowed my head.

Railan cupped my cheeks tenderly. 'Don't apologise, Isla. You never need to apologise for being here with me,' he said, his voice gentle and reassuring. 'But... won't you stay, just a little longer?'

I searched his face, but all I saw was an earnest, gentle longing, one that was now more restrained and innocent. I couldn't deny him something so harmless.

I nodded meekly, and a large, bright grin spread across Railan's face. He let out an elated sigh before he promptly fell back onto the bed, dragging me along with him. I let out a little squeak as I fell flat on his chest. He didn't seem to mind my weight as he wrapped an arm around me and pulled some of the blankets back over us. Even though I felt utterly embarrassed, it was nice and cosy and sweet. None of this was anything close to what I had expected our first official day in his estate to be like. This would complicate everything, but I just wanted to be selfish this one time.

I closed my eyes. I would figure it out later; for now, I just wanted peace and calm. The crackle of the fire, Railan's controlled breathing, and the calm beating of his heart—these were all things that brought me a very strange and unfamiliar sensation.

Not fear.

Just... release.

Strange and unfamiliar.

I let out a soft gasp as I whipped my head up to look at Railan, my eyes wide as I recalled the very strange and concerning situation in the forest.

'What is it?' He asked, barely opening one eye to look at me.

'Ah... my Lord-' I started, but Railan cut me off.

'I don't want you to call me that,' he said softly. 'Not when it's just you and me like this.'

I bit my lip, unsure of what he wanted from me. 'Raila-'

'You know that's not my actual name, right?' he let out a wistful sigh.

My cheeks blazed red as I buried my face against his chest. 'I know that...'

Railan let out an amused chuckle as he held me tighter. 'Hm, that expression is so... very arousing.'

'D-don't say it like that!' I only buried my head further, intent on hiding the source of his amusement.

Railan continued to laugh softly, the vibrations rumbling through his chest and into my cheek. 'Alright, alright, I'll stop teasing you,' he said, his voice still filled with amusement. 'But seriously, I only ever want you to call me by my real name from now on. At least... behind closed doors if that's alright with you...'

I nodded meekly, finding a single scrap of courage as I glanced up at him, 'I understand... Elieason.'

Railan's expression softened at the use of his real name. 'That's it,' he whispered, his fingers threading through my hair. 'I want you to know me, Isla. The real me.'

I swallowed hard, feeling a strange mix of excitement and trepidation. 'And... who is the real you?' I asked softly, my fingers tracing idle patterns on his chest.

Railan's eyes drifted shut as he let out a soft sigh. 'Sometimes, I don't even know anymore,' he admitted, his tone laced with bitterness. 'But with you... I feel like maybe I can find out.' He opened his eyes, looking down at me with a mix of vulnerability and determination. 'I want to try, at least.'

I nodded slowly, feeling a flicker of hope in my chest. 'I want that too,' I whispered, before leaning up to press a gentle kiss to his lips. It was a small, simple gesture, but it felt like a promise. A promise of something more.

I also realised that he had completely detailed my train of thought. Perhaps his charm was more powerful than I'd given it credit. I narrowed my eyes at him, giving him a small pout.

Railan chuckled softly, his fingers brushing lightly against my cheek. 'What is it?' he asked, his voice gentle. 'Oh, I interrupted you. Sorry... what were you going to say?'

I glowered at him, though a small smile tugged at the corners of my lips despite myself.

'It's okay... I just...' I composed myself, trying desperately to stay on track while I could remember anything. 'I just... I noticed that there were red... fire... witchlights in the forest where I found you... What happened? Were you attacked by something? Should I inform the city guard?' I asked, my tone oozing concern, the longer I spoke.

Railan blinked at me, an expression of brief confusion upon his face before recognition dawned on him and he gave me a small, almost embarrassed chuckle.

'Oh, that... no, it was just me.'

I gave him a confused look. 'What do you mean? Your.... Your focus is on water, isn't it?'

Railan nodded as he gave me a sheepish grin. 'It is...' he paused briefly, thinking carefully about what he wanted to say next. 'Do you know why I was chosen to be a Prime Mage?'

I pressed my lips into a line as I pondered his question. I knew Railan was powerful. I knew that he was a skilled warrior. I'd heard the rumours that he was a ruthless assassin. They were all equally viable reasons to draw the Celestial Lady's attention, but also perfectly mundane reasons. There had to be more; he had to be more than that.

'Because... you're a powerful warrior?' I said slowly, hoping he would correct me.

Railan gave me a light-hearted snicker as he shook his head. 'You're half right. But do you know what makes me powerful? The thing that sets me apart from all the other Prime Mages?'

'No,' I admitted.

'Magi are known for their ability to harness elemental power, but that is limited to the single element that awakens within them. For me, that was water, obviously.'

'I know what magi are,' I said quietly, annoyed at his condescending tone.

'That's not what I'm implying,' he quickly apologised. 'What I'm trying to say is, what if a magus could wield more than one element? Would that not be worthy of the Lady's attention?'

'That's impossible,' I frowned at him.

'Ah, but you see, it's not,' he said matter-of-factly.

'What?' I sat upright, looking at Elieason directly. 'What do you mean?'

Elieason flashed me a proud grin. 'What I mean is, I can wield more than just my awakened element. Well, for a time.'

I stared at him, my mouth slightly agape as I tried to process his words. Did he just say he could use multiple elements? That... wasn't possible. But he just said that it was. I couldn't refute him since my current evidence suggested that he was telling the truth. I couldn't deny my own eyes. Elieason seemed to be incredibly satisfied with his reveal and my subsequent reaction. My mind was a mix of awe and disbelief at Railan's words. If what he was saying was true, then he truly was a rare and powerful magus.

'How... how is that even possible?' I asked, still trying to wrap my head around the idea.

Railan shrugged nonchalantly. 'I... well, let's just say I know a little bit more about the Silvyan Order than what you compiled in your report.'

'What do you mean by that? I thought you didn't know much about them, hence the report?' I furrowed my brows in confusion.

What did he mean? Was he implying he had some kind of tie to the Silvyan Order? What did that implication imply? My mind raced with a thousand anxious thoughts.

'It's true, I don't know much about them. What I do know is the fact that I can imitate their techniques and manipulate multiple elements.'

Something about his words sent panic through me, as if he'd told me something that I shouldn't know. My first thought was whether or not Lady Amaranta knew about this, and that immediately spiked guilt within me. Why did I have to think about her when he just told me something important in confidence? That's because it was also my job. On the other side of the mask I wore right now was someone compelled to reveal all his secrets. To hunt for any indiscretions, any faults, any weaknesses that Lady Amaranta could exploit.

'You don't seem impressed by that, Isla,' Railan noted as he brushed his fingers over my cheek, a hint of disappointment in his tone. 'People are usually a bit more... ecstatic when they hear what I can do.'

'It's not that, I just... I don't know,' I shrugged. I couldn't tell him my thoughts, not yet, probably not ever. 'Maybe it's just the least impressive thing you've said in the last half hour.'

He raised a brow as his cocky grin returned. 'I haven't said anything that impressive, have I?'

I didn't know how to respond, so I simply turned away. I swear this man would make my cheeks melt off at his current rate of humiliation.

'I really should go, there are many things that need my attention,' I said simply. 'And you should rest.'

'What if I'm one of the things that needs your attention?' He gave me a sly smirk.

'I've just given you attention,' I said, lowering my eyes.

Railan's expression fell, and he let out a soft sigh. 'I understand,' he said softly. 'I'm sorry if I'm being too forward. I just... I can't help feeling drawn to you.'

I felt a pang of guilt at his words, knowing that my feelings towards him were complicated at best. 'It's not that, Elieason,' I said softly, using his real name without even thinking about it. 'I just...' I trailed off, unsure of how to articulate my thoughts. 'I have to go,' I repeated, before getting up from the bed and heading towards the door.

Railan watched me go, his expression unreadable. As I closed the door behind me, I couldn't help but wonder if I'd made the right decision in leaving.

Yes, of course I did.

I couldn't allow him to get into my head. He just wanted me to warm his bed, and I had actual work to do. Besides, if I wasn't careful, he would take advantage of me in more ways than one. I needed to keep a clear mind, remember why I was here. I hurried back to my office and locked the door behind me. I needed to come up with a solid plan for how I would let this play out. Railan might be the king on the chess board, but he could still take out a pawn like me if I got too close too soon. I needed to remain wary of his words.

I let out a heavy sigh, a dull ache radiating through my skull.

Why was this happening to me?

Chapter 15

I felt like a zombie as I ambled to my office, fresh coffee in hand. The aroma alone was usually enough to stir me, but today it was not. I had stayed up late and woke up early, much to my detriment. As much as I'd longed for the sweet reprieve of rest, my mind had refused, intent on replaying and overthinking the events of yesterday. Railan sure knew how to make things interesting, and I did not like that. I wanted stability, certainty, and he was chaos.

As I entered my office, my eyes were immediately drawn to an unusual envelope on my desk. It hadn't been there a few hours ago. I couldn't help but look around, as if expecting someone to be watching me, but there was nothing. I locked the door behind me before picking up the letter.

A red envelope.

I knew exactly what it meant. It was from Lady Amaranta, requesting a meeting with me at the Creed Citadel later that day. My heart sank as I read it. I knew there could only be one thing that she wanted. More information. But I hadn't learned anything that could be of use to her, not yet. In fact, my interactions with Railan had only left me more confused than before.

I sat down at my desk, staring blankly at the paperwork before me. My mind was foggy, and I couldn't concentrate on anything. I took a sip of my coffee, hoping it would help, but it only made me more jittery. I sighed, running a hand through my hair in frustration. What was I supposed to do? I could tell her about Railan's vague connection to the Silvyan Order, but I didn't exactly have any verifiable proof. Besides, was that really incriminating in any way? Knowing lost magic wasn't a crime; in fact, it was exactly the kind of thing that one would expect of a Prime Mage.

I dropped my forehead onto the desk. Lady Amaranta would have to be satisfied with what little information I did have. Besides, it hadn't been that long since my mission started. I needed time. These things couldn't be rushed. I needed to earn his trust. Though I had somehow managed to earn his wandering eyes since he had immediately professed his undying love for me. Love did not mean trust, and lust did not mean love.

I could feel my cheeks heating up, and I immediately covered them with my hands in an effort to ease the redness. There was no way that someone like Railan could ever be sincere. I was nothing, a mundus, used, dirty. I was simple, plain. There was nothing attractive about me. That was what Lady Amaranta liked about me, that I was so mundane that I could become invisible. Yet, Railan had somehow noticed me, and he shone a light towards me that I hadn't been expecting. He made me feel exposed, vulnerable, but not exactly scared. Perhaps he only wanted to use me simply because I was there. After all, I was convenient. If that was the case, he could have just asked me to arrange a mistress.

My chest tightened at the thought. His words had sunk their claws into my mind and my heart, and now I had doubts. I'd told him he could love me so long as he wouldn't be disappointed when reality sets in, and he's promised that would be the case. Except I knew that was a blatant lie. Feelings were messy; that was one of the first things I'd been taught when Lady Amaranta purchased me. But masking my feelings had never been my strongest attribute. My skills lie with books and paperwork. They were straightforward. Words written plainly could always be deciphered and understood. Feelings were inconsistent, always fluctuating, chaotic.

I let out an annoyed groan. None of it mattered. My only problem now was finding a way to meet with Lady Amaranta. It wouldn't be as simple as wandering down the street. Railan's estate was quite far from the city, perhaps too far to comfortably walk in a reasonable time. I could, in theory, borrow a sleigh, but would that not arouse suspicion? Perhaps I could come up with some excuse, like a sick family member or something along those lines. Maybe it would be a good time for Railan to prove his feelings are earnest. If I asked, would he let me just go to town? I would have to ask after work hours. But what if he asks to come along? He should be on bed rest, but I had a feeling he wouldn't pass up the opportunity to be alone with me again, and that would be useless. I pondered simply not going, refusing Lady Amaranta's summons. Surely she would understand. Yet, I knew she would be furious. To refuse her was to beg for punishment, and not just for myself, but also for my family. I couldn't do that. I knew what she could do, what she would do.

Lady Amaranta had a reputation for elegance, beauty, and grace, but she also had a reputation known only to those deep within the Creed. One that was cold, dangerous, and deadly. On the outside, she was a model citizen, a beloved Prime Mage, a merciful savant. But underneath the facade, I knew she delighted in destruction, in manipulating the scene, exploiting every single weakness, killing every thought and desire that did not serve her. She collected the poor and weak only to hold them hostage under the guise of charity. There was a reason she had been able to maintain her position as Third Prime Mage for so long. Her web of witchlights, of spies, was vast. She knew everything, and if she didn't, she would in time. If I defied her in any way, she would punish my family in my place. Would she starve them? Put them out on the streets? Torture them? Would she do to my sweet little sister what she did to me?

I had to push the thoughts aside. I would make it to her meeting, even if it meant walking in knee-high snow for hours. If she wanted to hear me summarise my report in person, then I would make it happen. In the meantime, I had legitimate work that I needed to get through. I nursed my coffee as I started on my pile of perfectly unsophisticated paperwork.

Knock!

I glanced up from my work to the door. It was locked. I let out a little sigh. I'd managed two hours of peace, but alas, the day was starting, and thus so was the trouble.

A second knock.

I stood and shuffled to the door, unlocking it.

'Yes?' I asked innocently.

To my surprise, Rosalind stood outside, her hands fiddling with her apron as she bit her lip nervously. Her eyes grew wide as I answered before settling back into a somewhat relaxed state.

'G-good morning, ma'am,' she gave me a curt bow. 'I-I was sent to inform you that you have been requested in the Master's office.'

My stomach dropped at her words. Really, he was requesting to see me so early? I checked my pocket watch. He shouldn't be awake this early.

'Is his Lordship alright?' I asked.

'I... I think so?' Rosalind stammered, as if my question had put her on the spot.

I let out what felt like my hundredth sigh for the day. He should still be resting. The doctor had said three days of bed rest. I'd cleared his schedule for just that reason. Why would he be in his office? If he were well enough, I shouldn't have bothered cancelling the next two days!

'Thank you for telling me. Is there anything else?' I forced out a polite smile despite my dread.

Rosalind shook her head.

'Alright, you may go. Don't work too hard, we won't be having any guests today,' I chuckled, a dark, annoyed undertone to my voice.

Rosalind furrowed her brows slightly but didn't enquire further as she bowed and left. I watched her go as I pondered simply ignoring Railan's summons. Perhaps I could get away with ignoring him, perhaps I couldn't. I wasn't sure how willing he was to abuse his power over me. He might not think of it that way, but I was still keenly aware of our positions. I could abuse his affection too, balance out the power discrepancy, but the thought made me queasy. I didn't want to do that. I didn't want to be used like that, and I wouldn't do the same to him.

I slumped my shoulders as I wandered back to my desk and grabbed my notebook. There was no winning for me. I had to go and see Railan, if not for business, then to at least make sure he was alright. Extreme mana exhaustion was a serious condition, deadly even. Just because he had seemed alright yesterday didn't mean his condition hadn't changed overnight. I probably should have checked on him earlier, but alas, I was purposefully avoiding him.

Defeated, I made my way to Railan's office. I clutched my notebook tight to my chest, uncertain what I was about to walk into. I stopped outside, pausing briefly as I considered simply walking straight on by, but I couldn't. I looked at the finely carved door, the only thing between us. I was overthinking things. It couldn't be that bad.

I knocked on the door as I steeled my nerves. 'My Lord, it's Isla. You summoned me?'

'Come in!' Railan called, his voice unabashedly cheerful.

I didn't want to. He sounded way too excited by my arrival. I turned the doorknob and stepped inside anyway.

Railan was sitting at his desk, but he stood up as soon as I entered the room. He was dressed in casual clothes, a far cry from the fancy outfits he usually wore, and he looked much better than the last time I saw him. He grinned widely at me as I walked in, and I couldn't help but feel a little bit of warmth spread through me.

'Isla! You came! I was starting to think you were avoiding me,' he said teasingly.

'I was busy,' I said, trying to sound as neutral as possible.

'Of course, of course,' he waved his hand dismissively. 'But I'm glad you're here. I wanted to thank you for yesterday.'

'Thank me?' I raised an eyebrow in confusion.

'Yes, for staying with me and taking care of me. You didn't have to do that,' he said sincerely.

'It is my duty,' I said stiffly, reminding him of our positions.

'Ah, right. Duty,' he said, his expression falling slightly. 'Well, regardless, I appreciate it.'

I nodded, not sure what else to say. The silence between us was thick, and my discomfort only continued to grow. I wanted to leave, to escape this room and his presence, but something was holding me back. Was this it? Was that really all he wanted to say?'

'But that's not what I actually wanted to ask you,' he spoke up. 'I was wondering if you could help me with some of this,' he gestured vaguely to the papers that were chaotically scattered upon his desk.

'If you need assistance, delegate them by priority, and I shall have Rosalind come and deliver them to my office,' I said as I turned to leave.

'Ah, wait, Isla!' Railan called after me.

I glanced back to see that he was coming for me. My heart raced slightly as he grabbed my hand and pulled me back to face him.

'It won't take that long. Please stay... just for a few minutes,' he pleaded.

He looked down at me through his long lashes, a reserved tenderness in his eyes. I could feel the heat returning to my cheeks once again, and I cast my eyes down. He squeezed my hand, encouraging me to give in to his request. A few minutes. A lot could happen in a few minutes. No, he said he would wait, and if he was indeed a man of his word, then it would be fine.

I nodded weakly, surrendering to my fate. Railan's face lit back up as a bright smile spread across his lips. He tugged on my hand and pulled me back to his desk. Before I could protest, he pulled me onto his lap and wrapped his arms around me. My face was well and truly red now.

'W-what are you doing, my Lord?' I stuttered.

'I told you not to call me that,' Railan muttered as he rested his cheek against my shoulder.

I tensed up, unsure of what to do. His embrace was warm and comforting, yet it also felt suffocating. I tried to push him away, but he only held me tighter. My mind raced as I tried to come up with an excuse to leave, but I couldn't bring myself to say anything. I was frozen, trapped in his hold. A witchlight caught in a web.

Railan shifted slightly, his breath tickling my ear. 'I just want to hold you for a little while,' he murmured.

I swallowed hard, feeling a mix of emotions. Part of me wanted to pull away, to run out of the room and never look back. But another part of me... another part of me felt safe in his embrace. It was a feeling I hadn't experienced in a long time. I closed my eyes and leaned into him, letting myself be held.

We sat like that for a few moments, the only sound in the room was the subtle sizzle of the fireplace and our breathing. It was a strange, intimate moment, and I didn't know what to make of it. I had to break the silence; I couldn't take it any longer.

'What, specifically, did you need help with?' I managed to mumble.

'Oh...' Railan abruptly snapped out of his daze as he fumbled to choose a document. "This, er, this one here,' he passed me a random paper. 'Could you please explain what it means? I'm afraid I'm not familiar with it.'

I narrowed my eyes at the sheet as I skimmed it over. I raised a brow as I looked back at Railan. 'You're unfamiliar with "Request for Fine Exemption Form"?'

A hint of red crossed his cheeks as he realised what he'd given me. However, he would not relent as he doubled down. 'Yes, I want you to explain it to me,' he somehow uttered the words with a straight face, and for a brief second, I might have believed him.

I let out a little sigh. If he wanted to play games, I would play along. I began a long-winded spiel detailing the meaning of every sentence, breaking down every meaning. I felt a little condescending, but this was what he'd requested. The words were clear, easy, and simple. They came to me so naturally and comfortably that I almost got lost in them as I spoke. For a brief second, I forgot I was still in Railan's arms. I blinked as I suddenly remembered, and my words trailed off, returning us to silence. Railan didn't say anything as he continued to rest against me, and I glanced down at him just to be sure I hadn't put him to sleep.

'You don't need me to explain this... do you?' I said quietly, almost embarrassed.

'No... I just wanted to hear your voice,' he admitted.

I didn't think my cheeks had stopped being red, but if they had, the redness returned once more. Why was he like this?

'It's nothing special,' I said quietly.

'It's beautiful and soothing, just like the rest of you,' he was quick to compliment me.

'You don't need to say things like that,' I snapped back as I looked down at my lap.

More pretty words. They pricked at my heart in a strange mixture of pain and elation. They were blatant lies, and I couldn't accept them.

Railan didn't respond immediately; instead, he lifted his head to look at me, his blue eyes piercing through me. 'Why can't I say things like that?' he asked softly.

I opened my mouth to reply, but no words came out. I didn't have an answer to his question. I didn't know why his words affected me so much.

'Is it so wrong for me to appreciate your beauty?' he continued. 'To be drawn to you? To want to hold you? To want you?'

I swallowed hard, my throat feeling dry. I didn't know how to respond. Part of me wanted to push him away, to tell him to stop. But another part of me... another part of me didn't want him to stop. It was a confusing, conflicting feeling.

'Eli...' I started, but he interrupted me.

'Isla, I know you're scared, that you've been hurt,' he said, his voice gentle. 'But please, believe me.'

I looked into his eyes, seeing the sincerity and vulnerability in them. I didn't know how to deny him. I nodded slowly, and he pulled me closer to him once again. I wondered how long this would last. How long until he grew bored with me? I was not beautiful, I was average at best, and I certainly wasn't attractive enough to hold his attention for long. Did he just want sex? There were far easier ways to get that than to play with me.

'I-if you desire intimacy... I-I can arrange for a visit from a lady of the night...' I could hardly bring myself to mumble the words aloud.

Railan's expression turned from tender to pained at my suggestion. 'Is that what you think I want from you?' he asked, his voice barely above a whisper. 'That I'm only interested in your body?'

I didn't know how to respond. I felt guilty for suggesting it, but I couldn't help but wonder if it was true.

'That's not it at all,' he continued, his grip on me tightening slightly. 'I don't want anyone else. I want you, Isla. All of you. I said I would wait, and I meant it. I want you to want me. Until then, I... I just want to be close to you.'

I felt my heart skip a beat at his words. It was both thrilling and terrifying. I had never been desired like this before. But at the same time, I was afraid of what it meant. What if I wasn't enough for him? What if I couldn't fulfil his expectations? I was only a mundus, could I ever truly hope to fulfil a magus, a Prime Mage?

'Eli...' I started again, but he cut me off once more.

'Just let me hold you for a little longer,' he whispered. 'That's all I'm asking.'

I hesitated for a moment, but then I relaxed in his arms once again. I felt guilty for even bringing up the subject. I decided to swallow a little bit of my pride, and I slipped my arm around his shoulder, pressing my forehead to his as I closed my eyes. His hair was soft against my skin, like silk, so fluffy. It was nice. If Railan desired a dream, I could give it to him, just not yet. I still needed time to think this through.

I also needed to go to the city tonight. I let out an internal groan. I would have to manipulate the situation. I opened my eyes slowly, letting my lashes flutter slightly as I brushed my fingers across Railan's cheek. His own eyes fluttered at my touch. For a brief moment, I let the bright blue of his eyes pour into me, like a wave washing over me. Beautiful and peaceful and drowning. I needed to drown just a little bit, to pretend. I could do it for just a second.

I let out a soft breath before I brushed my lips lightly against his. Railan responded immediately, deepening the kiss with a hunger that took me by surprise. His lips were warm and soft against mine, and I found myself getting lost in the moment, forgetting everything else. It felt like we were the only two people in the world, and nothing else mattered.

But then, just as suddenly as it had started, he pulled away. He looked at me with a mix of desire and sadness in his eyes.

'Isla, I...' he trailed off, and I could see the conflict written all over his face. 'I shouldn't have done that.'

I felt a pang of disappointment in my chest, but I tried to hide it. 'It's okay,' I said softly, trying to reassure him. 'I wanted it too.'

'But you're not ready,' he said, looking at me intently. 'And I don't want to push you.'

I appreciated his concern, but at the same time, I felt a sense of frustration. Why did he have to be so respectful all the time? Couldn't he just take what he wanted? But then, I reminded myself that he was different from the other magi I had known. He wasn't just after a quick lay; he genuinely cared about me.

'Eli, I...' I started, but I didn't know how to finish the sentence. I wasn't sure what I wanted to say or what I wanted from him.

'It's okay,' he said, cutting me off. 'Let's just take things slow.'

I nodded in agreement, and we sat there in silence for a few moments, just holding each other. It was comforting, in a way, to have someone to hold onto like this. I hadn't realised how lonely I had been until I met Railan.

But then, I remembered my plans for later that night. I had to go to the city, I had to see Lady Amaranta, and I couldn't put it off any longer. He was far too distracting for his own good. I cleared my throat as I quickly thought up a plan.

'I need to go out tonight,' I said, reluctantly pulling away from him. 'I-I was wondering if I could borrow the sleigh?'

'What? Why?' he asked, confusion written all over his face.

'I have some business to attend to,' I said vaguely, trying to keep my tone neutral.

'Can't it wait?' he asked, his grip on me tightening once again.

'No, it can't,' I said firmly. 'I promise to return before work tomorrow.'

Railan looked at me for a moment, as if trying to read my thoughts. I held his gaze, trying to look as convincing as possible. Eventually, he sighed and let go of me.

'Fine,' he said, sounding resigned. 'But be careful.'

'I will,' I promised, feeling a twinge of guilt for lying to him. 'Thank you.'

I gave him a quick peck on the cheek, a sort of peace offering, as I gave him a genuine smile. 'I suppose I should also get back to work. Though that does remind me. You should be in bed. The doctor prescribed bed rest, and working is not resting,' I scolded him lightly.

Railan chuckled softly, his eyes crinkling at the corners. 'You sound like my mother,' he said teasingly. 'But you're right. I'll head to bed now. You be careful out there, alright?'

'I will,' I said, nodding. 'Take care of yourself too... Eli.'

I blushed as I found to courage to say his actual name aloud, and his smile widened exponentially.

'I will, Isla,' he said softly.

I took my cue and finally escaped his grasp. I gave him one last glance before I slipped out of his office and into the halls of the mansion. I walked briskly towards my own office, my heart racing with both excitement and fear. I didn't like lying to Railan, but I had to do what I had to do. Lady Amaranta was expecting me, and I couldn't deny her.

Chapter 16

I made my way to the stables where the sleigh was kept. I quickly harnessed the horses and climbed into the driver's seat. The night was cold and dark, but I was driven by a sense of fearful determination as I set off towards the city.

As I rode through the snowy landscape, my mind raced with thoughts of Lady Amaranta and what she wanted from me. I had a feeling that it wasn't going to be pleasant, but I couldn't back down now. I had no choice in the matter. My stomach twisted into knots the closer I came. Every bump set me on edge. Every sound in the wind caused my panic to spike. I needed to remain calm. If I couldn't keep my composure, she would eat me alive.

Eventually, I reached the city and dropped off the sleigh at the Citadel. I then made my way to Lady Amaranta's mansion on foot to avoid drawing too much attention. The place was grand and imposing, with guards stationed at the gates. I approached them with a mixture of fear and trepidation, but they let me in without question. Of course, they knew exactly who I was and why I was there.

Inside, Lady Amaranta was waiting for me in her study. She was as beautiful as ever as red witchlights buzzed around her head, her silver hair draped loose over her shoulder. She wore an elegant, casual dress that accentuated her curves. Flanking both sides of her were two men

I immediately recognised, Dominick and Sergey. I froze for a split second as I saw them, my blood running cold. They had been some of my trainers in the past. Why were they here? This wasn't what I had expected. Lady Amaranta looked up as I entered the room, a small smile playing at the corners of her deep red lips.

'Isla, my dear,' she said, gesturing for me to take a seat. 'I'm so glad you could make it. I was almost worried you would be unable.'

'Of course, my Lady,' I said, trying to keep my voice steady as I sat obediently. 'I come at your command.'

A sly, satisfied smirk played across her lips as she regarded me for a moment. I averted my gaze, keeping my hands tucked neatly in my lap. She put down her pen as she leaned back in her chair.

'I received your report on Railan. It was very thorough, yet I couldn't help but think it was... lacking. Perhaps you'd like to elaborate further in person?' she purred as she continued to watch me.

'If that is my Lady's desire, please tell me which part you would like elaborated,' I said, my voice low as I tried to keep my tone neutral.

Lady Amaranta leaned forward, her gaze sharp and intense. "I want to know everything," she said, her voice dripping with honeyed malice. "Every detail you can remember about Railan's strengths, weaknesses, fears, and desires. You were tasked with getting close to him, were you not? Surely there is more you can tell me."

I swallowed hard, feeling a bead of sweat trickle down my forehead. I had expected this, of course. Lady Amaranta was not known for being satisfied with perceived half-hearted efforts. Even though I knew my report was thorough, I still had to defend it.

'As per my report-' I started, but Amaranta cut me off as she let out a snide laugh.

'I heard a whisper from a dear witchlight that Railan had a little accident yesterday. The doctor was called to his estate, and there was apparently quite a ruckus. What can you tell me about that?' she asked more pointedly.

'Lord Railan... he underestimated his abilities while out in the woods. He used too much magic and was diagnosed with a bout of Extreme Mana Exhaustion. He has received a mana potion supplement and been prescribed three days of bed rest,' I said matter-of-factly.

Lady Amaranta raised an eyebrow, her gaze sharpening. 'Extreme Mana Exhaustion? That's a serious condition. I've heard of mages dying from it,' her tone was dripping with scepticism.

'I can assure you, my Lady, that the doctor has given him the necessary treatment and he will make a full recovery,' I said, trying to remain calm.

'I hope so, for your sake. I gave you a simple task, Isla. Get close to Railan, gain his trust, and report back to me. And yet, it seems you have allowed him to wander off to do who knows what. How did he come to be in such a situation?' Lady Amaranta's voice was laced with disappointment.

My mouth felt dry as I licked my lips nervously. This was what I'd feared. Pointed questions that would point at me. I couldn't lie to her, not to her face. I clenched my hands into fists as I avoided Amaranta's gaze.

'Lord Railan was disgruntled and simply wanted to relieve some stress. However, he over-'

'Disgruntled? By what?' Amaranta cut me off once again.

My heart rate spiked as I struggled to find the words. 'He was... upset that I declined his advances...' I admitted quietly.

Lady Amaranta's eyes narrowed, and her lips curled into a smirk. 'I see,' she said, drawing out the words. 'And how did you handle this situation?'

'I... I told him that it was inappropriate and that I was only there to do my job,' I said, my voice barely above a whisper.

Lady Amaranta leaned back in her chair, regarding me with a mixture of amusement and disdain. 'Oh dear Isla, you disappoint me.'

My blood ran cold at her words. This was bad.

'You're supposed to get close to him, as close as he will allow you. If he wants you, then you are supposed to let him have you. You're supposed to let him go as deep and as thorough as he is willing. How else do you expect to become his confidant, to whisper my words in his ear?'

'I'm sorry, I-' I started in an attempt to defend myself, but Amaranta just let out a disappointed sigh as she snapped her fingers.

My eyes darted around the room as Dominick and Sergey suddenly moved into action, closing the gap between us as they grabbed my arms and threw me onto the ground.

'My Lady, please don't do this!' I cried out as they pinned me down.

'I'm not doing anything, Isla,' she said coldly. 'Do you find that you require additional instruction to jog your memory and remember your place?'

'N-no, it was a mistake!' I could feel tears pricking at my eyes as Sergey held my wrists above my head and Dominick slid his hands under my skirt.

'I honestly thought we had trained this resistance out of you, yet here you are trying to act coy. If you can't do your job, then you're useless to me,' Lady Amaranta sighed.

'My Lady, please, I can still fix this! H-he still wants me, I-' I let out a yelp as Dominick's hands wandered higher.

Lady Amaranta straightened up as she snapped her fingers again. Both Dominick and Sergey immediately released me and moved back into their positions beside Amaranta. I quickly pulled my skirt down as I sat back up, keeping my head down low. My heart raced, my breath was sharp and shallow. I needed to compose myself. I could hear the scraping of Amaranta's chair and the clicking of her heels as she stopped in front of me. She leaned down and grabbed my chin, forcing my head up to look at her. Her eyes were harsh and cold, full of malice and discontent.

'Don't disappoint me, Isla. You know that failure has consequences and not just for you. Think of your poor mother and father. Think of your poor sister. If you fail, well, I might just be forced to replace you with little Inessa,' she purred.

My eyes grew wide as my panic surged with every word. 'Please, I won't fail. I just need time,' I begged. 'Your faith in me is not misplaced. I'll have his ear and more if you give me enough time.'

Lady Amaranta released my chin and stood up straight, a look of contemplation crossing her features. 'Time,' she said finally. 'Time is a limited resource, but I suppose I've been a little hasty. Fine, take your time, but don't think I won't be keeping a close eye on you.'

I let out a sigh of relief, grateful for the reprieve. 'Thank you, my Lady. I won't let you down.'

'I certainly hope not,' she said, turning away from me. 'You're dismissed for now. Return to your duties.'

I stood up quickly and bowed deeply before turning to leave the room. As I walked away, I couldn't shake the feeling of fear and dread that had settled in the pit of my stomach. Lady Amaranta was not one to be trifled with, and I knew that I would have to be extra careful in my interactions with Railan from now on. Failure was not an option, not if I wanted to protect my family and keep my position.

I practically ran out of the Citadel, and my hands shook as I took up the reins of the sleigh. This was what I'd feared. For Lady Amaranta to doubt me. For her to force my hand. I'd really hoped that I would be able to do this mission as an honest person, a simple worker, a shadow. But she wanted me to pursue the light, to pursue Railan. That wasn't the person I wanted to be. But what I wanted didn't matter. I was just a means to an end. An end where Railan would be converted into nothing more than another one of Lady Amaranta's pawns. I was supposed to keep him in check, to watch and control him for her interests. If he resisted, I would rein him in, bend him to her will, using everything at my disposal. It was a mistake on my part to reject him when it would have made my job that much easier. But I didn't want to be used like that. Despite everything, I still clung desperately to the dream of being more than just an object. I just wanted to be a normal woman, nothing more and nothing less.

I returned to the estate, still shaken from tonight's events. I put away the sleigh and brushed off the horses before heading around to the staff entrance. A light snow had set in, and I hesitated as I stood in front of the door. I could run away right now, turn back, leave the country, and start a new life, one that was my own. I knew I could never do that. I needed to look after my parents. I needed to protect my sister. I wouldn't allow harm to come to them. I wanted my sister to have a good life, and I was the only one who could give it to her.

I let out a small sigh as I turned around and walked out into the gardens. I needed to clear my head, to get into the right frame of mind. Seduce Railan. That was easier said than done. He was willing, but I... I lacked the confidence to follow through. No amount of training or honeyed words could rid me of the disgust I felt for myself.

I found a nice, open spot and flopped down onto the ground, letting myself sink into the snow-covered earth. I took in a nice, deep breath of the chilled air and simply lay there for a moment. The night was quiet and peaceful, with only the subtle rustling of the forest around me. In the distance, I could make out the faint coo of an owl and the chirping of insects. Icy snowflakes fell upon me, melting and merging with the tears that fell silently down my face. If I stayed still long enough, I would fall asleep and forget about everything. But I didn't want to sleep. I spread out my arms and legs, making the impression of a fairy in the snow. A small, childish smile spread across my lips. Just a little bit of innocent fun wouldn't hurt.

I knew I wouldn't make a very good fairy, but in a way, I was like a fairy godmother, well, sister, to little Inessa. I would continue to watch over her and make sure that her dreams came true, no matter the cost. Though I had to admit, having magic would help greatly. I held my hand up to the sky, as if reaching for the stars. My family was mundi; not a single drop of magic flowed through our veins. Magic was the only true power in the world; everything else was simply the illusion of power. I clenched my fingers into a fist as I dropped my arm back to the ground with a crunch. I used to hope and pray to the Celestial Lady that I would receive the blessing of magic when I came of age, that I would awaken and be granted a new path. Alas, it never came. I suppose it was never a part of her plan. The Lady's motives were shrouded in mystery. I only knew that her favour opened up doors that one never even knew existed. That was Railan's path, to walk through the door revealed by the Lady, perhaps to glory or perhaps to ruin. The Lady's intentions had yet to be revealed, not that it was any of my business anyway. But it was my business. Lady Amaranta made it my business.

'Isla!' I heard a faint voice call my name, and I immediately sat upright.

I blinked. It was the middle of the night, and there shouldn't be anyone awake besides the groundskeeper. I whipped my head around, trying to find the source, but I saw nothing. I realised my glasses had a thin layer of ice on their surface and I quickly tried to wipe them clean. Being able to actually see might help.

'Up here!' The voice called again.

I put my glasses back on and glanced around towards the sky.

'Behind you!'

I finally turned to look behind me to find Railan leaning over his balcony, looking down at me with a wide grin.

Why.

What was he doing up at his hour, and how did he even know I was out here? I guess I should return inside. It was still rather cold, especially after lying in the snow. I stood to my feet and turned to leave without acknowledging him.

'Wait!' he called out to me.

I glanced up to see him climbing over the balcony. The air left my lungs as I watched him jump. I opened my mouth to scream, but nothing came out. A gust of wind whipped past me as it raced to swirl at Railan's feet, slowing his descent. He landed gracefully on the ground in front of me, the snow crunching under his boots. He looked up at me with an amused grin.

'Why are you out here all by yourself?' he asked. 'It's late.'

'Just needed some fresh air,' I replied, trying to keep my voice steady despite my heart racing in my chest.

I wanted to shout at him, scold him for acting so recklessly, but I couldn't bring myself to do it.

'You looked like you were having fun,' he said, gesturing towards my snow angel.

I shrugged, feeling a bit embarrassed. 'Just some innocent fun,' I said.

Railan chuckled. 'I remember doing that as a kid,' he said. 'Sometimes you just need to forget about everything and enjoy the little things.'

I nodded, feeling a bit more at ease with him. 'Yeah,' I said softly. 'I guess you're right.'

We stood there in silence for a moment, the only sound being the gentle snowfall around us. I shifted my weight from one foot to the other, suddenly feeling very self-conscious under his gaze. I looked up at him to find him studying me intently, a small smile playing at his lips.

'You're beautiful, you know that?' he said suddenly, catching me off guard.

I felt my cheeks heat up, and I looked away from him, feeling suddenly very shy. 'Thank you,' I said softly, forcing myself to accept the compliment.

'I mean it,' he said, stepping closer to me.

I felt my heart skip a beat as he reached out and brushed a strand of hair from my face. He leaned in closer to me, his breath warm against my cheek.

'Isla,' he whispered. 'I've been thinking about you all night.'

'You have? Why?' I couldn't bring myself to meet his gaze.

I knew I shouldn't resist, that I should be more receptive, that Lady Amaranta had told me to surrender to him. But my resistance was pure instinct. I didn't want to get hurt, and I certainly didn't want to hurt Railan.

'Because you're fascinating,' he said, his voice low and husky. 'You're not quite like anyone else I've met. You're... strange. In a good way, I mean. You somehow remain at the forefront of my thoughts long after everyone else has faded.'

I looked up at him, my heart pounding in my chest. His words had a way of making me feel both flattered and apprehensive at the same time. I couldn't deny that there was something alluring about Railan, something that drew me to him even as I tried to resist.

"I'm not sure I understand what you mean," I said, my voice barely above a whisper.

He smiled at me, a gentle expression that softened the hard lines of his face. "You don't have to understand," he said. "Just know that I find you intriguing."

I swallowed hard, feeling my resolve slipping away. Despite my misgivings, I couldn't deny the attraction I felt for Railan. He was dangerous, yes, but something was thrilling about being near him. I couldn't help but wonder what it would be like to give in to him, to let go of my fears and let him take me wherever he wanted to go.

'Ah, y-your nose,' I stammered as I noticed a fine trickle of blood had started to run down his face.

Railan seemed to snap out of his trance as he brought a hand up to his nose. He looked at the blood on his fingers with mild surprise before wiping it away with a handkerchief from his pocket.

'Thank you for pointing that out,' he said, his voice returning to its usual smooth tone. 'I guess I got a little too carried away.'

He shot me a reassuring grin, but I wasn't convinced. 'You should be in bed, not out here using magic. You're still not fully recovered from yesterday,' I grabbed his arm as I turned back towards the mansion. 'Please, let's go back inside. It's getting colder out here.'

Railan hesitated for a moment, studying me with a serious expression. 'You're right,' he said finally, nodding. 'I shouldn't be pushing myself like this. Thank you for looking out for me, Isla.'

I felt a twinge of guilt as he thanked me, knowing that my concern for him was born more out of self-preservation than genuine care for his well-being. But still, I couldn't deny that I wanted him to be safe.

Together, we made our way back inside, the warmth of the mansion enveloping us like a cocoon. As we walked, I couldn't help but steal glances at Railan, watching the way his muscles moved under his shirt, the way his eyes flickered with a hint of mischief. He thought I was strange, but he was truly the strange one.

We stopped outside his bedroom, a tense yet comfortable silence between us. I should just bid him goodnight and be done with it, yet I also couldn't help but wonder if I should join him in his bed right here and now. My heart fluttered at the thought, and I could feel the heat on my cheeks. I could offer myself to him, and I knew he would readily accept, but still I felt nervous. A cold shiver ran through me as I recalled Dominick and Sergey's hands upon me mere hours earlier. Railan surely wouldn't want me if he knew about that.

'Isla,' his voice sliced through my thoughts and brought me back to reality. 'Will you join me for dinner tonight?'

I felt warmth spread through me at his invitation. I blinked up at him for a second, my instincts screaming to say no. 'I... yes, I would like that,' I said, forcing a smile at him.

Railan's eyes lit up at my acceptance, and he gave me a small, charming smile. 'Excellent. I'll have my chef prepare something special for us,' he said, his hand resting lightly on my arm.

A soft flutter filled my stomach at his touch. I was both excited and nervous about the dinner, wondering what it would be like to spend more time with Railan in a more intimate setting. Would he try to make a move on me? Would I be able to resist him if he did?

As Railan opened the door to his room, he turned back to me with a mischievous glint in his eye. 'Until tomorrow then, Isla,' he said, his voice low and husky. 'Sleep well.'

I watched him disappear into his room before turning to make my way back to my own. My mind was racing with thoughts of Railan and the upcoming dinner, and I knew that sleep would be hard to come by tonight. But for now, I would have to content myself with the knowledge that he was thinking of me, just as I was thinking of him.

Chapter 17

The hour grew late, and the sun had started its daily descent behind the mountains. Dinner would be served soon, and my nerves grew exponentially with every passing minute. Perhaps accepting his request had been a foolish idea. I couldn't imagine what the rest of the staff were thinking. Would they think poorly of me? I couldn't tell so far since everyone had been acting normal all day. I could only assume they didn't know yet.

I made my way past the kitchen to see if things were on schedule, though I had nothing to worry about since Ivan had everything covered as usual. In fact, Ivan had his assistant, Bralon, stationed at the kitchen entrance specifically to stop me from entering. Ivan insisted that the meal was a surprise, so I supposed that meant that Railan really had come down and made a special request. I smiled inwardly, both curious about what he's chosen and also with a sincere sense of joy. He was already going out of his way so soon. I wondered how long that would last.

I slowly made my way to the dining hall, dragging my heels as I forced myself forward. I needed to stop resisting. I needed to do this, no matter what. Feelings didn't matter. I just needed to let him love me. Why was that so hard to accept?

As I entered the dining hall, I was pleasantly surprised to see Railan already there. My heart picked up as I saw him, and I was hit by a sudden wave of self-consciousness. Did I look alright? Yes, of course, what was I worrying about? I always looked impeccable, even if I looked as plain as white bread.

Railan stood up as I entered, his eyes trained on me instantly. 'Ah, there you are,' he said, a smile spreading across his face. 'You look absolutely stunning tonight.' He gestured for me to take a seat across from him at the table, which had been set with a beautiful array of dishes.

I couldn't help but feel a little embarrassed at his compliment. I didn't understand what he meant. I was still wearing the same clothes I'd been wearing earlier, the very same ones I wore daily.

I forced myself to smile graciously and took a seat. 'Thank you, my Lord,' I replied, trying to keep my tone soft.

'I told you not to call me that,' he reminded me.

I couldn't help but feel flustered as he put me on the spot. I glanced over to the other staff as they watched idly. Why was he forcing me to do this so... publicly? His eyes darted from me to quickly glance at the others in the room. A sort of recognition flickered across his features.

I couldn't quite decipher what he was thinking, but I couldn't dwell on it for too long as he began to speak again. "I hope you don't mind, but I took the liberty of selecting the dishes for tonight's meal. I wanted to surprise you with something special," he said, his smile widening.

I couldn't deny that I held a certain appreciation for his thoughtfulness. "Of course, my Lord- I mean, Elieason," I corrected myself quickly, not wanting to make the same mistake twice.

Railan's smile widened further, like a Cheshire cat, as I said his name aloud. He chuckled at my slip-up, though I was relieved at his lighthearted response. 'Don't worry about it,' he said, waving his hand dismissively. 'Now, let's dig in!'

We chatted amiably throughout the meal, discussing everything from politics to our favourite books. Of course, I fudged the details slightly; there was no way I could possibly tell him that my actual favourite book was a silly romance serial. I had to settle for my second favourite, a more academic piece on the history of the world.

As the night wore on, the conversation turned more personal. Railan delicately led me down a dangerous path, and I finally understood how he could charm everyone he encountered. I almost found myself divulging things involuntarily. But I was trained to resist such persuasions, and I caught myself just in time before I said something dangerous. He asked about my family, my childhood, and my hopes for the future. I lied about almost all of it. I couldn't tell him the truth. I told him my family was comfortable and that my childhood was happy. The only scrap of truth was my hopes for the future. I told him honestly that I wanted nothing more than to see him succeed, for the Celestial Lady to achieve her goals, and for Maentaea to thrive. My happiness would come from our success. At least, that was part of the truth. I deliberately left out the part about finally clearing my family's debts and giving them a better life. He didn't need to know about that.

Eventually, the meal came to an end, and the servers cleared the plates away. Railan stood up and offered me his hand. 'May I have this dance?' he asked, a mischievous glint in his eye.

I felt a thrill run through me at his request as I looked at his open hand, but then I also remembered that I could not dance. The one time at the ball had been a silly fluke, a side effect of Pavel's encouragement. It had been a long time since then. I didn't have the high of the atmosphere to back me up.

I hesitated. 'I thought you said you weren't much of a dancer?' I teased lightly to distract from my own shortcomings.

Railan chuckled. 'I never said I wasn't any good at it, just that I don't do it often. And besides, with you as my partner, I'm sure we'll make a fine pair.'

He held out his hand again, a smile on his face. 'Come on, don't be shy. It'll be fun.'

I took a deep breath and reached out to take his hand.

'I must warn you, I'm not very good. Don't act surprised if I step on your toes,' I gave him a nervous smile as we made our way to the centre of the room.

Railan simply flashed me an encouraging smile. 'Relax, it's just a dance. Follow my lead and you'll do fine.'

And so we began to dance, swaying to the music and moving in time with each other. Railan was a natural dancer, his movements fluid and graceful, and I did my best to keep up with him. I was less than graceful as I concentrated on not messing up. Understanding the beat did not come naturally to me. Luckily, Railan was a patient partner, willing to slow down just so I wouldn't make a fool of myself. As the music played on, I found myself moving more naturally. I soon began to lose myself in the moment, and before I knew it, I had forgotten all of my worries and was just enjoying the simple pleasure of dancing with a charming partner.

The dance came to an end all too soon, and Railan twirled me around one last time before bringing me in for a gentle embrace. 'You're a natural,' he murmured, his lips close to my ear. 'I knew you'd be a great dancer.'

My chest filled with pride at his words, despite knowing that his words were objectively false. We lingered in each other's arms for a moment longer, the warmth of his body seeping into mine.

'I have something important to discuss with you,' he said, his voice low.

I was instantly hit with a wave of apprehension at his words, but I tried to keep my expression neutral. 'Of course, my Lord- Elieason,' I corrected myself again.

Railan smiled briefly before his expression turned serious once more. 'I've been thinking about, well, everything,' he began, his gaze fixed on me. 'And I've come to the conclusion that I want to court you, publicly.'

My heart skipped a beat at his words, and I couldn't quite believe what I was hearing. 'What!? I...I don't know what to say,' I stammered, feeling a sudden rush of emotions.

He was still adamant about having me, and now he wanted to trap me under the scrutiny of everyone else. I knew the answer I needed to give, but my mouth felt dry.

Railan pressed me closer to him as he brushed a loose strand of hair from my face, his touch sending a shiver down my spine. 'Just say yes,' he whispered, his eyes locking onto mine.

'Y-yes... the answer is yes,' I murmured, my voice barely audible.

Railan's smile widened, and he leaned in to press a gentle kiss to my forehead. 'Excellent,' he sighed, his breath warm against my skin. 'You won't regret it, I promise.'

I couldn't help but feel a sense of apprehension at his words. While I was undeniably drawn to him, there was a part of me that knew this could only end in heartbreak. But for now, I pushed those thoughts aside and simply enjoyed the warmth of his embrace. We returned to our seats and continued to chat into the night, this time more relaxed than ever before. It felt as though a weight had been lifted from my shoulders. I'd done what was asked of me, and he was actively courting me. Hopefully, that would be enough to satisfy Lady Amaranta, for now.

It was getting late, and there was still a full schedule for tomorrow. We decided to call it a night, and Railan insisted on walking me back to my chambers. We stopped outside my door, and he turned to face me, a serious expression on his face. 'Thank you for tonight,' he said softly. 'It was everything I could have hoped for and more.'

I felt a flush rise to my cheeks at his words. It wasn't as if anything particularly amazing had happened, but I had to take him at his word. 'It was my pleasure,' I replied, trying to keep my voice steady.

Railan leaned in close, his hand reaching up to brush a strand of hair away from my face. 'I'll see you soon,' he murmured, before pressing a gentle kiss to my forehead and turning to leave.

I watched him go, a feeling of longing and anticipation stirring in my chest. I wasn't sure what kind of game he was playing, but I needed to be ready to make my own counter moves to keep myself safe. Even if we were technically on the same team, the board could be flipped at any time, and our positions could be changed. Railan's journey as Prime Mage had only just started. I had no idea where his position would lead him. I had to remain realistic, even if I longed to be optimistic.

Chapter 18

Railan had semi-formally declared his intentions to officially court me, and I had accepted. That meant I needed to be more receptive to his affections, no matter how hard it felt. I needed to accept him. That was easier said than done. I was scared, scared he would see past whatever illusions clouded his vision and see the real me. I was scared he would be disgusted by what he found hidden under my facade.

Worse still, while his intentions might have been honest, they also opened us up to scrutiny from, well, everyone. From the staff of the estate to the other Prime Mages. They would no doubt judge us harshly. It was very rare for a magus to pursue a mundus since such matches were generally frowned upon. "Tainting" the bloodline is what people would say. It would no doubt be exponentially worse since Railan was a Prime Mage, the most elite of the elite. Every eligible lady would have divines on courting him, and thus, I would become the enemy of every bachelorette in the entire country. I'd seen them swooning at the ball a while back. I didn't want to be in the spotlight like that. I was content to be his shadow. But Lady Amaranta had requested it; she wanted me to have his ear, and so I would try my best.

I made my way down to the private library. It was rather large, though most of the shelves were barren. A few boxes had been left to be unpacked later, but even with their scarce contents, the shelves would be painfully empty. I suppose Railan would build his collection over time. I didn't want to work in my office today. I wanted a change of scenery, which was a little sad considering I'd barely used my office for three days. Still, it wasn't as if I was being forcefully confined to one space. I technically had free rein of the staff quarters and most of the ground floor. I was sure I only needed to ask, and Railan would grant me access to every room in the entire estate. No doubt, he would probably do anything and everything I asked of him. That was a dangerous precedent. Lady Amaranta would take advantage of that fact within a heartbeat.

For now, I didn't want to think about any of it. I found myself a nice little corner by one of the large pane windows, and I made myself a comfortable little nest. I carefully placed my stack of paperwork beside me and flipped open my notebook. I glanced outside. It was snowing rather heavily. I hoped that didn't mean a snowstorm was settling in. They could last a whole month if it were particularly bad. Not that I needed to worry, the estate had more than enough supplies to survive, but I was concerned for how my family would fare. Their weekly rations were just that, weekly rations. I let out a heavy sigh. I couldn't think about that either. Lady Amaranta would take care of them in my stead; it was part of our contract.

I focused on work, filling out everything as necessary and writing out small reports. The needs of the household were numerous, yet the work was comforting. It was simple, easy, and uncomplicated. I didn't need to impress anyone or pretend to be someone else. The paperwork didn't care who or what I was or wasn't. I found myself lost among the pages and, without realising it, my eyes fluttered as I leaned my forehead against the window. The cold glass was refreshing. Just a momentary break, I told myself as I closed my eyes.

I heard a soft voice call out somewhere nearby, and I stirred. Had I fallen asleep? I swear I'd only closed my eyes for a second. Yet as I opened my eyes, I could see the sun was now much lower in the sky despite being obscured by the raging snow flurry.

'Isla,' Railan's silky voice drew my attention, and I quickly whipped my head around to see him kneeling beside me.

'Ah, E-Eli!' I let out a small, startled squeak.

Railan chuckled softly at my reaction, his smile warm and fond. 'Did I wake you?' he asked, reaching out to brush a strand of hair from my face.

I blushed at the intimate gesture and quickly sat up, straightening my papers in the process. 'No, no, I was just...resting my eyes,' I said, my voice slightly breathless.

Railan's eyes flickered over my work, his brow furrowing slightly. 'You've been working all day,' he commented. 'You should take a break.'

'I'm fine,' I said quickly, not wanting to be seen as lazy or unproductive. 'I was just... lost in thought.'

Railan's gaze softened, and he took my hand, squeezing it gently. 'You don't have to pretend with me, Isla,' he said softly. 'We agreed to a certain degree of honesty, didn't we? You can tell me if something's bothering you.'

I hesitated for a moment, unsure if I should open up to him so soon. But something in his eyes, something warm and genuine, made me want to trust him. 'It's just...' I trailed off, unsure of how to phrase my fears.

'Just what?' Railan prompted gently.

'It's just...this,' I said, gesturing to us. 'This courtship. It's...it's not normal, is it? For a magus, a Prime Mage no less, to pursue a mundus?'

Railan's expression turned serious, and he reached up to cup my cheek, his thumb stroking my skin gently. 'I won't deny that it's rare,' he said. 'But that doesn't mean it's wrong. Isla, I don't care about your bloodline or your status. I care about you. I mean it.'

I felt tears prick at the corners of my eyes, and I blinked them away, not wanting to seem overly emotional. 'It's just... there will be people who will judge us... you,' I said, my voice barely above a whisper. 'Aren't you worried about your perception? It can very easily be used against you...'

'Let them judge,' Railan's expression hardened slightly, his hand dropping from my cheek. 'I am aware of the risks, Isla,' he said firmly. 'But I will not let the opinions of others dictate my actions, especially when it comes to matters of the heart. I am not ashamed of my feelings for you, nor will I hide them. I want what I want and I won't let anything or anyone get in my way.'

I swallowed, feeling a rush of admiration and gratitude towards him. He was so confident, so steadfast in his stance. I wished I could share the same convictions, but I was weak, scared.

'I... I just don't want to cause you any trouble,' I whispered, my voice barely audible over the howling wind outside.

Railan's smile returned, the corners of his eyes crinkling in gentle amusement. 'You're not trouble, Isla,' he said. 'You're a delight.'

My cheeks warmed at the compliment, and I looked away, feeling embarrassed. Railan chuckled softly and leaned in, pressing a soft kiss to my temple. 'Come on,' he said, standing up and offering me a hand. 'Let's go for a little walk. I want to discuss some things with you.'

I glanced at his hand, apprehension swelling in my stomach. What did he want to talk about? I would have to find out as I gingerly took his hand. He pulled me up with ease, pressing me briefly to his body. My cheeks brightened at the motion. I let him hold me close for just a moment before I leaned back slightly.

'I-I need to return these first,' I said as I reached back for my notebook and paperwork.

Railan nodded as he let me collect my things. I quickly gathered everything and clutched the work to my chest as I turned back to him.

'Ready,' I said quietly.

'Alright, we'll drop these off, then I want to take you somewhere more private,' he said casually.

Private?

My blush burned, but I kept my composure as I gave him a small nod.

We made our way through the halls in silence before we reached my office. I quickly put everything away as Railan leaned against the doorframe, waiting intently for me. He wanted to take me somewhere private. He had said he would wait for me to be ready, but what if he changed his mind? What if he decided that he no longer wanted to wait? What if his urges were too strong? I would have no choice but to give in, but it was so soon. I still wasn't prepared for him to see me like that. I found myself slowing, trying to delay the inevitable, but there was only so much I could pretend to do.

'You ready?' he asked, a small smile upon his lips as he raised a brow.

I nodded weakly as I returned to his side.

'Good, let's get out of here,' he grabbed my hand and pulled me down the hall.

As we walked, I couldn't help but feel a mix of nervousness and excitement. I didn't know where he was taking me, but the idea of being alone with him made my heart race. We passed by several staff members, some of whom gave us curious looks, but Railan didn't seem to pay them any mind. He led me to a small room at the end of the hallway and opened the door, gesturing for me to go in first.

I stepped inside, my eyes adjusting to the dim light. The room was small and yet to be furnished, as the only fixture was a daybed that had been built into the bay window. The true appeal of the room was the large window that took up most of the far wall, giving a stunning view of the expansive gardens below. I walked over to it, gazing out at the flurry that surged in the environment. No doubt it would be exceptionally beautiful when the storm stopped, but even still, it was a magnificent view.

'It's beautiful,' I said softly.

Railan came up behind me, placing his hands on my waist. 'Not as beautiful as you,' he murmured in my ear.

I felt a shiver run down my spine as his breath tickled my skin. I turned to face him. His deep blue eyes poured down at me through his long lashes, a look of tender desire swimming within them. My heart pricked up, and I felt the sudden urge to kiss him. But before I could act on it, he spoke up again.

'I brought you here to talk about us,' he said, his tone serious.

What did he mean?

'Is something wrong?' I asked, my voice shaking slightly.

Railan shook his head, his expression softening. 'No, nothing's wrong. I just wanted to make sure we're both on the same page.'

'The same page?' I asked. 'What page do you think we're on?'

I was curious to hear his answer.

'You've agreed to our courtship and you know exactly how I feel about you, Isla. But I want to know what you actually think... about us, about everything. You said that you couldn't be honest with me, but I don't think that's entirely true.'

I took a deep breath as I tried to gather my thoughts. I couldn't push him away. I should just say what he wants to hear, but that wouldn't be entirely honest. I needed to lace the lie with truth, but what was the truth? What did I really think of us? That it could never work out, that the power imbalance was too vast? That he would hate me if he knew I was simply a spy sent to watch and control him? That I was never going to be good enough for someone like him? That he could never truly be fulfilled by someone like me? Every emotion I felt was overwhelmingly negative. I needed something positive. I couldn't deny I found him attractive, that despite everything, I was still a simple woman with my own desires.

'I...' I started, unsure where I wanted to go. 'It's true that I can't be entirely honest with you about many things. I have a... complicated life. But I do know that there is one truth I can tell, and that truth is that I want to be with you, by your side, everything. I am constantly ruled by fear, but I don't want to live like that anymore. I want to be free, to be more, to be valued, to be loved by you and only you. I don't want to care about anyone else. I want to surrender to you completely, fully, as long as you can promise me that you won't discard me, no matter what happens, no matter what I do, no matter how much I hurt you,' I said passionately, letting my emotions run wild.

Railan's expression softened as he listened to my words. He took my hand and pulled me closer to him, his eyes never leaving mine.

'I promise, Isla,' he said firmly. 'I won't discard you. I won't hurt you. I'll always be here for you, no matter what happens, no matter what you do. I need you by my side, always.'

His words filled me with a sense of warmth and security that I hadn't felt in a long time. I had never felt so vulnerable, yet so safe at the same time. I looked up at him, my heart swelling with love for this man. He drew me into his chaotic presence, and I knew it would consume me until there was nothing left, yet I would gladly drown in his ocean if he held me in his embrace. This was it, I couldn't turn back.

I pushed up on my toes and brought him into a soft, cautious kiss. Railan responded to my kiss with a fervour that sent shivers down my spine. It was as if he had been waiting for this moment for a long time, and now that it had finally arrived, he was determined to make the most of it. Of course, he'd already made it clear that he desired me. I knew he didn't want to wait, that he wanted all of me as soon as possible. I wasn't supposed to deny him, and I wasn't sure I could keep up my futile resistance any longer. His hands roamed over my body, pulling me closer to him, and I melted into his embrace, lost in the sensation of his touch.

He pressed me back against the sunbed, and my heart raced as he kissed me deeper, harder, with a fierce hunger. I could feel the coolness of the glass against my back as his hands slid under my skirt and up my thigh. At that moment, I knew that there was no turning back. I wanted him as much as he wanted me, and I was willing to give myself to him completely. But there was still a small voice in the back of my head that warned me about the consequences of my actions. What would happen if he found out the truth about me? Would he still want me? Could he forgive me for lying to him? Could he save my family? These questions lingered in my mind, but I pushed them aside for the moment, lost in the passion and intensity of the moment.

Railan's lips moved down my neck, trailing hot kisses that sent shivers down my spine. His hands were everywhere, exploring every inch of my body as he plucked at the fastenings of my clothes. My cheeks burned like fire at every touch, every kiss. I could do this, I could give in. It would be alright. Just let him have what he wanted. It would be over soon enough.

I felt a jolt of electricity pulse through my body as his fingers slipped between my thighs. I let out a small, surprised gasp as he caressed me gently, the sensation completely unfamiliar.

'W-What are you doing?' I stuttered breathlessly.

Railan lifted his head, his eyes dark with desire as he looked down at me. 'What does it feel like I'm doing?' he asked, a sly smile playing at the corners of his mouth.

I bit my lip, trying to suppress the moan that threatened to escape my lips. 'I-I've never...' I trailed off, feeling embarrassed and exposed. 'D-Don't you just want to...' I trailed off, unable to utter the words aloud.

Railan's smile softened as he cupped my cheek with his hand. 'I want to make you feel good, in every way possible,' he said, his voice low and husky. 'I want to explore every inch of your body, and discover all the things that make you gasp and moan.'

I felt a wave of desire wash over me at his words, and I knew that I wanted him to continue. I nodded, biting my lip in anticipation, and he leaned down to capture my lips in another searing kiss. His fingers continued their gentle exploration, tracing patterns over my most sensitive areas and sending sparks of pleasure through my body. I gasped and moaned, unable to control the sensations that were coursing through me as I clung to him desperately.

As the pleasure mounted, I felt myself on the brink of something I had never experienced before. I arched my back, my fingers tangling in Railan's hair as I cried out his name. At that moment, I knew that there was no going back. I was his, completely and utterly, and I had never felt more alive.

'I love it when you say my name,' he murmured in my ear as I tried to catch my breath.

'Eli...' I brushed my lips against his ear as I held him close.

I expected him to continue, to take what was his, but he didn't; he simply held me tight. I didn't understand what was happening. Why would he care about my pleasure without receiving his own? This wasn't a part of my training.

'D-do you want to... continue?' I asked softly.

Railan pulled back slightly, looking down at me with a small smile on his lips. 'Of course I do, Isla,' he said, his voice low and husky. 'But not now. Not when you're not ready.' He brushed a strand of hair away from my face, his gaze searching mine. 'I want you to feel completely safe and comfortable with me.'

I felt a sense of relief wash over me at his words. He wasn't going to force me. Still, a part of me wanted to continue, to see what he would do to me.

'I-I am ready...' I mumbled even though I could feel my hands tremble with every word.

Railan's expression softened as he looked at me, his hand caressing my cheek. 'No, you're not. I can still sense your hesitation,' he placed a gentle kiss upon my forehead. 'This is enough for now. But when the time is right, I promise I will make you feel like you've never felt before,' he said, his voice filled with warmth and tenderness. 'But for now, let's just stay like this.'

He pulled me closer to him and rested his head upon my chest. I could feel the steadiness of his breath against my skin as he closed his eyes. In that moment, I felt safe and protected, like nothing could harm me as long as I was with him. I closed my eyes and let myself relax, enjoying the comfort of his embrace.

No one had ever cared about my desire, comfort, or safety like this before. Had I really underestimated him that badly? Or had I simply been in a shroud of denial, refusing to see what was truly before me? Was I dreaming? I certainly felt like I was living in a dream.

After a few moments of blissful embrace, Railan lifted his head slightly so he could rest his forehead against mine. 'Isla, I want to host a ball here at the estate. I want to announce my intentions to the world, to make a public declaration.'

My heart skipped a beat at the mention of a ball. Did he really want to host a ball to announce our courtship? I didn't think that was a good idea. I knew he didn't care what anyone else thought, but still, the idea incited anxiety within me. I would be a pariah, a mundus blatantly trying to rise above her station. Everyone would know what kind of woman I was, or they would assume so. They would assume the worst. I suppose it wouldn't be unwarranted for them to think badly of me, as I was acting disgracefully.

'Eli, I don't think that's a good idea,' I said, my voice barely above a whisper. 'People will talk, and not in a good way.'

Railan's eyes searched mine, his expression unreadable. 'I understand your concerns, Isla. But I won't hide our relationship, not when it means everything to me. I want the world to know that you are mine, and I am yours.'

I felt a sense of warmth spread through my chest at his words. He wanted the world to know that I was his. I never thought I would have someone like Railan in my life, let alone be with him. But still, the thought of being in the public eye, of being judged by others, terrified me.

'I understand, I...,' I said, my voice trembling slightly. 'It's just... our reputation will be on the line, and I don't want to be the cause of any scandal or controversy. I know you don't care, but I can't not. It's still a part of my job to advise you, and doing this would invite unfavourable opinions. I'm... I'm not sure I can handle that.'

Railan sighed and pulled back slightly, looking at me with a pained expression. 'Isla, I understand your concerns, but I won't let anyone dictate my life or my happiness. I won't let their opinions, their judgments, or their prejudices stop me from being with the woman I love. And that woman is you.'

He took my hand and brought it to his lips, kissing it gently. 'I know it won't be easy, but we'll face whatever comes our way together. We'll stand by each other and support each other. And as for your job, Isla, I don't see it as advising me; I see it as us working together as partners. You're not just my advisor, you're my confidante, my friend, and my lover.'

He leaned in and kissed me softly on the lips, his eyes never leaving mine. 'Please, Isla. Trust me, and let's do this together. Let's show the world that love knows no bounds.'

I looked into his eyes, seeing the sincerity and love in them, and I knew he was right. I couldn't let my fears hold us back. I took a deep breath and nodded. 'Okay, Eli. Let's do it.'

Railan smiled and pulled me into his arms again, holding me close. 'Thank you, Isla. You won't regret it.'

I knew that his unbridled confidence would be his undoing, but I had warned him, and that was all I could do.

Chapter 19

Railan had wanted to host the ball as soon as possible. His excitement was almost unbearable. Luckily, I had convinced him to wait at least a month in order to make appropriate preparations. Still, one month felt like a short period to arrange such a big event, especially since every other aspect of life was back to business as usual.

My only solace was Lady Amaranta's overwhelming approval. She'd even approved my request to let my family into my care for the night. That alone filled me with dread. I hadn't exactly told them about Railan and his intentions. No doubt they would be shocked. I, myself, was still shocked. I never imagined I would be pursued by a Prime Mage, yet here I was, helping with preparations for a ball in honour of our courtship.

Oh, great Celestial Lady, help me!

I needed strength to get through this. I had already met Railan's family at our first ball, and while it had been rather informal, it still counted in my books. Now I needed to arrange for him to meet mine. I dreaded the idea. Surely he would know what kind of woman I truly was once he walked into the gilded cage of Lake Village. Everyone knew what that place was, a prison for unfortunate souls masquerading as a pretty picture of charity. Perhaps he would finally realise that I wasn't worth anything, that my value was in the negatives, and he would give up on this silly notion of love. Still, a part of me couldn't bear the thought. He'd promised not to discard me. I had to cling to the hope that that was true. Perhaps one day he might even be able to buy my freedom, though I doubted it greatly.

There was a sudden knock on my office door, and I perked up. My mind immediately went to Railan. Was he here to see me?

'Come in,' I said a little too eagerly.

The door swung open, and to my disappointment, it wasn't Railan, but instead one of the young butlers, Leonid. I quickly hid my disappointment and greeted him.

'Leonid, what can I do for you?' I asked.

He seemed to be somewhat distressed as a frown sat upon his brow. 'Sorry to bother you, ma'am, but, er, there's a problem in the foyer.'

I tilted my head, confused. 'Oh? What problem?'

'There's, er... an unexpected visitor,' he seemed hesitant to tell me.

'A visitor?' I pulled out my pocket watch and checked the time. 'Lord Railan is already in a meeting. We aren't expecting the next guest for another hour at least. Send them away.'

'We, er, tried, but they insist on meeting with his Lordship. Now,' Leonid fiddled with his hands as he spoke with a shaky voice.

I frowned, annoyed at the audacity of this person. 'I see,' I stood from my seat. 'I shall handle this,' I said firmly.

I got Leonid to take me to this mysterious visitor. My mind raced, and I had no idea who would be so bold as to try and disturb a Prime Mage in his own home. Then my heart sank and my chest tightened as we crested the top of the grand stairs.

In the foyer stood an ominous figure, one that I immediately knew. I recognised him instantly as the silver-masked Prime Mage from the ball so long ago. I couldn't remember his name at the moment, but I only knew that his aura sent a shiver down my spine. He still wore the same mask, no doubt a gift from the Celestial Lady. I had to steel my nerves as I made my way down the stairs. Leonid followed behind me, but I could feel his fear as he stayed a few steps shy.

'Good evening, my Lord,' I greeted him with a bow as I came to a stop a few feet away. I wanted to keep some distance between us. 'I'm afraid Lord Railan is currently engaged and not expecting an additional guest at this time.'

The man stood tall, a similar height to Railan, and he wore a heavy fur coat in the more regal Creed style. His light blue hair was cropped short, and his skin was as pale as the snow outside. His eyes were hidden behind his mask, but I could feel them piercing me as a chill-inducing smirk spread across his lips.

'Ah, yes. You must be the assistant,' his voice was deep and smooth. 'I am aware of Lord Railan's schedule. However, my business with him cannot wait.'

I raised an eyebrow. 'And what business would that be?'

He suddenly closed the distance between us in one quick step and leaned in uncomfortably close, the smirk still present. 'That is between Lord Railan and me.'

I didn't like the way he spoke to me, but I had to maintain my composure. 'I'm sorry, but without an appointment, I cannot allow you to disturb his Lordship's meeting.'

The silver-masked Prime Mage let out a chuckle. 'You do not understand, I am not here for an appointment. I am here to deliver a message, one that Lord Railan would not want to miss.'

I didn't like the sound of that. 'I assure you, my Lord, if it's urgent, I can relay the message to him personally.'

He shook his head. 'I'm afraid it cannot be delivered by anyone but me. It's a most urgent Prime Mage matter.'

My heart sank even further. 'I see.' I took a deep breath, trying to steady my nerves. 'I'll have to consult with Lord Railan first. I'll ask him to make time for you as soon as possible.'

The silver-masked Prime Mage's smile widened. 'Of course, I trust you'll deliver the message promptly.'

I nodded. 'May I have your name, my Lord, so I may pass it on?'

'Tell Railan that the Doctor is here to see him,' he grinned, as if expecting me to understand.

I gave him one last glance before I bowed again. 'I will see to it, my Lord.'

I made my way back up the stairs, barely able to stop myself from running. I couldn't shake the feeling of unease. What message could be so important that it couldn't wait? And why was this Prime Mage so confident in his delivery of it? I had a feeling that this would be the beginning of a wave of trouble for Railan. Was this other Prime Mage really ready to strike against him so soon? Amaranta had gotten her fangs in from the very first second, so I didn't have any doubts. Still, if moves were being made, that meant I needed to be prepared.

I stopped just outside Railan's drawing room, where I could hear the muffled sounds of his current meeting. My stomach felt heavy. I'd never interrupted him before. But I had no choice. I knew better than to cross a Prime Mage.

I knocked on the door, and as expected, there was no answer. I took a deep breath and entered anyway. Both Railan and his guest turned immediately to stare at me as I strode to my Lord's side. A frown sat upon his brow as he eyed me. I tried my best to keep my expression neutral as I stopped beside him.

'Isla?' He asked, a hint of concern in his voice.

'Forgive me, my Lords,' I bowed deeply before I glanced at Railan. 'I have an urgent message,' I struggled to keep my tone steady as I leaned over to whisper in his ear. 'A man claiming to be the Doctor insists on seeing you.'

I wasn't sure if he would know what that meant, but I didn't have much more information to offer.

Railan's expression darkened as he straightened up, his eyes flickering to the door as if he could see through it. 'The Doctor,' he muttered, more to himself than to me. 'I see,' he turned back to his guest. 'My apologies, it seems something important has come up regarding another Prime Mage. I'm afraid I must cut our meeting short.'

Railan's expression was serious, more serious than I would have expected, and his guest didn't bother to offer any protest or resistance.

'Ah, well, we were just wrapping up anyway,' the man gave a curt nod as he stood and shook Railan's hand.

I wasn't sure if that was true or not, but the man promptly left without a word.

Once we were alone, Railan turned to me with a furrowed brow. 'You did well. Thank you for bringing this to my attention. I'll take care of it from here,' his voice was firm but not unkind, and I knew better than to push any further.

I nodded and turned to leave, but Railan quickly grabbed my hand. I glanced back at him. A small, reassuring smile sat upon his lips.

'Give me a little bit of courage, won't you?' he asked, and my cheeks blushed pink.

I nodded meekly before leaning up and placing a small kiss upon his lips. He squeezed my hand before letting it go.

'Good luck, Eli,' I whispered as I turned to leave once more.

Railan followed me out of the room, and I watched him head towards the foyer from the corner of my eye before I walked back to my chambers. I couldn't shake the feeling of unease that lingered in my gut. I didn't know who the Doctor was, but if it was urgent enough to warrant a Prime Mage's visit, it couldn't be good news. I could only hope that Railan was prepared for whatever was coming his way.

I tried my best to return to my work, but I couldn't shake the feeling of anxiety that lingered in the back of my mind. I let out a heavy sigh as I put down my pen. It was late in the evening, bordering on dinnertime. I wasn't going to be productive until I could put my mind to rest, so I decided to do a little snooping.

I wandered down to the kitchen and greeted Ivan and his helpers.

'Good evening, has his Lordship come down for dinner yet?' I asked casually.

'No, not yet, ma'am,' Ivan shook his head.

I frowned. 'I see, I shall have to take it to him then.'

'You needn't worry yourself with something so trivial, ma'am. I can arrange for one of the maids to service his Lordship.'

I shook my head. 'No need. I have a few things to run by His Lordship anyway. Two birds, one stone,' I insisted with a gentle smile.

'If you insist,' Ivan simply shrugged. 'I shall prepare something right away.'

'Thank you, I will be back in a little while to pick it up,' I said before I exited the kitchen.

I continued my rounds to the staff quarters. To my pleasant surprise, Rosalind was just returning after her shift. She seemed equally surprised to see me as she let out a little squeak.

'M-ma'am,' she stuttered. 'What are you- I mean, I...' She stopped herself before she could ramble further.

'Rosalind,' I flashed her a friendly smile. 'How are you?' I asked her casually.

'I... I'm doing well, ma'am,' she seemed to relax slightly.

'I was wondering, have you seen his Lordship around?' I tried to keep my tone cool and impartial.

She immediately shook her head. 'Last I saw, he was still in the drawing room with that scary-' she quickly covered her mouth. 'S-sorry, I didn't mean any offence.'

I let out a small chuckle to reassure her that she was fine. 'You may speak your mind to me. I agree our unexpected guest is rather scary, but I'm sure his Lordship can handle his own.'

Rosalind still looked on edge, but she forced a small smile anyway. 'Yes, ma'am. I'm sure everything will be fine.'

I nodded in agreement. 'You take care of yourself, and remember, you may come to me about anything if you need to.'

She nodded, and I soon left her to get some rest.

At least I'd learnt something valuable. Railan was still with the Doctor. Worry poked at me, and I swung back around to the kitchen to pick up the meal I'd requested. I wanted to know what was happening, and I could now use the guise of the meal as a reasonable excuse if I should get caught.

I quietly made my way to the drawing room and saw that the door was still shut. I tiptoed to it, and I could hear whispers coming from inside. My heart raced with adrenaline as I carefully placed my ear to the door to try and overhear what they were saying.

As I listened in, I could barely make out what was being said. It sounded like a discussion about some sort of deal, but the details were too muffled for me to catch. I considered trying to peek through the keyhole, but I didn't want to risk getting caught.

I took a step back from the door, deep in thought. I had to find a way to get more information without arousing suspicion. Maybe I could try to eavesdrop from a different angle, or even talk to Railan directly. I was sure he would tell me if I just asked, but still, the thought made me nervous. I didn't want him to become wary of me or my intentions.

As I pondered my options, I heard footsteps approaching from down the hall. I quickly stepped away from the door and tried to act casual as the footsteps drew nearer. It was Leonid the butler. I stood straight and tried to look like I was exactly where I was supposed to be. Leonid gave me a curious look once he noticed me.

'Ma'am?' He asked as he glanced down at my tray of food.

'Good evening, Leonid. How are the rounds?' I tried to keep my nerves in check as I greeted him.

He regarded me silently for a moment before he seemed to lighten up. 'Good, ma'am, everything is as it should be. Are you alright?'

'I'm fine, just making sure his Lordship is taken care of,' I gestured to the tray. 'Alas, work never ends around here,' I chuckled in an effort to distract him.

'Indeed, ma'am, I'm sorry to disturb you,' he said simply.

Leonid didn't say anything further as he walked away. I watched as he moved past me and out of my sight. I just stood there for a moment, trying to calm my racing heart. I knew I had to be careful, but I couldn't let my curiosity get the best of me. I needed to find out what was going on, no matter the risk.

With a determined sigh, I took a deep breath, dumped the tray, and made my way back to my quarters. I needed to come up with a plan, and fast. As curious as I was, curiosity would also get me killed. I decided that my questions could wait until the morning. Patience and subtlety were the keys to success in this world.

Chapter 20

I awoke early after a particularly sleepless night. The first thing I did was check the drawing room. To my relief, the room was empty. That meant the other Prime Mage had finally left. Their meeting had drawn on into the night. Exactly how late, I didn't know. But what I did know was that several other important meetings had needed to be rescheduled. That meant even longer days as I'd managed to squeeze them into the late evening.

I made my way to Railan's chambers. I didn't intend to wake him just yet. I simply wanted to confirm he was actually getting some rest. Talking could wait until later, even if my curiosity was driving me crazy.

As I approached Railan's chambers, I noticed that the door was slightly ajar. I hesitated for a moment, wondering if I should just let him sleep or check on him anyway. In the end, my concern won out, and I pushed open the door to peek inside.

Railan was lying on his back in bed, his arms folded behind his head. He looked peaceful and content, and for a moment I felt relieved that he was finally getting some much-needed rest. But then he opened his eyes and looked straight at me, a small smile on his lips.

'Good morning, my dear Isla,' he said, his voice soft and warm. 'Did you sleep well?'

I felt my cheeks heat up at the sound of his voice. 'Not really,' I admitted, stepping inside and closing the door behind me. 'I had a lot on my mind."

'Same here,' Railan replied with a sigh. He rubbed his eyes and yawned, then turned to look at me. 'Want to join me?' he patted the edge of the bed beside him.

I hesitated for a moment before I wandered over to the edge. I sat gingerly, as if I shouldn't dare to do so. My reservations didn't matter as Railan grabbed my hand and pulled me to his chest. I let out a startled yelp as he wrapped his arms around me. He let out a small, contented sigh as he snuggled me.

'So soft...' he whispered against my hair.

'Eli...' I started, unsure what I wanted to say.

Railan tightened his hold on me and rubbed his cheek against mine. 'Shh, don't worry about anything right now,' he murmured. 'Just relax and let me hold you.'

I closed my eyes and let myself sink into his embrace, feeling my worries and anxieties start to fade away. For a few minutes, we just lay there in silence, his arms wrapped tightly around me.

Eventually, I stirred and pulled away slightly to look up at him. 'Thank you,' I said softly. 'I needed this.'

Railan smiled up at me, his eyes warm and gentle. 'I know,' he said. 'So did I.'

He leaned up and brushed his lips against mine in a sweet, tender kiss that left my heart racing. I leaned into him, deepening the kiss, and for a few blissful moments, nothing else mattered but the feel of his lips and the warmth of his body pressed against mine. When we finally pulled away, I couldn't help but smile.

'I'm glad you're here,' I said, my voice barely above a whisper.

Railan's smile widened. 'I'm not going anywhere,' he promised. 'I'll always be here for you.'

I rested my head on his chest once more, feeling safe and content in his arms. Damn it, he'd done it again, distracted me from my actual purpose. That charm of his would give me grief if I let him walk over me like that too often.

I propped my head up on my elbow, gazing down at his sleepy face. 'Actually, I wanted to ask you about yesterday... about the Doctor,' I said quietly.

Railan's expression turned serious as I mentioned the Doctor. He sat up slightly, releasing his hold on me, and ran a hand through his hair.

'What about him?' he asked, his voice guarded.

'I'm just curious... You were talking for a very long time,' I said, trying to keep my tone casual. 'I was a little worried.'

Railan's expression softened as he looked at me. 'I appreciate your concern, but there's no need to worry,' he said. 'The Doctor and I go way back, and we had some catching up to do.'

'Catching up?' I repeated, my curiosity piqued.

Railan nodded. 'Yeah, we haven't seen each other in years. We were just reminiscing about old times, nothing important.'

I studied Railan's face for a moment, trying to read between the lines. Something in his tone suggested that there might be more to the story, but I didn't want to push too hard. Instead, I decided to change the subject.

'I see... I'm glad it wasn't anything too serious. Though he had implied that it was,' I gave Railan a small huff. 'I had to cancel the rest of your day and assuage some very upset nobles.'

Railan let out a chuckle. 'Yeah, he does tend to exaggerate things,' he said. 'But don't worry, I'll make it up to you and those nobles.'

I smiled at him. 'I do not doubt that you will.'

Railan leaned in and kissed me again, a soft and gentle gesture that made my heart skip a beat. 'So, there's still a little bit of time before the first meeting, what would you like to do?' he asked, pulling away slightly.

What did I want to do? I hadn't expected to do anything. I pondered the question for a moment.

'Oh, um, I suppose I do have another question...' I started.

I wasn't sure I even wanted to ask it. The thought made my blood pressure rise. Could I really just ask him to meet my family? He would meet them at the ball, but still, I didn't just want to spring everything on them all at once. They at least needed a little bit of time to prepare for the farce that was to come.

'What's on your mind?' he asked as he brushed my cheek.

'I... well, with the ball and... everything,' I could feel the heat upon my cheeks, but I needed to stay strong. 'D-don't you think it's only right that we tell my parents in person, about u-us, that is, b-before the ball?'

Railan's expression turned curious as he considered my request. 'Of course, Isla. I think it's important to meet your parents before the ball,' he said. 'When would you like to arrange the meeting?'

I breathed a sigh of relief, grateful that he was willing to accommodate my request. 'Thank you,' I said, leaning in to kiss him on the cheek. 'I was thinking we could do it tomorrow night, after work is over for the day, so that it doesn't inconvenience you more than everything else already has.'

Railan smiled at me. 'That sounds perfect,' he said. 'I'm looking forward to meeting your parents.'

I smiled back, feeling a mix of nervousness and excitement at the thought of introducing Railan to my family. 'I'm sure they'll love you,' I said. 'Just... be prepared for a lot of questions.'

Railan chuckled. 'I'll do my best to answer them all,' he said.

We spent the next few minutes talking about the logistics of the meeting, and I felt a sense of relief wash over me as we made the arrangements. It was a weight off my shoulders to have that conversation out in the open, and I was grateful for Railan's understanding and willingness to make it work.

We spent the rest of the morning together, talking and laughing, enjoying each other's company. As we parted ways to attend to our respective duties, I couldn't help but feel a sense of excitement at the thought of introducing Railan to my family. It was a step forward in our relationship, and while I wasn't exactly sure if I was ready to take it, I was going to do it regardless.

Chapter 21

The night of the introductions arrived all too soon as I packed away the last of my paperwork. I needed to get ready, and once again, I was dragging my feet in an effort to postpone the inevitable. I couldn't help but stress over what Railan's reaction might be once he put two and two together. Would he abandon his promise and discard me, or would he turn a blind eye? I was sure he would have his own questions, and I wasn't sure if I would be able to answer them. I wanted to be honest with him, but Lady Amaranta's threats still lingered in the back of my mind. If I did something she didn't like, my family would suffer the consequences. I had to be careful, remain vigilant.

I ambled to my room and rummaged through my clothes. A deep sigh passed through my lips before they pursed up into a pout. That's right, I didn't exactly have anything... nice. Just the same old uniforms in varying shades of brown. Casual dress was not something I was accustomed to. It usually meant forgoing my jacket, but I would need that for the trip into the city. I sighed again as I simply freshened up. My family wouldn't care what I looked like, and I knew Railan felt the same. It was simply another excuse to waste time.

There was a sudden knock on my door and I jumped in surprise.

'Isla, it's me. Are you ready yet?' Railan's all-too-excited voice called from the other side.

The time was here. No more delays. I swallowed hard as I prepared myself to face the situation head-on. I opened the door and greeted Railan with as much of a smile as I could muster.

'I'm ready,' I said.

His eyes glanced over me with a tender glee. 'Beautiful as ever,' he said simply as he held out his hand.

Always one to give out unearned compliments. I felt a mild heat touch my cheeks as I avoided his gaze. I just wanted to get this over and done with. I took his hand and let him lead me out into the entrance, where the sleigh was already waiting. I blinked as the driver was obviously missing.

'Where's Henry?' I asked as I looked up at Railan.

He gave me a light chuckle, a glint of mischievous intent in his eyes. 'I gave him the night off. I'll drive us, it'll be less conspicuous.'

I raised a brow as I felt my stomach sink slightly. 'You, less conspicuous?'

'Ah, you wound me, my dear,' he continued to smile as he feigned pain. 'Relax, I've got this.'

I searched his face for a moment, but all I found was his usual cocky bravado. I nodded meekly and prayed this would go smoothly. Railan helped me onto the sleigh before sliding on next to me. He took the reins, and I felt the slightest bit nauseous as we started to move.

To my relief, he stuck to the road, avoiding any suspicious detours, and I felt myself slowly relax. I leaned against his arm as the gentle bumps lulled me into a false sense of security. The wind was nice and cold against my face, and the crunching of the snow under the horses' hooves was almost musical against the gentle breeze. It was just Railan and me, alone in the woods together with no watching eyes, no pressure, nothing. If only things could always be like this, maybe then we would stand a real chance.

We soon entered the city, and I nervously directed him towards Lake Village. I hoped he wouldn't notice, but then I remembered the literal gated checkpoint that bordered the ward. He would surely realise I was worthless then. My heart raced as we drew closer and the iron gates came into view. I held my breath as we pulled up just outside, and he helped me down from the sleigh. A smile was still plastered upon his lips, and I was scared to find out how long it would take to fade.

I made my way up to the guards and showed them my Creed emblem. They looked from me to Railan as I felt my stomach twist anxiously. They seemed to be almost on edge as they immediately recognised him. They let us in without question, and I quickly pulled him through the streets of Lake Village.

I could feel the weight of Railan's gaze on me, but I refused to look back at him. I didn't want to see any judgment or disappointment in his eyes. As we walked, I couldn't help but feel a sense of guilt and shame wash over me. Was I doing the right thing by bringing him here? Did I really want to ruin everything? I tried to push those thoughts away. It was too late to have reservations now.

I made my way to my family's house. It was a small, unassuming flat that was part of a larger housing tenement. All the streets and houses looked the same here, a maze of basic structures with no hint of personality or boldness. Everything was bland and mundane, as deserved by its inhabitants. I paused briefly as hesitation took hold. I needed to get this over with. I swallowed hard and knocked on the door. I heard shuffling from inside before the door burst open. A young girl with chocolate brown hair stood in the doorway, her eyes wide as she saw me. At first, she seemed shocked, but then her expression abruptly shifted into one of joy before it returned to shock as she laid eyes upon Railan.

She let out a shrill scream as she abruptly turned and ran back inside the house. 'Ah! Issy's home and she's brought a strange man with her!' my little sister screeched at the top of her lungs for the whole neighbourhood to hear.

At that moment, I regretted every decision in my life that had led me to this point as my cheeks burned the colour of a lobster. I wanted nothing more than to fade into the aether, never to be seen ever again. Railan let out a deep chuckle beside me, clearly finding the situation amusing. I couldn't even bring myself to look at him. I was far too red and embarrassed. My embarrassment only rose further as Inessa circled back around to the front door, a big, bright smile upon her little face as she ran straight into me and flung her arms around me.

'Issy! Issy! I can't believe you're here!' She couldn't control her excitement as her voice boomed loudly.

'Nessy, calm down,' I forced an awkward chuckle as I hugged her back.

'And who is he?' Inessa asked with the bluntness of a child as she pointed straight at Railan.

'Um...' I bit my lip, unsure how exactly to answer.

Railan stepped forward, a charming smile on his face. "My name is Eli. I'm a very good friend of your sister," he said, crouching down to her level. 'And who might you be, little lady?'

Inessa looked at him sceptically for a moment before her expression softened and she smiled back at him. 'Inessa, but you can call me Nessy!' she beamed, seemingly satisfied with his answer.

'Isla!' A second voice called out to me, and I saw my father poking his head out from around the corner. 'I can't believe my eyes, it really is you!' He seemed extremely happy to see me as he hobbled over to usher me inside. 'Come inside, it's cold out,' He paused briefly as he finally caught sight of Railan. 'Oh, I... I didn't realise we would be having a guest.' His eyes flicked from me to Railan and back, a hint of confusion within them.

I did as he asked and dragged Inessa and Railan with me as I closed the door.

I could see the hint of tears in my father's eyes as he tentatively embraced me.

'I wasn't sure you'd actually make it when they said you wanted to visit,' he said quietly.

'Of course I'd make it, it has been far too long,' I hugged him tight.

'We've missed you, sweetheart,' my father held me just a little longer before finally pulling back. 'And who is this young man? I don't believe we've met.'

'Um, Papa, this is...' My mouth felt dry, and I glanced at Railan, hoping he would introduce himself once again.

On cue, Railan stepped forward and took the lead with his usual air of confidence. 'Ah, good evening, sir. You must be the man I have to thank for bringing such a wonderful woman like Isla into the world,' he grabbed my father's trembling hand firmly. 'I am Elieason Railan, the twelfth of the Prime Mages.' He flashed my father a wide, warm smile.

'A Prime Mage! Wow!' Inessa gasped in awe.

My father looked visibly uncomfortable as he shot me a confused glance. I returned his look with my own subtle pleading. I just needed him to remain calm, and everything would be ok, well, I hoped so. If the introduction alone was this tense, I could only imagine their reaction when we broke the news of our courtship.

'Well, that's... It's a pleasure to meet you,' my father finally blurted. 'Come, make yourselves at home,' he turned to me. 'Your mother is waiting in the kitchen.'

I nodded as I stepped over to his side and grabbed his arm, keeping him steady. I smiled tenderly, feeling the warmth of my family as I felt their love permeate my very essence.

'Come on, let's go see Mama,' I smiled, and Nessy eagerly led us to the kitchen.

I shot Railan a small, sincere smile as I ushered him to follow.

My mother was busy hovering over the stove, so engrossed in the cooking that she didn't even notice us entering. Inessa ran straight up to her and pulled on her skirt with excitement and energy that only a child could have.

'Mama, mama, Issy is here and she bought a Prime Mage with her!' She chirped.

My heart felt like it was going to burst from all the embarrassment that coursed through it. My mother looked like she was about to scold Inessa for just a second before she comprehended her words, and she snapped around to see me. My mother was less restrained as her eyes immediately filled with tears as she laid eyes upon me, though they soon turned cold as she saw Railan.

'Issy...' she muttered as her eyes darted between us.

I took a deep breath and stepped forward, taking my mother's hands in mine. 'Mama, it's been too long,' I said softly, trying to ease the tension in the air. 'I'm sorry I didn't tell you I was coming sooner, but I had to come see you and Papa.'

My mother's gaze softened a little as she pulled me into a tight embrace. 'I've missed you so much, my darling girl,' she whispered into my ear.

I hugged her back, feeling the warmth of her love enveloping me. 'I've missed you too, mama.'

As we pulled back, I saw that my mother's eyes had turned to Railan once again. 'And who is this young man?' she asked, her voice laced with suspicion.

'Mama, this is Eli,' I said, introducing him. 'He's... a friend of mine.'

My mother raised an eyebrow, clearly not convinced. 'A friend?'

I nodded, hoping to keep things simple for now. 'Yes.'

Railan stepped forward, bowing slightly. 'It's an honour to meet you, ma'am,' he said politely.

My mother eyed him warily, but didn't say anything else. Instead, she turned back to the stove and resumed her cooking. 'Well, dinner will be ready soon,' she said, her tone curt.

I glanced at Railan, silently urging him to follow my lead and not cause any trouble. He seemed to understand, as he simply nodded and followed me to the table. Inessa immediately claimed the seat next to him and began to interrogate him with a barrage of questions. I smiled at Inessa's enthusiasm, glad that she was able to lighten the mood. I turned to my father, who had been silent throughout the exchange, and gave him a grateful smile.

'I've really missed you, it's been so long,' I said quietly, feeling a sense of peace wash over me.

My father smiled back, his eyes crinkling at the corners. 'It's good to have you home, Isla. I know your studies have been long and arduous, and now you're working... but you really need to remember to take a break now and then.'

'I know,' I admitted as I fiddled with my hands. 'Things have been rather... hectic to say the least. How is your leg?' I diverted the conversation away from me.

'Ah, still as bothersome as ever,' father grumbled. 'But the extra money you've been sending has been a blessing. I've been able to get some ointment to ease the pain.'

I gave him a warm smile as my chest felt lighter. 'I'm glad to hear that. I want to send more, but...' I trailed off.

'You shouldn't have to worry about us,' my father sighed heavily as he placed his hand on top of mine. 'I'm sorry we're such a burden on you.'

'No, you're not. Don't ever think that,' I said hastily, my voice a little louder than I'd like. 'Let's not talk about this now...' I glanced towards Railan.

He seemed to be distracted by Inessa, and I let out a small sigh of relief. My father looked over to Railan, and his expression grew guarded as he squeezed my hand.

My mother soon served dinner, and a palpable tension rose in the air with every bite. Inessa seemed completely unaware as she continued to chatter nonstop. Railan had a wide smile on his face, but I could sense there was something else going on behind the facade. Did he realise what I was? That I was a slave, that I was unworthy of him. I ate quietly, unable to find my courage.

'Oh, I'm so excited for the ball! Are you going to take Issy, Mr Eli?' Inessa's question suddenly cut through my thoughts and reminded me why we were here.

Railan nodded eagerly. 'I am... that's actually part of the reason why I've come to visit.'

My mouth felt dry again.

Oh no, this is it.

No matter what he said, I knew there would be some kind of fall-out. I looked down, unable to meet his eyes. But then he reached over and grabbed my hand, giving it a reassuring squeeze.

'I actually have an announcement to make,' Railan spoke up with an excited fervour. 'I plan to officially announce my intentions to court Isla at the ball, and I'm here to seek your approval to do so.'

My heart fluttered at the conviction in his words. My parents both looked stunned, their expressions frozen in shock. Inessa, on the other hand, squealed in delight, clapping her hands together.

'Ah, I knew it!' she exclaimed. 'Does this mean you're going to buy us?'

I felt a cold shiver run down my spine at Inessa's words.

'Nessy!' I hissed as I shot her daggers.

Did she really just say that? My father's face turned red with anger, but before he could say anything, Railan spoke up.

'No, Inessa, I'm not buying anyone,' he said firmly. 'I simply want to court Isla with the intention of hopefully marrying her someday.'

My mother looked at me with concern in her eyes. 'Isla, is this what you want?'

I hesitated for a moment, unsure of what to say. On one hand, I couldn't deny that I was attracted to Railan and that I had enjoyed spending time with him. But on the other hand, I couldn't help but feel like it was all a cruel joke, that he would never truly see me as his equal. Regardless, I was in too deep now to turn back.

'Yes,' I said firmly as I squeezed his hand back. 'We've mutually agreed to this decision.'

Railan smiled warmly at me, and I could feel my heart skip a beat. In that moment, I allowed myself to believe that maybe, just maybe, this could work out. My parents still looked hesitant, but they seemed to be warming up to the idea.

'Well, if that's what you both want,' my father said finally. 'Then we'll support you.'

My mother nodded in agreement. 'Just promise me that you'll be careful,' her eyes then darted to Railan, a stern gleam in them. 'You're dragging Isla into a very dangerous situation. Can you swear that you will protect her from all that is to come?'

'Mama...' I started.

Railan squeezed my hand once again as he replied. 'I understand your concerns, Mrs. Marielle,' he said calmly. 'But I assure you that I will do everything in my power to keep Isla safe. I care for her deeply, and I would never intentionally put her in harm's way.'

My mother's expression softened slightly, but she still looked wary. 'I hope you're not just saying that, Lord Railan,' she said pointedly. 'Because if anything happens to Isla, you will have me to answer to.'

Railan nodded seriously. 'I understand, and I take full responsibility for Isla's safety. You have my word.'

The rest of the dinner passed in a blur. Inessa continued to chatter excitedly about the upcoming ball, while my parents and Railan discussed various topics, including the state of the city and the political climate. I couldn't concentrate on anything they were saying; my mind was consumed with thoughts of what the future might hold. Could I really have a chance at happiness with Railan? Or was it all too good to be true?

As the night drew to a close and we prepared to say our goodbyes, the creeping feeling of unease clawed at the pit of my stomach. What if he changed his mind and was just too polite to say so in front of my family? As I hugged my parents and made my way to the door, I found myself filled with dread. I was scared to be alone with Railan, to find out how he really felt. I clung to my sister a little longer than I should have in an effort to put off what I knew was coming. I wanted to strangle her for yapping too much, but she was just so innocent. She didn't understand what any of this meant. She didn't know that her words could ruin me.

'Good night, I'll see you all at the ball,' I bid them farewell as I stepped over the threshold and into the cold night.

I started towards the gates, my pace a little faster than usual as I tried to maintain a distance between Railan and me. I could hear the crunching of his boots behind me, so I knew he was following along. As we walked in silence, I couldn't help but feel a knot in my stomach. I was unsure of what to say to him or how to act. My mind was racing with questions, but I didn't know how to voice them. Finally, Railan spoke up.

'Isla,' he said softly. 'Are you okay?'

I stopped in my tracks, turning to face him. 'What do you mean?'

'I mean...' he hesitated for a moment before continuing. 'I don't know...' he trailed off.

I lowered my gaze and turned back to face the gate that loomed ahead. This is where I belonged, in a cage, never to be free, never to have anything. I could feel tears swelling in my eyes. I couldn't cry right now, it was just so embarrassing. I started walking again, but was stopped as Railan grabbed my arm.

'Isla, wait,' he said softly, turning me around to face him again. 'If something's wrong, you can tell me.'

I tried to hide my fear, but I could feel it written all over my face. 'It's nothing,' I lied. 'I'm just tired.'

Railan frowned, clearly not believing me. 'Isla, please. You can tell me anything.'

I looked up at him, and in that moment, I saw something in his eyes that made my heart skip a beat. It was warmth, kindness, and something else... something that I couldn't quite put my finger on. But it made me feel safe, and it made me want to trust him.

'I'm scared,' I admitted finally, my voice barely above a whisper.

Railan's expression softened, and he pulled me into a warm embrace. 'I know,' he said quietly. 'But you don't have to be scared. I'm here for you, and I'll always be here for you.'

I wrapped my arms around him, letting myself sink into the safety of his embrace. For a few moments, I allowed myself to forget about everything else. The ball, the politics, the danger... all of it faded away, leaving only me and him.

'I'll protect you, Isla,' Railan whispered, his breath warm against my ear. 'I promise.'

I pulled away from him, looking up at his face. 'How can you be so sure?'

Railan looked at me with a fierce determination in his eyes. 'Because I love you,' he said simply.

I felt my heart skip a beat at his words. He said it again.

Love.

Could he really mean it? But then my mind reminded me of my place in society, of the fact that I was a slave and he was a Prime Mage. How could someone like him love someone like me? I tried to push those thoughts away, but they lingered like a dark cloud hovering over us.

'I... I-I... love you too,' I stuttered, my voice almost inaudible.

A part of me didn't want him to hear, for my words to simply be lost in the wind. Railan's eyes widened in surprise, but a smile quickly spread across his face. He pulled me into another embrace, this one more intense than the last. I could feel his heartbeat against my chest, and it was racing just as fast as mine.

'Isla,' he said, pulling away slightly to look into my eyes. 'Do you mean it? Do you really love me?'

I nodded, unable to speak as tears streamed down my face. The weight of my emotions was overwhelming, but at the same time, I felt lighter than I had in years. This was the first time I had ever allowed myself to love someone, to feel that kind of connection with another person. And even though the circumstances were far from ideal, I knew that I was willing to suffer the consequences.

Railan leaned in, pressing his lips to mine in a tender kiss. It was like fireworks going off in my head, and I couldn't help but melt into his embrace. For that moment, I was content to just be with him, to forget about the rest of the world.

But eventually, we pulled away, both of us breathing heavily. 'Isla,' Railan said, his eyes shining in the moonlight. 'Let's get out of here.'

I nodded, and I let him lead me back to the sleigh. I cast one last glance at the gilded cage of Lake Village as we pulled away. A sliver of sadness pricked at my heart despite my happiness. Maybe things would be fine, maybe they wouldn't. I was feeling both lost and found. It was a very strange sensation.

We sat in relative silence as we drove through the city streets. It wasn't uncomfortable, but it wasn't entirely comfortable either. Railan was constantly reassuring me, but why was it so hard to accept? Why couldn't I just accept his love freely? Why did I have to live in constant fear?

A sudden jolt shook me out of my thoughts, and I saw that Railan had taken us off the main road and into the Maentaean forest. The uneven terrain jostled me about, and I soon clung to Railan. I looked at him, unsure what he was doing.

'Where are we going?' I asked, a hint of uncertainty in my voice.

Railan gave me a reassuring smile. 'Just trust me,' he said. 'We're going to a safe place.'

I nodded, trying to calm my nerves. As we drove deeper into the forest, I noticed that the trees grew denser and taller, casting dark shadows over the terrain. A sense of foreboding clung to the air, like we were venturing into a forbidden realm. It was truly a different place at nighttime.

Then I saw it, a vibrant, rainbow glow in the distance. It started small as tiny witchlights perched on the trees around us, but slowly grew as more and more witchlights gathered, coating entire trees in their soft glow. The forest soon gave way, and I immediately recognised the small clearing. It was the long-forgotten menhirs that Railan had shown me some time ago.

A safe place.

I couldn't stop the smile that spread across my lips. It was even more beautiful at nighttime, where the witchlights could shine in all their glory. Railan pulled up the sleigh just on the outskirts of the clearing and helped me down. I stared in awe as the air buzzed with the soft hum of a thousand witchlights of all elements. They were almost reminiscent of stars. Railan led me over to the menhirs, and I let out a small gasp as I saw the intricate sigils that were now revealed by the witchlights. I hadn't noticed them during the daytime. Now I could see very clearly that each menhir was carved with magic runes of all types. I finally understood why the witchlights were so attracted to this place. I knew it was magical, but I thought it had been a little more innate in nature. My eyes flicked to the statue at the centre. Every inch of it was covered in a twinkling rainbow.

'It's so... it's even more beautiful at night,' I mumbled.

Railan nodded, a soft smile on his face. 'It is, isn't it?' He took my hand and led me closer to the statue. 'I didn't exactly tell you much about this place last time, did I?' He motioned for me to sit, and I obeyed without question.

He joined my side, his arm pressed firmly against mine. I took the initiative to lean my head upon his shoulder as I laced my fingers with his.

'You did not,' I said softly as I watched the witchlights flutter and rearrange themselves.

Railan chuckled. 'Well, it's a long story. But in short, this place was once a sacred site for the Silvyan Order. They used to gather here to perform rituals and ceremonies, and the menhirs were believed to be imbued with the power of every element. But over time, the site was forgotten and left to decay.'

I listened intently, my eyes never leaving the glowing statue. 'But it's still so beautiful,' I said.

'Yes, it is,' Railan agreed. 'And it still holds a great deal of power. But that's not why I wanted to bring you here.'

'Why did you bring me here, then?' I asked, tilting my head up to look at him.

'Isla...' he started, but hesitated as he struggled to find the words. 'I need you to be as honest with me as you can.'

I felt my chest tighten at his words. Oh no. My eyes fluttered as I understood what he wanted. I managed a weak nod, encouraging him to continue.

'About what your sister said...' Railan spoke softly, gently, as if he was being cautious. 'I know you have your secrets, but... what did she mean by "buy" you?'

My throat felt dry as I hid my face against his sleeve. This was it, the thing I'd been dreading. I couldn't tell him the truth, not the whole truth.

Railan rubbed soothing circles on the back of my hand, waiting patiently for my response. I took a deep breath and tried to find the right words, the ones that would reveal the least amount of information but still satisfy his curiosity. I needed to find the perfect balance between truth and lies. I took a deep, steadying breath as I looked up to the stars. They were vast and far removed from the problems of humans, of magi and mundi.

'I told you... everything about me is a lie, a dream. I'm not who you think I am...' my voice was barely above a whisper as I stared at the sky, unable to look at him. 'I have to protect my family from the consequences of my actions. To protect Inessa from ending up in the same situation... my life... it's not my own. I'm not free, nothing I do is of my own volition...' I could feel my tears rolling down my cheeks, their heat turning cold as the chill set in. 'I'm a thing to be used and discarded, over and over, until there is nothing left.'

Railan's expression softened as he listened to my words, his thumb still rubbing soothing circles on my hand. 'Isla,' he said softly. 'You are not a thing to be used and discarded. You are a person, and your life is your own. You deserve to be happy, to be free.'

I shook my head, unable to meet his gaze. 'You don't understand,' I whispered. 'There are things I have to do, things I can't avoid. And if I don't do them, if I don't play my part, then my family will suffer.'

Railan's hand stilled, and I could feel his concern radiating off of him. 'What kind of things?' he asked quietly.

I hesitated, biting my lip. I couldn't tell him everything, but maybe I could give him a little bit more. 'Things that I'm ashamed of,' I said finally. 'Things that would make you hate me.'

Railan's eyes searched mine, trying to understand. 'I could never hate you, Isla,' he said firmly, his tone reassuring. 'I promised I would never discard you, and I keep my promises.'

I felt a flicker of hope at his words, but it was quickly snuffed out by the weight of my secrets. 'You don't know what you're saying,' I said, my voice shaking. 'If you knew, you would hate me. And you would never look at me the same way again.'

Railan released my hand, and a chill ran down my spine. Was he starting to realise the truth? My eyes widened as I felt his fingers on my chin, tilting my face up so that I was forced to meet his gaze. 'Isla,' he said firmly. 'Nothing you could tell me would ever make me hate you. I love you more than anything else in this world.'

His words made my heart ache with longing, but I couldn't let myself hope for too much. 'I know... but I'm just so used and dirty.' I sobbed quietly.

Railan's expression turned pained as he saw my distress. He pulled me into a tight hug, holding me close as I cried against his chest. 'You are not dirty, Isla,' he whispered fiercely. 'You are not used. You are a beautiful, strong, and brave woman. And I love you for who you are, not for any perceived worth or usefulness.'

I clung to him as if my life depended on it, and in a way, that was true. One half of me prayed that he would be my salvation, but the other half knew he would never be strong enough.

'Eli... I... I belong to someone else, I mean... I was sold into slavery a very long time ago...' I admitted aloud.

Railan's arms tightened around me at my confession, and I could feel his shock and anger radiating through his body. 'What do you mean, you belong to someone else?' he growled. 'Who?'

I shook my head, feeling overwhelmed by the emotions that were threatening to consume me. 'I-I can't...' I said, my voice barely above a whisper. 'I've already said too much.'

Railan's grip on me loosened slightly, and I could sense his frustration. 'Isla, please,' he pleaded. 'I want to help you. I want you to be mine and mine alone. I'll do anything to make that happen, anything.'

I took a deep breath and steadied myself before answering. 'It's impossible.'

Railan's expression darkened, and I could see the fury in his eyes. 'Why?' he demanded.

I looked up at Railan, seeing the anger and frustration etched on his face. 'Because there are some things that not even you can undo,' I murmured. 'I belong to someone else, and I always will. There is a debt that must be paid, and I must pay it.'

Railan's eyes narrowed, and his grip on me tightened again. 'Who is it?' he asked, his voice low and dangerous. 'Tell me, Isla. I need to know. If this is about money, then I will pay it. I'll spend every coin at my disposal.'

I hesitated, unsure if I could trust him with such sensitive information. But as I looked into his eyes, I saw the fierce determination and love shining there, and I knew that I had to tell him a part of the truth. Just a little more.

'It's not about money, not really... no amount of money in the world would ever be enough to release me. I may be nothing, but the things I can do are worth more than anything to my master. The things... I can do to you,' I mumbled as shame surged through me.

Railan's expression softened as he understood the weight of my words. 'Isla, I don't care about what you can or cannot do to me,' he said firmly. 'I care about you and your well-being. Please, tell me who your master is. I need to know. I can protect you and your family, I swear it.'

I took a deep breath, gathering my courage. If I did this, everything would collapse. I would be handing myself from one master to another. Did I trust Railan enough to betray Lady Amaranta? Could he really protect me? Could he protect my family? He was only the Twelfth Prime Mage, the most precarious of positions. Could he really go up against the Third Prime Mage? Or would I be dragging him down with me?

'Promise me you won't say anything, promise me that you'll keep everything I say a secret,' I begged him softly.

'I promise,' he said firmly, his tone full of conviction.

I let out a small breath as I slipped my hands onto his shoulders, pressing him down slightly so I could whisper into his ear. 'My master is... Lady Amaranta.'

Guilt rocked through me, and I could feel my body trembling slightly. I shouldn't have said anything. Railan's muscles stiffened under me, and for a second, I thought he might push me away. But he didn't; instead, he held me tighter, burying his face in the crook of my neck. I could feel his breath against my skin and the subtle torment that swirled within him. No doubt he understood the implication of my words.

'Lady Amaranta,' he repeated, his voice low and dangerous. 'I should have known. That woman has always been trouble. But... why you, Isla? Why would she choose you?'

I swallowed hard, trying to control my emotions. 'I... I don't know,' I said weakly. 'A long time ago, she said that she saw something in me, something that would be useful to her.'

Railan's eyes bore into mine, searching for any sign of deception. But all he saw was the truth, raw and unfiltered. 'You deserve so much better than this, Isla,' he said, his voice gentle. 'And I will make sure that you get it. I promise you that.'

I looked up at him, seeing the determination in his eyes. And for the first time in a long time, I felt a glimmer of hope. Maybe, just maybe, there was a way out of this. Maybe Railan could help me escape Lady Amaranta's grasp and start a new life. Maybe there was a chance for me to be free.

Railan's grip on me loosened slightly as he pulled away, looking down at me with a mix of concern and determination. 'We need to figure out a plan,' he said firmly. 'Lady Amaranta is not someone to be taken lightly, and I won't let her harm you or your family.'

I nodded, grateful for his concern. 'But how?' I asked, my voice barely above a whisper. 'How can we go up against the Third Prime Mage? You haven't had any time to establish yourself, and I... well, I'm not sure I can do anything.'

Railan's expression turned grave as he contemplated the question. 'We'll need allies,' he said finally. 'People we can trust, people who are willing to stand up against Lady Amaranta.'

I bit my lip, feeling the weight of the situation. Finding allies wouldn't be easy, especially with Lady Amaranta's power and influence. But if there was anyone who could do it, it was Railan. He was well-respected and well-liked, even by those who didn't agree with his politics. And with his magic, he could sway people to his side.

'But... the only allies who can go up against her are the other Prime Mages and... I don't think you can trust them either,' I said slowly.

Railan nodded grimly. 'Yes, they all have their own agendas and alliances. But there are others who are not part of the Prime Mage circle who have their own reasons for opposing Lady Amaranta,' he paused, considering his words carefully. 'I have a few contacts outside of the Council who might be willing to help us. It won't be easy, but it's our best chance.'

Allies outside of the Prime Mages? That didn't exactly fill me with much hope. Lady Amaranta was firmly, safely in her position. She maintained it through her vast network of witchlights, spies, and agents. No one could be trusted. Not even the most mundane of the mundi.

'Eli... you really can't trust anyone. Not even me... not when she still has her claws so firmly planted within me.'

Railan gave me a small smile as he brushed a stray strand of hair from my face. 'I do trust you, Isla. I know that this isn't your fault. I can see the torment in your eyes every day. I want to see the light within you, I want to fight for you, no matter what.'

'I don't know if there's much of anything left within me, but I want to give it to you. I want you to save me,' I admitted.

'I will, I promise,' he hugged me tight once more.

I almost felt relieved, like a weight had finally been lifted from my shoulders. He knew the truth, and he still wanted me. This man was truly something else, and he wanted to be mine. I would have to do my best to overcome my fears, my doubts. I couldn't let my trauma sabotage my future anymore.

'Lady Amaranta can't know that you know the truth. I need to act as if everything's the same as usual, and that includes... reporting on your every move,' I mumbled.

Railan nodded. 'I understand. You need to do what you must, but we can do it together. Does... does she know about... us?'

'Yes...' I admitted quietly. 'She's... she's the one who told me to pursue you after, well, after the incident in the forest...'

Railan's expression hardened. 'Of course she did. She wants to keep tabs on me and use you as a pawn in her game. But we won't let her. We'll find a way to break free from her grasp.'

'Yes, I want to break free with you,' I mumbled against his ear.

Railan held me tighter, his warmth enveloping me. 'We will, Isla. We will find a way,' he pulled back and looked at me intently. 'But I... I just want to know how you really feel about me, about us. I want you to want me, but only if it's by your own volition.'

My eyes fluttered as my cheeks flushed red. 'I... I meant what I said earlier tonight. If everything else is lies, then the one truth is that I truly, sincerely do love you. That is my choice and mine alone.'

Railan's eyes softened as he gazed at me. 'That's all I needed to hear,' he whispered before pressing his lips gently against mine.

The kiss was sweet and tender, yet filled with a deep longing that I could feel in every fibre of my being. We broke apart, both of us breathless, but the warmth and intensity between us lingered.

'We'll figure this out,' Railan said, his voice low and determined. 'Together.'

I nodded, feeling a sense of comfort and security in his words. For the first time in a long time, I felt like I wasn't alone in this battle. We may be up against Lady Amaranta, but I had to have faith in Railan, faith in us.

'Together,' I echoed.

I wanted to believe that we could do anything so long as we were together. I felt like the Celestial Lady had finally answered my prayers, that she had specifically sent Railan to me. I knew that couldn't possibly be the truth, but still, I felt blessed for the first time in my life.

'I want us to be together, always,' I breathed against his lips as I kissed him again.

Railan's arms tightened around me, pulling me closer as our lips met again. 'Always,' Railan echoed between kisses, his voice filled with conviction.

I knew that he was the one. The one I would give my heart to. My past, present, and future, none of it mattered so long as I was his and he mine. I deepened our kiss, finally feeling free of all my reservations, all my doubts. Railan responded with equal fervour, his hands roaming over my body, igniting a fire within me that only he could spark.

Our love was passionate and intense, but also filled with tenderness and understanding. He was kind and respectful and everything I could have ever hoped for. I needed him to understand that.

I let him push me gently into the snow, clinging to his neck to keep the warmth of his breath close as his mouth trailed across my skin. My heart raced as I felt his lips on my neck, his touch sending shivers down my spine. I moaned softly, unable to contain my pleasure, as he continued to explore every inch of my body. It was like we were the only two people in the world, lost in our own little bubble of passion and desire.

I bit my lip, and while I felt nervous, I also felt sure. 'P-please... please take me, now,' I murmured against his hair.

Railan paused, his lips still against my skin, and looked up at me, his eyes full of concern. 'Are you sure?' he asked, his voice soft and gentle.

I nodded, my heart racing with anticipation. 'Yes, Eli. I'm sure.'

He searched my face for any sign of hesitation or uncertainty. When he found none, he nodded, his eyes filled with love and understanding. He leaned in and kissed me deeply, his hands running through my hair. I moaned softly as I felt him harden against me, his desire for me evident. He pulled up my skirt, and I felt a shiver run through me as the cold air touched my legs. Railan paused, pulling back slightly as he blinked for a second before he returned my skirt to its original position, a sheepish grin on his lips.

'Perhaps I ought to take you home first.'

I blushed at his words, not expecting him to hesitate. But he was right. I couldn't help but feel a little embarrassed at how caught up in the moment we had both become. Railan helped me up, brushing the snow off my clothes before offering me his arm. He led me back to the sleigh, and we began the journey back to his estate. My heart still raced the entire ride as I leaned against his arm. We rode in silence, but it wasn't uncomfortable. We'd said what needed to be said; all that was left between us now was sweet, blissful peace.

As we arrived at his estate, Railan helped me out of the sleigh and, to my pleasant surprise, swept me up into his arms. I blushed harder, feeling like I was perhaps a little heavy, but he seemed to carry me with ease. I could feel the strength in his arms and the power in his stride as he brought me up to his room. He placed me gently upon his bed but did not immediately join me.

'Are you sure you're ready?' he asked again, giving me one last chance to back out.

I nodded, feeling my heart racing in my chest. A bright, tender smile touched his lips before he pressed a soft kiss to my forehead. He slowly, tenderly, began to undress me. Every touch was deliberate, every movement filled with care and reverence. I knew that he was treating me with the utmost respect, and it only made my love for him grow stronger. I felt myself surrendering completely to him with every touch, wanting nothing more than to be close to him. He took his time to explore every inch of my body with his hands and lips. I felt completely exposed under his gaze, but it was a good feeling. I felt a rush of pleasure course through me as his fingers slipped between my thighs, and I couldn't stifle the moan that escaped my lips. Railan kissed me hard, his tongue exploring my mouth as more moans tried desperately to escape. He pulled back slightly, his breath heavy upon my cheeks, before he began to trail kisses down my neck and chest, nibbling at my flesh, savouring every inch.

'Say my name, Isla,' he whispered against my skin.

He flicked his eyes up at me, a smouldering, hungry desire burning within their depths as he looked at me expectantly.

'E-Eli!' I gasped as he stroked me at just the right spot.

His eyes narrowed with an almost primal satisfaction as he brought me to the brink of ecstasy. I didn't know how much more I could take. My eyelashes fluttered as my breath became shallow, desperate. Railan continued to pleasure me, his touch becoming more urgent as he brought me closer and closer to the edge. I couldn't hold back any longer, and I cried out his name, my body convulsing with pleasure.

He held me close, his arm wrapping around me as he continued to stroke me, prolonging the pleasure until I pressed gently against his shoulder, signalling for him to stop.

He pulled back and looked at me once more, his eyes filled with love and desire. 'I love you,' he whispered. 'I want you.'

I didn't know if I could take any more, but for him, I would do anything.

'P-Please take me. I want to feel you, all of you,' I murmured through shaky breaths.

Railan's eyes darkened with passion as he gazed at me, his hands gently caressing my body. Without a word, he moved to position himself above me, his eyes never leaving mine. Slowly, he entered me, and I gasped at the sensation of his hard, hot flesh filling me completely. He moved slowly at first, allowing me time to adjust to him, but soon his movements became more urgent, more demanding. I clung to him desperately, lost in the intensity of the pleasure he was giving me. All other sensations disappeared, my mind completely devoid of anything but ecstasy.

As he thrust into me, our bodies moving together in perfect harmony, I felt the true depths of our connection, as if we were two halves of a whole. He was my everything, my lover, my friend, my soulmate. I knew that I would never be able to love anyone else the way I loved him.

As we both reached the pinnacle of our passion, we cried out in unison, our bodies shaking with the intensity of our release. Railan collapsed beside me, his breath raspy and his cheeks rosy. We lay there for a few moments as we tried to catch our breath, our hearts still racing, before Railan pulled me close to him. His fingers traced lazy circles on my back, and I felt completely at peace. This was where I belonged, in his arms, with him beside me. I never knew that I could feel so beautiful, that I could feel so loved.

'I love you,' Railan murmured, his lips pressing against the top of my head.

'I love you too,' I replied, snuggling closer to him as tears pricked at the corners of my eyes. 'Always.'

Chapter 22

The next morning, I woke up to find Railan watching me with a warm, affectionate smile on his face. He brushed a strand of hair from my face and leaned in to kiss me softly.

'Good morning, my love,' he whispered.

I smiled back at him, feeling happier than I ever had before. 'Good morning, Eli.'

Railan wrapped his arms around me and pulled me close, nuzzling his face into my hair. 'I love you so much, Isla,' he murmured.

'I love you too, Eli,' I replied, my heart swelling with emotion.

We lay there for a few moments, lost in each other's embrace, before Railan reluctantly pulled away.

'The first meeting will start soon,' he said regretfully. 'Can I just cancel everything and spend the day with you instead?' he joked, though I could sense a hint of earnest sincerity laced through his words.

'No, if you have any more cancellations, you'll never have time for me,' I teased him back lightly. 'Besides, I also have work to attend to. Though...' I bit my lip as I thought about our schedule for the day. 'We do have a meeting with Master Pompanov after lunch to discuss the finalisation of the decor for the ball. You will see me then.'

Railan smiled at me, his eyes bright with amusement. 'I look forward to it,' he said before leaning in to give me another kiss.

As Railan pulled away, he got out of bed and started to get dressed. I watched him as he moved around the room, admiring the way his muscles flexed with every movement. He was so very handsome. I absentmindedly let my eyes follow him until he caught me looking and smirked.

'Like what you see, Isla?' he teased me.

My cheeks blazed with heat, and I quickly pulled the blanket up over my face. Railan chuckled as he finished dressing, then walked over to me and pulled the blanket down.

'Don't be embarrassed,' he said, his voice gentle. 'I love it when you look at me like that.'

I smiled up at him, feeling my heart flutter with affection. 'I can't help it,' I said softly. 'You're just so...' I trailed off, unable to find the words to express the way I felt about him.

Railan leaned down and kissed me again, his lips soft and warm against mine. 'I know,' he whispered against my lips. 'I feel the same way about you.'

He pressed his forehead against mine, resting there for a moment, soaking in the warmth of my skin. He let out a contented sigh before pulling away.

'Will you meet me at my office before Pompanov arrives? I want to see you first,' he asked.

'Yes, if that's what you want,' I nodded meekly.

'Good, I'll see you then,' he gave me a bright, mischievous grin before he left to start the day.

I couldn't help but smile to myself as I rolled over in his bed. My heart felt full and weightless at the same time. I was happy, and for a brief moment, I wasn't scared of anything. I brought his pillow up to my chest, hugging it tight as I breathed his scent into my lungs.

Eli.

I never would have ever thought that I would get swept up in a whirlwind romance like those featured in the Dastardly Dandelion serial. Romance only happened to, well, other people. Yet here I was in the bed of a Prime Mage, one who had professed his undying love for me, a nobody. Of course, things were going to be exponentially more difficult now. But right now, at this very second, I was happy.

Unfortunately, reality called, and I lazily rolled out of bed to get dressed myself. As much as I wanted nothing more than to warm his bed all day long, I, too, had work to do. I made the bed before I stuck my head out of the door, peering around to make sure no one saw me. I would die of embarrassment if someone said anything right now. I still had to wrap my head around everything myself.

I ambled to my office in a sort of lovesick daze, and while I tried my best to work, my mind was constantly being pulled back to thoughts of Eli. I could still feel the warmth of his skin on mine, the pressure of his lips, and the gentle touch of his hands. My cheeks were hot as usual, and I patted them to try and get them to cool down. Alas, every thought I had only seemed to make them redder. No doubt, Railan would be amused if he knew what he did to me.

As the time approached for my meeting with Railan, I found myself oddly excited. Usually, I would be nervous, uncertain, but now I felt an unfamiliar sense of warmth, a sort of good anxiety. Perhaps I was still riding the high of last night, but now I was actually looking forward to seeing him again. My pep only continued as it carried over to my every step. His office had never seemed so far, and yet I was practically skipping there.

I stopped briefly outside his door, taking a deep breath to try and calm myself before stepping into Railan's office. Railan looked up from his desk as I entered, a warm smile lighting up his face.

'Hello, my love,' he greeted me, standing up to come over to me.

'Hey,' I said, my voice barely above a whisper.

He closed the gap between us almost immediately as he swept me up into his strong arms. He pushed the door closed behind me before locking it. As soon as he was certain we wouldn't be easily disturbed, he gently grabbed my chin and tilted my head up so that he could place an eager kiss upon my lips. My knees went weak at the touch of his lips on mine, and I leaned into him, my arms wrapping around his neck. He pulled me closer, deepening the kiss, and I felt a rush of heat spread through my body. This man had a way of making me feel so alive, so wanted.

'There are a few minutes...' he breathed against my skin as his mouth moved down my chin to my neck.

'W-What?' I stuttered as my cheeks blazed with the heat of a thousand suns. 'Here? Now?'

Railan pulled away from me, a mischievous grin on his lips. 'Why not?' he said, his voice low and sultry. 'No one can disturb us here, and I can't think of a better way to spend the time,' he leaned in again, his lips trailing down my neck, sending shivers down my spine.

I felt a rush of desire coursing through my body as his hands roamed over my back, pulling me closer to him. My heart was racing, my breathing becoming more and more shallow. I knew I should be worried about getting caught, but all I could think about was how good it felt to be in his arms, to be wanted by him.

'Eli...' I moaned as his hands moved down to my hips, pulling me up against him.

'Shh...' he whispered against my ear, his hot breath sending shivers down my spine. 'Let me have you.'

And with that, he lifted me and placed me onto his desk, his lips finding mine again as he pulled me in for another kiss. I wrapped my legs around his waist, pulling him closer to me, wanting more of him. In that moment, nothing else mattered. All I could think about was him and how much I wanted him. Railan's hands moved with haste as they went straight for the hem of my dress and pulled it up and out of the way. I broke the kiss, gasping for air as I looked at him. He smiled at me, his eyes filled with desire and a hint of mischief. He knew exactly what he was doing.

'W-what if someone comes?' I asked him, my voice trembling with excitement.

'The only one who will be coming is you,' he purred as his hands slipped under my thighs, pulling them into position. 'I want you, and I want you now.'

I felt exposed and vulnerable, but also incredibly aroused. Railan's lips moved down my neck, leaving a trail of kisses and nibbles. His fingers worked their way up my inner thigh until they got to my sweet spot. I let out a sharp gasp as he touched me gently, slipping his fingers into my wanting slit.

'You're already so very wet. Have you been thinking about me?' he murmured against my neck.

I bit my lip as I pulled him closer to me. My body responded immediately to his touch, arching up against him. I moaned softly, unable to control the pleasure that was building inside of me. Railan's fingers moved expertly, teasing and caressing me in just the right way. I could feel my release building, and I knew that it was only a matter of time before I exploded.

'Eli...' I gasped, my voice barely audible.

'Shh...' he whispered again, his voice full of lust. 'Just let go, my love.'

And with that, I let go, my body convulsing in pleasure as I came undone under his skilled touch. Railan didn't stop there, though. He continued to pleasure me, his fingers moving faster and harder, sending me over the edge again and again. I lost track of how many times I came, but each time was better than the last.

Finally, Railan withdrew his fingers and leaned back, a smug smile on his lips as he looked at me. I was a mess, my body still trembling with the aftershocks of my orgasms. I looked at him, feeling a mix of emotions. Part of me was embarrassed that I had just let him finger me on his desk, but another part of me was incredibly turned on by the whole experience. I couldn't deny that Railan had a way of making me feel things that I had never felt before.

'That was...' I started, not sure what to say.

'Amazing?' Railan finished for me, a twinkle in his eye.

I nodded, feeling a smile tug at the corners of my lips.

'Good,' he said, leaning in for a kiss. 'Because we're just getting started.'

'B-but the meeting...' I could hardly form the words. My head was so fuzzy.

'It'll be fine if we're a little late,' he shrugged as he unfastened his belt.

I couldn't bring myself to watch as Railan pulled down his pants and stepped closer to me. My cheeks were full of burning heat as I covered my eyes.

'Don't be shy,' he chuckled, his hand moving to gently remove mine from my face. 'Look at me.'

I opened my eyes to find Railan standing in front of me, his eyes dark with desire. He leaned in and kissed me, his hands moving to cup my face. I kissed him back, my hands resting on his chest. I could feel his hardness pressing against my thigh, and I knew that I wanted him just as badly as he wanted me.

'Are you ready?' he asked, his voice low and husky.

I nodded, feeling a mixture of excitement and nervousness. Railan positioned himself at my entrance, slowly pushing into me. I gasped at the sensation, feeling full and stretched in the best way possible. Railan started to move, his thrusts slow and deliberate at first, but then became faster and harder as he picked up the pace. I wrapped my legs around his waist, pulling him closer to me, wanting to feel even more of him.

'You feel so good,' he keened, his hands moving to grip my hips. 'I could do you all day.'

I moaned in response, unable to form coherent words. The pleasure was overwhelming, and I knew that I was close to coming again. Railan must have sensed it, because he started to move even faster, his thrusts becoming more erratic as he chased his own release. And then, with one final thrust, he came, his body shaking with the force of his orgasm.

I fell back onto the desk, pulling Eli with me. We were both panting and sweating. He rested his head upon my chest as his arms shook, barely able to keep him from completely collapsing onto me. We stayed like this for a few moments, entwined in each other's embrace as we tried to catch our breath. I kissed the top of his head, feeling his silky hair upon my lips. I was so very much in love with this man.

Knock!

I let out a sharp, startled gasp as our intimate moment was abruptly interrupted. Railan let out a frustrated groan as he lifted his head from my chest. The knocking continued.

'Give me a minute,' Railan almost growled as he let out a deep sigh and finally pushed himself off me.

I quickly stood and straightened out my clothes as best as I could. My legs were weak, and I let myself fall into the nearby chair, hoping that I looked unassuming. Railan pulled up his pants, not nearly as concerned about his appearance as I, as he made his way to the door. He glanced back at me for just a second before he unlocked the door and cracked it slightly.

'Yes?' he said quietly, his tone cold and unyielding.

'S-Sorry to bother you, my Lord, but Master Pampanov is waiting in the sitting room,' I recognised the voice as Leonid, the young butler.

Railan's expression softened slightly as he recognised the name. 'Ah, Leonid. Thank you for letting me know. I'll be out shortly,' he replied in a more cordial tone before closing the door. He turned back to me with a sly smile. 'Are you ready for some ball preparations, my love?'

I nodded. I knew this was coming. I stood a little too quickly, and my legs wobbled. Railan came back to my side and slipped his arm around my waist to keep me steady. I gave him a sheepish smile as I tried to hide my embarrassment. I wasn't sure I could make it to the sitting room, least of all arrive there without arousing suspicion.

I shouldn't have let him talk me into this little rendezvous, but it was too late now.

Railan chuckled softly as he led me out of the room and towards the sitting room. 'Careful there, my love. Don't want to attract any unwanted attention,' he whispered with a hint of amusement, his hand warm against my waist.

As we walked down the corridor, I couldn't help but feel a little nervous. The last thing I wanted was for anyone to preemptively spread malicious rumours. I wanted to remain in control of the narrative. If we weren't careful, we could show our hands too early and leave ourselves open to the machinations of the other Prime Mages.

When we arrived at the sitting room, Master Pampanov was already waiting for us. He looked as nervous as I felt as he hastily stood as we entered. Beads of sweat had already formed on his head, and he quickly patted at them with his handkerchief before he made his way over to us.

'Lord Railan, I hope you're as excited for this ball as I am.' Pampanov gave Railan a light, anxious smile as the two men shook hands.

Railan returned the handshake, a charming smile on his face. 'Of course, Master Pampanov. I'm looking forward to finalising the details,' he replied smoothly.

I smiled politely, trying to keep up appearances. I needed to blend into the background. I was just Railan's assistant at the moment.

Pampanov then turned to me, his expression slightly hesitant. 'And madam, I hope you are feeling well?'

'Yes, thank you,' I replied, trying to hide my discomfort as Railan's hand moved to my lower back in a subtle gesture of possession.

Pampanov seemed to pick up on the tension between us and quickly changed the subject. He launched into a discussion about the upcoming ball, going over every detail of the event and any last-minute changes. Railan listened intently, occasionally interjecting with a suggestion or question. I tried my best to follow along, but my mind kept drifting back to our interrupted tryst. I could feel Railan's subtle glances and the threat of a knowing smirk upon his lips. I had to remain calm.

As the meeting went on, I began to relax and focus on the details of the ball. Pampanov was a meticulous planner and had thought of everything, down to the smallest detail. Railan was equally attentive, making sure that all of my suggestions were heard and incorporated; the ball was, after all, secretly in my honour.

As the meeting drew to a close, Pampanov stood up and shook our hands. 'Thank you for your time, Lord Railan, madam. I look forward to seeing you both at the ball,' he said with a slight bow before exiting the room.

Once he was gone, Railan turned to me with a mischievous glint in his eye. 'Well, that was fun, wasn't it?' he said with a smirk. 'Are you satisfied with the final order?'

I couldn't help but smile at his playful tone. 'I suppose,' I replied, trying to keep my composure. 'I am if you are.'

Railan chuckled, his hand still lingering on my lower back. 'Of course, my dear. It's your ball after all,' he said, leaning in closer to me. 'But let's not forget about our unfinished business from earlier,' he whispered, his breath warm against my ear.

A shiver ran down my spine at his words, a mixture of anticipation and nervousness. 'You still have half a day of meetings,' I said hesitantly, trying to keep my voice steady.

Railan's smirk widened. 'I'll make it quick,' he said, his hand trailing down to my hip. 'Unless you want me to take my time?'

I felt a flush creep up my neck at his suggestive tone. 'I think... quick is good,' I managed to reply, trying to suppress a smile as I bit my lip.

Railan chuckled again, his hand tightening on my hip. 'Good girl,' he murmured as he pushed me down on the couch.

I let out a small gasp as Railan's lips found mine, his hands roaming over my body with a fierce hunger. Then, just as abruptly as he had started, Railan pulled away and made his way to the door.

'I'll see you later then,' he said with a wink before disappearing out of the room, leaving me there alone and completely flustered.

I took a deep breath, trying to steady my nerves as I quickly righted myself. This was dangerous territory, but I couldn't deny the excitement that came with it. I had to remind myself that I still had to be careful. I couldn't afford to let myself become too careless. If I made one mistake, Lady Amaranta would know. I couldn't let anything compromise our positions or the safety of my family. We just needed to hold out until the ball.

But the ball itself was like a dark shadow that loomed over me. I was excited but also scared. Railan would announce his intentions to the whole city, and that would no doubt invite the scrutiny and ire of not only the other Prime Mages, but also the gentry, the Creed, and everyone, really.

Relationships between magi and mundi were generally frowned upon. "Tainting" the bloodline was what people said. It's one of the reasons that the radical group, Magi Primacy, exists. They believe in magi purity and view us mundi as lesser, like animals. I felt doubt creep into the back of my mind, and I wrapped my arms around myself. It was too late for doubts; I was already in too deep to back down now. Railan had promised to protect me, and I had to believe in him. Even still, he was only the twelfth Prime Mage, the most unstable position. His favour with the Celestial Lady only hung on by a thread; any wrong move would see it break, and the Lady would discard him. I didn't want to be responsible for destroying all of his hopes and dreams.

I needed to stop thinking about such things.

Chapter 23

The ball was fast approaching, and only one detail remained: our outfits. I noticed an appointment had been made to visit Aizel. I felt a slight pang of jealousy as I got ready for the visit. I would have to try and find something within my budget while Railan was hashing out his grand design. I couldn't expect him to get me something fancy, especially from there. The cost would be astronomical. Besides, Lady Aizel's talents would be wasted on me since I was still confined to shades of brown. Brown could be beautiful, but it still felt lacklustre when I thought about the sea of rainbows that would be all the other guests.

I waited nervously in the foyer for Railan as he finished up his last meeting for the day. Lady Aizel's work was not to be rushed, and so the entire evening had been cleared just to see her. The front door was wide open as craftsmen and other contractors shuffled in and out, bringing with them decor and other important articles for the ball. The main ballroom was buzzing as physical preparations had already begun. The head butler, John, was busy directing people to where they needed to be, and Leonid was helping as best as he could. They looked a little flustered but were otherwise doing their jobs expertly. I couldn't help but smile to myself. The staff were truly next level here.

I was grateful to work with competent people, even though I had initially prepared myself for complete incompetence.

'Are you ready?' Railan's voice cut through my thoughts, and I let out a little squeak as I looked up at him.

I quickly composed myself and stood up straight, smoothing out my dress. 'Yes, I'm ready,' I replied, trying to sound more confident than I felt.

Railan gave me a small smile before gesturing for me to follow him outside. As we walked towards the waiting sleigh, my nerves continued to grow. I wondered if I would be able to find anything nice or if I would simply end up wearing my slightly fancier uniform.

As we pulled up outside Aizel's, I caught myself staring in awe. Here I was visiting such a high-end store for the second time. I never thought I'd visit it once, let alone twice. It was just as dazzling as last time, with new, more luxurious dresses and suits propped up in the windows. Lady Aizel was truly a master of her craft. I stepped off the sleigh and turned to face the street where the more, er, accommodating stores stood.

'Shall I meet you here at your scheduled end time?' I asked Railan.

Railan gave me a puzzled look. 'Where are you going? You're coming in with me?'

'Ah, I, um, I need to find something to wear, so I figured I'd just browse somewhere else while you were with Lady Aizel...' I muttered, feeling slightly flustered.

Railan frowned slightly, his expression one of confusion. 'What are you talking about? This appointment is just as much for you as it is for me,' he said, his voice tinged with smug affection. 'I want you to look your best for the ball.'

I felt a flush creep up my neck. 'I-I don't want to inconvenience you or spend too much,' I said, looking down at my feet. 'Lady Aizel's talents would be wasted on me anyway.'

Railan let out a small chuckle, shaking his head. 'You really don't understand, do you? You're not an inconvenience, and as for the cost, don't worry about it. I want you to feel confident and beautiful at the ball. Don't forget, it is our courtship ball, you're the one who will be in the spotlight. And believe me, Lady Aizel's talents are not wasted on anyone,' he took my hand and placed a kiss upon it before he led me towards the entrance of the store.

I blushed hard, uncomfortable with his public display of affection. We were supposed to be keeping things on the down low. I knew he would simply do what he wanted regardless, but still, I had some sense of self-preservation. The subtle scent of roses and fabric hit my nose as soon as the door opened, and the place was just as beautiful as I remembered. I couldn't let myself get distracted. I was technically still working, and so I scanned the room for Lady Aizel's attendant. I let out a small sigh of relief as I spotted the familiar-looking woman already making her way over to us. She was as professional and calculating as last time as she walked straight past me before I could make Railan's introduction.

'Lord Railan, it's a pleasure to see you again,' the woman purred. 'Lady Aizel is waiting for you now,' she said as she reached out to brush against his arm.

Railan gave her a polite smile but didn't seem to reciprocate her flirtatious behaviour. 'Thank you, I'm looking forward to our meeting,' he replied smoothly. He then turned to me, offering his arm. 'Shall we?' he asked, his tone warm and reassuring.

The woman's eyes flicked over to me, and I could feel her assessing, judging gaze. 'Please follow me,' she said, gesturing towards the back of the store.

The opulence of the store was overwhelming, and I couldn't imagine anything in here being within my price range. But I reminded myself of Railan's words and tried to relax. If he wanted to buy me something from here, could I really deny him? It did seem like a waste, though.

We reached a door at the end of a long hallway, and the woman knocked softly before opening it and ushering us inside. Lady Aizel was seated at a large desk, poring over sketches and fabric swatches. She looked up as we entered, a warm smile spreading across her face as her calculating eyes flicked from Railan to me and back.

'Lord Railan, how lovely to see you again,' she said, standing up and extending a hand towards him. 'And this must be Lady Isla. It's a pleasure to meet you.'

I shook her hand, feeling a little awestruck. Lady Aizel was a legend in the fashion industry, and I was honoured to be in her presence.

'J-Just Isla, my Lady,' I corrected her.

'Oh, of course,' she continued to smile warmly at me as she turned her attention to Railan. 'So, I gather you're here for something special for your little ball?' she asked, settling back into her seat and gesturing for us to take a seat opposite her.

Railan cleared his throat. 'Yes, I was hoping we could discuss outfits for the upcoming ball,' he said, his eyes flicking towards me for a moment before returning to Lady Aizel.

'Of course,' Lady Aizel said, clasping her hands together. 'I have been anticipating your appointment since I received the invitation. It is such a wonderful opportunity to showcase my designs,' she paused for a moment before continuing. 'And what kind of look were you envisioning, Lord Railan?'

Railan hesitated for a moment before responding. 'I was thinking of something elegant and eye-catching, but not too flashy, perhaps something similar to the last suit you made me,' he said. 'Though that's not my main concern,' he said as he placed his hand gently on the small of my back. 'I want Isla to be the focus of the night.'

I blushed at his words, feeling utterly embarrassed by the attention. Lady Aizel, however, seemed pleased by the challenge. 'I see,' she said, her eyes glinting with excitement. 'And what is your vision, my dear?'

She pulled out a sketchbook and readied her pencil as she waited eagerly for my response. I opened my mouth to speak, but no words came out. What did I want? I didn't know.

'I... I, um, I suppose something in brown,' I mumbled nervously as I played with my hands. 'Something... subtle.'

Lady Aizel and Railan both raised their brows at me, and I wanted to melt into the couch and disappear.

'A-A mundus must wear brown, that is the rule of the Creed,' I tried to justify myself.

Lady Aizel's expression softened, and she placed a reassuring hand on mine. 'My dear, I'm well aware of the rules,' she said kindly as she flicked her eyes to Railan.

I could feel his grip tighten around my waist as he pulled me closer. 'You needn't worry about that silly rule, Isla. You are going to be my consort and therefore you are entitled to wear my colours.'

I wanted to die as he uttered the words, and I leaned back slightly, looking at him in disbelief.

'It's ok, Lady Isla. Lord Railan has already informed me of your situation,' Lady Aizel tried to reassure me, but her words only filled me with more dread.

'My situation?' I asked as I raised my brow at Railan.

What exactly had he been telling people without my knowledge?

Railan cleared his throat, his grip on me relaxing a little. 'As my fiancée, you have certain privileges associated with my rank as Prime Mage...' he trailed off, unsure of how to continue.

Fiancée?

I was internally screaming. Why would he say that? I'd agreed to courting, not an engagement. I could feel my heart racing as I looked at Railan, my mind trying to make sense of his words. Had he really just called me his fiancée? I had only barely agreed to courting because he'd begged me, and now he was talking about an engagement? He said he would take it slow, but this was not slow. Panic started to set in as I wondered what I had gotten myself into.

'Railan, what do you mean by fiancée?' I asked, my voice shaking slightly.

Railan looked at me with a mixture of concern and confusion, as if he didn't understand why I was asking such a question. 'Isla, I thought we had discussed this. You agreed to court me, which is a step towards engagement,' he said, his tone gentle but firm. 'And as my consort, it is only natural that people would refer to you as my fiancée.'

I felt a lump form in my throat as I tried to process his words. Had I really agreed to such a thing? No. I'd agreed to courting, just courting. Why was he doing this? I could feel my heart pounding against my ribs painfully. And why did he have to do this here, of all places? I didn't know if Lady Aizel could be trusted.

'I...I don't know,' I stammered, feeling a sudden wave of fear and uncertainty wash over me. 'I think I need some time to think about all of this.'

Railan's expression softened, and he gently cupped my cheek, his thumb stroking my skin. 'Of course, my dear. We can talk about this later. But for now, we are here for an appointment. I just want you to understand that you can choose any colour your heart desires.'

Later? I wanted to talk about this now. I wanted to shake him silly for his recklessness, but he was right; we were here for business. I cleared my throat as I tried my best to compose myself. Lady Aizel was watching, and I didn't want to embarrass myself any more than I already had.

'No need to worry, Lady Isla, this is a safe space,' Lady Aizel tried to reassure me. 'Now, let us focus on the task at hand. Tell me about your preferences. Excluding brown, do you have a preferred colour? Any style dos and don'ts?'

I bit my lip as I tried to think of answers. I'd never had to think about what I wore. Varying versions of my Creed uniform had been the only thing I'd worn for the last nine years. I didn't know what looked good, I didn't know what I liked.

'I-I don't know, I've never thought about it,' I admitted. 'I suppose I'm partial to blues and greens, but I have no idea about style.'

Lady Aizel smiled understandingly. 'Not to worry, Lady Isla. That's what I'm here for. Let's start with your measurements, shall we?' She looked to Railan as she stood and offered me her hand. 'We shan't be too long, my Lord.'

I took her hand almost a little too eagerly as she helped me up and whisked me away to a more private room. As Lady Aizel took my measurements, I couldn't help but feel a little overwhelmed. This was all so new to me, and I didn't know how I was supposed to act or what I was supposed to say. What would Lady Amaranta think about this? Would she be enraged or elated? Marrying Railan would be as close as I could ever possibly get to him; there was no closer position. Yet, I couldn't help but feel like she would be unhappy. Even though Railan had said he would do everything in his power to free me from her hold, it didn't change the fact that she still owned me and my family. I knew that Lady Amaranta held similar views to those of the Magi Primacy, viewing the mundi as tools rather than real people. My thoughts left me feeling terrified.

Lady Aizel seemed to sense my unease and did her best to put me at ease, chatting pleasantly about various styles and colours as she worked.

Once she had finished, she gestured to a rack of dresses that had been set up in the corner of the room. 'Now, let's see what styles will suit you best.'

I approached the rack hesitantly, unsure of what I was supposed to do.

Lady Aizel stepped forward and began flipping through the dresses, holding them up to me and assessing them critically. "What about this one?" she said, holding up a deep blue gown with delicate beading along the bodice.

I looked at it uncertainly. It was certainly beautiful, but I wasn't sure if it was my style. I hadn't exactly worn anything without sleeves before.

'I'm not sure,' I said hesitantly. 'It's very...' I wanted to say immodest, but I also didn't want to offend Lady Aizel. 'Maybe something, um, more conservative,' I suggested, feeling a little self-conscious.

Lady Aizel nodded understandingly. 'Of course, my lady. Let's see if we can find something that fits your preferences,' she continued to flip through the rack, pulling out various gowns in shades of blue and green. Some had sleeves, while others had high necklines or more coverage.

As she held each dress up to me, I couldn't help but feel a little out of place. These dresses were so elegant and refined, and I felt like I was playing dress up in them. But as Lady Aizel encouraged me to try them on, I began to feel a little more confident.

After trying on several dresses, we finally settled on a simpler, classic design. Long sleeves and a high neckline, but still elegant and flattering. That felt more like me. Lady Aizel sat down with her sketchpad in hand as she eagerly scribbled down designs.

'Now for the final touch, what theme would you like?' she asked, her eyes shining with inspiration.

'Theme?' I frowned, unsure what she meant.

'I like to incorporate subtle themes, ideas, or concepts into my designs. For example, I recently designed a dress with a moon and stars motif for a client who loved stargazing. It can be anything that resonates with you or represents a special memory or interest,' Lady Aizel explained.

I thought for a moment. A theme? I'd never thought about anything like it before. I understood what they meant; I'd read about them before. What motif did I have? None. Railan had said I could use his colours, but what about his motifs? What was his motif, now that I thought about it? I closed my eyes, trying to visualise what kind of theme would complement us both.

Railan.

He was so... strange. He had eyes that were as deep and intense as the ocean, and his personality was just as volatile. He was like surging waves in a storm, but also as calm and cool as turquoise shallows when he wanted to be. He had hidden depths that I wasn't sure I'd ever be able to reach. He was the sea and I... what was I?

A tiny ship sailing into the unknown? No, I was more like a gentle breeze going along with the flow. I could stir the sea, make it rage if necessary. Alone, I was nothing, harmless, a simple gust through the trees. But with Railan, I could make waves, I could ask him to make a hurricane, and he would do it. It didn't matter what games he was trying to play. I was in far too deep; the undertow had already taken hold.

'Wind and water,' I finally said, my voice quiet. 'More specifically, the breeze that stirs the sea.'

Lady Aizel's eyes lit up at my suggestion. 'Oh, I love it! That's such a beautiful and unique theme. I can already imagine the designs,' she exclaimed, flipping through her sketchpad and jotting down notes.

My mind buzzed with excitement as she worked. It was amazing how Lady Aizel was able to take my vague idea and turn it into something tangible and beautiful. And the thought of wearing a dress that represented my connection with Railan made my heart race.

After several minutes of scribbling and drawing, Lady Aizel turned to me with a smile. 'I have some ideas for the design, but I would love to hear your input as well. What do you think of this?' She held up a sketch of a flowing gown in shades of blue and green, with delicate swirls and curls that evoked the movement of wind and water.

I gasped in delight. It was perfect. 'I love it,' I said, feeling a huge smile spread across my face. 'It's beautiful.'

Lady Aizel grinned. 'I'm so glad you like it. I can't wait to get started on the final design,' she flipped through her sketchpad, showing me more designs and colour schemes inspired by our theme of wind and water. I felt myself getting more and more excited with each page.

Each design subtly drew my thoughts back to Railan. I wondered what he would think of the dress, of the theme. Would he understand what it meant to me, how much he meant to me? I couldn't wait to find out. Even if he was rash and forward with his desires, I knew he only had me in mind. His passion had opened up doors for me that I never knew existed. He wanted to bring me into his world, a world that would otherwise be impossible. I wondered if he would like to match my theme. I knew he was partial to blues since they went well with his hair and made his eyes pop.

Lady Aizel wrapped up my design, and we returned to her main studio. Railan sat casually, his chin resting on his palm, an almost bored expression upon his features. He immediately sat up, his face lighting up as he saw us.

'How did you go, my love?' he asked eagerly.

'Great, Lady Aizel is truly a master,' I said meekly.

Railan grinned, his eyes shining with pride. 'Of course she is. I knew she would be the perfect designer for you,' he said, reaching out to take my hand. 'So, what did you come up with?'

I couldn't help but smile, a hint of heat upon my cheeks as Lady Aizel showed him the sketch she had made. 'We came up with the theme of wind and water,' I said, watching his face carefully for any signs of disapproval or confusion.

Railan's eyes widened in delight as he studied the sketch. 'Wow, this is amazing,' he said, his fingers tracing the lines of the dress. 'It's perfect for you, my love. Beautiful, just like you.'

A warm flush spread across my cheeks at his words. 'I'm glad you like it,' I said softly, squeezing his hand. 'I was thinking of you.'

Railan's gaze flickered up to meet mine, his eyes softening with affection. 'You were thinking of me?' he repeated, his voice low and husky.

I nodded, feeling my heart beat faster in my chest. 'Yes,' I said, unable to look away from his intense gaze. 'I-I wanted the dress to represent us. Powerful and free like the ocean, but also gentle and calming like the wind.'

Railan's expression grew even softer as he listened to my words, his fingers tracing patterns on the sketch. 'That's beautiful,' he said, his voice filled with admiration. 'You always know how to make me feel special, my love.'

I smiled, feeling a sense of warmth and contentment settle over me. 'I just want to make you happy,' I said as I lowered my gaze.

Railan leaned in closer, his hand lifting my chin so that I had to meet his gaze once again. 'You already do, my love,' he said, his eyes searching mine. 'You make me happier than I ever thought possible.'

I felt my heart swell with love and affection as I looked into his eyes. 'Y-you shouldn't keep Lady Aizel waiting, she still needs to design your outfit,' I mumbled quietly.

As much as I wanted to be close to him, now was not the time or place.

Railan chuckled softly, his thumb brushing over my cheekbone. 'You're right,' he said, his gaze lingering on my face for a moment longer before he pulled back and turned to Lady Aizel. 'I'm ready whenever you are,' he said, his tone friendly and relaxed.

Lady Aizel nodded, a small smile playing on her lips. 'Wonderful,' she said as she motioned for him to follow her. 'We have a lot of work to do, but I'm confident we'll come up with something truly spectacular.'

I watched as Railan and Lady Aizel disappeared into the depths of the studio, feeling a sense of anticipation and excitement building within me. I knew that the next few days would be a whirlwind of activity and preparation, and while I didn't feel ready for it, I would do my best. More importantly, I needed to remember to clarify things with Railan. He wanted to marry me, and while the thought made me excited, it also filled me with fear. Courting and marriage were two very different things, and I wasn't sure if I was ready for the latter. We hadn't even known each other that long. I could feel an intense blush spreading across my cheeks. I needed to confront him.

Chapter 24

By the time we had finished at Aizel's, the sun had already set for the day, and the street lamps cast the city in a soft gold and blue tone. I didn't waste any time admiring the view; it was one I'd seen many times. I stepped into the sleigh, and Railan followed close behind, his body close to mine as he sat next to me. As the sleigh started moving, I took a deep breath, trying to calm my nerves. I knew I needed to talk to Railan, but I wasn't sure how to bring up the topic without making things awkward between us.

'Well, that was fun,' Railan mused as he looked out the window at the snow-covered streets as they passed.

He reached out to grab my hand, squeezing it as he placed it on his lap. I looked at our hands entwined, comfortable, as if they were made for each other. I needed to speak up, but the words were caught in my throat. I closed my eyes and took in a shallow breath as I leaned into his arm, hiding my face against his cloak. I could talk to him about anything, yet that didn't stop me from feeling scared.

Railan must have sensed my hesitation, as he turned his head to look at me, concern etched on his features. 'Is everything alright, my love?' he asked softly, his hand rubbing soothing circles on the back of my hand.

I lifted my head, my gaze meeting his. 'E-Eli... there's something I need to talk to you about,' I said, my voice barely above a whisper as I forced out the words.

Railan's expression softened as he turned his body towards me, giving me his full attention. 'Of course, what is it?' he asked, his voice gentle and reassuring.

I took a deep breath, gathering my thoughts. 'It's about... about what you said earlier,' I started, feeling my cheeks flush with embarrassment.

'About us getting married?' Railan finished for me, his expression serious as he waited for me to continue.

I nodded, grateful that he understood what I was trying to say. 'I-I don't know if I...' I struggled to speak as my throat felt dry. 'You're going too fast... I'm not sure I'm ready or able to do something like that given my situation...' I admitted, my voice barely audible as I looked down at our intertwined hands.

That's right, I was still a slave. I couldn't make decisions like this for myself.

Railan's expression softened, his thumb stroking the back of my hand gently. 'I understand,' he said, his voice calm and reassuring. 'I never meant to pressure you into anything, Isla. I just... I love you, and I know that I want to spend the rest of my life with you. It may seem irrational to you, but I know you are my other half, the one who makes me whole.'

My heart skipped a beat at his words, and tears prickled at the corners of my eyes. Why did he have to be so... I couldn't even describe the way he made me feel.

'Eli... I love you, I do, it's just... You don't seem to understand my position,' I whispered as I let out a soft sigh. 'I agreed to be courted by you, but... we both know that relationships like ours are meant to be unspoken. This ball, calling me your fiancée, those are dangerous things, things that make me scared... and you should be too.'

Railan's expression turned serious as he listened to my words. 'I understand the risks, Isla,' he said, his voice low and firm. 'But I refuse to let anyone or anything dictate what I can and cannot do. I promised I would free you and your family, and I will. Please don't doubt me. I would do anything for you. I would do anything to prove my love to you. I would take the stars from the sky, the heart from the sea, I would even turn against the Celestial Lady for you if you asked for it.'

His words left me breathless, and I felt a warmth spread throughout my body. He was so passionate, so determined, and it was hard not to be swept away by his intensity. But at the same time, I couldn't ignore the danger of his words. I quickly put my hand over his mouth to stop him from spouting further heresy.

'Please don't say things like that...' I pleaded quietly.

Railan removed my hand from his mouth and took it in his again. 'I'm sorry,' he said softly. 'I get carried away sometimes.'

I smiled weakly at him, trying to lighten the mood. 'It's alright, Eli. I know you mean well.'

'But you're still afraid,' he said, his voice barely above a whisper.

I nodded, feeling tears prick at the corners of my eyes. 'Yes, I am,' I admitted, my voice shaking slightly. 'Everything... It's just a lot all at once... I need time to think, to understand how I actually feel.'

Railan squeezed my hand gently, his eyes full of understanding. 'I understand, Isla,' he said softly. 'I'm sorry... I'll try to be more patient. I don't want you to be uncomfortable.'

I looked up at him, my heart full of gratitude for this man who had shown me nothing but kindness and love despite everything. 'Thank you, Eli,' I whispered, feeling tears slide down my cheeks. 'I... I don't know what I'd do without you.'

Railan gently wiped away my tears with his thumb before pulling me into a tight embrace. 'You'll never have to find out,' he whispered into my hair. 'I'll always be here for you. Always.'

In that moment, wrapped in Railan's arms, I felt safe and loved. Did everything really matter that much? Was I overthinking everything? Maybe, maybe not. Regardless, I was done thinking about it for now. I just wanted to enjoy the comfort of Railan's warm embrace.

We sat in comfortable silence for the rest of the ride back to his estate. He didn't let me go, not even for a second. A part of me wished I didn't have any doubts, that I could just say yes and let him make me his wife, but I knew it wouldn't be that easy. The sleigh finally came to a stop, and Railan helped me out. The cold air was somewhat refreshing as my boots crunched into the snow. He held my hand firmly, refusing to let go as we entered the mansion.

'It's late, we should head to bed,' I said as I stopped, expecting him to let me go.

'We should,' he nodded in agreement, but didn't let me go; instead, he continued to pull me along behind him.

'I mean... I should go to my room,' I rephrased.

Railan stopped and turned towards me, his expression serious. 'I know,' he said, his voice low. 'But... can you stay with me tonight?'

I hesitated, feeling a mix of emotions. On one hand, I wanted nothing more than to be close to him, to feel his warmth and comfort. On the other hand, I didn't want to do anything that would compromise our position.

'I... I don't know, Eli,' I said, my voice barely above a whisper. 'What if someone sees us?'

Railan cupped my face in his hands, forcing me to look at him. 'I'll protect you, Isla,' he said, his eyes full of sincerity. 'No one will ever know.'

I looked into his eyes, seeing the love and passion there. It was hard to resist, hard to deny him anything when he looked at me like that. 'Alright,' I whispered as I gave him a small nod, feeling my heart rate increase.

Railan's face broke out into a wide grin as he pulled me close, wrapping his arms around me. 'Thank you, Isla,' he said, his voice full of gratitude. 'I promise, nothing will happen that you don't want to happen.'

I nodded as I was overwhelmed with sudden excitement and fear. This was dangerous, this was wrong. I knew that I shouldn't give in to him like this, yet I couldn't help but fall harder. Being with him was right, it felt right. We made our way to his room, his hand never leaving mine. When we arrived, he closed the door behind us and locked it before he turned to face me. His eyes were already dark with a burning desire that threatened to outshine even the flames of the fireplace. I felt my breath sharpen as I looked at him. I knew what he wanted, and as much as I wanted it too, I didn't feel like I was in the right state of mind. The day had been a whirlwind of emotions that left me feeling drained.

'Are you sure you want to do this, Isla?' he asked, his eyes searching mine for any signs of doubt.

I took a deep breath, shaking my head slowly. I hadn't denied him for quite some time, and I found myself nervous to see how he would react.

'N-no...' I said softly, my voice shaking like a leaf. 'I-I think I just want to sleep right now...'

Railan's face fell slightly, but he quickly composed himself and nodded. 'Of course, my love,' he said, his voice gentle and understanding. 'We can just sleep.'

He led me over to his bed and pulled back the covers, motioning for me to climb in. I took a moment to undress, shedding my many layers until all that was left was my slip and glasses. Perhaps it was cruel to tempt him like that, but as I placed my glasses on the nightstand and plunged myself into relative blindness, I felt grateful for this little reprieve. Railan stripped his own clothes before he climbed in beside me and wrapped his arms around me, pulling me close.

'Just rest, Isla,' he murmured. 'I'm here. Always.'

I could feel the heat of his skin sinking into mine, and the steady beating of his heart was like a gentle lullaby to my ears. I closed my eyes and allowed myself to sink into the warmth and safety of his embrace. It was a relief to have a moment of calm amid all the chaos. As

I drifted off to sleep, guilt plagued my mind for denying him, but I knew deep down that it was the right decision for me at that moment.

I dreamt that I was a little witchlight flying free through the Maentaean forests. I was shrouded in vibrant hues that shifted through the colours of the rainbow. It was strange but beautiful. I felt light, free, and curious. The forest was vast, and yet I found myself floating amidst a field of ice flowers, their blooms sharp and crystalline. A gentle breeze encouraged me forward, and I followed it willingly.

However, I soon found myself frozen in place. The world had stopped moving, and it left me confused. But then I saw that I had become entangled in a spider's web. The delicate threads were nearly invisible, and though I buzzed and jingled, I could not get free. My panic soon summoned the spider, big and black. Its glossy eyes were like cold, malicious voids as they stared at me, hungry for my flesh. Slowly, it crept forward, its long, pincer-like legs sending a shiver down my spine.

No!

I didn't want to be consumed. I wanted to be free.

'There you are. I've been looking for you everywhere, Sil,' a familiar, gentle voice called.

Suddenly, I felt gentle fingers around my waist, and the spider was moving away from me, or more like I was moving away from it. I looked back to find Railan clutching me close to his chest. He held me close, tenderly, as if he was scared I would break. I felt warmth rush through me, warmth that was happy and peaceful and content. I still wanted to be closer to him. I could feel the ebb and flow of magic that surged through his veins, and I longed to be a part of him-

I awoke with a gasp, my head fuzzy as the dream remained fresh in my mind.

What a strange dream.

I closed my eyes, but I soon opened them again. Railan still held me close, his arms like steel bands around me, making it hard for me to move. I tried to wiggle out of his grasp, but he only held me tighter.

This was fine, except now I was feeling uncomfortable. I needed to change position, but now I was stuck.

'Eli,' I whispered, nudging him slightly. 'Please let me go.'

He shifted slightly, his arms loosening their grip on me. 'I'm sorry, my love,' he murmured sleepily. 'Is something wrong?'

'No, it's just...I can't get comfortable, I want to be the big spoon,' I admitted, feeling a flush rise to my cheeks. It was silly, I knew, but I couldn't help the way I felt.

Railan chuckled softly, his breath tickling my ear. 'Well, we can't have that,' he said, his voice full of amusement. 'Let me help.'

He finally released me as he shifted his weight and rolled over onto his side. I let out a small sigh of relief, feeling a little freer. I rolled over and slipped my arm around his waist as I tucked my head against his back. He was so very warm. I could feel the steady rhythm of his heartbeat beneath my ear, and the rise and fall of his chest was soothing.

'Is that better?' he mumbled.

I nodded, feeling a sense of contentment wash over me. 'Yes, thank you,' I said softly.

We lay like that for a while, just enjoying the closeness and comfort of each other's embrace. As I drifted off to sleep again, I knew that I was making the right decision by denying him earlier. We would have other nights for passion, but tonight was just for comfort and rest. And in that moment, that was all I needed.

Chapter 25

I woke up to the sound of Railan's gentle snores and the soft light of the rising sun peeking through the curtains. I turned to face him and smiled as I watched him sleep. He looked so peaceful, so content. I wanted to freeze this moment in time, to stay here with him forever. But I knew that wasn't possible.

I watched him for a while, my mind wandering back to thoughts of yesterday. He had said he would do anything for me, even turn on the Celestial Lady. But was that really true? I had many questions, and I wouldn't be able to seriously consider his proposal until I had answers. But for now, I would let him dream a little more.

I gently untangled myself from his arms and got dressed, trying to be as quiet as possible so as not to wake him. As I stood by the door, ready to leave, Railan stirred and opened his eyes. He looked at me and smiled sleepily.

'Good morning, Isla,' he said, his voice still thick with sleep.

'Good morning,' I replied, my voice quiet.

'Where are you going? There's still a little time before my first meeting,' he patted the bed beside him, beckoning me to return.

'I'm going to work,' I informed him.

'Work can wait,' he groaned.

'Not for me,' I said simply.

'What if I said it could?' he said playfully.

'Are you asking me as Eli or are you commanding me as Lord Railan?' My tone was frosty. For some reason, I wasn't in the mood to play with him.

Railan's smile faltered slightly as he realized he had crossed a line. 'I apologize, Isla. I was just trying to be playful,' he said softly.

'I know, and I appreciate it,' I replied, softening my tone. 'But I have responsibilities that I can't ignore.'

'I understand,' he said, nodding. 'I'll see you later then.'

I nodded and left the room, feeling a mix of emotions. On one hand, I was glad that I had stood my ground and not let him influence my decisions. On the other hand, I couldn't help but feel a pang of sadness as I walked away from him. Our time together was always so fleeting, and I didn't know when I would be able to see him again.

But I couldn't let those thoughts consume me. I had work to do, and I needed to focus on that. As I made my way to the office, my mind drifted back to the dream I had had last night. The spider's web, the warmth of Railan's embrace, the sense of contentment and peace. It was all so vivid, so real. Maybe it was just my subconscious trying to tell me something, or maybe it was just a silly dream that didn't mean anything.

Either way, I knew that I needed to focus on reality and not get lost in my fantasies. Railan was a complicated man, and I had a lot to consider before making any decisions. But for now, I would just focus on my work and try to push those thoughts aside.

I spent the next two days carefully avoiding Railan. He tried to get me alone, what felt like an infinite number of times, even going so far as to recruit the other staff for his little schemes to woo me back to his side. He didn't understand that I needed time and space to think. His meddling was also making it hard for me to work. I knew that I shouldn't ignore him, that he probably genuinely wanted my help with the ball preparations, but I was confident he could handle things by himself for just a little while.

I was still trying to decide what I wanted to do. Everything was too complicated. I'd written down a bunch of questions that I needed him to answer, and now I was simply putting it off. But I knew I couldn't put it off forever, and with the ball mere days away, I figured I should make a definitive decision before then.

I knew Railan would be free after dinner tonight, and that seemed like the perfect time to turn the tables and ambush him with my questions. I felt a little devious, but I was also determined to see it through. I wouldn't let him derail me. I was going to stand my ground.

Yet as I stood outside his bedroom door, I couldn't stop from trembling slightly. My stomach felt heavy as if it was filled with stones, and my throat was dry despite just having a drink before arriving. No, I couldn't allow myself to talk myself out of doing this. I needed this. I took a big gulp of air, letting my lungs fully expand before exhaling.

Calm.

You can do this, Isla.

I knocked on the door sternly. 'My Lord, it's me, Isla. May I come in?'

Railan's response was almost immediate. 'Yes, of course!' his voice was as smooth as ever, but there was a hint of something else there, something that I couldn't quite place.

I pushed the door open and stepped inside. The room was dimly lit, the only light coming from a few candles scattered around the room and the dying fireplace. Railan was sitting in a plush armchair by the fire, focusing on a book in his lap. I paused as I saw him, my breath catching. The shadows made his features appear sharper, more dangerous in that sensual kind of way. His freckles almost seemed to glitter as if he were some kind of mythical creature.

No, stop being distracted.

I quickly shook my head as he looked up at me, his eyes tightening playfully before a small smile played at the corners of his lips.

'I've been waiting for you,' he said, setting the book aside and greeting me.

'I know... I just needed some space,' I said, my voice steady despite the nervousness I felt inside. 'But I'm ready to talk now, if you'll let me.'

Railan's expression softened as he approached me. 'Of course! You may have noticed, I've been hoping to speak with you as well,' he gestured for me to take a seat on the nearby couch, which I did.

I watched him carefully as he sat down next to me, my fingers tightening around my notebook as his leg brushed my skirt. He reached out to take my hand, but I simply leaned back and out of his way. I didn't want to be distracted, and I knew I would be if I let him touch me.

Railan noticed my reaction but didn't comment on it, instead choosing to speak. 'What would you like to talk about, Isla?' he asked, his tone gentle but tentative.

I took a deep breath and opened my notebook, flipping to the page where I had written my questions. 'I have a few things that I need to ask you, Eli,' I said, my voice firm. 'And I need you to be completely honest with me.'

Railan nodded slowly, his eyes fixed on me and filled with just a hint of uncertainty. 'Of course... ask away.'

I nodded and cleared my throat before I spoke. 'If I am to even consider your proposal, then I need to know that we have similar life plans. I want your honest answers,' I said, watching him intently for his subtle reactions.

Railan nodded once more, his expression now serious with just the slightest hint of relief behind his eyes. 'I understand. Please, ask me whatever you need to.'

I took a deep breath and began. 'Firstly, do you plan on having children?' I asked, trying to keep my voice steady even though my cheeks blushed red.

Railan's expression now had the subtle hint of a smirk on his lips. 'Yes,' he said, almost too quickly. 'I haven't given it much thought in terms of how many, but I've always known I've wanted a family of my own.'

My eyes fluttered slightly at his response. A family of his own. I kept my face neutral, though I had a big smile on the inside.

'Say that I was hypothetically pregnant, you understand that there's a chance our children will end up as mundi like me. How do you feel about that? Would you play favourites based on blood purity? Or gender?'

Railan's expression became serious as he listened to my questions, and he took a moment to consider them before answering, clearly trying not to rush. 'I don't plan on playing favourites,' he said firmly. 'Every child is precious, regardless of their abilities or gender. I want to love our many children equally and do everything in my power to ensure that they have the best possible life,' he paused for a moment before continuing. 'I don't care about blood or magic or any of that nonsense. I want to love our family for who they are, Isla, and that is not based on their usefulness or potential.'

I felt a weight lift off my shoulders at his answer, and the hint of a smile spread across my lips, though I quickly pushed it back down. 'I see,' I said, keeping my cards close to my chest. I took a deep breath, feeling a little more at ease now that we had addressed some of my concerns. 'And what if... I'm unable to bear your children?'

Railan's eyes widened for a split second before he reined himself in. It appeared the idea hadn't exactly been something he had considered. 'What... do you mean by that?' he asked, his voice more guarded.

'I mean, what if I can't have children? Would you still want me then?'

I saw the subtle hitch in his breath, the way his throat clenched just a fraction. He turned his face away from me for a second, his gaze landing on the dying embers of the fireplace.

'That won't happen,' he said, almost under his breath. 'I know you'll be able to...' he faced back towards me, his eyes ablaze with determination. 'We will have children together. I know it, so please don't suggest otherwise.

'Eli...' My fingers tightened around the pages of my notebook, crinkling them slightly. 'I'm asking what if...'

'No,' he shook his head. 'There is no "what if".'

He seemed so certain. But then his expression softened slightly as he saw the seriousness on my face. I wanted a real answer, not what he wished to be true.

'I... but, hypothetically... if that isn't possible, then...' he hesitated as if the mere thought were painful. But then he pushed forward. 'We... we will find other ways to create a happy and fulfilling life together, regardless. There are... so many other ways we can enjoy each other's company and build a life together. Also... I am sure many children in orphanages would... benefit from our care and lifestyle.'

A wave of relief washed over me at his words. I could see that the idea of not having children of our own was hard for him to grasp, but it was still at least a little reassuring to know that he was willing to adapt to whatever life may bring us.

Railan must have been able to see my relief as he reached over and took my hand, squeezing it gently. 'I love you, Isla...' he spoke softly as he brought my hand up to kiss my knuckles, his lips lingering upon my skin. 'And truly, all I want is nothing more than to build a happy life together. I have a plan of how I want things to go, but I'm also prepared to tackle any curveballs thrown our way, no matter how... hard or painful.'

I squeezed his hand back, letting it linger in his grasp even as his touch made my heart race. 'And what if... something bad happens?' I asked, my face wrinkling with a slight grimace. 'What if... what if me... or our children... end up sick... or disabled?'

My father immediately flashed to the forefront of my mind. The way his injury had not only ruined his own life, but also my whole family's life and future. It was the thing that had led me here, the only reason I was even in this situation to begin with. I shuddered at the memory, the slight prickle of pain in my chest.

Railan seemed to pick up on my distress as he gently coaxed me to come and lean against him. I was reluctant for a moment, not wanting our conversation to derail. But I also couldn't deny that I needed that little bit of comfort. So I leaned in closer, letting my head rest against his shoulder as he lightly wrapped his arm around my waist to keep me close.

'That won't happen either...' he murmured against my hair.

I shook my head in firm disagreement. 'Don't pretend to be so naive...'

He let out a soft sigh. 'Fine... nothing bad will happen to us, but if it did... of course I would still be here to love and support you and our family. I'm not going to abandon you, not now and not ever. I'll do everything in my power to make sure that we figure things out. And even if I can't do anything... I'll still love you.'

His words were reassuring, and my heart swelled with comfort knowing that he would be there for me and our family no matter what challenges we might face. I snuggled just a bit closer to him. 'You'll always love me, hm?'

'Of course I will. I've made up my mind on that much,' Railan chuckled softly, brushing a bit of stray hair back from my face.

'And is that what you think marriage will be? Just... loving me? But... is that it?' I tilted my head slightly into his palm as his fingers brushed against my ear.

Railan took a deep breath before answering, his expression softening. 'I... I hope so, honestly. I want to just love you and not worry about anything else,' he admitted. 'But I know that's not... realistic,' he sighed. 'Maybe I just hope that things don't change too much from how they are now, you know?'

'So just us... sneaking around and living in the shadows?' I raised a brow.

'What? N-No, that's not what I meant!' he said defensively. 'I mean I'd like to keep feeling the same way I do now, just in the light... proudly and openly.'

Proudly and openly.

To love me proudly and openly was the most dangerous part, yet my heart continued to sing with joy at the thought of what would inevitably be our mutual destruction.

'And what happens... if you grow sick of me?'

Railan's face softened, and he pressed me tighter against his side. 'I love you, and I want to be with you. I want a family with you. I want to share an interesting and long life with you. I don't want to discard you. I don't want to think of a time without you,' his grip on my face tightened as he gently turned my face up to look at him. 'There is no more life without you, without us. Because that is the only life I can see as worth having.'

I wanted to cry a little, as this is exactly what I wanted to hear. It filled me like a bottle held empty for so long.

'And... What about outside temptations?' I asked quietly, my throat catching at this question.

Railan remained firm yet tender in the face of my bombardment. 'Temptation...' he repeated the word, making a face as if the mere thought was sour. 'I consider myself lucky to even have you. Besides, there's no point in having a mere snack when you have a feast at home, you know what I mean?'

I chuckled softly at his comparison. I wasn't sure how I felt about being called a feast, but it did make enough sense to me. 'I suppose I do,' I paused, my voice growing quiet again. 'But what if... I reject you? I don't want to, but I... can't promise that I won't in the future, for whatever reason.'

Railan looked at me intently, his eyes searching mine. 'I will wait then. You know that I will always wait for you. My bed -and my heart- is a place you will always be welcome. Besides...' he smiled and leaned in a bit closer so that his breath ghosted over the shell of my ear, 'you can't resist me for long.'

There was no stopping the blush that crept over my cheeks. Dammit, Railan! He always had a way with words. I swallowed hard, fighting back temptation with everything I had.

'I have one last question... what would you do if you lost the Celestial Lady's favour because of me?'

Railan's smile faltered before hardening, and he took a deep breath before answering. 'I would sacrifice everything for you, including my wealth, status, and even my life. What's important to me is our life together.'

I felt a lump form in my throat at his words. It was both reassuring and scary to know that he was willing to give up everything for me. 'I don't want you to lose everything because of me,' I said softly, feeling a subtle pang of guilt.

Railan pressed me into his side once more, his chin rubbing gently against the top of my head. 'I don't want that either. But I want you to know that my love for you is more important to me than anything else. I will always choose you, no matter the cost.'

I looked into his eyes and saw the sincerity and love reflected in them. It was a powerful feeling, knowing that someone loved me that much. I felt my heart flutter. It felt as if the weight of the world had finally been lifted from my shoulders. We were on the same page, even if he wanted to move faster than I did. I wasn't entirely confident in my decision to accept his proposal yet, but I did feel completely and utterly confident in my love for him. I placed my notebook to the side and threw myself into his arms, hugging him tight as tears threatened my eyes.

'Thank you, Eli,' I whispered against his chest. 'I love you, always.'

Railan wrapped his arms around me, holding me close. 'I love you too, Isla,' he whispered back. 'Always and forever.'

I held him close for a little while; the subtle movement of his chest was calming, and the sound of his heartbeat was soothing. Everything was perfect. Well, as perfect as reality could be. I felt light and relaxed as all the tension between us seemed to disappear. I pulled back slightly and gave him a shy little smile.

'Would you like to know my answers?' I blushed, feeling a little vulnerable.

Railan smiled at me, his eyes shining with love and curiosity. 'Of course. I want to know everything about you,' he said, his voice warm and gentle.

I fluttered my eyelashes as I thought about my answers. These were questions I'd never thought I'd be able to answer, not now and certainly not with someone like Railan.

I bit my lip as I prepared to tell him my most intimate thoughts and desires. 'I want my own family too. I've always wanted to have children of my own. I would have as many as the Celestial Lady is willing to bless me with, especially with you as their father,' I almost felt faint. My cheeks were so intensely on fire. 'I'm glad you don't care about blood purity because that's not something I can change, even if I wanted to. A-and even if it didn't happen, I would be sad, but I know there are other ways to make a family.'

Railan looked at me with a soft smile on his lips, his eyes filled with love and adoration. 'Isla, you make me so happy,' he said, his voice low and gentle. 'I want that too, a family with you. I don't care about blood purity or any of that nonsense. As long as we love each other, that's all that matters,' He leaned down and kissed my forehead, his lips warm against my skin. 'And if we can't have children, we'll find another way to make a family. I promise you that.'

Relief and happiness washed over me. It was so wonderful to be with someone who accepted me for who I was and didn't judge me for things that were out of my control. He was truly a strange and remarkable young man. I didn't need nor want to think anymore. Time was a construct that didn't matter. Being with him was right, the only right thing in my life. I couldn't put into words the way he truly made me feel. He made me feel alive and real, seen and heard, loved and respected, and so much more.

I leaned up and placed a soft kiss upon his lips, a small, simple expression of my affection. Railan responded to my kiss with a gentle one of his own, his lips soft and warm against mine. It was a sweet and tender moment, filled with love and trust. We pulled away, still holding each other close, our foreheads touching.

'I have a question of my own,' Railan said, his voice serious but gentle.

'What is it?' I asked, looking up at him with curiosity.

'I haven't asked you properly yet, but... will you marry me?' he asked, his eyes shining with hope and love.

I felt my heart skip a beat, and my breath caught in my throat. This was it, the moment I had been dreading for so long, yet now it only made my heart swell with happiness. I looked at him, really looked at him, and saw the love and sincerity in his eyes. I didn't need to think about my answer; I already knew it.

'Yes,' I said, my voice barely above a whisper. 'I will marry you, Elieason Railan.'

Railan's face lit up with joy and relief as he pulled me close again. 'Thank you, Isla. You've made me the happiest man alive,' he said, his voice filled with emotion.

I wrapped my arms around his neck, feeling happy and content in his embrace. This was where I belonged, in his arms, with his love to guide me through life. For the first time in a long time, I felt hopeful and excited for the future.

I brought myself up to kiss him once more, this time more intensely and filled with more emotion. I wanted to pour everything I had to offer into this man, my love, my devotion, my body, everything. Railan responded to my kiss eagerly, his arms tightening around me. I pulled back slightly and allowed myself to slip onto his lap, my thighs straddling his hips, before I returned my mouth to his. I let one hand run through his silky hair as the other began to unfasten the buttons of my dress. I wanted to show him how I truly felt. I wanted him.

Railan's hands trailed down my back, his touch sending shivers down my spine. As I pushed the dress off my shoulders, he pulled back slightly and looked at me with wonder in his eyes. For a brief moment, a wave of self-consciousness washed over me, but he quickly dispelled it with a gentle touch to my cheek.

'You're so beautiful, Isla,' he murmured, his hands trailing up my sides to cup my breasts.

I felt a blush creep up my cheeks at his words, but I also felt a sense of pride and confidence. This man loved me for who I was, flaws and all. With that thought in mind, I leaned in for another kiss, more passionate than the last. He was always so attentive to me, and now it was my turn to show him just how attentive I could be. With a blazing blush upon my cheeks, I moved my hands down his chest to his waist, my fingers finding the buckle of his belt, unfastening it and the clasp of his pants before I let my fingers trail down to his hardened erection.

Railan let out a low moan as my fingers wrapped around him, stroking him slowly at first, then increasing in speed and pressure as he grew harder in my grasp. I felt a surge of power and pleasure at the effect I was having on him, and it only made me want him more.

I leaned in to whisper in his ear, 'Do you want me, Eli? Do you want to be inside me?'

He let out a ragged breath, his hands gripping my hips tightly as he pulled me closer. 'Yes, Isla, yes, I want you, I want to be inside you,' he moaned, his lips finding mine once more in a fierce, possessive kiss.

With a shy grin on my face, I lifted myself slightly and positioned him at my entrance, slowly lowering myself onto him. A sharp moan escaped my lips at the feeling of him stretching and filling me, and I felt him grasp my hips tightly as I took his full length. I began to grind my hips against his, slowly at first, savouring the sensation before I picked up the pace, my body moving to its own rhythm. Railan's hands found my hips, and he began to guide me, his movements syncing with mine. We moved together in perfect harmony, our bodies moving as one.

I felt the tension building within me, the pleasure coiling tight in my stomach. Railan must have sensed it too, because he began to move faster, his motions becoming harder and more insistent. I could feel myself getting closer and closer as he swelled within me. I knew he was close as he pressed me close to him, his breathing laboured as his muscles tensed. I knew exactly what I needed to do to push him over the edge.

'E-Eli,' I moaned against his ear, my body trembling slightly.

He let out a low, almost primal, growl in response, his hands tightening on my hips as he thrust deeper inside me. I could feel his breath hot against my neck as he whispered my name like a prayer, urging me to let go. And then, with one final thrust, he lost control, and I felt the rush of warmth within me as his seed filled me to the brim. The force was enough to send me over the edge, my body trembling as a blinding wave of pleasure surged through me. I collapsed against him, my vision hazy and my breath heavy, as he wrapped his arms around me, holding me close. A fine layer of sweat coated our skin, and our hearts raced. I snuggled against his neck as I ran my fingers through his hair.

'I love you, always,' I whispered breathlessly against his ear.

Railan let out a contented sigh, his arms holding me even closer as he replied, 'I love you too, Isla. Always and forever.'

We stayed like that for a few moments, simply enjoying the feel of each other's presence and the aftermath of our lovemaking. Eventually, he shifted slightly and pulled out of me, and I couldn't help but let out a soft whimper at the loss. He chuckled softly and pressed a gentle kiss to my forehead before getting up to grab a towel to clean us both up. Now that the moment was over, I found myself back to feeling an overwhelming sense of shyness. I quickly pulled my slip back in place, grateful for its minimal coverage as I pressed my thighs together. I was glad we were on the same page about our future, especially given the frequency of our encounters. It was also probably for the best that I accepted his proposal, since I didn't exactly want to get pregnant out of wedlock. A tender blush spread across my cheeks at the thought. A family of my own with the man that I loved. Were such things truly possible, or was this all simply a dream? The heat within my body told me this was all too real.

Railan returned with the towel and cleaned us both up, his movements gentle and loving. Once he finished, he tossed the towel aside and scooped me up off the couch and into his arms. He carried me over to his bed and lay me down gently before climbing in beside me. I nestled against him, feeling his warmth and the steady beat of his heart against my cheek.

'You don't mind spending the night here?' he asked softly.

I shook my head. 'No, I want to be here,' I murmured.

Railan smiled softly and kissed the top of my head. 'Good,' he said. 'I want you here with me.'

I snuggled closer to him, feeling safe and content in his embrace. We lay like that for a while, talking softly about our future together and all the things we wanted to do. It was a peaceful and intimate moment that I knew I would treasure forever. Eventually, exhaustion overtook me and I drifted off to sleep in his arms, feeling happier and more loved than I ever had before.

Chapter 26

Today was the day of the ball. My stomach was twisted in knots with a mixture of excitement and dread. Railan would announce our engagement to all of Maentaea later tonight, and while it made my heart feel full, I also knew that it would cause more than a little stir within the community. How would my parents react? We had only just told them we were courting barely a week ago. I hadn't even told Lady Amaranta. Her reaction was the one that filled me with the most dread. I knew Railan would be able to protect me and my family tonight, but once the night was over, my family would be at her mercy. I also knew that a few of the gentry on the invite list had views that aligned with those of the Magi Primacy. Would they cause trouble for Railan because of me? What about the other Prime Mages? I couldn't help but wonder just how badly this would go.

A high-pitched scream snapped me out of my thoughts, and I blinked as I refocused my vision. My little sister's eyes were as wide as the full moon as she ran into the estate foyer. A wholesome smile settled onto my lips at her reaction.

'Issy, Issy, this is where you live?' Inessa gasped in awe as her eyes darted around frantically, unable to settle on any one spot for more than a second.

I chuckled at her response. 'Sort of, this is Lord Railan's estate. I work here and I have my very own room in the staff quarters,' I explained, carefully leaving out the fact that I also shared his bed.

'Wow, it's so big and fancy! I've never seen so much space!' Inessa spun around on her heels in the middle of the foyer, making sure to get in the way of the butlers and maids as they hurried about finishing off the last-minute preparations.

'Nessy,' I growled lightly as I took her hand. 'Be careful, everyone else is still busy. We mustn't get in their way.'

'Sorry, sorry! It's just so...!' She gave me an apologetic grin as she squeezed my hand. 'I want a tour!'

'Soon,' I said. 'We need to wait for Mama and Papa.'

'Sorry to keep you waiting on us, my darlings,' my father apologised as he finally made his way to the front entrance.

My mother had her hand on his waist, keeping him steady as he hobbled along with his cane. I couldn't help but feel a pang of guilt for having made him travel so far.

'No, I'm sorry that it's so far, Papa,' I dragged Nessy over to our parents.

'Nonsense, I would walk the world for you, my darling girl,' my father reassured me firmly.

I couldn't help but smile as warmth spread through me. 'Luckily, I only ask you to make it through the night,' I said light-heartedly. 'I've arranged a room for you to get some rest before the actual party starts.'

My father looked grateful for my thoughtful reprieve. I led my family to their arrangement for the night, a nice, simple guest room in the staff quarters. I let my parents get ready while I distracted Inessa with a sort of mini tour of the estate. Seeing her little face light up at every little thing simultaneously made my heart flush with joy, but also sadness. This was the first time in a very long time that she had even been allowed to leave Lake Village. The outside world was so foreign to her, and that made my heart ache. She was so curious and energetic, knowing she was locked up day after day, it hurt me more than words could describe. I needed to stay strong. Railan had promised me he would find a way to truly free me and my family from Lady Amaranta's clutches.

I checked my pocket watch and saw that the time to get ready was fast approaching. I collected my mother and the three of us retired to a separate room to get dressed. To my surprise, Lady Aizel was already waiting for me, box in hand, containing the custom dress she had made for me.

'Lady Aizel, I wasn't expecting to see you,' I said as I shut the door behind me. 'Please allow me to introduce my mother and sister, Inessa.'

Aizel gave me a warm smile, the wrinkles of her eyes crinkling deeply. She looked absolutely stunning in a simple but elegant dark purple dress that clung to her figure perfectly. Her silver hair was styled up, and she was definitely a vision of high-end fashion as she came over to greet us.

'I just had to personally see to the delivery of your dress, my dear Isla. I'm so very excited to see you in the finished product,' she beamed.

It had looked extravagant at the fitting, and I, too, found myself excited and nervous to see the product of her skilful efforts. My mother gave Lady Aizel a deep bow as she came over to join us. Inessa watched on from the bed she had immediately thrown herself upon. I stripped down into my slip as Lady Aizel undid the magic that kept the dress safely within its box. Both mother and Inessa let out shocked gasps as the beautiful dress of wind and water unfurled before their very eyes.

Inessa let out an elated squeal as her face lit up once more. My mother, on the other hand, looked horrified. I felt my stomach sink at her expression.

'What is that?' she frowned. 'She can't wear that, there must have been a mistake.'

'Mama...' I started, unsure where to start to explain.

'There is no mistake, Mrs Marielle. This is the masterpiece commissioned by Lord Railan himself for Lady Isla,' Lady Aizel explained calmly.

My mother let out a nervous scoff. 'Nonsense, we all know that colours are forbidden to people like us,' my mother looked at me, her face etched with concern.

'Lord Railan has given his express permission for her to wear his colours, you needn't worry about such things,' Aizel tried to reassure my mother, but she remained incredulous.

'Isla, my sweet, Isla, you understand what you are doing?' My mother's voice was low, almost begging me to reconsider.

But I couldn't. I was already firmly committed; she just didn't know yet.

'I do,' I reassured her. 'I understand the implications and the consequences, but this is what Lord Railan wants. What I want.'

My mother shook her head as she let out a deep sigh. There was a brief look of defeat in her eyes, and I moved to her side and wrapped my arms around her tightly. She was stiff for a second before finally relaxing into my embrace.

'If you're sure... just promise you'll be careful,' my mother finally relented as she smoothed my hair.

'I promise,' I said firmly. 'Now, will you please help me get ready?'

My mother nodded curtly. I could tell she was still scared, but she put on a brave face nonetheless. With the expertise of the two older women and the minor hindrance of my little sister, I was eventually ready for the ball. I felt tears prick at the corners of my eyes as I did a twirl in the mirror. I'd never looked or felt so beautiful in my life. The dress was perfect. It perfectly invoked the feeling of the wind upon the sea, as if I were standing on the beach right then and there. My hair was styled half up and half down and adorned with matching flowers. I even had subtle, shimmering makeup on my face. It was perhaps a little wasted since I had to wear my glasses, but I didn't care.

'One last thing!' Lady Aizel spoke up as she pulled a small pouch from her bag.

She pulled out a pair of small clips that looked like a mixture of butterfly wings and a mermaid tail. She came over and clipped them onto the sides of my frames, and I blinked in stunned awe. I hadn't even thought that something so small could make such a difference. I was perfect, like a fairy princess.

'Thank you, Lady Aizel,' I breathed, trying to keep myself composed despite the rush of emotions that stirred within me.

'You are a true vision of the wind and sea. I think you're perhaps my greatest work in a long time,' Lady Aizel gave me a heartfelt smile as she squeezed my hands. 'Now, I shall see you downstairs soon. We mustn't keep everyone waiting.'

'Thank you,' I repeated as I watched her grab her things and make her way out of the room.

'You look absolutely beautiful, my darling,' my mother's voice was barely above a whisper as she held back her own tears.

'I want to be a princess too when I'm older,' Inessa chipped in.

I let out a soft chuckle. 'I'm sure you will have your chance, Nessy.' I grabbed her hand before I offered my other hand to my mother. 'Shall we get going? I'm sure Papa is already waiting for us.'

My mother gave me a weak smile and took my hand with a nod. I led the pair to the prearranged meeting spot, and I almost stopped dead in my tracks as my father came into view, followed by Railan. I felt my chest tighten as my heart fluttered, the air briefly leaving my lungs, as I lay eyes on him.

Lady Aizel had really outdone herself. His matching suit clung to him in all the right places, with long tails that almost reached the floor and silver embroidery that invoked the depths of the ocean. His suit was a deep blue in contrast to my shades of green and teal.

Wind and Sea.

He stood straight and confident as usual as he chatted idly with my father. His vibrant orange hair was somewhat slicked back, and his features were sharp. Of course, Railan was as handsome as ever.

'Mr Railan!' My sister squealed as she tugged her hand out of mine and ran up to him.

''There you are, Miss Nessy, where's-' Railan flashed her a smile as he greeted her.

He didn't finish his sentence as his eyes flicked up to me. They grew wide as he took in a sharp breath before a smile that would eclipse the sun spread across his lips.

'Isla...' he was barely able to utter my name as I closed the distance between us.

I could feel the heat on my cheeks as I averted my gaze. I knew I had nothing to be nervous about, yet that didn't stop my heart from racing and my hands from shaking lightly.

'My Lord,' I gave him a small bow.

He quickly composed himself as he took my hand in his and brought it up to his lips to place a small kiss upon my knuckles. The gesture was small and simple, but it only made my blush deepen.

'You look absolutely radiant, Isla,' he said quietly.

'Y-you too,' I stuttered, feeling awkward that that was all I could manage to say.

Railan chuckled softly, his warm breath ghosting over my skin as he leaned in closer. 'You always have a way with words,' he teased, his eyes sparkling with mirth.

I couldn't help but smile, even if he was teasing me. He squeezed my hand before he returned his attention to my family.

'Feel free to go ahead, the ballroom is open. I just need a moment to speak with Isla,' he said firmly, a slightly commanding tone to his voice.

My sister opened her mouth to speak, but was quickly silenced by my mother as she grabbed Inessa's hand.

'Of course, my Lord,' my mother gave Railan a small bow as she tugged Inessa along behind her.

She shot me a concerned glance but ultimately let us be. My father quickly hobbled over to me, placing a small kiss upon my cheek.

'See you soon, my darling,' he whispered before joining my mother and sister.

I watched them round the corner. As soon as we were alone, he pulled me close to him, pressing my body close to his as he slipped a hand around my waist.

'You are absolutely ravishing, my love,' he whispered in my ear. 'Can we just skip the ball and escape to my room?'

I knew he was joking, and I let out a soft chuckle as I pressed back against his chest. 'Have you changed your mind about the announcement? We don't have to go through with this if you have.'

I tried to keep my tone light, even though a part of me was asking honestly.

'I think it's a little late for that,' he said, giving me a reassuring smile. 'I'm determined to announce my love for you to the world, Isla. Besides, this will allow me to weed out my potential allies from my foes.'

My heart fluttered once more at his words. 'I know...' I returned my gaze down.

'Are you worried?' he asked, sensing my discomfort.

'Of course,' I admitted with a little sigh.

'Don't be, I'll protect you, no matter what,' he reassured me as he cupped my chin and tilted my face up.

He leaned down and placed a sweet kiss upon my lips, careful to avoid smudging my makeup. I gave him a small smile as he pulled back. His words filled me with the slightest sense of ease.

'Alright, shall we go and join in the festivities? We are the guests of honour, after all,' Railan offered me his hand once more, giving me a small bow.

'Yes,' I nodded as I took his hand and he led me towards the ball-room.

I was nervous as we crested the grand staircase; a few of the newly arriving guests glanced up to look at us before turning to gossip quietly to each other. I wanted to run away. I should be blending into the background, yet here I was being paraded around for all to see. Railan kept his grip on my hand, holding me steady with an understanding gentleness. I squeezed his hand as we stepped off the stairs and started towards the ballroom proper. He gave me a reassuring grin as he returned the gesture.

As we entered the ballroom, the music grew louder, and the chatter of guests filled the air. My eyes took in the grandeur of the room, with its glittering chandeliers, sweeping curtains, and drapings of rainbow colours everywhere. It was hard to believe we were still in Railan's estate. The room felt foreign, as if ripped straight from a fairytale. Master Pompanov had really, truly outdone himself. Everything was so grand and elegant, more so than Railan's debut ball had been. I felt like an impostor amidst the sea of regal colour. My anxiety was only fueled further as people naturally turned to look at us as we made our way through the crowd. Of course, everyone had been waiting for Railan to arrive; he was the host after all. I could feel the curious, judging eyes of everyone around us.

Railan seemed unfazed by the attention and walked with a confident stride, nodding and exchanging pleasantries with various guests as he made his way towards the center of the room. I followed his lead, smiling politely and trying to ignore the way my heart was pounding in my chest. It was all so overwhelming. I naturally wanted to slink backwards into Railan's shadow, but he kept me firmly by his side. I was stunned by the sheer number of people who had turned up. Railan truly was quite popular. To my surprise, I even spotted a group of Silvyan Order representatives huddled up on the balcony. They were out of the way, content with not interacting with the rabble. I recalled the only other time I had seen them was at Railan's debut ball. They had been just as frosty and antisocial then, too. Nevertheless, it was impressive that he could somehow draw them into the open like this.

'Ah, there you are, Railan,' a distinct, chilling voice interrupted our current conversation.

I didn't want to turn around, I didn't want to acknowledge him, yet I was forced to as Railan turned to face him, The Doctor.

Railan's expression changed to one of polite indifference as he greeted the Doctor. 'Good evening, Cygmonde. I trust you are enjoying the festivities?' he asked.

Cygmonde's thin lips curled into a smile that didn't reach his eyes. 'Oh, indeed. Your generosity is well-known, and the decor is quite exquisite,' he replied, his gaze flickering over to me briefly before returning to Railan.

Railan noticed the direction of Cygmonde's gaze and stepped slightly in front of me, subtly positioning himself as a barrier between us. 'I am glad to hear it. Is there anything in particular you would like to discuss?' he asked, his tone polite but guarded.

Cygmonde's smile widened slightly. 'Oh, no need for business tonight, Railan. I simply wanted to congratulate you on your engagement,' he said, his eyes lingering on me once more.

I felt my cheeks flush and my stomach drop. Engagement? Why would he say that? Railan and I had only just agreed barely two days ago; no one should know. Had he told Cygmonde already? I glanced up at Railan, silently pleading for an explanation.

Railan's expression remained carefully neutral as he replied, 'I am not engaged, Cygmonde. I am simply hosting this ball as a celebration of our recent success.'

Cygmonde's smile faltered for a moment before he quickly regained his composure. 'Ah, my apologies. I must have misunderstood,' he said smoothly before excusing himself and slipping back into the crowd.

I let out a relieved breath as he left, and Railan turned to me with a small smile. 'Don't worry, Isla. I haven't told anyone about us yet,' he reassured me quietly.

I nodded, feeling an overwhelming mixture of stress and anxiety. Now I only felt worse, as if I wanted to be sick. Were we too obvious? I found my eyes frantically searching the crowd for Lady Amaranta. Would she suspect the shift in our relationship? She knew we were courting, but our engagement was something I had carefully hidden until tonight. Railan wanted to make a statement to her by announcing his intentions of marriage in front of everyone in attendance. He wanted her to know that he was going to take me from her, whether she liked it or not. I'd hesitantly agreed, but now I was regretting my decision.

Railan must have sensed my unease as he took my hand and led me towards a quieter area of the room. 'Don't worry, Isla. Everything will be fine,' he murmured, his voice low and comforting.

I looked up at him; his eyes rested upon me with confident reassurance, yet they did not quell the fear that raged within me. I knew that Lady Amaranta was not one to take kindly to someone trying to take away something she believed was hers, and Railan's bold move could have serious consequences. I knew this all along. I knew this when I'd told him the truth about who I was, when I agreed to be with him. But thoughts and feelings were a different beast when faced with the reality of the situation. Somewhere in the crowd, she was watching, waiting; they all were. Hidden under painted faces and cheerful smiles, I knew everyone was waiting for us to fall, to make a mistake. If I fell, then I would become trapped under their boots forever.

'I'm scared,' I said softly, unable to meet his gaze.

Railan squeezed my hand gently. 'Trust me, Isla. I have everything under control.'

I wanted to believe him, but the nagging feeling of doubt wouldn't go away.

Railan must have sensed my hesitation because he pulled me closer to him, wrapping his arm around my waist. 'I understand it's overwhelming. But you don't have to worry about anything. I won't let anything happen to you,' he murmured, his voice low and soothing.

I leaned into him, the warmth of his embrace calming me down slightly. 'I trust you, Eli. It's just that... what we're doing is risky. Lady Amaranta won't just let us be,' I said, my voice barely above a whisper.

Railan chuckled softly, the sound sending shivers down my spine. 'Of course not. But that's why we have to be smart and stay ahead of her. We have to show her that we're not afraid of her, that we won't back down,' he replied confidently.

I looked up at him, his eyes ablaze with a determination that only inspired more of my admiration for him. He was always so sure of himself, so confident and charismatic. It was easy to see why he was already a highly revered Prime Mage.

I nodded weakly, clinging desperately to his warmth and the promise of his words. 'I trust you, I do. I think... perhaps a drink or two might help calm my nerves,' I tried to be lighthearted, to swallow my fear, but a part of me really did want a drink at this point.

Railan chuckled again, but this time it was a genuine sound of amusement. 'I think that's a great idea. Let's go get ourselves a drink,' he said, leading me back into the crowd to find a server.

We pushed through the crowd until Railan was finally able to snag a couple of glasses of sweet wine.

I took a sip of the wine, the sweetness soothing my nerves slightly. 'Thank you,' I said, offering him a grateful smile.

He grinned back at me, his eyes sparkling mischievously. 'Don't thank me yet. We haven't even begun to have fun,' he said, taking a long sip of his wine.

A pang of excitement tickled my stomach at his words, despite my lingering fears. Being with Railan always seemed to bring out a sense of adventure in me that I never knew existed before.

'What do you have in mind?' I asked, curiosity getting the better of me.

Railan's grin widened, and he gestured towards the dance floor. 'Let's dance, Isla, and show these people how it's done,' he said, offering me his hand.

I hesitated for a moment, recalling my lack of rhythm. I also recalled our last dance and its relative smoothness. If Railan was leading me, I knew I would be just fine, and as I looked back at Railan, his eyes shining with excitement, I knew that I couldn't say no.

I took his hand, letting him lead me out onto the dance floor. The band began almost on cue as Railan spun me into position. The floor filled up quickly as the music swelled, but I hardly noticed as I lost myself in the moment, forgetting all about my fears and worries. For a brief moment, it felt like nothing else in the world mattered except for the two of us, dancing together under the bright lights of the ballroom. He was such a good partner, leading me with confidence but also keeping things simple so I could easily follow along. Joy swelled in my heart as he twirled me around. Combined with the wine, the dance was just the thing I needed to relax. The music slowed, and so did we. The dancefloor thinned slightly as we moved onto an interlude, but I hardly noticed as Railan consumed my entire world. I was almost breathless at this point, my cheeks rosy as I smiled at him with genuine happiness.

'Ahem!' Someone cleared their throat behind Railan before I saw them tap him on the shoulder. 'May I cut in?'

I blinked, both flustered and surprised as I recognised the figure.

Lauralai.

I hadn't seen her since the last ball. She looked absolutely stunning, even in brown. Her bright green eyes latched onto me, a smile upon her red lips.

Railan turned to face Lauralai, a hint of surprise at the corners of his eyes as he gave her a warm smile. 'If the lady wishes, I will oblige,' he said, looking at me expectantly.

I gave him an almost sheepish smile, feeling a little bad that I was about to snub him so soon into the night. 'I do. Just one dance,' I gave his hand a reassuring squeeze before letting it go. 'I'm unsure if you are acquainted, but this is my fellow scholar, Lauralai,' I hastily introduced her.

'I don't believe I got the chance to introduce myself at your debut ball, Lord Railan,' Lauralai gave him a curtsy. 'I hope you don't mind if I steal Isla away for a little while?'

Railan smiled politely. 'Not at all, Miss Lauralai. It's a pleasure to finally make your acquaintance,' he said, bowing slightly. 'Please, enjoy your dance together. I'll be around if you need me,' he added, before turning and disappearing into the crowd.

I let out a small sigh as I watched him go, feeling a little guilty for leaving him so abruptly. But at the same time, I couldn't deny the excitement that coursed through me as Lauralai took his place, taking my hand and pulling me closer to her.

'It's been a while since we last saw each other, Isla. How have you been?' she asked, her eyes scanning me up and down as her lips curled into a sensual grin.

'I've been... good," I replied, a bit taken aback by her sudden attention. 'And how about you? You look like you've been doing well.'

Lauralai grinned. 'Oh, I have. I've been busy with work, but it's been going well. And speaking of work. How's that going?' she asked, a hint of curiosity in her voice.

'It's been... interesting,' I said, not wanting to give too much away.

Lauralai raised an eyebrow. 'Interesting? Sounds like there's more to it than that. Care to elaborate?' she pressed, a playful glint in her eye.

I hesitated for a moment. 'What can I say, there's never a dull day when you work for a Prime Mage,' I shrugged nonchalantly.

Lauralai let out a musical laugh. 'I do agree. Speaking of, would you look at that, it would appear our Lords have found each other,' she darted her eyes to the side.

I felt the air get caught in my throat at her words. Lord? I followed her gaze to see that Railan was talking with another man, one who was slightly taller with regal features. I recognised him from the previous ball: Lord Drakoryon.

My heart skipped a beat in recognition, and I whipped my head back to look at Lauralai. She was still perfectly content as she watched the men. She hadn't told me that she worked for a Prime Mage. A sudden unease settled in my stomach, wondering what Lauralai's true intentions were. Was she also one of Lady Amaranta's spies? Was she like me? Or was she something else?

'Lauralai, I didn't know you worked for Lord Drakoryon,' I said, keeping my tone even.

She shrugged nonchalantly, her eyes still fixed on Railan and Drakoryon. 'I thought you knew, it's not a big secret or anything,' she said, finally tearing her gaze away from the men and looking back at me.

I couldn't help but feel a little betrayed, but I also didn't understand why. She had offered her help when I was doing research, and I had accepted it. Nothing malicious had happened between us, but still, I couldn't shake the wariness that stirred within me. The other Prime Mages were not to be trusted.

'I see,' I said, my voice barely above a whisper.

Lauralai seemed to sense my unease, and she placed a comforting hand on my arm. 'Isla, don't worry. I'm not here to cause you any harm. Just because we work for different Prime Mages doesn't mean we can't be friends,' she said, her tone sincere. 'We're entitled to have relationships outside of business.'

She was right, there weren't any real reasons that we couldn't be friends. But even still, what if she was also working for Lady Amaranta? I had let my guard slip, and that could leave me in an even more vulnerable position than the one I was currently in.

I gave her a small nod as I forced a smile onto my face. 'Yes, our personal lives are indeed very separate from our work.'

Lauralai smiled back at me, her hand still resting on my arm. 'Exactly,' she said. 'And besides, I think it's important for people like us to stick together. We're both mundi in a magi-dominated world, after all.'

I gave a small nod in agreement. She was right. It was tough being a mundus in a world where the magi held most of the power. But as much as I appreciated Lauralai's words, I couldn't shake the feeling that there was something she wasn't telling me. I decided to tread carefully, keeping my guard up but not showing any outward suspicion.

'You're right,' I said. 'It's good to have someone who understands the challenges we face.'

Lauralai nodded in agreement. 'So, Isla, what do you say we go grab a drink? We can catch up properly and talk about anything and everything except work.'

I hesitated for a moment, but then I thought that maybe it would be good to spend some time with Lauralai in a more casual setting. 'Sure, that sounds great,' I said with a smile.

Lauralai's face lit up, and she linked her arm with mine. 'Let's go then,' she said, leading me towards the buffet.

As we walked, I couldn't help but feel a sense of unease. I still didn't trust her completely, but at the same time, I didn't want to miss out on the opportunity to get to know her better. I decided to keep my guard up, but also to keep an open mind. Maybe Lauralai really was just a friend.

We shared a few drinks and more than a few laughs, and I soon felt all the fear and unease slipping away. I found myself forgetting all about the judgmental stares of those around me, of Lady Amaranta, of the consequences of Railan's announcement.

Railan!

I'd almost lost myself in Lauralai's infectious musings. The night was wearing on; surely it would be almost time for him to make the announcement. I sat up straight and put my glass down on the table before me, giving a frazzled grin.

'Ah, it's getting late! Lord Railan has something important to do, and I need to find him,' I said as I stood, my body swaying slightly.

'Aw, are you going so soon?' Lauralai pouted before she shot me a mischievous grin. 'I understand, duty calls.'

'It does indeed,' I gave her an awkward wink that made her chuckle.

'Good luck,' she raised her glass to me, and I nodded back at her before I slipped into the crowd to find Railan.

As I made my way through the throngs of people, I caught snippets of conversations. Most of them were about Railan. Some speculated about the occasion for the ball, while others whispered about their plans and ambitions towards him. It was clear that everyone was here for their own reasons, and I supposed I was no different. I was here because I wanted to be with him. I whipped my head around, scanning the crowd for his signature orange hair. As I moved deeper into the crowd, a gnawing feeling started to prick at the back of my neck, like I was being watched and not just subtle stares. It felt as though someone was watching me intently. I tried to make my way to the edge of the room, but was soon stopped as someone grabbed my arm. It felt like someone had zapped me with a bolt of lightning, and I whipped around to find myself face to face with one of the Silvyan Order representatives.

They didn't say anything as they stared at me, their face entirely concealed by their signature silver mask. I frowned, expecting to feel frightened, but I didn't feel anything.

'May I help you, my Lord?' I asked, giving them a nod of acknowledgement.

The representative stared at me for a few seconds more before they pointed towards the couples dancing. I followed their finger, and it clicked. They wanted to dance. But why with me? My eyes fluttered in confusion. I wasn't sure if it was a good idea, but I did recognise that it could be a good chance to foster relations between the Creed and the Silvyan Order.

'A dance?' I said aloud. 'Of course,' I extended my hand out in a friendly manner.

They did not speak as they tilted their head slightly, looking at my hand. Had I been mistaken? They did not seem to speak my language, and I did not know Silvyan. I felt my nerves returning. I didn't want to offend them. To my abrupt surprise, they suddenly took my hand and pulled me towards the dance floor. They paused for a moment, glancing around the room before taking up the lead position. I obliged as I too fell into position, unsure what to expect. We paused for a moment as the music lulled. As soon as the music began to swell again, they pulled me along into a simple dance. It felt familiar, but I couldn't put my finger on it. The representative spun me around, holding me a little too close. Then it hit me, they were perfectly mimicking Railan's moves from earlier in the night. Had they been watching us dance earlier?

I felt my cheeks grow hot, uncertain how I felt about all this.

'L-Lord Railan is very grateful that you could make it tonight,' I decided to make some light conversation.

The representative continued to remain silent as we continued to dance. Now I was beginning to feel a bit awkward. What should I do now? I didn't know what I was doing. Thankfully, the music started to lull again, and we came to a slow halt. They released me from their grasp and brought their hand up, pointing at me.

'Sil,' They spoke for the first time.

I let out a soft gasp. Their voice was light and breezy, as if it had a slight echo. I was stunned they would speak to someone like me.

'Me?' I asked, unsure what was happening.

They nodded before they looked around the room. They then pointed off into the distance. I followed their finger, and to my shock, I saw a flash of orange.

Railan?

'Lord Railan?' I raised a brow.

They nodded again. 'El.'

'El?' I tilted my head curiously.

They then held up their pointer fingers before bringing them together side by side. 'Elsil.'

I blinked, utterly lost.

'I'm sorry, I don't understand,' I apologised.

The representative pointed at Railan and me before bringing their fingers together again. 'Elsil,' they repeated.

What were they trying to say? Were they implying something about Railan and me? I focused on their motions as they repeated them. Was "Elsil" some kind of term for a relationship? I thought back on my Silvyan Order research. "Sil" had referred to someone of great importance, if I was remembering correctly. Was "Elsil" also a reference to someone important? What did I have to do with it?

I pointed my finger towards Railan. 'Elsil?'

The representative shook their head before pointing at us both simultaneously. 'Elsil,' they then pointed only at me. 'Sil.'

Did they think I was someone important? I gave them a light smile as I shook my head. 'I think you've mistaken me for someone else.'

They tilted their head, regarding me quietly before they abruptly turned and left. I frowned as I watched them leave, uncertain what had just happened. Had I offended them? I hoped not.

As the representative disappeared into the crowd, my unease returned. What did they mean by "Elsil"? Was it a term for a relationship, or was it something else entirely? And why did they seem to think that I was important? I glanced around the room, trying to see if anyone else had noticed the exchange, but no one seemed to be paying us any attention.

I took a deep breath and tried to push my thoughts aside. I was here for Railan, and I didn't want to let anything distract me from that. I scanned the crowd once more, searching for a glimpse of his orange hair, and finally spotted him at the far end of the ballroom. He was surrounded by a group of people, all vying for his attention, but he seemed to be ignoring them all as he stared intently at something in the distance.

I quickly made my way towards him, weaving my way through the crowd, and as I approached, he finally looked up and caught my eye. His expression shifted as he saw me, a bright grin spreading across his lips as he excused himself and strode to meet me. My heart skipped a beat as he did so. I'd been without his company for far too long.

'There you are, my love,' Railan whispered into my ear as he slipped his arm around my waist. 'I was getting worried you'd gotten lost in this crowd.'

'No, I just got distracted,' I leaned into him, standing on my tiptoes to whisper back to him. 'I ran into someone from the Silvyan Order.'

Railan's grip on me tightened slightly. 'What did they want?' he asked, his voice low and guarded.

'I'm not entirely sure,' I admitted. 'They didn't say much, but they kept pointing at us and saying something about "Elsil". I have no idea what that means.'

Railan's brow furrowed in confusion. 'Elsil? Hm... I don't recall it.'

'Me neither,' I replied, feeling even more puzzled. 'But I thought it might be related to something important. They seemed to think I was someone else.'

Railan's expression softened as he looked down at me. 'Well, you're definitely someone important to me,' he said, his hand reaching up to brush a strand of hair out of my face. 'Let's not worry about it for now, okay? We have other matters to attend to.'

I nodded, feeling a sense of relief wash over me. With Railan by my side, everything seemed a little bit easier to handle.

'I believe all the guests have arrived. I've seen the Grand Cardinal and several of the other Prime Mages. I think now should be a good time for our little announcement.' Railan's breath tickled my ear, and his words filled me with a mixture of dread and excitement.

'A-are you sure?' I asked once again.

'I've never been more sure about anything in my life,' he said firmly as he squeezed my waist. 'Just follow my lead. I'll keep you safe, I promise.'

I nodded despite my fear. I wanted to see this through. I didn't want to let fear rule me any longer, and I knew as long as Railan was by my side, I could push through.

'I'm ready,' I said quietly as I resigned myself to my fate.

Chapter 27

Railan gave me a reassuring smile before he led me towards the centre of the ballroom. As we walked, I could feel the eyes of everyone in the room on us. The other Prime Mages, their agents, the wealthy merchants and nobles, all of them were watching us closely. It made me feel nervous and exposed, but I kept my head held high, trusting Railan to guide me through this. The chatter in the room quieted as we approached the elegant dias that had been set up. All eyes turned to us as we stood above the crowd. I wanted to desperately melt into the shadows, but right now I needed to be a beacon, a symbol for Railan's plans.

'Ladies and gentlemen,' Railan began, his voice carrying easily across the room. 'I have an announcement to make.'

Hushed silence fell across the crowd, and Railan strategically paused for a moment, letting the anticipation build, before continuing.

'As many of you know, I am Elieason Railan, Twelfth Prime Mage of the Creed. But tonight, I stand before you not just as a Prime Mage, but as a man. A man who has found something worth fighting for. A woman who has captured my heart and I hers.'

He turned to me, taking my hand and pulling me closer to him. I could feel the collective scrutiny of the crowd as they stared at me, judging me. I kept my head high and my face neutral. I could only pray they didn't notice the slight tremble of my hands. For a split second, I caught Lady Amaranta's eyes in the crowd. Her expression was dark and hidden as she watched with furious curiosity. Railan's speech was intentionally trying to stir her, to subtly jab at her, and how he intended to take me from her grasp.

'Tonight, I am here to declare that I intend to marry this beautiful woman beside me, Isla Marielle,' Railan continued, his voice strong and resolute. 'I know there may be those among you who disapprove, who believe that our union is unwise or even dangerous. But I ask you to trust in my judgment and my love for her. Together, we will be stronger than we ever could be apart.'

The room was silent for a moment, as if everyone was holding their breath. Then, a murmur started to spread among the guests. Some looked shocked, some excited, and some were furious. I could feel the weight of their eyes on us, judging and analysing our every move. But Railan didn't falter. He continued to hold my hand tightly, a sign of his commitment and determination.

'I understand that some of you may have questions,' he said, addressing the murmurs in the room. 'But I assure you that our love is true and strong. We are willing to face any challenge that comes our way, together.'

I looked up at him, my heart full of emotion. Despite my fears, I felt a surge of pride and joy at his words. He was willing to risk everything for me, to declare his love to the world. And I knew that, no matter what happened next, we would face it together.

'Objection! This is heresy!' a loud voice boomed.

A large man pushed his way to the front of the crowd, his face red, as an enraged snarl sat upon his features. It was the Grand Cardinal. My heart immediately sank.

'That woman is a mundus; she cannot marry a Prime Mage. It's sacrilegious, an insult to the Celestial Lady! I cannot condone this union in good faith,' he boomed, filling the room with an air of tension that seemed to spread like wildfire.

People started to join in, announcing their objection and outrage. Railan didn't flinch at the Grand Cardinal's outburst; instead, he stood tall and held my hand tighter. He turned to face the Cardinal and spoke in a calm and measured voice.

'Respectfully, Cardinal, your opinion on the matter is noted, but I must remind you that I am still a Prime Mage of the Creed, and as such, I have the right to choose my partner. Our love is not sacrilegious, nor is it an insult to the Celestial Lady. It is simply two people choosing to be together, and I refuse to let anyone tell me otherwise.'

The room was still tense, but Railan's words seemed to have some effect on the crowd. A few people looked at each other with uncertainty, as if reconsidering their initial objections. I could feel the hope start to build in my chest.

The Grand Cardinal sneered, his eyes narrowing. 'Your infatuation clouds your judgment, Railan. You are endangering not only yourself but the entire Creed. This is a disgrace to our faith and our people. I cannot and will not allow it.'

Railan's jaw tightened, but he didn't back down. 'I understand your concerns, Cardinal, but I assure you that I have thought this through carefully. I love this woman, and I believe she will be an asset to the Creed. Our union will only make us stronger.'

The Grand Cardinal scoffed. 'Love is a fleeting emotion, Railan. It cannot be trusted, especially not in matters of the Creed. You are putting your desires above the safety and stability of your people.'

Railan's grip on my hand tightened even more, and I could see the fire in his eyes. 'Love may be fleeting, but loyalty and devotion are not. I am devoted to the Creed, and I will do whatever it takes to protect it. And that includes marrying the woman I love.'

There was a tense moment of silence as the Grand Cardinal and Railan faced off. The rest of the crowd watched with bated breath, unsure of what would happen next. The Grand Cardinal suddenly shifted his fury towards me.

'You, woman, you should know better. If Lord Railan cannot see reason, then what of you? Put a stop to this foolishness right now. You know there will be consequences for your actions. Would you really taint such a pure and strong bloodline?' He demanded as his eyes seared into me.

I could feel tears brimming at the edges of my eyes as he called me out. My heart felt like it was going to burst. It was beating so fast. I could hardly catch a breath. Why did the room suddenly feel so small? Hateful, resentful eyes roamed over me.

'I-I...' The words felt like they were trying to choke me. I needed to speak, I needed to defend myself, defend Railan. 'I love him, is that really wrong?' My voice was barely audible over the murmurs of the crowd.

The Grand Cardinal's sneer deepened, and he leaned in towards me. 'Love is not a justification for disobedience and heresy. You are a mundus, and your place is not with a Prime Mage of the Creed. Do not let your foolishness blind you to reality. You are inferior in every possible way, and you are overstepping your place. You will be condemned for this. Do you really want to risk Lord Railan's position, to drag him down with you?'

I could feel the weight of his words crushing me, suffocating me. He was right, I was inferior, but Railan didn't care about that. He wanted me anyway.

Railan stepped forward, standing between me and the Grand Cardinal. 'I will not let you speak to her that way. She is not inferior; she is my equal. And I will stand by her, no matter what the consequences may be,' his voice was strong and unwavering, filled with conviction and love.

The Grand Cardinal's eyes blazed with fury, and for a moment I thought he might dare to strike Railan. Everything was descending into pure chaos.

I took a deep breath, trying to steady my shaking voice. 'I understand what I am, my Lord, but I also know that my place is by Railan's side, always. I have always been faithful and devoted to the Creed, just as I plan to remain faithful and devoted to Railan. All I seek is this one small happiness, is that really so offensive if Railan is willing to grant it of his own volition?' I urged the Grand Cardinal to reconsider his stance as I stole a glance at Lady Amaranta.

Her face was cold, and I could see the rage that swelled behind her eyes.

'Impure!' Someone shouted, and I felt my heart race as the crowd swelled.

'Blood traitor!' Yelled another.

I clung to Railan's arm as more yelling ensued.

Railan stood tall and resolute, shielding me from the angry crowd. 'Silence!' His voice boomed through the room, and the crowd gradually quieted down. 'You dare to insult her, the woman I love? Isla is not impure, and I am no blood traitor. She is a kind and caring person, more pure of heart than any of you,' he glared at the crowd. 'You seem to be forgetting, Grand Cardinal, that I have been chosen by our goddess. Your challenge of me is also a challenge of her divine judgment,' he stood firm, daring the crowd to challenge him.

'And you forget that I am also close to the Celestial Lady. Mark my words, she will hear about this blasphemy and you will find out exactly how little she cares for blood traitors like you,' the Cardinal shot back.

Railan's eyes flashed with anger. 'I will not stand idly by while you insult me and my beloved. The Celestial Lady will hear of your behaviour, and she will judge accordingly. But in the meantime, I demand that you retract your accusations and apologise for your slanderous words,' he said firmly.

The Grand Cardinal's face contorted with rage. 'How dare you speak to me in such a manner? You are nothing but a foolish boy who has been seduced by the wiles of this mundus. I will not retract my words or apologise for speaking the truth,' he spat.

Railan's hand tightened on mine, and I could feel the tension in his body. The situation was rapidly spiralling out of control, and I didn't know what to do. All I could do was hold on to Railan and pray that everything would turn out okay in the end.

More shouts erupted from the crowd, with people surging forward towards the dias, reaching out to us and clawing at my dress.

Railan stepped forward, his voice thundering over the commotion. 'Back off! Do not lay a hand on her, or you will face the consequences of your actions,' his eyes flickered around the crowd before landing on Lady Amaranta, silently pleading for her help.

She did not move nor acknowledge him.

'Enough!' Another, unfamiliar voice echoed loudly around the room, plunging the crowd into immediate silence.

A small, frail-looking elderly woman pushed her way to the front of the dias, batting people with her ornate cane as she forced them to move. She made her way up onto the stage, her face stern as she regarded the crowd.

'This display is unbecoming of our order. You all forget that we are here to serve our goddess, not to bicker amongst ourselves like common peasants,' her voice was cold and firm. 'We will retire for the evening, and in the morning, we will resume our duties with renewed focus and dedication. But know this: any further insubordination or disrespectful behaviour towards our fellow members will not be tolerated. Is that understood?' Her voice was calm and measured, but there was an underlying edge that made everyone in the room take notice.

'Lady Fenril...' the Grand Cardinal seemed almost hesitant to continue his tirade. 'You know this is wrong. I will have words with the Celestial Lady about this.'

My eyes widened in recognition, and I thought I might collapse right then and there. Lady Fenril. As in Lady Fenril, the first of the twelve Prime Mages. The one who was closest to our goddess above all others.

'Have your words, Grand Cardinal, but until then, I think we are done here,' she said firmly, her glare enough to kill a man.

The Grand Cardinal gave her a disgruntled sneer but ultimately backed down in the face of her superior position.

'Mark my words, there will be consequences. I strongly urge both of you to reconsider this madness,' the Cardinal threw out before he relented and turned to leave.

His entourage hurried after him, followed by those who shared his sentiments. The crowd began to disperse, some still casting angry glances in our direction as they left the room. Lady Fenril turned to Railan and me, her expression softening slightly.

'You two sure know how to put on a show,' she said, her tone carrying a hint of amusement.

'Lady Fenril,' Railan offered her a deep bow, and I did the same. 'I appreciate your assistance.'

Lady Fenril waved off his thanks with a small smile. 'It's nothing, my dear. It's my duty as First Prime Mage to maintain order and peace within our ranks.'

She then turned to me and regarded me with a curious expression. 'And who might this lovely young lady be? I don't believe we've had the pleasure of meeting before.'

I introduced myself, my voice trembling slightly from the recent events. 'My name is Isla Marielle, my Lady.'

Lady Fenril's eyes softened as she placed a gentle hand on my shoulder. 'Isla...' she said my name slowly, as if committing it to memory. 'My dear, I'm sorry you had to witness that. The Grand Cardinal can be quite...difficult to deal with at times.'

I nodded, still in shock from the realisation that I had just witnessed a clash between two powerful factions within the church. Lady Fenril gave me a reassuring smile before turning back to Railan.

'Now, I believe you have some important matters to attend to, Railan. I won't keep you any longer. But do take care of this young lady, won't you?'

Railan nodded, his expression grateful. Lady Fenril then made her way off the stage, her cane tapping against the marble floor as she left.

Railan turned to me, his expression serious. 'Are you alright?'

I took a deep breath, feeling a sense of relief now that the chaos had subsided. 'Y-Yes, I think so... What just happened?'

Railan's lips pressed into a thin line. 'Exactly what I expected and more,' he cast his gaze out to the small crowd that still lingered. 'Now we know where to start with potential allies,' he pulled me closer to whisper in my ear. 'I will set you free, I will keep my promise.'

'I know, I believe in you,' I whispered back as I wrapped my arms around his chest and held him tight.

'You!' a harsh voice called out behind us, and I looked up to see my mother storming towards us, her face red with a mixture of worry and fury.

She marched straight up to Railan and me, her whole body shaking. Her eyes bore down upon Railan, blazing with rage like I'd never seen before. I opened my mouth to speak, but she cut me off immediately.

'How dare you do this!' she hissed quietly, her voice laced with venom. 'Do you have no regard for Isla at all? Why would you do this to her?'

'Mama-' I started, but she whipped up her hand to silence me.

'Do you understand what you've done? Your actions have consequences, not just for you, but for all of us. Did you even think about your father and me, your sister?'

'Of course I did!' I was quick to defend myself. 'I'm always thinking of you.'

'Then why would you allow this man, Prime Mage or not, to ruin us?' She let out a bitter scoff. 'Does he even know what you really are?'

'Railan isn't going to ruin anyone. He's going to help us. Mama, he knows. He knows everything,' my voice was barely a whisper.

My mother's eyes searched my face, the anger subsiding slightly as it was replaced by sadness. 'Issy... you're a foolish girl,' she shook her head before she cast her scrutiny back on Railan. 'You knew and yet you still did this? You have provoked a power that is beyond even you. I hope you can both live with the knowledge that you have doomed us. As soon as we walk out of here, we will never be able to come back...' My mother's voice grew quiet and sombre.

'Please stay, Mama. Railan has promised to protect you all. He won't let anything happen to us...' I reached out to her, but she pulled away, shaking her head.

'There is a debt to be paid, and if you can no longer pay it, then someone else will have to do it,' tears threatened her eyes. 'Why would you do this to your sister, Issy... she's still innocent...'

I felt a lump form in my throat as my mother's words hit me like a ton of bricks. I had never wanted to hurt my family, but I had thought that what I was doing was for the greater good. Now, seeing the pain and disappointment in my mother's eyes, I wasn't so sure anymore. I had been selfish, so selfish. Something about Railan made me want to be free, to be something other than what I was.

'I'm sorry, Mama,' I said softly, feeling tears prick at my eyes. 'I never wanted to hurt anyone. I just...'

My voice trailed off as I struggled to find the right words to explain my actions. Railan stepped forward, his expression serious but gentle.

'Lady Fenril is right, your daughter has done nothing wrong,' he said firmly, addressing my mother. 'I understand your concerns, but I promise you that I will do everything in my power to protect your family.'

My mother looked at him sceptically, but Railan's confidence seemed to ease some of her worries.

'What an unfortunate turn of events,' Lady Amaranta's voice suddenly cut through the air.

I felt my blood turn cold, and I turned my eyes to the ground, unable to bring myself to look at her. Railan's hand tightened around mine, offering me some comfort as Lady Amaranta approached us. She circled around us slowly, her aura reminiscent of a predator toying with its prey. I could feel the intense weight of her gaze as she fixated on me.

'You have caused quite the stir,' she said, her voice laced with amusement as she flicked her eyes to Railan. 'I knew you were one for theatrics, but I never expected something like this. And you, my darling Isla, I never knew you could be so bold. It's quite a surprise.'

I clenched my jaw, feeling a mix of fear and anxiety boiling inside me. Lady Amaranta's words made it seem like everything that had happened was just some kind of game to her, and I knew that it was. She lived for this, the thrill of intrigue. I wanted to make up some excuse, but I knew there was nothing she would believe. She knew, and now I was worthless to her. My heart raced. We had made a terrible mistake.

'There's no need to flatter me, Lady Amaranta,' Railan said coolly, his grip on my hand reassuring. 'I simply wanted to declare my love to the world. I wasn't expecting a riot over something so simple and unimportant.'

'Simple and unimportant?' Lady Amaranta raised a brow, her eyes brimming with amusement. 'On the contrary, it's the most important matter. The Cardinal was not wrong; there will be consequences for your actions. But I'm curious, Railan, why would you risk everything over a silly girl? There will be many, many more that will occupy your time, so why be so stubborn about this one in particular? Love is not enough, so there surely must be something else,' Lady Amaranta deliberately coaxed him, and I could feel his muscles tensing slightly at her words.

I looked at him, uncertain why she would choose those words. Railan's jaw tensed as he glanced at Lady Amaranta, his eyes narrowed in suspicion. 'Love is the only answer,' he said firmly, his voice carrying a hint of defiance.

'Then you're a liar,' Lady Amaranta shot back, a wicked grin upon her lips.

Railan's expression darkened, and his grip on my hand tightened. I could feel the tension in the air, the atmosphere charged with hostility. Lady Amaranta's words seemed to have struck a nerve in Railan, and I could tell that he was struggling to keep his composure.

'I am not a liar,' Railan said through gritted teeth. 'My feelings for Isla are genuine.'

'Oh, I'm sure they are,' Lady Amaranta replied with a sly smirk. 'But there's more to it than that, isn't there? Something that you're not telling us, or at least, that you're not telling her,' her eyes quickly darted to me for a brief second, and I felt my blood run cold. 'Besides, Love is a fleeting emotion, Railan. It fades with time, leaving nothing but regret and bitterness. You should know that better than anyone,' she continued casually.

I could feel Railan's grip on my hand trembling slightly as he struggled to maintain his composure. What did she mean that was more to his feelings than just love? Was she implying there was something else that Railan had an interest in? But what? I was nothing. My position with Lady Amaranta was compromised, and all that was left was just me, nothing of note. Whatever it was, it was important enough for Railan to risk everything for it. I could sense the tension in the air between them unfurling like a suffocating smog. Whatever was happening was no longer just about me. There was a history between Railan and Lady Amaranta that I didn't understand, but it was clear that their relationship was complicated.

Railan's jaw tightened as he looked at Lady Amaranta, his eyes filled with anger. 'You know nothing about my feelings,' he said through gritted teeth.

Lady Amaranta chuckled softly, her eyes dancing with amusement. 'Don't be so defensive, my dear Railan. It's not becoming of you,' she said, her voice dripping with honeyed sarcasm. 'In fact, one would think you were hiding something, don't you agree, Isla?' Her dark eyes poured over me.

I didn't say anything as I kept my head down. She was trying to provoke something, and I wasn't going to feed into it any more than I already had this night.

Railan's grip on my hand loosened slightly as he turned to look at me. 'Isla knows everything she needs to know,' he said firmly, his voice laced with determination. 'And whatever you think you know, Lady Amaranta, it's none of your business.' his tone was sharp and cold, and for a moment, I saw a glimpse of the dangerous Prime Mage that he was known to be.

Lady Amaranta shrugged nonchalantly, but her eyes continued to bore into me. 'I think you'll find that this matter is my business, dear Railan. If you think you can just swoop in and take what is mine under the guise of "love," then you would be mistaken,' she said, a hint of amusement in her voice. 'Isla belongs to me, and I think it is time that I requisition her. If she's so important to you, then whyever would I just let you have her?'

I felt like I was on the verge of a heart attack. She wanted to requisition me? That could only mean terrible things for me and my family. If I left with her now, I knew that I might not make it through the night. I leaned into Railan's arm, silently begging for him to put a stop to this, to save me and protect me and my family just like he'd promised. I didn't care about ulterior motives or secrets so long as he would keep his word.

'My Lady-' my mother started, but Lady Amaranta shot her a death glare that stole her voice.

'This is between Railan and me,' she said coldly.

Railan's grip on my hand tightened again, a clear indication of his anger and protectiveness. 'I will not let you take her from me, Lady Amaranta,' he said firmly. 'I made a promise to protect her and her family, and I intend to keep it. You have no right to requisition her; she's not some object to be passed around like a trinket.'

Lady Amaranta's eyes narrowed, the amusement in her expression replaced with a cold fury. 'I think you will find that she is, dear Railan,' she said icily. 'I own her and I want her back. You may have some power on the battlefield, but do not think that it extends beyond that. Isla is mine, and you have no right to interfere.'

Railan's eyes narrowed as he stared at Lady Amaranta, his grip on my hand almost painful. 'You have no idea what you're dealing with, Lady Amaranta,' he said, his voice low and dangerous. 'You dare to come into my home, accept my hospitality, and threaten me and my staff. I suggest you leave now, before things get out of hand.'

Lady Amaranta laughed, a cold and bitter sound that echoed through the room. 'Oh, Railan, you are so dramatic,' she said, her voice dripping with contempt. 'But if you wish to call upon the laws of hospitality, so be it. I shall leave for now, but mark my words, Railan. This matter is not over.' With that, she turned on her heel and looked at my mother. 'After you, Mrs Marielle. You'll find your husband and daughter are already waiting for you,' her voice oozed with malicious victory.

My mother looked at her, disappointment and resignation on her face. I felt my panic surge to new heights, and I let go of Railan's hand as I stepped forward.

'No,' I finally spoke up, my voice low as it trembled. 'Please don't do this. Please don't hurt them. They are innocent in this.'

Lady Amaranta glanced back at me, a smug smirk upon her lips. 'Oh, Isla,' she said, her tone patronising. 'I thought I taught you better than all of this. It appears you still have much to learn about the world, my dear. But don't worry, you will learn soon enough.' With that, she turned and started to walk out of the room.

My mother cast me one more glance before she followed after Lady Amaranta, her demeanour demure in contrast to her earlier fury. I moved to follow after them, but found myself held in place as Railan grabbed my hand. I turned to look at him, confusion and fear rushing through me. If my mother left, I would never see her again. I understood Lady Amaranta's words clearly, and I knew that she did not hold back on her threats.

Railan's eyes were fixed on mine, his expression one of deep concern. 'Isla, listen to me,' he said, his voice soft and urgent. 'You must trust me. I will not let anything happen to your family, I promise you that. But you need to stay here, with me. You are safer here than anywhere else right now.'

I shook my head, tears pricking at the corners of my eyes. 'No, Eli,' I said, my voice a mess. 'If I let them go now... I need to protect them.'

Railan's grip on my hand tightened, his eyes pleading with me. 'Isla, please,' he said, his voice barely above a whisper. 'I need you to stay here. I can't protect you if you're out there. You're not safe, not with her.'

I looked up at him, searching his face for any sign of deception or dishonesty. But all I saw was sincerity and worry etched into his features. I knew that he was right, that I would be safer here with him. But the thought of my family being taken away from me, of being separated from them forever, was too much to bear. I tore my eyes away from him and shook off his grasp.

'Lady Amaranta, please wait!' I called after her. 'If you want me so badly, then I will give myself to you, but on one condition. Please release my family into Railan's care.'

Lady Amaranta stopped in her tracks, and at first, she was quiet, as if contemplating my offer. But slowly, quietly at first, a laugh escaped her lips. It grew loud and obnoxious as she turned back to look at me, her eyes glowing with pleasure.

'Do you really think you're in any position to make demands?' she mocked me.

I stood my ground, trying to keep my voice steady despite the fear and anger that bubbled up inside of me. 'I know I'm not in a position of power, but I am asking for mercy. You've already won, you've already taken what you want. Please, just let my family go.'

Lady Amaranta chuckled again, clearly amused by my words. 'Oh, my dear Isla. You are truly innocent, aren't you? Mercy is not something I offer, especially not to those who try to betray me. You know, when I told you to give yourself to that boy, I didn't mean literally. Now look at where we are,' she shook her head in disappointment. 'All of my efforts, wasted. Nevertheless, you knew these would be the consequences. Accept them.'

I felt my heart sink as I realised that Lady Amaranta would not be swayed by my words. The hope that had briefly flickered within me was extinguished, leaving only a deep sense of despair. I knew that I had made a mistake allowing things to go this far, that I had put not only myself but also my family in danger. I knew the whole time, and yet I still did it. I'd allowed myself to be naive, to be swayed by pretty words and promises.

Railan stepped forward, his hand still outstretched towards me. 'Please, Isla,' he said. 'Come back to me. I'll protect you. I'll fix this.'

But I couldn't move. I was paralyzed by fear and uncertainty, unsure of what to do next. I felt a tear roll down my cheek as I watched Lady Amaranta turn and leave the room, my mother following close behind her as if being pulled by an invisible chain. Why had I ever dared to dream of being free? Had I just swapped one gilded cage for another? I knew Railan loved me, I knew he was sincere, but I couldn't help but wonder if everyone was right; love was not enough. Railan's power would never be enough to save me.

Railan's expression softened as he saw the tears on my face. He stepped closer to me, gently wrapping his arms around me as I collapsed into his embrace. 'I'm so sorry, Isla,' he murmured into my hair. 'I never wanted this for you. I didn't mean for things to turn out this way.'

I clung to him, my body shaking like a leaf as I sought solace in his touch. But even as he held me, I could feel the roots of fear and despair had already begun to tear me apart. It felt like I was trapped, like there was no escape from this life of fear and uncertainty. Was this really all there was to my life? Was I destined to always be at the mercy of others? Was I always meant to be a slave, an object to be used?

Railan held me for a few more moments before gently pulling away, his eyes searching mine. 'I know this isn't what you wanted, Isla. But I promise you, I'll find a way to fix this. I won't let anything happen to you or your family. Just trust me, please.'

I looked up at him, my heart heavy with doubt and fear. Could I really trust him? Could I trust anyone in this world? I didn't know anymore. All I knew was that I was tired of feeling powerless, tired of feeling like a pawn in someone else's game. But what could I do? What choices did I have left?

'I do trust you, Eli...' I whispered. 'But... this is too much... you've provoked Lady Amaranta. But not just her, also the Grand Cardinal, the Magi Primacy, everyone... and now...' I trailed off, unable to finish as I continued to sob quietly.

Railan's expression was pained as he watched me cry. He took my hand in his, giving it a gentle squeeze. 'I know it's a lot to take in, Isla. But we aren't as alone as it feels. Your family will be safe for now. Lady Amaranta would not be foolish enough to harm them when she thinks she has the upper hand. I'll get them back before anything can happen, I promise. As for everyone else, they don't matter. If they wish to take me on, then I will let them. Then they will see the true power of my fury. They will be reminded why I was chosen by the Celestial Lady.'

I looked up at him, my eyes filled with tears. There was a fierce, sincere determination that burned within him. I knew there was a reason he was favoured by our patron goddess, but even still, he remained her least favourite out of the twelve Prime Mages. He was a powerful magus, but that didn't mean he was more powerful than Lady Amaranta. She had been in this game for a very long time. Railan was still young, barely a man. He hadn't had enough time to grow and establish himself. I shouldn't have trusted his pretty words. I was foolish to let his charm enthral me.

'It won't be enough...' I shook my head.

Railan's grip on my hand tightened. 'It will be enough, Isla. I will make it enough. I won't let them take you away from me. I won't let them hurt you or your family.'

I could see the fire in his eyes, the passion and determination that burned within him. But I couldn't help feeling like it was all for nothing. Like we were just two small fish in a vast ocean of power and politics. What could we possibly do against the might of Lady Amaranta and her allies?

'I don't know... I don't know anymore,' I said softly. 'I...'

My head felt simultaneously light and heavy. The world seemed to be closing in on me as dark shadows crept into the corners of my eyes. My lungs burned and refused to expand. I couldn't breathe. It was all too much. My knees grew weak, and my eyes fluttered as I struggled to remain standing. I wanted nothing more than to collapse, to disappear, to turn back time.

Railan quickly caught me before I could fall, holding me steady. 'Isla, are you okay? What's wrong?'

I shook my head, tears streaming down my face. 'I don't know... I don't know...'

He held me close, murmuring soothing words as he stroked my hair. 'It's okay, my love. I'm here. Just breathe. Take deep breaths. You're going to be okay.'

It took several moments, but eventually, I managed to calm down enough to take deep breaths and steady myself. Railan held me the entire time, his warmth and strength a comfort. When I was finally able to speak again, I pulled away from him, wiping my eyes.

'I'm sorry... I just... I can't...' I trailed off, unable to finish my sentence.

Railan cupped my face in his hands, forcing me to meet his gaze. 'You don't have to do anything, Isla. You just have to trust me. I will handle everything.'

His words were both reassuring and terrifying. I knew I was in over my head, but I also knew that I had no other choice but to trust him. Lady Amaranta had made her move, and now it was up to Railan to make his. All I could do was watch from the sidelines, hoping and praying that he would be able to come out on top somehow.

I nodded slowly, still feeling faint. 'I just... I think I need to lie down.'

Railan nodded understandingly. 'Of course, my love. You rest, and I will take care of everything.'

He swept me up into his arms and carried me up to his room. He lay me down gently and made sure I was comfortable before placing a soft, loving kiss upon my forehead.

'I'm sorry...' he whispered.

I gave him a vague nod as my eyelids faltered and the exhaustion of the night finally took over.

Epilogue

I didn't want to dream, and yet here I was, a little witchlight in a vast forest once again. I sat perched upon a branch, content to simply watch from a distance as life went on. But as I looked out into the forest, I felt the subtle sensation of longing. I longed for something that was not here. I thought for a moment, but I couldn't recall what it might be.

I watched a pair of birds soar through the canopy and down to a small puddle that had formed amidst the underbrush. One was brown while the other had striking blue and black markings. I recognised them as fairy wrens. They were round and small, but they also looked happy as they took turns playing and washing in the water.

'Wake up...' a faint, barely audible voice rang out seemingly all around me.

I looked around, but I didn't see anyone but the birds.

'When will she wake up?' another voice echoed.

'When she's ready,' another remarked.

'But he needs her.'

'She will awaken when she's ready.'

What were they talking about? Who needs whom? Someone was asleep. I didn't understand. Perhaps they weren't talking to me, after all, I was simply a little light in the treetops. There was a crunch somewhere nearby, and the little birds scattered back up into the safety of the canopy. I was a little sad to see them go. I looked towards the sound.

To my surprise, a figure had appeared. A dark shroud covered them from head to toe, with only their silver mask visible from my perspective.

They turned their head to me, as if to acknowledge my presence. I remained still as they made their way over to my tree. They stood beneath me for a moment, regarding me, before they eventually extended a hand up to me. I looked but did not move. I did not feel compelled to join their side.

'Won't you wake up, Sil?' they finally spoke.

A beat...

The figure solemnly retracted their hand before moving to their mask. The silver glinted in the sunlight as the metallic covering fell away.

'Sil.'

Eliason wasn't asking; he was commanding.

And my eyes finally opened as recognition coursed through me.

'El...'

To be continued in book 2.

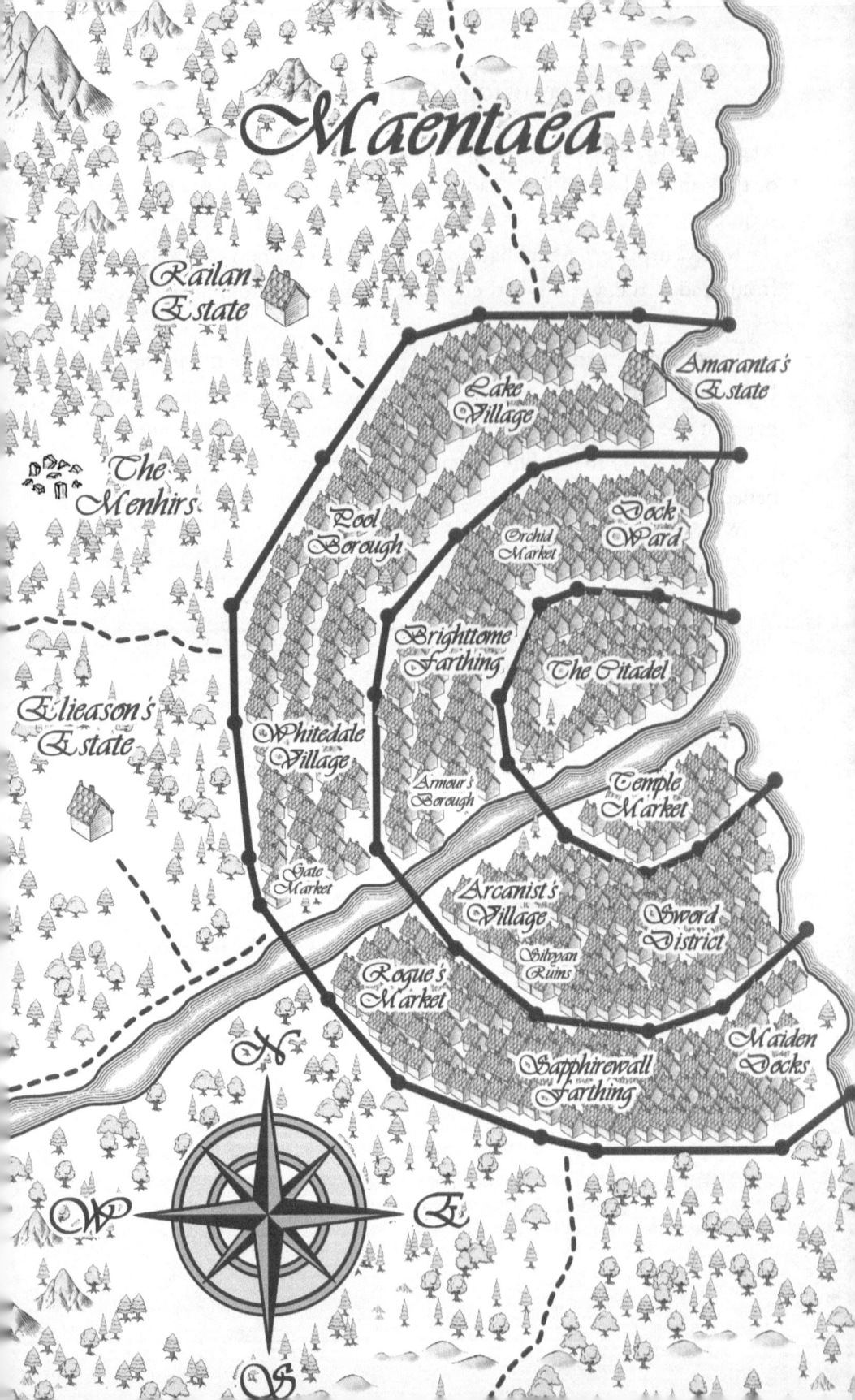